"Twins?"

Becca's voice cracked. "I'd just gotten used to the idea of one child. And now there are two babies. The rules keep changing on me here. Or should I say the reality keeps changing. And multiplying."

Nick smiled at her. The smile reached his eyes, making them crinkle at the edges. Ooh, those incredible hypnotizing brown eyes that looked darker and more soulful than ever right now.

"Obviously I'm no expert, but I hear change is par for the course with children. Just when you think you have it all figured out, everything changes."

He shrugged.

"For someone who claims to know nothing about children, you sound pretty wise. But are you sure you're ready to do this?"

What a dumb question. They didn't really have any choice now. Or at least she didn't. She was still bracing herself, preparing for the moment that he changed his mind. And if learning that there was not one but two babies didn't send him running... She couldn't quite let down her guard and let herself go there yet.

* *

HAMMERSME

D1144259

Let's get this party started!

HIS TEXAS CHRISTMAS BRIDE

BY
NANCY ROBARDS THOMPSON

MILLS & BOON

All rights reserved including the right of reproduction in whole or in part in any form. This edition is published by arrangement with Harlequin Books S.A.

This is a work of fiction. Names, characters, places, locations and incidents are purely fictional and bear no relationship to any real life individuals, living or dead, or to any actual places, business establishments, locations, events or incidents. Any resemblance is entirely coincidental.

This book is sold subject to the condition that it shall not, by way of trade or otherwise, be lent, resold, hired out or otherwise circulated without the prior consent of the publisher in any form of binding or cover other than that in which it is published and without a similar condition including this condition being imposed on the subsequent purchaser.

® and ™ are trademarks owned and used by the trademark owner and/or its licensee. Trademarks marked with ® are registered with the United Kingdom Patent Office and/or the Office for Harmonisation in the Internal Market and in other countries.

Published in Great Britain 2015
by Mills & Boon, an imprint of Harlequin (UK) Limited,
Eton House, 18-24 Paradise Road, Richmond, Surrey, TW9 1SR

© 2015 Nancy Robards Thompson

ISBN: 978-0-263-25182-1

23-1115

Harlequin (UK) Limited's policy is to use papers that are natural, renewable and recyclable products and made from wood grown in sustainable forests. The logging and manufacturing processes conform to the legal environmental regulations of the country of origin.

Printed and bound in Spain
by CPI, Barcelona

National bestselling author **Nancy Robards Thompson** holds a degree in journalism. She worked as a newspaper reporter until she realized reporting "just the facts" bored her silly. Much more content to report to her muse, Nancy loves writing women's fiction and romance full-time. Critics have deemed her work "funny, smart and observant." She resides in Florida with her husband and daughter. You can reach her at www.nancyrobardsthompson.com and facebook.com/nancyrobardsthompsonbooks.

This book is dedicated to Cindy Rutledge and
Renee Halverson. You make writing so much fun!

Chapter One

Becca Flannigan wasn't a gambler. For as far back as she could remember, she usually leaned toward the tried and true. She'd choose dependable, low-risk options over games of chance any day.

That's why it was particularly baffling when she discovered peace and the meaning of unconditional love with the simple flip of a coin.

Figuratively, of course. But she'd heard it said when you're uncertain about something, you should flip a coin. Even before the result turns up, you'll know what you want.

It was true.

The trip to Celebration Memorial Hospital's emergency room had been Becca Flannigan's bright, shiny quarter spinning in the air.

As she lay on the emergency room bed, one hand curled into the sheet and the other splayed protectively over her belly, she knew exactly what she wanted: she wanted—no, she *needed*—her unborn baby to be safe and healthy and unharmed by the bout of food poisoning that had landed her here in the hospital.

So, *this* was unconditional love, Becca thought as she tried to make sense of the foreign emotions that had commandeered her heart.

She'd never known a conviction like the one that had rooted itself deep in her soul; a certainty that she would die for the little being growing inside of her. But in this case, she couldn't die, because now there was something so much more important than herself to live for.

A few hours ago, the stabbing pain from the food poisoning had been so bad that death might have seemed preferable. But the terrifying realization that being this sick might cause her to lose the baby transcended the discomfort and became all consuming.

At barely three months pregnant, she hadn't been sure how she felt about her *situation*. Single and alone, she'd called it a predicament, a dilemma, a mess, a pickle—a gamble she'd taken and lost. She'd called it all those things, but she hadn't called it love until she'd faced the very real possibility of losing her child.

Here, under the harsh lights of the ER, something had cracked open inside her, and her previously muddied feelings had spilled away and everything important had crystallized.

Despite the fact that she didn't know how to find her child's father. She hadn't told her parents. Kate Thayer, her boss and best friend, was the only one who knew. The only reason Kate knew was because she'd been there with her in the ER when Becca had told the doctor.

Now the only thing that mattered was that the child growing inside her was safe and healthy.

This child was her everything.

At twelve weeks, she wasn't showing yet—although her body had started changing, a subtle transformation, adapting itself for the nine-month journey. She was thicker and her clothes fit snugly. People probably thought she'd gained weight. Just last week, her mother had made a snide comment about Becca spending too much time with Ben & Jerry's. Little did she know.

As Becca lay there with IV tubes in her arm and various machines beeping and humming, a restrained orchestration to accompany the chorus of emergency room sounds and voices on the other side of the cubicle curtain, she took back every negative or uncertain thought that had ever crossed her mind about this unplanned pregnancy.

She was single and only twenty-five years old. A baby hadn't been part of her plan at this juncture. They'd used protection that night. She wasn't supposed to take away a living, growing souvenir.

But now, faced with the possibility of losing her child, everything was suddenly different. If she lost this baby, this new capacity to love would surely die right along with it. Becca closed her eyes against the thought.

It wasn't going to happen. She wouldn't let it happen.

"How are you feeling, hon?" Becca opened her eyes to see Kate standing at the opening in the privacy curtain. Kate had driven Becca to the emergency room as soon as the nausea and pain had started.

The onset had hit Becca like an iron fist. One moment she was fine, walking from her desk to Kate's office with the mail, just as she did every single day, and the next thing she knew, she was doubled over in pain. Sensing something, or maybe Kate had heard Becca whimper, Kate had insisted on taking her to the hospital. "I got you some ice chips," Kate said. "I tried for water, but this was the best I could do. The nurse said she wants to make sure you can handle ice before she lets you have the hard stuff. They're pretty busy out there, and they're getting ready for a staff change. She said she'll try to pop in before she clocks out, but if she can't, she said the doctor who's coming on duty will be in to see you."

Becca did her best to smile as she accepted the white foam cup from Kate's outstretched hand. She felt like a wrung-out dishrag, but she was stable and the baby was okay.

Now she just wanted to go home.

"Thank you," Becca said, trying to steady her thin, shaky voice.

"I'd feed them to you, but—" Kate crinkled her nose as she held up her hands, motioning around with one "—it's a hospital and I haven't washed my hands. Plus, you'd probably bite me if I tried."

She smiled her sweet Kate smile. Becca did her best to smile back.

"Feeding me would be going above and beyond. I can handle it, thank you."

As Kate sat down, Becca lifted a piece of ice to her mouth, letting it linger on her parched lips. It melted on contact, leaving behind a cool, clean moisture. As she licked the droplets of water, Becca thought it was possibly the freshest, most delicious thing she'd ever tasted in her life. She placed another chip on her tongue. Surely this was what they meant when they'd said *nectar of the gods*.

Whoever *they* were. The ones who imparted such great wisdom about flipping coins and drinks fit for deities.

"How's the ice settling?" Kate asked.

Becca turned her head toward her friend, who had seated herself on a chair in the tiny space.

"I can't recall ever tasting anything so good," Becca said. "I highly recommend it."

She smiled at Kate, but Kate's smile didn't reach her worried eyes. "I'm glad you and the baby are going to be okay."

She knew her friend's words were sincere, but an unspoken question hung between them.

"No one else knows," Becca said. "About the baby, I mean. No one except you. And the doctor and nurses."

"You haven't told your family yet?"

Becca shook her head. She moved the cup of ice chips from her stomach to rest on the side of the bed. She needed to tell them. She probably should've already told them—before anyone else.

She'd wanted to be sure she'd make it through the first trimester…though, if she were being honest with herself, she hadn't really thought about telling them until now. But it made sense. No use in causing a family uproar for naught.

The thought made her shudder. She drew in a deep breath. Not only had her little one survived the first trimester, he or she had made it through this bout of food poisoning. This was a tenacious little being.

The words *meant to be* skipped through her head.

She would tell her parents.

Sometime soon…

As soon as she figured out how to explain.

They would ask about the father. That was the tricky part. What should she say? That his name was Nick and he was tall, gorgeous, and he'd swept her off her feet?

She'd met him at this very hospital the evening her nephew Victor had landed in this very emergency room that fateful evening three months earlier.

Nick. Nick who? Nick of the sultry brown eyes and the secret tattoos. Nick, who had been kind and generous in body and spirit and comfort. He'd been at the hospital that day interviewing for a job, which he hadn't taken or hadn't been offered. For whatever reason, he didn't work there now. Personnel wouldn't tell her why. They offered no help finding him. Of course, she hadn't told them she was pregnant. Not that it would've done any good. The woman with the horn-rimmed glasses had been so tight-lipped she might as well have been head of security at the Pentagon. She wasn't giving anything away. Oh, sure, she'd taken Becca's number and offered to pass it along. But Nick hadn't called.

Big surprise. They'd spent one night together. A night when her emotions had been raw. It was crazy because, judging by outward appearances—those tattoos, the motorcycle and that dark, penetrating gaze—he wasn't her type at all.

And what exactly was her type? It had been so long

since she'd been on a date that she couldn't really remember. Working at the Macintyre Foundation, she'd been so busy that she didn't have time for much of a social life. But that night with Nick, something intense and foreign had flared inside her. It hadn't mattered that he wasn't her type or that she didn't even really know the guy. She'd been inexplicably drawn to him, and in the midst of the rush, *type* hadn't even factored into the equation.

Of course, explaining this to her family would go over like a turd in the punch bowl. She was the good girl. She didn't do things like *that*. Especially not after her sister, Rosanna, had gotten pregnant in high school. Nope. Rosanna had been the bad example, the cautionary tale about why you didn't sleep with men who didn't love you.

Becca's hand found her stomach again. If she'd stayed at the hospital the night of Victor's accident, life would be drastically different right now.

"Do you want to talk about it?" Kate asked.

She shrugged. "I do, but not here."

"Of course." Kate sat forward on her chair. "There's no privacy here. And you're probably not up to it right now. But, Becs, I'm here for you. Okay?"

Kate reached out and squeezed Becca's hand.

"Whatever you need," she added.

Becca forced a smile. She recalled how her mother used to tell her it took more muscles to frown than it did to smile. At the moment, nothing could have felt further from the truth.

"Thank you, Kate. You've already done so much for me today."

And she had. Kate had spent the afternoon in the

emergency room with her. By now, Kate's family would be home. Her husband, Liam Thayer, was head of Celebration Memorial pediatrics. He was one of the bigwigs at the hospital. Becca had thought about asking him to do a little sleuthing on her behalf to help her locate Nick.

Now that Kate knew, maybe she would. She'd be asking Liam to break the rules. And of course, she'd have to offer a pretty darned good explanation as to why she wanted personal info about a doctor who had interviewed at the hospital three months ago. That would mean she'd have to admit to Liam she'd slept with a man without even knowing his last name.

Other than pride, she couldn't think of a good reason not to ask Liam to help her get an address or phone number, something more to go on than simply *Nick, the hot doctor from San Antonio.*

He was the father of her baby. He deserved to know.

But she and Kate would have that conversation another time. She couldn't chance someone who worked in the ER overhearing them plotting to infiltrate hospital human resources.

Right now, her throat and lips were too dry to talk, and she was utterly exhausted. It took all the energy she possessed to place another ice chip in her mouth and close her eyes.

She wasn't sure how long she'd been lying there drifting in and out of light sleep, dreams merging with the sounds in the ER; dreams of the night of Victor's accident when her sister had been crazed with worry and had taken it out on Becca. She dreamed of Rosanna screaming at her, telling her to get out.

Blaming her for what happened. And then the dream morphed into meeting Nick, making love to Nick…

That's why she wasn't sure if she was dreaming or if she really had sensed him standing there. But when she opened her eyes at the sound of someone pulling open the curtain surrounding her bed, Nick *was* standing there.

"Hi, Ms. Flannigan. I'm Dr. Ciotti." He was looking down at the tablet in his hands, not at her.

It was *him*. All tall six-foot-something of him. Slightly longish brown hair. The lab coat and green scrubs didn't hide the mile-wide shoulders, but they covered up the tattoos on his biceps.

God, those tattoos. One of them, a single word—Latin, she thought, but she wasn't sure. The other was an ornate Celtic cross, which she found fascinating—especially now, because based on his last name, Ciotti, Nick Ciotti—his background might be Italian.

She'd memorized those tattoos. Just as she'd memorized the feel of the long, lean muscled planes of that body. Despite her weakened state, recalling these details had her feeling the same brand of hot and bothered she'd felt *that night*, the night they'd first met.

And now he was standing in front of her. As if she'd conjured him.

Becca blinked. What was he doing here? When she'd tried to find him, the people in the human resources department had sworn there was not a doctor with the first name of Nick employed at Celebration Memorial.

Maybe he was some dark angel who'd been sentenced to serve purgatory in emergency rooms… Okay, she wasn't so out of it that she didn't realize how delusional that sounded. Or that she probably had never looked worse. Maybe he wouldn't recognize her.

And that would be preferable?

Maybe.

"I've just come on duty after a shift change, and I wanted to look in on you before signing your release papers."

Had she conjured him? Or maybe she was hallucinating?

"How are you feeling?" he asked as he keyed something into the tablet, still not looking up. "I understand you're pregnant. Are you feeling strong enough to go home?"

She didn't quite know what to say. Especially since her entire body had gone numb at the sight of him.

When he finally looked up, their gazes met. His upright professionalism gave way to recognition. Recognition morphed into something that resembled utter shock. But it took only a couple of beats for him to compose himself. Becca could see the virtual wall go up around him.

"Hello," he said. "It's, uh—it's nice to see you again."

His words were clipped and matter-of-fact. There was no trace of the sex god who had zapped her of all common sense and discretion *that night*.

"It's been a while, hasn't it?" She tried to keep her voice light. It wasn't an easy task, lying there on a gurney in a hospital gown, with parched lips and a dry mouth. How many times had she imagined running into him at a park or in a restaurant—in her imagination he was always dining solo, of course, waiting for her and overjoyed by the reunion. But the one scenario she'd never imagined was running into him as a patient in the emergency room, looking as she felt right now.

God, just kill me now.

She instantly regretted the figurative words. Her hand automatically moved to her belly in a protective stance.

She took a deep breath and reframed. This wasn't the time for vanity. So what if her hair was a mess and her makeup had washed away hours ago? No matter what she looked like right now, she had important matters to discuss with him.

"How long has it been?" he asked. His shock and surprise had settled into a professional half smile that put miles of space between them. The expression established that they were acquaintances. That he was the doctor and she was the patient, and doctors didn't sleep with their patients.

But until now, she hadn't been his patient. He had only helped her out by answering questions about her nephew's condition. Medical terms she hadn't understood and he'd explained to her.

"It's been three months," Becca offered. "Twelve weeks, almost exactly to the date."

Dr. Nick *Ciotti* glanced down again at the tablet in his hands. He scrolled with his fingertip. "Yes. So, it's been…three months."

She could see him doing the math in his head.

Nick turned to the nurse, whom Becca had just noticed, and Kate. "Would you give me a moment with Ms. Flannigan, please?"

Ms. Flannigan? What?

As if she didn't feel unattractive enough, now he was making her feel like the mean woman who ran the orphanage in *Annie*. Wait, no, that was Miss Hannigan. Still, no one called her Ms. Flannigan. Especially not the hot guy who'd gotten her pregnant.

The nurse cast him a look.

"It will be fine, Sally. Becca and I are old friends. We need to catch up."

Old friends? She forced herself to not look at Kate. If she looked at Kate, she was sure Sally would be able to see everything in the glance they'd exchange.

Nick met Becca's eyes again. "I'm sure your friend won't mind giving us a moment, will she?"

Becca opened her mouth to answer. However, suddenly, she didn't want Kate to leave.

But she and Nick needed to talk. The thought of being alone with him knocked the wind out of her.

"Becca?" Kate asked. "Is that okay?"

What was she supposed to say? *No? Don't leave me?*

God, she was so unprepared for this. Then again, it seemed as if she'd been unprepared for everything these past three months.

Just another day in her life. Only this one included the father of her child. The thought sent her free-falling.

She nodded. "It's fine."

Sally looked dubious, but she motioned for Kate to follow her. "Are you sure you're okay?" Kate asked.

"I'm fine," Becca repeated.

"We shouldn't be long," Nick said, his gaze trained on the tablet in his hands.

Kate cast an uncertain glance at Nick, but she followed Sally out into the emergency room. Once they'd cleared the curtain, an awkward silence stretched between Nick and Becca.

Nick lowered his voice. "It's good to see you again."

"Quite a surprise," she said. "I didn't realize you'd taken the job."

"I didn't at first," he said. "But we finally came to a meeting of the minds. So, is there something we need to talk about?"

"Yes, we have quite a bit to talk about," Becca said. As Nick watched her lips move, he tried to process what was happening.

Becca Flannigan looked like the girl next door with her silky brown hair and piercing blue eyes with golden flecks and a navy circle around the iris. They were the kind of eyes that tempted a guy to stare a little too long. That's what had happened the night he'd met her, when her sister had been screaming at her, telling her to leave the hospital, blaming Becca for her son's accident, even though the kid had admitted he'd been drag racing. As he was on his way out after interviewing for the ER job, he'd witnessed Becca trying to ask a question about her nephew's condition, and then he'd watched the boy's mother tear into her. He probably shouldn't have—he should've left well enough alone and gone back to his hotel—but as Becca had been walking away, he'd called her back and answered her question.

She'd looked so fragile that night, some protective instinct had sprung to life. He'd wanted to help her, set her mind at ease.

Even now she stirred that same visceral reaction that had previously attracted Nick. And when he'd walked into Bentleys across from the hospital to get some dinner before going back to his hotel and saw her sitting there, she'd been a ray of sunshine on his gray horizon of plans.

And he realized Becca had been talking, but he hadn't heard a single word she'd said—except for *pregnant* and *yes, we absolutely need to talk*.

In the span of five minutes his entire world had upended. He couldn't be a father. Well, yeah, he could be, but they'd used a condom. How had this happened?

He raked a hand through his hair as unsavory words galloped through his mind. What if this wasn't his baby? What proof did he have other than one night with her around the time of conception? How well did he know this woman? He didn't, beyond the fact that he'd been mesmerized by her that lone night three months ago.

He set his jaw to ensure his thoughts didn't become words and escape into the ether.

Instead, he said, "Would you like to tell me how this happened?"

Becca frowned at him as if he was an idiot, and he realized how that must've sounded. *Idiotic.*

"Never mind," he amended. "I'm—"

Something clattered on the other side of the curtains—a dropped supply tray, maybe, or something else metallic and noisy. Somewhere in the distance, a child cried, "I want my mommy." He could hear one of the nurses in the adjacent area conversing with a patient as if she were standing next to him talking in his ear.

Suddenly, everything seemed amplified. They couldn't talk about this here. Nick trained his eyes on the patient chart tablet for a long moment, trying to gather his thoughts—looking for something, anything, that might right this rapidly sinking ship. Her emergency contact was her friend Kate, or at least he assumed it was Kate. Kate Thayer, the chart read, friend. No husband or boyfriend or significant other. Becca had named her parents as next of kin. Which completely eliminated the possibility that she'd gotten married since the last time—the only time—he'd seen her. But wait—he scrolled back up to the top of her chart to check. Yes, marital status was listed as single.

He looked back at Becca.

She was the last person he'd dreamed he'd run into today.

He'd wanted to see her again. In fact, he'd thought about her often since that night. When he'd finally accepted the job, he'd planned on trying to look her up. How many Beccas could there be in Celebration, Texas? But he hadn't had much spare time lately. Between wrapping up his job in San Antonio and moving to Celebration, he'd been slammed. He'd been in town only five days. His possessions were still in boxes stacked inside his apartment because he'd hit the ground running since moving.

And here they were. Reunited.

And she was three months pregnant. He didn't need a calculator to do that math.

"When did you get back into town?" she asked.

Her question answered something that had been lurking in the back of his mind. Had she come here looking for him?

Of course she hadn't. It said right on her chart

that food poisoning had brought her into the emergency room.

Then another question elbowed its way into the forefront of his mind: When had she planned on telling him? Was it even part of her plan? If he hadn't changed his mind and accepted the job, would he have even known about the pregnancy?

"I've been here less than a week."

"I see." He glimpsed a note of sadness in her eyes. Or maybe she was simply mirroring his own confusion back at him.

She looked small and fragile lying there. Despite everything—the bombshell, the uncertainty—he still had the damnedest urge to gather her in his arms and protect her.

Wasn't that how they'd gotten into this situation in the first place?

With that thought firmly in mind, he reminded himself that he was at work. In this moment he was her attending physician. Thoughts like that were off-limits. She was off-limits.

"Sally will be here in a moment to check your vitals. When everything checks out, you can go home. You'll want to follow up with your obstetrician, and, of course, if you start feeling ill, call your doctor. Or come back to the emergency room. If it's an emergency."

She was quiet while he updated her chart.

When he'd finished, essentially signing off as her doctor, he said, "When are you available?"

"Excuse me?"

"We need to talk."

She shrugged, then lowered her voice. "Listen,

I'm not going to try to force you into anything you don't want to do."

"Let's not talk about this here."

Even though he hadn't meant to offend her, and he wasn't putting her off—he was on the clock, and they needed privacy—she looked offended.

"When are you available?" he repeated.

"I don't know. I guess, whenever I feel stronger."

Really, there was no sense in delaying.

"How about tomorrow?" he said.

Chapter Two

Thirty minutes later, Becca was in Kate's car on her way home. It was cold outside on this mid-November evening and she felt the chill down to her bones. It amplified how weak and vulnerable she felt.

Despite how she'd wanted to reconnect with Nick, how she'd tried to find him right after she'd found out that she was pregnant, she hadn't been prepared for the reunion to happen this way.

Even though he deserved to know the truth, she'd wanted the disclosure to be on her terms. The vulnerable side of her wished she was still safe in her cocoon, the only one who knew about the baby. No one to please. No one to convince that this child was wanted and dear and loved—even if he or she was a surprise. She had just come to terms with the situation herself. Now things had suddenly gotten complicated again.

Becca stared out the passenger-side window into the inky sky. The trees were beginning to shed their leaves and stood stark and bare in the chill night.

How symbolic, she thought. Exposed. Stripped down to the naked branches with nothing to hide what lay beneath. Somewhere from deep inside, a voice reminded her that some of these trees had lined Celebration's Main Street for centuries. They'd endured winters and storms and climate changes to see another season.

This was simply a new season of her life.

Nick was coming over tomorrow to talk. While she understood that he needed time to digest the news—just as she had—he hadn't seemed very happy about it. And she wasn't sure she was ready to deal with that right now. But if not now, when?

When they stopped at a red light, Becca felt Kate's gaze on her. Kate was such a good friend. This was all fresh news to her—huge news that her best friend was pregnant and going it alone. Well, not exactly alone. Not anymore. So, it was actually a double bit of juiciness, and not once since they'd left the hospital had Kate pushed her to give up the goods.

Becca knew she didn't owe anyone an explanation, but Kate did deserve to know what was going on.

"So, I'm pregnant," Becca offered. "And Nick is the father."

Kate's eyes were wide, but all she did was nod.

"I probably should've told you sooner so that you didn't find out like this, but I wasn't ready to tell anyone. Still, I hope you know how much I appreciate all you've done today. You're such a good friend, Kate."

"I'm glad I was here for you today," she said. "For

the record, you don't have to tell anyone anything until you're ready."

The two sat in silence and Becca let the solidarity wash over her.

"But he is a good-looking guy," Kate added. "I can see the temptation."

A hiccup of a laugh escaped Becca, and for a moment the tension lifted. "I know, right?"

Kate's curiosity was almost palpable.

"Liam's never mentioned Dr. Ciotti."

The statement was a question. Kate was testing the water to see how Becca would warm to telling her more. The light turned green, and Kate accelerated at a gentle pace.

"He hasn't even been at the hospital a week," Becca said. "Since they're in different departments, I'm not surprised he hasn't mentioned him. They may not have met yet."

That was a long shot. The hospital wasn't large. Most of the staff knew each other at least by sight.

"How did you two meet?" Kate ventured. "You don't have to answer that if you're not ready to talk about it."

The cat was already out of the bag. She couldn't blame Kate for being curious. If the situation were reversed, she'd want to know. Then again, Kate was married to a fabulous man. It was a relationship made in heaven, though it hadn't started out that way. Her husband, Liam, had been a widower when Kate had first met him. He came with adorable twin teenage girls and the expected amount of baggage that a man who had lost his first love much too young would bring to a new relationship. But Liam and Kate were soul mates. Despite fate's cruel curveball, they'd been given a chance at happiness, and they'd taken it.

Becca tried to keep her mind from wandering to the possibility that she and Nick might be soul mates.

She really shouldn't go there. For her own peace of mind.

The best way to make sure she didn't was to tell Kate the story of the night she met Nick.

"No, it's okay. I don't mind. Remember the night that Victor got in the drag racing accident?"

"Yes."

"That night at the hospital Rosanna was so mad at me."

Kate slanted her a glance. "Why was she mad at you? You weren't driving."

"I wasn't, but I was the one who taught Victor how to drive a standard transmission."

They came to a stop sign, and Kate shot her a glance that conveyed she clearly didn't understand Rosanna's anger.

Really, who did understand her sister? It seemed as if she was angry most of the time.

"She said if I hadn't taught him, he wouldn't have been tempted." Becca shrugged. "That's Rosanna logic for you. But I know she was just upset. Victor was banged up pretty badly. Anyhow, when the doctor came to give us the prognosis, I asked him to clarify something, and Rosanna tore into me. She told me I didn't get to ask questions. She told me to leave.

"I wanted to give her some space, so I walked away. I went over to the nurses' station to get a cup of coffee. I just wanted to give her a chance to calm down. When I was pouring the coffee, this guy—this drop-dead-gorgeous guy—was standing there, and he told me he didn't mean to butt in, but he couldn't help but overhear the exchange with my sister. Everybody had heard her, I'm sure. He told me he was a doctor, and he explained what Victor's doctor had said."

"That was Nick?" Kate asked.

Becca nodded.

"And then what? Did he ask for your phone number?"

Becca ran a hand over her eyes. *Ugh.* This was so embarrassing. Kate knew her well enough to know she didn't sleep around. In fact, the last time she'd had sex was with her boyfriend two years ago.

"Not exactly. I went back over and rejoined my family, but Rosanna was just hysterical. My dad suggested that it might be a good idea to give her some space. He told me to go get something to eat, which really meant I should disappear for a while. He said he'd call if there were any changes in Victor's condition.

"So, I walked over to Bentleys across the street from the hospital. I was just going to sit there for a while, get a decent cup of coffee—the stuff at the nurses' station tasted like dirty water, and it was only lukewarm. I was going to bring some coffee back for my folks and Rosanna. A peace offering. I just wanted to give her a little time.

"And who do you suppose walked into Bentleys?"

"Nick?"

"How did you guess?" Becca laughed, but the sound was dry and brittle. It wasn't funny. It was embarrassing. Kind of pathetic, really.

"That night Nick and I seemed to be on a trajectory toward each other. I came in and sat down at a booth and ordered my coffee. And for some reason everything that had been bottled up began spilling out. I started crying, and I couldn't stop. I mean, I wasn't making a scene or anything, but the tears just wouldn't stop. The next thing I knew, I saw Nick through the window. He was parking a motorcycle, and a minute later, he was standing by my table, offering me a napkin for my tears."

"And the rest is history?"

"After he'd told me what the doctor had said, he'd checked on Victor and learned that, though he was banged up pretty badly, he was stable. He was going to be fine. And then the rest is history."

Even though they were both adults, and she knew Kate wouldn't think badly of her, Becca couldn't look at her friend. Instead, she stared straight ahead.

"I've never had a one-night stand before," Becca said. "I do, and look what happens."

They were in front of Becca's condo now. Kate killed the engine and reached out and put a hand on Becca's arm. "Honey, I'm not judging you. You're a grown woman, and you're free to do whatever you want with your body. As long as you're *safe*—"

"We used protection." She hadn't meant to sound so defensive. She took a deep breath and tempered her tone. "Obviously, something went wrong."

Kate nodded. "What are you going to do now?"

Becca shrank into the shadows as she watched two of her neighbors, Mrs. Milton and Mrs. Cavett, who had the condos on either side of her, extract themselves from Mrs. Milton's ancient Cadillac Deville. Mrs. M's late husband had purchased the car brand-new, and she was still so proud of it she'd tell anyone who'd care to listen. If Becca had heard the story once, she'd heard it twenty-five times.

For that matter, both of her neighbors loved to gossip. People affectionately called them the Busybody Twins. Between the two of them, they prided themselves on knowing everything about everyone who lived in the sixty units at Lake Celebration Landing Condos. What they didn't know, they made up.

Once they learned of Becca's pregnancy, word would be all over the tiny condo complex.

Becca shouldn't care. She shouldn't let other people's opinions of her matter. But it did matter. She'd always been the good girl, the one people could count on, the community-minded good example.

Now she'd be known as the one who got knocked up.

Well, it is what it is.

She just needed to make sure her baby didn't grow up feeling like a mistake.

"I'm going to have a baby," she said. "Tomorrow, Nick is coming over, and we're going to figure it out."

Nick steered his motorcycle into a parking space at the Lake Celebration Landing Condominiums, a neatly landscaped, compact grouping of townhomes on the east side of Celebration.

His gaze picked out unit four. Becca's place. Glossy ceramic planters with yellow and rust-colored flowers flanked the red front door, which sported a wreath of wheat stalks and small pumpkins—or were those gourds? It was hard to tell. Whatever they were, they screamed fall and hinted that Becca took a lot of pride in her home.

The amber porch light glowed in the dusk. She was waiting for him. Or she was home, at least. Of course she was; she was expecting him, even if last night as he'd signed her discharge papers she hadn't seemed overly eager to see him. He swung his leg over the bike's seat and stood, hesitating a moment.

Was a person ever really ready for a conversation like this? Yesterday morning when he'd opened his eyes, he'd had no idea how his life was about to change.

But they had a lot to talk about. He'd made a list. Because he knew if he didn't write down the important things he might get distracted. Becca Flannigan made him stupid like that.

Nick hated acting stupid. Stupid equaled out of control, and out of control usually ended in disaster.

He reached in the storage console on his bike and pulled out a paper grocery bag. It contained chicken noodle soup and a small box of saltines. Becca was probably sick of bland food by now. But at least it was something. He wasn't showing up empty-handed, he thought as he knocked on the door above the wreath.

He heard a dog bark and then a soft murmuring he imagined was her way of gently quieting the animal.

Funny, he knew so little about this woman. As he stood on her front porch, it almost felt like a blind date. However, when she answered his knock, and he saw her there, looking much more like herself, or at least more like the woman who had swept him away when they'd met, he felt that attraction, that visceral pull that had hit him hard that first night.

She wore blue jeans and a simple blue blouse that brought out the color of her eyes. She'd pulled her golden-brown hair away from her face with a black headband. She didn't wear much makeup. The color had returned to her cheeks, and her skin looked so smooth he had to fight the urge to reach out and touch her.

"Hi," he said.

"Hi, Nick." The dog, a red-and-white, low-to-the-ground model, barked a greeting and jumped up on his leg.

"Hey, there, buddy," Nick said.

"Priscilla, get down. I'm sorry about that. Just tell her no, and she'll stand down."

"It's okay." He dropped to one knee, setting the bag down so he could use both hands to scratch the dog behind her ears. The animal showed her appreciation by jumping up again and licking Nick's nose.

"Priscilla. Stop it," Becca said. "Mind your manners."

"She's a corgi?" Nick asked as he got to his feet.

"Yes. A very spoiled corgi who needs to learn how to listen."

Nick smiled. "We had a corgi when I was growing up. They're great dogs."

"Yes, they are. Come in."

She stepped back to allow him room to pass. As he stepped into the foyer, he could smell the faint scent of her perfume—something floral—which brought him back to that night. As it had before, it tempted him to lean in closer and breathe in the essence of her. His mind flashed back to how she'd looked as he'd made love to her—soft and sweet and incredibly sexy in an understated way that had driven him mad.

He blinked away the thought and held out the bag.

"What's this?" she asked.

"It's for you. Although you probably don't need it now. You look like you're feeling better."

He'd been at the hospital from 7:00 p.m. to 7:00 a.m. And then he'd gone home to get some sleep. When he'd called her this afternoon to confirm she was up for meeting this evening, she'd said she was fine. She'd taken the day off from work to rest. Since they were meeting tonight, it hadn't made sense to drop it by earlier. Besides, it might've given her the wrong idea. That he wanted more than he was prepared to give.

It was all true and valid.

So, why did he feel like a jerk?

"Thanks." She accepted the grocery bag and peered into it. "Ah, soup and crackers. Thank you. I'm almost completely back to normal, except for being a little tired. But that's par for the course lately."

She shrugged and ducked her head as she turned away to shut the door. Her body language made her seem a little vulnerable in the wake of her admission.

Nick had taken a few steps out of the small foyer and into the nicely decorated living room before she caught up with him. The room, which featured shades of greens and blues, had a traditional feel, but it certainly wasn't old stodgy traditional. It looked as if she'd put a lot of thought into the decor. Still, it wasn't so decorated that he couldn't imagine kicking back and watching the Cowboys or the Mavericks on a flat-screen on a lazy Sunday afternoon.

His mind tried to lead him to other things they could do on a lazy afternoon, but he reminded himself why he was here tonight, and the thought was instantly sobering.

"Sit down." She gestured toward a couple of chairs

arranged across from the couch that were upholstered in a blue-and-green geometric pattern. The couch—a big, overstuffed number —looked a hell of a lot more comfortable, but tonight wasn't about comfort. It was about figuring things out.

He took a seat on the closest chair.

The dog had trotted into the room with a rawhide in her mouth and plopped down next to his feet, ready to do some damage to her chew toy.

"May I get you something to drink?" she asked.

He wondered if she meant wine or beer or something tamer like water or coffee. The only thing they'd had the night they met was coffee. He didn't even know if she drank.

His gaze drifted over her stomach for a quick moment. Of course she wouldn't imbibe alcohol now.

"I'm good," he said. "But thanks."

She sat on the couch across from him.

"You worked today?" she asked.

So, they were going to make small talk before they got to the heart of the matter. Okay, for a few minutes. His ex-wife had told him he wasn't good at chitchat. According to her, he wasn't good at communicating. Period.

It was true; he usually didn't have the patience for meaningless conversation. What was the point? That's why he didn't care for cocktail and dinner parties, and it was a big part of the reason he was divorced now.

That and his tendency to be a workaholic. Delilah had complained a lot about him never being home. He'd told her that was life with an ER doctor. Eventually, she'd left him for his best friend, who also happened to own the lawn service that did their yard.

He wasn't sure which was sadder…the fact that their breakup had been such a cliché—the only thing that could've been worse was if she'd left him for the pool boy—or the overwhelming sense of relief he'd felt after he'd signed the divorce papers.

After that, he'd buried himself in work. Emergency medicine suited him so well. It was fast-paced and involved a revolving door of patients. He could keep it all about work and not get too personal. He'd make sure they were stable and hand them off to their primary care doctor.

It was clean and simple. No need for small talk or building relationships beyond the situation that had brought them into his emergency room.

"I've worked twelve-hour shifts for the past five days. Actually, it's my first night off since I took the job."

"Are they ganging up on the new guy?" She smiled and her dimples winked at him.

"No, they've been so shorthanded that the other doctors haven't had much time off in a while."

She was quiet for a moment and he could see the wheels turning in her mind. She glanced at her hands, which were in her lap, before looking back at him.

"Why didn't you take the job at first?" she asked. "Because they did offer it to you, didn't they? Please, tell me you didn't decline because of what happened between us."

A pretty shade of pink bloomed on her cheeks.

"Wait, don't answer that," she said. "It's a dumb question. Of course you didn't turn down a job because of me. It's just that I tried to get in touch with you after I found out I was pregnant, but all the hospital would tell me was that you didn't work there."

He nodded. So she'd tried to find him. He wondered if she'd been discreet when she was doing her detective work. No one had told him that a woman claiming to be carrying his child had been there looking for him. Then again, how would an employer break that news to a new hire? And would she really have told a complete stranger *why* she was looking for him? Not likely.

"I couldn't justify relocating on the first offer," he said. "But I could work with their counteroffer. So, just in case you were still wondering, no, my turning it down had nothing to do with you or what happened between us."

"I didn't even know your last name," she said.

Exactly. They hadn't exchanged much personal information beyond first names. He'd thought that was the way she'd wanted it, and it had made their meeting sexy and exciting.

"So, I take it you're keeping the baby."

"Of course I am. I have a good job. This place isn't a palace, but it's big enough for a child and me."

They sat in silence for a moment. The furnace ticked and then clicked on. A car honked somewhere outside.

"Look," she finally said, "I won't try to force you to be part of this child's life. We will be perfectly fine on our own. I just thought you should know."

"Would you be willing to take a paternity test?"

"Excuse me?"

"A paternity test. Would you take one?"

Her mouth opened and shut before she could utter a word.

It wasn't an unreasonable request, but the way she glared at him made it seem as if he'd asked her to move to Mars. The look in her eyes cut him deeply.

But he couldn't go there. Or rather, he couldn't let her work her way into that soft spot where instinct and feelings lived and eclipsed common sense. Instinct and feelings had never served him well. That's how they'd gotten themselves into this mess in the first place. He made a mental note not to call the pregnancy—or the baby—a mess. If she was reacting this way to a paternity test, she'd probably smack him if he called the situation a mess.

It was all so new that the pregnancy and baby didn't seem as if they were one and the same. That *his* child might be growing inside Becca…

The thought hit him like a punch in the gut. He would not make a good father. He was married to his job. Children were too unpredictable. They were too fragile. He knew for a fact he did not do well with unpredictable and fragile. He'd learned the hard way. The ER was a different type of unpredictable. It was based in science and methodical procedure. He never knew what he'd get one night to the next in the ER, but no matter what was thrown at him, he could follow procedure and tame the chaos. He could fix people.

But being a father? Raising a child? God help him. Or more accurate, God help the poor child.

That's as far as he could go right now.

He simply couldn't wrap his mind around it. But

there was no sense in getting shell-shocked until he had the facts in hand.

He knew he sounded like a first-class jerk, but the sad truth was he wouldn't be able to wrap his mind around the pregnancy until he was certain the baby was his.

Yes, she was three months pregnant. Yes, he'd slept with her twelve weeks ago. But they'd been together one night. He didn't know her or how many guys she'd slept with or when she'd slept with them. Even though he didn't want to believe she'd try to saddle him with another man's kid.

But he didn't really know her. Because of this, he reminded himself, it wasn't out of line to ask for proof that he was the father.

"We used a condom," he said. "I just don't see how this could've happened."

She squinted at him and did a little head jut.

"Hello, you're a doctor. You, of all people, should know that condoms aren't one hundred percent fail-safe."

He shrugged. "You're right. They aren't foolproof. But they do prevent pregnancy most of the time. I need a paternity test for my own peace of mind. It's not you, it's me. When you get the test and the results come back, you can tell me I'm a jackass and say *I told you so* as many times as you want."

She scoffed and shook her head, obviously disgusted with him.

"Becca, don't be mad, please."

"I'm not mad at you. Because even though I don't sleep around, Nick—before you, I'd never had a one-night stand, and after I got the news, I wished I never had—you couldn't possibly know me well enough to know that. So I'm not mad at you. I'm mad at myself for sleeping with a man who doesn't know me well enough to know that."

Chapter Three

Just as Nick had maintained that he was within his right to ask Becca to take the paternity test, she was justified in feeling offended and irritated by his request.

However, the all-too-rational part of Becca's brain knew without a doubt how the results would come back. It would prove that Nick was the father. So, why argue?

Why?

Insult and exasperation kicked up again. *Do the words* it's the principle of the matter *not mean anything to you?*

Her heart had broken a little bit after Nick's visit. Still tender, it tried to overrule that sickeningly reasonable voice in her brain.

She didn't *have to* take the test if she didn't want to. He wasn't strong-arming her. She didn't need to

prove herself. But wouldn't it look as if she had something to hide if she held out? The truth would set her
free.

Or would it?

Handing Nick proof positive would not guarantee
he'd be any happier about it than he was right now.
But that was the chance she'd have to take. She'd
meant it when she'd told him she wouldn't try to
force him into anything he didn't want to do. And
she wouldn't.

In the end, vindication trumped justification. The
next day she went to the lab in Dallas that Nick had
recommended and let them draw blood for a non-
invasive prenatal paternity test. They told her they'd
have the results back in two business days.

After the longest two days of her life, Becca braced
herself for the news. She wasn't sure why she was
anxious, since the results wouldn't be a surprise. But
last night she'd dreamed that the lab had gotten her results mixed up with another person's, and she couldn't
seem to make Nick understand that it was a mistake.
That the lab had messed up.

All her life Becca, who'd been a straight-A student
up through college, had had recurring nightmares of
failing tests. They'd only served as incentive to work
harder. But this test was out of her control.

As she took the parking garage elevator into the
lobby of the Macintyre Enterprises building, she took
a deep breath and tried to get in touch with her rational mind, which still seemed to be fast asleep this
morning.

Her foolish, emotional, battered heart was not only
wide-awake and beating like a cymbal-banging mon-

key, it had been making her do crazy things like check her email every fifteen minutes since five-thirty this morning. If her rational mind cared to show up, it would convince her that, much like pressing an elevator button repeatedly when waiting for a slow car, refreshing her email browser every fifteen minutes before the workaday world had poured their first cup of coffee was fruitless.

But sometimes exercises in futility were therapeutic.

She stepped off the garage elevator into the lobby and turned toward the bank of elevators that would carry her up to her office on the top floor of the building.

The Macintyre Foundation was housed in a twenty-five-story glass-and-chrome building in the heart of downtown Dallas. The Macintyre Family Foundation shared office space with Macintyre Enterprises, which belonged to Kate's brother, Rob Macintyre. The foundation mostly served the community of Celebration, Texas, which was located about twenty minutes outside of downtown Dallas. But since Rob Macintyre owned the Dallas-based building, they couldn't beat the cost of rent.

Every time Becca stepped into the massive glass-enclosed lobby, she looked up. She couldn't help herself, even after all these years. The ceiling seemed to stretch miles above her head, reaching toward the heavens. All around a gentle green-tinted light filtered in. Even in the soft morning sunshine, it reflected off the chrome furniture, fixtures and giant fountain in the center of the atrium.

Everything about the space was sleek and polished, and this morning it felt particularly cold and fed her anxious nerves, which just proved she needed a hot beverage to warm her up, because there wasn't anything cold about the Macintyre family. They did a lot of good for the Celebration community.

Becca tightened her cashmere scarf and turned up the collar on her red wool coat to stave off the chill that had worked its way into her bones. She'd worn her favorite gray tweed skirt and ivory cashmere sweater to bolster herself against the emotional day. The ensemble was soft and warm, a comfort outfit, if there was such a thing, even if it was fitting a little snug these days.

She took off her hat, smoothed her hair into place and waved good morning to Violet, the receptionist who tended the lobby concierge desk. Even though Violet was small, young and pretty and very feminine, she was the gatekeeper, and she took her job seriously. No one got past her unless they had an appointment or possessed a preapproved security badge. Nobody wanted to tangle with Violet.

The heels of Becca's boots tapped a cadence on the marble floors. The sound seemed to carry and echo in the cavernous lobby. Today, all of her senses were heightened. Even so, she tried to walk a little more carefully to muffle the noise.

When Becca finally reached the twenty-fifth floor, the office was quiet. Kate, Rob and his wife, Pepper, who was in charge of the foundation's community relations department, obviously hadn't gotten to work yet. Becca was so early even their receptionist, Lisa, wasn't there.

After Becca turned on the office lights, she made her way to the kitchenette, where she started a pot of coffee for the office and brewed herself a cup of herbal tea.

God, the coffee smelled good. It took every ounce of strength she possessed not to toss the tea—a spicy, fruity blend that Kate had brought in for Becca after she'd learned about the pregnancy and Becca's subsequent caffeine sacrifice.

Caffeine wasn't good for the baby. That was the only incentive she needed to fortify her willpower. She grabbed her caffeine-free infusion and headed straight to her office away from temptation. At least the insipid liquid was hot and had begun to take the edge off the chill she'd experienced as she drove into work.

Fall was one of Becca's favorite seasons. She loved everything about it, from the pumpkins and the autumn leaves as they shrugged off the last vestiges of summer green and donned glorious harvest colors, to the nip in the air and the way the community seemed to come together even more at football games and festivals. Becca had decorated her office to set a festive mood. A garland of leaves and straw artfully woven together festooned her office door, and she had brought in her pumpkin-spice-scented candle. Before she sat down at her desk, she turned on her electric candle warmer.

She had a long to-do list to plow through today, lots to accomplish to make sure Celebration's fourth annual Central Park tree-lighting ceremony, an event the foundation sponsored the day after Thanksgiving, went off perfectly. The event had become a beloved tradition for the Celebration community, and if Becca had it her way, she'd do her part to make it better and better every year.

But even that had to wait. Because the first thing she did after she booted up her computer was check her email to see if there was any word from the lab.

The tech had given her a password and told her that after she received the email alerting her that her test results were ready, she was to go to a website, enter the password and retrieve her exoneration.

He'd called it results, of course, not exoneration, but that's how she'd come to think of it.

Of course, since it wasn't even nine o'clock, the email hadn't yet arrived. She took a fortifying sip of tea and uttered a silent prayer that they wouldn't make her wait until the end of the day.

But wait—what if she'd miscalculated? Was today considered day two? Or was that tomorrow? The cymbal monkey kicked in again, and her heart virtually rattled at the thought. She didn't know if she could bear to wait another twenty-four hours.

She minimized the screen of her inbox and pulled up the file for the tree-lighting ceremony. She had so much to do today that, really, she should have enough to keep her mind occupied. But as she read the bids from the professional tree decorators, her mind invariably drifted to Nick.

How would he act once he had proof positive that he was the baby's father? Would he choose to be part of his child's life? Would he believe that despite their night together she didn't sleep around? Whatever he did, Becca fully intended to play the I-told-you-so card once she had the results in hand.

Nice. That'll entice him to stay. It'll make you very pleasant to be around.

She shook away the thought, clicked on her inbox and refreshed her browser again.

Still nothing.

So she picked up a red file folder that contained her notes for the ceremony.

"Good morning." Becca looked up to see Kate, dressed in a smart black pantsuit, holding a cup of coffee and standing in the doorway of her office.

"Hey," she said.

"Dare I ask?" Kate grimaced as if she were bracing for Becca to throw something at her. "Any news yet?"

Great. As if she needed any more nervous encouragement, but she knew Kate meant well. Becca didn't have the heart to sigh and tell her to go away. And to take her coffee with her.

Instead, she mustered her sweetest smile.

"Not yet."

Kate nodded, then took a sip from her mug. "Good coffee. You really are a saint for having it ready. Since you can't drink it, you really don't have to do that."

Becca closed the red folder. "I don't mind." She sipped her tea as if to prove she didn't need the high-octane fuel, and the fruity, spicy stuff served her much better.

"Come in for a minute." Becca pointed toward the chair. "Sit, please. Talk to me. Distract me. Stop me from checking my email at the top of every minute."

Becca happened to see the clock on the bottom right corner of her computer screen turn over to nine o'clock. So, she hit the refresh button once more.

"Okay, I did it again." Becca held up both hands, palms forward in surrender. "Stop me, please."

"Okay, Britney Spears. I wish there was some way I could rig your computer so that every time you check your email Britney would sing, 'Oops!… I Did It Again.' That would make you think twice, wouldn't it?"

"And how," Becca said.

"Of course, I could always come in here and sing to you every few minutes. A couple of rounds of Britney therapy will probably work like touching a hot stove. After you experience it, you just know better."

Becca laughed. "Darn, I wish I would've brought in the karaoke machine. I knew I was forgetting something."

"I'm happy to sing a cappella. That would probably have the biggest impact."

"Do you make house calls?" Becca asked. "I could've used you last night."

"Why? It was a little early to start the test result watch last night, wasn't it?"

"No, it wasn't that. I wasn't actually looking, but I was anxious about it. To take my mind off things, I let myself binge-watch classic movies. Turner Classics was having a James Dean film festival."

Kate narrowed her eyes and cocked her head to one side. "Sorry, hon, I'm not following you. Why is James Dean bad?"

Why? Becca shrugged.

"I know this sounds crazy, but there's something about Nick that reminded me of James Dean—with a modern spin and maybe with shades of Adam Levine and biceps and tattoos.

"But more rugged, though, less metrosexual," Becca added.

They paused for a moment of quiet appreciation, slow smiles spreading over their faces.

Actually, Becca had drawn the James Dean-Adam Levine parallel the first time she'd set eyes on Nick Ciotti. Well, actually, that's what she'd thought the second time she'd seen him. The first time, she hadn't really *seen* him. She'd been distraught over Victor's accident and the way Rosanna was trying to ice her out. She'd needed answers. But then when he'd walked into Bentleys, that's when she'd *seen* him.

After noting the James Dean comparison, her next thought had been that he had to be one of the best-looking human beings she'd ever laid eyes on. Bad-boy dangerous and take-your-breath-away gorgeous, with that shock of dark hair that was just a tad too long.

Sigh.

"I can totally see it," Kate said. "Did you sit and brood over James Dean last night?"

Becca tried to shrug it off. "I did and it's so stupid. I just need to get Nick out of my head. I keep going back and forth between being furious with him for pushing this paternity test issue and thinking that this guy and I are going to be irrevocably connected because of the baby. And despite it all, I want that. I really want it. But what he must think of me to insist on this test."

Kate looked at Becca for a long moment, and Becca could see the wheels turning in her friend's head.

"What?" Becca asked. "Just say what you're thinking. I've already admitted I'm a hot mess."

"I know it was hard for you to go get the test done. It probably felt as if he was questioning the very core of your character. I know that must've felt really crappy. But there are some women who—" Kate paused and winced. "How do I say this? Just don't hate me for it, okay?"

"Just say it."

"There are women out there who might try to trap a man like Nick."

"A man like Nick? What do you mean? I don't understand."

"He's a good-looking guy with a nice income and secure job. You know, a doctor."

"You sound like Jane Austen." In her best high-pitched British accent, Becca said, *"It is a truth universally acknowledged, that a single man in possession of a good fortune, must be in want of a wife."*

Kate laughed. "Well, not exactly. I was trying to say that there are certain women who think a man in possession of a good job, especially a doctor, would make a good husband. Okay, I guess that did sound a little Austen-ish. Remember Liam's neighbor Kimela Herring, and how she set her sights on him after his first wife passed away? That woman was shameless. She would've done anything—and I mean anything—to get her hooks in him. She's the reason I ended up bidding ten thousand dollars for him at that bachelor auction that funded the new pediatric wing at Celebration Memorial Hospital. Remember how she drove up the bid?"

Becca sat back in her chair and squinted at her friend while she tried to ignore the annoyance sparking in her solar plexus. "I remember, but I'm not quite sure where you're going with this trip down memory lane. Because surely you're not comparing me to Kimela Herring."

Kate looked genuinely surprised. Becca knew she sounded defensive, especially when Kate burst out laughing.

"Hardly," Kate said, a broad grin commandeering her face. "But what I am saying is, even though you are far from being a Kimela Herring and I know this is tremendously hard for you, you might want to cut Nick some slack. Women like Kimela throw themselves at men like Nick and Liam, and that might be one of the reasons Nick is so wary."

Becca wasn't quite sure what to say. She could always count on Kate to give it to her straight, but she was having a hard time swallowing what Kate was dishing up. Okay, so Nick was a doctor. That didn't make him better or worse than anyone. Even if certain women had a tendency to fling themselves at men like Nick. It certainly didn't absolve him of his responsibility.

Kate must've read that on her face, because she waved her hand as if she were erasing her words. "That didn't come out right. I feel like I just set back womankind two hundred years."

Becca cocked a brow. "Maybe three hundred years." But she smiled to let Kate know she wasn't taking it personally. She couldn't. Because even though Kate's words rankled her, Becca could step back and see that there was some truth to the matter. Gold diggers were real. They weren't the stuff of urban legends. She didn't like it, and she certainly didn't like the thought of Nick thinking of her that way.

"You're right," Becca said. "He doesn't know me."

"So please don't be too hard on him, or on yourself, for that matter, okay?" Kate said.

Becca offered a one-shoulder shrug but nodded. He'd see the truth soon enough. She wasn't trying to force his hand. Even if they were having a baby, she didn't want to marry a man she didn't love or a man who didn't love her.

For a moment her heart tried to eclipse logic with quiet protestations. How did she know she couldn't love Nick? She didn't even know him beyond that one earthmoving night, which proved that there had certainly been plenty of raw material to work with then.

And, oh, how it had worked.

As if the heavens were seconding that motion, a notice that she had a new email popped up on her computer screen.

She clicked over to her inbox.

The results were in.

After working the 7:00 p.m. to 7:00 a.m. shift the night before, which he would repeat tonight, Nick's days and nights were mixed up, but such was the life of someone employed in emergency medicine.

His schedule was as unpredictable as the cases that presented themselves each night in the ER. Some weeks he worked the graveyard shift, others he pulled the more civilized 8:00 a.m. to 8:00 p.m. one. Even though Celebration Memorial usually scheduled attendings four days on and three days off, sometimes the workweeks were longer, and he never knew what he'd be working one week to the next. That was fine because he was married to his job. Emergency medicine was a possessive spouse.

But now he was going to be a father.

He'd picked up Becca's text after he woke up around two o'clock. He hadn't even had a chance to grab a cup of coffee. So he was still a little groggy as he read the news. It was force of habit to check his phone the minute he rolled out of bed to make sure he was on top of things at the hospital, to make sure he hadn't missed an important call or text.

In this case, he had.

Becca had called. Then, when he'd slept right through that, she'd texted. Her message had said, The results are in. She'd included a link to a website and a password.

He'd known what the results would be before he'd typed in the first character. He'd known in his bones that Becca wasn't the kind of woman who would try to pawn off another guy's child on someone else. He supposed he'd known the truth since the moment he'd set eyes on her again in the emergency room, but he hadn't been able to wrap his mind around it.

A father. He was going to be a *father*. He couldn't imagine a worse person for such an important job. The kid deserved better than anything he could offer. Of course he would provide for the child, but love? How could he love someone else when he didn't even like himself sometimes?

The bald reality rolled around inside his gut, cold and heavy like a large ball bearing. To make it stop, he pushed up off the sofa bed and made short order of putting the couch back together, tossing the cushions into place. The chore had become a routine because if he didn't put away his bed, it dominated the living space in the tiny efficiency apartment that sat above George and Mary Jane Hewitt's garage. He'd rented the place on a month-to-month basis, figuring he'd find something more permanent once he got settled in his job and got to know the area. Since the place came fully furnished, he'd had the movers unload everything he owned, except his clothes, into a storage shed.

He didn't spend much time at home, and as the modest apartment came with everything he needed, he really hadn't missed the stuff that was stashed in those boxes. The Hewitts' granddaughter was coming to live with them in January. So they wouldn't offer more than a sixty-day lease. By that time, Nick figured he'd be settled in at the hospital and have a better read on the town. He'd even planned on looking up Becca.

It didn't make any sense to unpack only to pack it all up again when he moved again after the first of the year. It felt good and light and free to not be weighed down by worldly possessions, even if temporarily.

But he hadn't counted on the news that Becca was carrying his child.

He was going to be a father.

Maybe if he repeated the words to himself enough it would start to sink in. *Yeah.* No, that hadn't happened yet.

As Nick made his way into the tiny kitchenette, he uttered a silent oath that was utterly unfatherly. He braced his arms on the edge of the slip of kitchen counter, where the coffeemaker and toaster lived. He knocked his head against the cabinet in front of him for not being more careful.

But he had been careful. They'd used protection. Short of being celibate, how much more careful could he be?

The only thing that was crystal clear now was, with Nick as its father, this poor kid was screwed. Nick wasn't cut out to be a dad or a family man. The most devastating part of the equation was that this child hadn't asked for this, hadn't selected him. He or she—*God, this was a person, a living, breathing human being* whom he could screw up—deserved so much more than such a poor excuse for a father.

But like it or not, this child would arrive in about six months. There was no changing that. He squeezed his eyes together and raked both hands through his hair, which was still sleep mussed. Then he grabbed his phone and called Becca.

The phone rang three times, and he thought it might go to voice mail, but she answered.

"Hi, it's Nick."

There was a beat of silence, and for a moment he wondered if the call had dropped. He was just pulling the phone away from his ear to look at the screen when he heard her.

"Hi, Nick." Her voice sounded neutral, almost businesslike. Of course, she was probably at work. And nearly four hours had passed since she'd texted him this morning.

"I just picked up your text."

"Okay."

She wasn't going to make this easy on him, was she? Well, why should she?

Okay, so he had some smoothing over to do to convince her he wasn't a first-class creep. But he still felt justified asking for proof positive. He hoped Becca would understand that the test results were the first step in moving forward.

"We have a lot to talk about," he said.

"Do we, Nick?"

Her tone wasn't hostile, just calm, eerily calm, a matter-of-fact answer to his feeble attempts to meet her halfway.

"I would ask you to have dinner tonight, but I have to work at seven. Would you have time to meet for coffee after you get off work?"

"Meet me in Central Park in downtown Celebration at five o'clock."

He released a slow, controlled breath, both relieved and surprised that she'd agreed to see him. But she had, and that was the first step. They'd take it from there.

"I'll see you then."

"Nick," she said. "I don't expect you to marry me. So, don't worry."

What was he supposed to say to that? It was one of those damned if you do, damned if you don't situations, and he wasn't going there. This impassive front she was projecting was probably just a defense to gain control over a situation that felt way out of control. He felt out of control, too.

Becca had just told him he was off the hook. She'd just handed him a free pass. If he knew what was good for him, he'd take it and run. But he couldn't. And that made him feel so out of control it was as if his world was spinning, and all he could do was hang on or risk being flung off into parts unknown.

Actually, maybe that had already happened. Maybe this weird alternate universe was where he'd landed.

"I'll see you at five."

He arrived at the park a little early. He left his motorcycle in a parking space along the street and sat on a bench, looking at the fall decorations adorning the gazebo. Kids played in the park, running and laughing and chasing each other, as he sat there trying to gather his thoughts before Becca arrived.

Her words *I don't expect you to marry me* rattled in his brain. If Becca Flannigan was one thing, it was sincere. If she said it, she meant it. Nick knew he should've been relieved, but he wasn't. He wasn't sure what exactly he was feeling—

Until he saw her walking across the grass toward him in her red coat and boots. Something pinged in his gut. Awareness flooded his senses, and his body tightened in response.

An image of the night they were together played through his mind. A guy like him would be wise to ignore feelings like this. He shouldn't lead her on and make her think he was promising things he couldn't deliver. Becca and the baby deserved better than anything he had to offer. He had a history of tearing things apart, of ruining anything good that had ever come into his life.

She deserved to be married to the father of her child, if she wanted to be. Deserved to have a traditional family, a traditional life. The house with the white picket fence with dogs and cats in the yard, if that's what she wanted.

He didn't know for sure, because he didn't know her at all. Even if every cell in his body tried to convince him otherwise. As he stood to greet her, he shook off the unbidden memory of their night together—holding her, kissing her, making love to her. He had to man up and knock it off.

She offered a shy smile as she approached.

He had to fight the urge to hug her. He mentally scoffed. What the hell was wrong with him? He wasn't a hugger. He had to do something to lighten the mood and preempt the awkwardness.

"Go ahead and say it."

She squinted at him as she fidgeted with the scarf that hung around her neck. "Say what?"

"You can say *I told you so*. Twice if you want."

She nodded solemnly. "I thought about it, actually." She shrugged and looked away.

Maybe he shouldn't have tried to make a joke out of it. He was only trying to lighten the mood. A group of six preschool-aged kids ran ahead of their mothers, landing and tumbling in the grassy area directly in front of Nick and Becca.

Their mothers stopped at another bench about ten yards away and waved to Becca. She waved back. The three huddled for a moment, talking, then in unison they looked back at Nick and Becca. Then huddled up again.

"Friends of yours?" Nick asked.

"Acquaintances," she said. "I don't usually hang with the playgroup set. I guess that will change soon."

One of the kids, a little girl with white-blond curls,

let loose an earsplitting shriek, and two of her friends followed suit before they started chasing each other and shrieking even louder as they ran.

"Oh. Uh. Do you feel like walking?" he asked.

"Sure." Becca cast another glance at the three women and waved goodbye.

When they were safely out of earshot, Becca said, "This is so uncomfortable. So, I'm just going to say it and get it out into the open. I'm not going to force you to do anything you don't want to do, Nick. Neither of us planned this. And I know I've had more time than you to sit with this and come to terms with it, but I have to say, I'm happy now. I can't say I always was, but that night I was in the emergency room, I was so afraid I might lose the baby that it all suddenly became crystal clear. I want this child. I hope you'll be part of its life. I firmly believe a child, whether it's a boy or a girl, needs a father figure."

"Me? A father figure?" He shook his head. "Way out of my league. I would probably scar the poor kid for life. Maybe your dad or brother, if you have one, can be the father figure."

He meant it as a joke, something to lighten the mood. But she didn't laugh. She didn't even smile.

"Disregard that. It came out sounding wrong. I was trying to be funny, but I should know better."

"Just so you know, my parents don't know about the baby yet. Not many people do. Only you, Kate and maybe her husband, who also works at the hospital. But you don't have to worry about him saying anything to anyone."

"Who is he?" Nick asked.

"Liam Thayer. He's in charge of the hospital's pediatric unit."

"I haven't met him yet. But then again, I'm in my own little world in the ER unless a specialist consults. But Celebration isn't a very big town. Aren't you afraid, even if a couple of people know, word might get out before you tell your parents?"

"I trust Kate and Liam." She shrugged. "Telling my folks is easier said than done."

"You're a grown woman. What are you afraid of? It's your body and your life. Do you really care about what they think?"

"They're my parents, Nick. Of course I care."

"Sorry. That's a perfect example of just how bad I am at family relations."

"You're not close to your family?"

The question hit him like a punch to the gut. "No. I'm not."

"How come?"

He shook his head. "That doesn't really matter. Not right now, anyway. What is important is that you know that I will take responsibility for our child. I can't promise that I'll be a great father, but I will provide financially. I'm going to do what's right. You and the child will never want for a thing."

She stared at him with disappointed eyes.

"I don't understand why you're so sure you'd be a bad father."

"Once you get to know me, you'll understand."

She looked at him dubiously.

"For some reason I don't believe you. But you do bring up a good point. We need to get to know each other better."

One thing he was beginning to realize about Becca Flannigan was that she seemed to think the best of people. She saw the silver lining, when he tended to be too jaded to even see the clouds. He wasn't necessarily a pessimist. More of a realist.

But what could it hurt to get to know her better? After all, she was the mother of his child.

"That's a good idea. Since I'm just getting to know you and the town, maybe you can show me something that's typical of Celebration, Texas?"

He might've been imagining it, but he could've sworn he saw a half ton of tension lift from her shoulders. Those blue eyes of hers that could hypnotize him if he wasn't careful seemed to have regained some of their sparkle.

"I know you have to go to work. But I'll think of the most quintessential Celebration thing I can and let you know. But first, I have an appointment with my OB doctor tomorrow in Dallas. Will you go with me?"

His first thought was to say no, to back off—way off. But why should she have to go this alone? Especially after he'd just promised her that he would do what was right?

"Sure, let me know what time."

"Thank you. I'm so glad you're coming."

Before he knew what had hit him, she'd turned to him and hugged him. For a moment he didn't want to let her go.

Chapter Four

The next day, Becca glanced around her obstetrician's office at all the happy pregnant couples who were in for appointments. There was a man and woman who were heartbreakingly tender toward each other. The husband—Becca guessed they were married because they wore matching wedding rings—sat with his arm protectively around his wife, gently stroking her shoulder.

If Becca had to wager, she'd bet that this was their first child, because they were young and seemed so much in love.

Another couple had brought their four kids with them. The little ones were playing in the children's area in the far corner of the office. Their father was sitting with them quietly keeping them in line.

As she glanced at Nick, who was sitting next to her reading a newspaper, she was torn. On one hand, she was happy he had agreed to come for the sonogram, but on the other, she felt like a fraud sitting there as if they were a couple who had conceived a baby as a by-product of their love. It shouldn't really matter. Nick was there, wasn't he?

He caught her staring, and he smiled at her, his eyes lingering on hers before they dropped down to her lips and then found their way back to his newspaper. She wasn't trying to fool anyone. They were here together because they were having a baby. Their relationship was nobody's business but their own.

Becca glanced around the waiting area at the posters adorning the walls—some featured tips on women's nutrition, there was a public service announcement that reminded women over thirty-five to get mammograms, and there was a watch-your-baby-grow poster addressing prenatal development and care.

Becca eyed the rendering of the three-month-old fetus. The poster said at this stage, her baby was about three inches long and had fingerprints.

Hmm. Only three inches? How could something so tiny make her feel so big already?

Becca's attention was momentarily shanghaied by a young woman who had just entered the office. She looked to be in her late teens or maybe early twenties, and she was very pregnant. She looked as if she might go into labor any moment. Becca noticed she wasn't wearing a ring on her left hand.

It shouldn't matter, but lately every time she saw a pregnant woman, she found herself looking at her left ring finger and sorting her into two categories: married and single.

She knew it was none of her business, and, yes, if she knew somebody was sorting her into categories, she probably wouldn't like it. But she wasn't judging. She just wanted proof that she wasn't the only one going this road alone.

Well, given the fact that Nick was here with her today, she wasn't exactly alone. But as much as the little voice inside of her wished it were different, they weren't a couple, either. They were certainly far from married.

After the young woman signed in, she turned and walked in Becca's direction. Her young face looked pale and drawn, as if she were exhausted down to her bones or maybe just plain weary. She was tall and waif thin, except for the basketball-sized baby bump protruding off her middle, which was visible only from the front and side. From the back, you couldn't even tell she was pregnant. She took a seat somewhere behind Becca, and if she wanted to continue watching her she'd have to turn around or relocate.

It was probably a good thing that she sat behind her, because Becca didn't want to stare. It was just that when she discovered a woman in the same situation she was, she felt an automatic need to bond with her—even if it was only with a smile of solidarity or an empathetic nod.

But this one had looked away as she had passed. Refusing to make eye contact. Probably because Becca had a man with her. As if on cue, Nick shifted his weight as he rested his elbow on the chair's armrest. His upper arm pressed against Becca's. The feel of his body pressed against hers caused heat to prickle a little on the back of her neck.

When he didn't immediately shift away, she gazed up at him, and he gave her a lopsided grin. The look in his eyes made her a little weak and melty on the inside, but she did her best to play it cool.

"Do you like football?" she asked.

He put down his newspaper and slanted her a glance, but his shoulder stayed right next to hers.

"I do."

She liked the warmth of his arm on hers. It made her think about how their bodies had felt skin to skin, and a little frisson shivered its way through her.

"I was thinking about how you wanted me to show you something typically Celebration. Maybe we could go to the football game Friday night. That is, if you're free. I know it's a weekend, and you might have to work or you might have plans."

She wondered if he was dating. Was there anyone else in his life?

Of course that's when the nurse chose to open the door and call them back into the exam room.

"Think about it," she said. "But no rush. You can let me know tomorrow."

Even though Nick was a doctor, he still felt a little out of place in the obstetrician's office. He wasn't sure what Becca had told them about him— the baby's father—the last time she'd been in for a checkup, but when she introduced him, the staff didn't seem to bat an eye.

Either it was commonplace for some fathers to not be involved, or the staff was very professional.

That helped him breathe easier. She shouldn't have to go this alone. Even if he wasn't much help. Maybe having someone there for support was something. Especially since she hadn't yet told her family. He, of all people, knew that sometimes family could be a bigger hindrance than help. Even though she hadn't said much, it sounded as if she and her folks had their challenges. That surprised him because Becca seemed warm and together, but maybe her family was as dysfunctional as his.

Nick's mind flashed back to his brother, Caiden, and that day when everything changed. The usual heavy feeling of guilt showed up and threatened to weigh him down, but he mentally shook away the thought. He wasn't going to bring his heavy baggage here. Today he was going to hear his child's heartbeat for the first time—maybe even see the sonogram picture.

With due respect to Caiden, he locked memories of his late brother in the recesses of his heart as he followed Becca through the maze of stations and stops, where they performed tests and took her vitals before finally showing them to an exam room.

"The doctor will be right in," said the nurse. "Make yourself comfortable."

Becca settled herself on the exam table. Nick didn't know how anyone could be comfortable sitting there.

"Are you sure you don't want the chair?" Nick asked, surprised by the protective feelings that had come to life inside him.

"Oh, no, thanks," she said. "I'm fine here. They'll do a sonogram. So I'll need to be on the table for that. I might as well stay here."

"How often do you have to come in for checkups?" he asked.

"Once a month right now, but the closer I get to my due date, the more often I'll have to come in. You're a doctor. You didn't know that?"

"In case I forgot to mention it, obstetrics isn't my specialty."

"Yeah, I think you mentioned it." She smiled at him. "Nick, I'm really glad you came with me today. I know this probably seems a little overwhelming, but having you here has made it so much easier for me."

"I haven't really done anything."

"Yes, you have. Just by being here."

She looked small and fragile sitting on that table. Nick had to fight the overwhelming urge to pull her into his arms and tell her he was willing to do anything he could to protect their child. But he didn't want to lead her on, and he didn't want to promise her anything he wasn't 100 percent certain he could deliver.

Memories of Caiden rattled that cage in the back of his mind, reminding him it probably wasn't in anyone's best interest—certainly not Becca's or the baby's—to promise more than financial support.

Becca had no idea how foreign the concept of family closeness was to him. Very few things scared him, but that was one of the things that did. Only because it was so big and so crucial—and in his experience, very unforgiving. One misstep and not only did you screw up your own life, but the person, the people who were counting on you, too...

Stop. You're not doing this now.

"By the way, I'm off Friday night," he said, taking his thoughts in a 180-degree turn.

Her face brightened. "Do you want to go to the football game?"

"That would be fun."

"It's a high school game. Is that okay? But the entire community turns out. I can't think of anything more typically Celebration than that."

"Sounds…fun."

"Did you play when you were in high school? Or even college?"

"Who, me?" He shook his head. "No. I didn't play sports."

"Too busy studying? When you were in high school, were you one of those übersmart guys who ruined the grade curve for everyone else?"

He'd ruined a lot of things for a lot of people when he was a teenager, but the bell curve wasn't one of them.

"No, I had to work much harder just to keep up. I had a part-time job that edged closer to full-time when I was in school, and then right after high school I joined the marines."

Her eyes widened, and her mouth formed an O. "Yet another thing I didn't know about you. You're a constant surprise, aren't you?"

He winked at her. "I try my best."

"Well, during football season the whole town shows up for Friday night football games. This year, Celebration High has a pretty good record. It's the first time since I can remember that they've been contenders for the district championship. It should be fun. I'm glad you want to go."

"What time does the game start?"

"Seven."

"Would you like to grab a bite to eat before the game?" he asked.

"That would be great. If you're up for the full experience, we could grab something there. The band boosters grill burgers and hot dogs and sell chips and sodas."

"Sounds like a meal fit for a king. How about I pick you up at six?"

Someone rapped on the door, and the doctor and his assistant entered the small room.

"Hello, Becca," he said. "How are we doing?"

He cast a curious glance at Nick, who was trying his best to disappear in the corner.

"Hi, Dr. Stevens. I'm feeling great, thank you. I'd like to introduce you to Dr. Nick Ciotti, the baby's father."

Nick recognized the practiced nonchalance with which Stevens greeted him. He was congenial, but there wasn't a trace of surprise that, at the three-month mark, Becca had finally produced the baby's phantom father.

After they shook hands and exchanged generic pleasantries, Becca told Stevens about the food poisoning and he got down to business asking her a series of questions.

"Have you felt the baby move yet?"

Becca shook her head. "No, not yet. Should I have already felt this?"

"No. Not necessarily. For a first pregnancy it could happen as early as fourteen weeks, but generally it happens between sixteen and twenty-five weeks."

"That's a wide range."

"Each pregnancy is as individual as the parents."

He asked her questions about morning sickness— she told him it had gone away; about fluid leakage and spotting—no to both; and whether she'd been taking her prenatal vitamins—religiously.

Then the doctor pulled over the fetal Doppler machine. Nick knew this machine because they had them in the emergency room. Dr. Stevens held a small probe against Becca's slightly rounded belly and moved it around until they could clearly hear the heartbeat.

The doctor listened for a moment and frowned.

"Is everything okay?" Nick asked.

The doctor moved the probe around more, seemingly lost in what he was doing.

"Dr. Stevens?" Becca said. "What's wrong?"

"Don't get your hopes up, because we need to do an ultrasound to confirm it, but I believe I hear two heartbeats. There's a chance that you might be pregnant with twins."

"Twins?" Her voice cracked. "I'd just gotten used to the idea of one child. And now Dr. Stevens confirms there are two babies. The rules keep changing on me here. Or should I say the reality keeps changing. And multiplying."

Nick smiled at her. The smile reached his eyes, making them crinkle at the edges. *Ooh*, those incredible hypnotizing brown eyes that looked darker and more soulful than ever right now.

"Obviously, I'm no expert, but I hear change is par for the course with children. Just when you think you have it all figured out, everything changes."

He shrugged.

"For someone who claims to know nothing about children, you sound pretty wise. Are you sure you're ready to do this?"

What a dumb question. They didn't really have any choice now. Or at least she didn't. She was still bracing herself, preparing for the moment that he changed his mind. And if learning that there was not one but two babies didn't send him running… She couldn't quite let down her guard and let herself go there yet.

"I don't see how either of us really has a choice," he said.

She couldn't read him. Or maybe she simply didn't want to because she couldn't handle any more changes until she digested the fact that they were having *twins*.

If it had thrown *her* for a loop, how in the world must he really be feeling?

An hour later, as they walked to the parking lot, the toe of Becca's boot caught an uneven edge of sidewalk and she did an awkward little stumble-dance to keep herself from falling.

An instant later, Nick's hand was around her waist steadying her. Her body was warm where he touched her. Or maybe it was just that the stumble had awakened the cymbal-banging monkey, and it was playing a wild staccato in her chest.

"I'm fine. Thanks." Her voice was a squeaky octave too high. She flashed him an awkward smile as heat crept up her cheeks, and she quickened her step away from him.

Gaaa! Leave it to her to be klutzy at the worst possible moment. She took a deep breath and blew it out as the burn of indignity taunted her.

"I guess I'd better get used to the uncertainty of parenthood," she said. "Just when I think I have it figured out, I realize I don't even know how I feel. I mean, I'm trying not to get too freaked out over his comment about twins making it necessary to classify the pregnancy *nearly normal*. Why? I should've asked questions, but I was too stunned. Now that everything is sinking in, I have a million questions. I'm going to stew about them until my next appointment. Do you know what he meant by *nearly normal*?"

"Do you want to go back in and ask him?"

"I hate barging back in. It would throw off their schedule. I'll call them tomorrow."

"He mentioned that Southwestern Medical Center specializes in high-risk deliveries. I can check into it for you—for us."

Nearly normal pregnancy. High-risk delivery. Just hearing the words made her head swim.

She was so glad Nick had come to the appointment with her, and good grief, how would she be feeling right now if he'd left her to go this alone?

She needed to at least pretend as if she was in control of her emotions. But her body still tingled where he'd touched her, and a tear had leaked out of the corner of one eye and was meandering down her cheek, and then another one followed. She tried to take a deep breath, but it sounded so shuddering and pathetic.

She attempted to turn away before Nick could see how ridiculous she was being, but before she could, he'd caught her and had drawn her back into his arms.

"It's going to be okay," he said. "Let's just take this one step at a time. I promise I will do everything in my power to make sure you don't have to worry about anything."

His words were soothing, and she stayed in his

arms until she had regained her composure. She pulled back a little to wipe her eyes, but first she looked up at him. His gaze snared hers, and then he was looking at her mouth, and she was leaning into him.

When he took her chin in his hand and drew her closer, she felt his warm, mint-scented breath so near that every feeling—every dream and desire she'd had since the first moment she'd set eyes on him that night at the hospital—played out before her eyes. Since then, since learning she was pregnant, since finding him again, one of the things she tried not to think about was the way his arms would feel around her, protective and strong. The way his lips would taste... That taste that was so uniquely Nick.

Then he kissed her. Despite everything, the kiss surprised her. The tentative touch and softness of his lips were a sexy contrast to his masculinity—even better than she remembered from that night at Bentleys. The warmth lingered, melting the chill in the air. His mouth was so inviting, and even though a voice of reason sounded in a distant fog in the back of her mind, saying she really shouldn't be doing this, she couldn't quite make herself stop.

He pulled her closer, enveloping her in his arms.

Again, he dusted her lips with a featherlight kiss, as if he were trying to kiss away all of her doubt and insecurity. When his mouth finally covered hers, he kissed her with such an astonishing passion, she was sure it had to have come from his soul.

It was a deep, demanding kiss, and it sent all of her senses reeling and let loose a yearning that consumed her entire body. The way he touched her—one hand in her hair, holding her protectively in place, while the other slid down, caressing her back, edging its way underneath the hem of her blouse until the skin-on-skin contact made it too hard for her to catch her breath.

A low groan of desire broke through the sounds of the cars whooshing by on the highway and a horn honking in the distance. She realized the moan had come from her. If she knew what was good for her, she'd stop now before she got too attached to this man who might or might not choose to be in her life—and even if he did stick around, he might want things to be strictly platonic. Unlike this very *not* platonic kiss.

She pulled back, muttering something about it being late and needing to go and not wanting to keep him from the hospital.

She knew the contrast was jarring, and she saw the confusion on Nick's face as she drove away. When she looked in her rearview mirror, he was still standing there watching her.

Chapter Five

Nick paid for their football tickets, and they entered the gates at Denison Field. She hadn't been to many football games lately, but the field looked exactly the same as when Becca had gone to Celebration High School.

It was hard to believe it had been seven years since she'd graduated. Yet stepping through those gates it felt as if she were transported back in time. She had gone away to college at the University of Florida, and yet she'd chosen to return to her hometown.

Celebration was a place like no other. Even though everybody knew everything about everyone in town— for the most part, though she'd managed to keep her pregnancy a secret, for now, anyway—it was nice to be part of something bigger than she was, something exactly like this town.

"Welcome to Denison Field," she said to Nick. They had arrived a half hour before the game was supposed to start, and the place was already filling up. "I spent a lot of time here as a teenager. As you can see, the whole town turns out for the games. Especially when the team is doing well."

She laughed.

"Everybody loves a winner," Nick said.

"Don't they, though?"

Becca inhaled the scent of flame-grilled burger. "*Mmm*, smell that? It's the best burger in town."

The left side of Nick's mouth turned up in a sardonic grin. "If the best burger in town is cooked by a bunch of band parents, should I be worried about my new hometown?"

"Absolutely not. The dads have gotten together and they run a food truck on weekends to raise money for the band. They've managed to buy a fleet of new tubas and outfit seventy-five kids with brand-new marching uniforms."

"That's enterprising. I hope they can cook as well as they can fund-raise."

"Are you kidding? Apparently, the burger recipe is one that Stubby Blanchard's great-grandmother came up with decades ago. Rumor has it that Ray Isaac, the chef at Bistro St. Germaine, offered to buy the recipe and exclusive rights from Stubby, but Stubby wouldn't sell. Now Ray has made it his mission to figure out the recipe on his own. The town has been calling it burger wars. The funny thing is, even though Ray graduated from Le Cordon Bleu in Paris, he can't seem to figure it out."

"It's probably some strange ingredient we'd never think of, like peanut butter or baking soda," said Nick.

"Baking soda? Don't say that out loud around Stubby. Because he gets uneasy about people trying to deconstruct his burger—and baking soda?"

First, Becca made a face, and then she shrugged. "Watch the secret ingredient turn out to be just that!"

"Becca Flannigan? Is that you?"

Becca turned to see Lucy Campbell, an old high school friend she hadn't seen since graduation.

"Lucy! How are you? When did you get back into town?"

"Just last week. I moved back from California. I went out there to try my hand at starting my own fabric line."

"You always were so artistic," Becca said. "How did it go?"

"Well, the cost of living is so high, I had to take another job to support myself, and it was difficult enough to find time to devote to my designs, much less take time off work to meet with potential investors. So I decided to move back and concentrate on my art. And who's this?"

Lucy all but batted her lashes at Nick. He seemed to have that effect on women.

"Lucy Campbell, this is Nick Ciotti. Lucy and I were good friends in high school. I can't believe we lost touch over the years."

Lucy offered Nick her hand; Nick shook it.

"Nice to meet you," he said.

"Nice to meet you, too, Nick. *Sooo*—" Lucy looked back and forth between Becca and Nick. "Are you two dating?"

The subtext to Lucy's question was *is Nick taken or is he fair game?* Even though Becca knew that Lucy was a harmless flirt, she couldn't help but feel a tad territorial. Because the truth was she didn't know what to say.

Actually, Lucy, tonight is our first date. Unless you count going to the obstetrician together and the night we slept together three months ago when I didn't even know his last name. Oh, did I mention that we're having a baby? Actually, we're having two babies. Twins!

Good Lord.

Not unless she wanted the news broadcast all over town. Sure, Lucy was harmless, but it was the rare soul in this town who could keep a juicy secret like good-girl Becca Flannigan getting knocked up. Especially if they were the one who got to break the news.

Becca figured the best way to head off the question was simply not to answer it.

"Lucy, it was great to see you. We need to run, but let's get together sometime soon and catch up. Okay?"

Maybe by then she would know what to say. Because right now she hadn't given up hope that maybe she and Nick might figure it out and make it work. The thought cued the cymbal monkey in her chest, and it began banging away again.

Becca gauged right. Lucy had enough class to know better than to push the question.

"Absolutely," she said. "I can't wait to catch up. I'm staying with my sister until I get settled. You remember Hannah, don't you?"

Becca nodded.

"Let me give you my cell number." As Lucy rattled off the number, Becca added it to the contacts in her cell. "Please, give me a call, and we can set up something."

Becca was never so glad to get away from anyone. As she and Nick walked away, the sinking feeling hit her that bringing him here had probably been a bad idea. A very bad idea. How the heck had she figured she and Nick would get lost in the crowd when every night at a Celebration High School football game was like homecoming? Especially when most of the people in town had never met Nick and probably thought she didn't even date.

She wondered for a moment if it was too late to suggest that they do something else. In fact, she glanced up at him ready to ask him if they could leave, but his eyes met hers, and in that split second she didn't care if the two of them stayed or went. She didn't care if people asked questions or wanted to meet the new guy.

Things would work themselves out the way they were meant to.

But tonight, he was there with her.

That was all that mattered.

"I noticed how you evaded her question," Nick said. He looked as if he was trying not to laugh.

"You think it's funny, huh? What was I supposed to say?"

Her heart dared her to tack on the words *boyfriend*, *fiancé*, *baby daddy*, but her mouth chickened out.

"Actually, I thought it was pretty skillful."

"And I noticed that you just skillfully evaded my question," she said.

He smiled at her again. "Did I? I guess I didn't understand the question."

"I'll give you that. It's sort of a hard one to understand, isn't it?"

Thank God the color announcers chose that moment to inform the crowd that tonight was senior night and that the football players, cheerleaders and band members would have their photos taken on the field with family members during the halftime break.

"Oh, shoot," Becca said. "I completely forgot it was senior night."

"Did you forget you were supposed to have your picture taken at halftime?" Nick teased. "After we get our food, I'll hold your cheeseburger for you if you need to go freshen up. Although if it's as good as you say it is, I can't guarantee it'll still be here when you get back."

"Very funny. My nephew Kevin is on the football team, and he's a senior."

"You have two nephews? Victor, the one who was in the emergency room that night, and Kevin?"

"Three, actually, and a niece. Victor belongs to my sister. Kevin and Marshall, who is a junior, are my brother Mark's sons. They're all on the football team. My niece, Nora, who is Mark's daughter, is a cheerleader." She waved it away. "I have a big, complicated family. If my sister realizes I'm here and I avoided the photo, it could cause a pretty bad scene. But the funny thing is, if I wanted to be in the photo, she would probably find a reason that I shouldn't. You remember my sister? She's the one who threw me out of the emergency room the night we met."

"Oh, right. I do remember her. She was kind of scary. Although, I have thought about thanking her for throwing you out, because if she hadn't..."

Oh. *Oh!*

Becca could read a whole lot into that. Again, her brain wanted her to ask him if he realized that if Rosanna hadn't been in such a rage that night, they probably wouldn't be expecting twins next May. But her mouth couldn't ask the question. And if she couldn't ask the question, he couldn't refute or clarify exactly what he meant, and she could go on believing that he was happy they *met.*

Thank goodness her parents wouldn't be there tonight. She wouldn't have suggested going to the game if she thought they'd be here.

They never went to the games when the temperature dipped below sixty degrees, which it was tonight and on most Friday nights in November. Her mother had suffered a case of pleurisy ten or fifteen years ago. The cold aggravated the condition—even after all this time. Becca suspected Isabel used it as an excuse to avoid certain functions—such as football games, which were at the bottom of her mother's list of fun things to do, along with root canals and gynecologist appointments.

Of course, Rosanna would be there because Victor was second-string varsity. He didn't play much, if at all, but it was rare for a freshman to make the varsity team. Even if he rode the bench, he did it proudly. Rosanna would be holding court in the bleachers with the other football moms.

Since it would be shoulder-to-shoulder crowded, Becca didn't worry about running into Mark and Rosanna. And, honestly, it wouldn't be the end of the world if she did. She'd simply introduce Nick and tell them—tell them what?

* * *

As they made their way toward the concession area, Becca saw Kate and Liam heading toward them. Kate's eyes flashed, and a broad smile overtook her face when she caught sight of them.

"You're here," she said, greeting Becca with a warm hug.

"We are," said Becca. "Nick asked me to show him something quintessentially Celebration. Since the entire population of the town will be here tonight, I thought I would give him Celebration in one fell swoop."

"You're a brave man, Dr. Ciotti," said Liam. "I didn't attend my first game until my daughters made the cheerleading squad."

They all looked down at the track.

"Amanda and Calee are so excited to be cheering with Nora this year," Kate said. "Nora is Becca's niece. Did she tell you? And her nephews are on the team."

"She did," Nick said.

"Ooh, I can't watch." Kate gestured toward the cheerleaders. They were organizing to do one of their stunts. Nora and one of Kate and Liam's girls were at the base of the pyramid holding the leg of Liam and Kate's other daughter, who was teetering high on top.

Becca winced right along with her. "They're adorable and so athletic, but I can't watch them do those stunts. I'm always so afraid they will fall and get hurt."

Kate sighed. "But their coach is all about safety. So we've all agreed that as long as they're vigilant and they play by the rules, we won't embarrass them by hiding our eyes when they perform stunts and acrobatics."

"We'd rather them be here than out who knows where." Liam slid his arm around Kate's shoulders. "Not that we would let them go to *who knows where*, but it is good that they are involved in something that takes up so much of their time."

Kate had married into her ready-made family and adopted Amanda and Calee when she and Liam wed. Liam had lost his wife in a tragic accident, and both he and the girls had benefited from Kate's nurturing touch.

"Are you two coming over on Sunday night?" Kate asked, directing her question mostly toward Nick.

"What's going on Sunday night?" Nick said.

"You are new to the area, aren't you?" Liam teased.

"Every Sunday night we get together to watch the Dallas Cowboys play football. Well, the guys watch the game, and the ladies usually gather in the dining room. This week, we're making wedding favors for Anna Adams and Jake Lennox's wedding. You might know them from the hospital. Anna is a nurse, and Jake is an attending."

"Right. I met them on my first day at the hospital, actually," said Nick.

"Well, then, in addition to football on Sunday night, you might want to mark the Sunday of Thanksgiving weekend on your calendar."

"Is the whole town invited?"

"Pretty much," said Kate. "A lot of people from the hospital are on the guest list. I hope you have a nice suit. You can be Becca's date."

Becca felt her face heating up. She wished she

could grab one—or maybe she'd need two—of her niece's pom-poms so she could stuff them in Kate's mouth to shut her up.

"Since I'm the new guy, I'll probably get the honor of working that night. Someone will have to hold down the fort."

"We will have to see about that," said Kate. She flashed a smile that Becca knew meant *you can thank me later.* "They've made arrangements for the shifts to be covered."

"We'd better find a seat before kickoff," said Liam. "If we stay here much longer, this one will be planning your wedding."

"Okay, let's hear it for my friends Mr. and Mrs. Awkward, guaranteed to make everyone feel uncomfortable. We're going now. Bye-bye."

"You're welcome to sit with us," Liam called after them.

"Thank you, but if we wanted to be tortured all night, my sister is right over there." Becca gestured with her head toward the crowd in the center of the bleachers, the area that was reserved for the Celebration Quarterback Club. Then she hooked her arm through Nick's and steered him away.

"See you Sunday," Kate called.

Becca waved goodbye without looking back at her friends. She knew Kate and Liam meant well, and she wasn't mad at them for being so forward. In fact, Becca hoped Kate hadn't scared off Nick and that he wanted to come to the football gathering Sunday night. The five couples who got together every Sunday night in the fall were some of her best friends.

Over the years she'd watched them meet and marry their sweethearts. She was the last single in the bunch.

Now that she thought about it, if Nick didn't want to come, she wasn't going to push him. The two of them would be the lone singles swimming in the sea of married couples. That would levy an altogether different kind of pressure than what Kate and Liam had joked about tonight.

Once they were a good distance away, Becca withdrew her arm from Nick's.

"I'm sorry about that," she said.

"About what?" he asked.

His question threw her for a moment, but she recovered.

"They love to joke around. The football parties are fun. It's a great excuse for everyone to get together. I don't want you to get the wrong idea and think that it would be a night full of pressure, of them pushing us together. It's mostly guys in one room and women in another—especially this week, since we'll be busy with the wedding favors. With as many people as Jake and Anna are inviting, it's going to take a village to get them done on time."

Before he could answer, they walked into the midst of a rush of latecomers who had just purchased tickets and were streaming into Denison Field, obviously intent on getting to the bleachers to find seats before kickoff. Becca and Nick were momentarily separated. But once Becca found her way through the crowd, Nick was waiting on the other side for her. Her stomach did a little stutter-step—as it did every time she saw him. There was this momentary rush of disorientation over the fact that this gorgeous man—this man who looked dark and a little bit dangerous—was actually very kind and caring, even if he was still a bit of a mystery.

Nick knew Kate and Liam's good-natured banter was just that—good-natured banter. He also knew they wouldn't say things like that if they didn't welcome him into their inner circle. Sure, there was a grain of seriousness to it, and if he let it, it might bother him—only because he wasn't used to other people being so into his business. But as he looked around at all of the people who'd turned out tonight for the football game, he realized living in a small town like Celebration meant people would be in your business. It was a given. Celebration wasn't like San Antonio, where it was easy to be a face in the crowd. Here, new faces stood out in the crowd, and the community made it their business to find out about their new neighbor.

His gaze snared Becca's as she walked toward him. Someone stopped her and greeted her with a hug. It gave Nick a chance to watch her without her realizing he was staring. She looked gorgeous in her tight jeans and blue-and-white Celebration High School Wildcats spirit shirt. Her navy blue peacoat hung open so that the T-shirt underneath was visible. He couldn't help but notice how the V-neck emphasized her breasts, which had been sexy as hell before the pregnancy, and appeared to be even fuller now.

A man would have to be dead not to notice how good she looked. And damned if that same aching need that had drawn him to her that first night didn't threaten to consume him again.

When she reached his side, he took her hand. "We wouldn't want to get separated again. I might not be able to find you amid the throng of sports fans here tonight."

She smiled at him, and they found their way to the small outbuilding to the right of the bleachers where the band boosters were selling food.

The smell of grilled burgers and hot dogs filled the air, and Nick's stomach rumbled. He wasn't sure the concessions would feed what he was hungry for, but for now it would have to do. They got in line just in time for the marching band to begin playing "The Star-Spangled Banner." All of the cooks put down their spatulas and removed their hats; the money takers stood and put their hands over their hearts. Everything stopped until the piccolos trilled the last trill and the cymbals put the final exclamation point on the national anthem.

When it was all over and the announcer started speaking, Becca asked, "What are you going to have?"

He smiled at her, tempted to say, *The same thing I had that night at Bentleys.* But she had acted so jumpy over Liam and Kate's teasing that he didn't want to push it.

Right now, he was content to be out with her on this beautiful, cool fall evening, holding her hand and enjoying her company.

"I think I'll have a cheeseburger and fries. They must be serious if they're operating their own Fry-Daddy."

"Best fries in town. I highly recommend them."

The crowd went wild as the team ran out onto the field. The announcer informed everyone that if the

Wildcats won the game tonight they would advance to the semifinals for the district championship. The crowd cheered again, and several people leaned on air horns. The band broke into a rousing round of what must've been the school's fight song. After another exuberant cheer, the crowd settled down until the Wildcats won the coin toss and elected to kick the ball to the visiting team.

"It's nice that the town supports the team so well," Nick said. "I guess in its own way Celebration isn't really the sleepy little town that I thought it would be."

"No, the people around here tend to make their own fun. It may not be a wild party—unless you come over to Kate and Liam's for football Sunday—but it's nice."

It was nice. It was everything he imagined being part of a small community would be. He wasn't exactly sure how he felt about that. If truth be told, the small-town closeness was one of the reasons he had turned down the job in the first place. But when they came back with an offer he couldn't refuse, well, he simply couldn't refuse.

They ordered their food—two cheeseburgers, two orders of fries, a bottle of water for Becca and a can of cola for himself—and made their way over to a group of high-top patio tables that were off to the side but still allowed them a partial view of the field.

Since most of the people in attendance had crowded into the bleachers, the area where they enjoyed their meal was mostly empty except for a small knot of teenagers who obviously had no interest in watching the game.

"Does Kate know about the latest development in our little adventure?"

"No, we were busy today, and… I don't know. I guess I'm still getting my head wrapped around our growing family."

"Rebecca?"

The voice came from behind him, so he couldn't see who it was, but good grief this woman was popular. Granted, Celebration was a small town; Becca Flannigan obviously knew everyone who had ever lived here.

But he only had to take one look at her face to realize she wasn't thrilled to see this person.

Nick turned around and saw an impeccably dressed woman with the same basic bone structure and clear blue eyes as Becca. At that moment he caught a glimpse of what Becca might look like in twenty-five or thirty years. This had to be Becca's mother. The distinguished man with silver hair at her side had to be Becca's father.

"Rebecca, you're here. Good. I meant to call you today to remind you that tonight is senior night, and Kevin is getting a family portrait made on the field, and we all need to be in the picture. Make sure you meet us at the half."

The woman stopped abruptly and trained those piercing blue eyes on Nick. The way she tilted back her head gave her the appearance of looking down her aquiline nose.

"Rebecca, who is this? Please, introduce your friend to us."

Even though it was more of a command than a request, Nick stood. "Hello, Mr. and Mrs. Flannigan, I'm Nick Ciotti. Very nice to meet you."

As he greeted Becca's mother and shook her father's hand, some of the missing pieces to the puzzle fell into place.

While the Flannigans were cordial, they were also a bit cold and aloof. The way they carried themselves and the way they dressed suggested affluence. Nick could see through the stuffy, polite veneer to the judgmental subtext lurking below.

Later at halftime, as he stood at the chain-link fence that separated the track and football field from the bleachers, he watched the dynamics among the Flannigan family. As Becca joined her nephew's senior night photograph, he realized that he and perfect, beautiful Becca Flannigan were more alike than he'd realized. Even though she was part of a big, wealthy family—the opposite of his working-class parents—he sensed that Becca felt just as alone in the world as he did.

Chapter Six

Two nights later Becca sat at Kate's dining room table sipping caffeine-free pumpkin spice chai tea and chatting with five of her best girlfriends as they filled mini mason jars with monogrammed candy.

Anna and Jake had gotten engaged over the summer and had planned on getting married the following spring, but Regency Cypress Plantation and Botanical Gardens, which was booked out for nearly two and a half years, had an unexpected cancellation, and Anna and Jake had been able to grab it.

The only problem was now all plans were on the fast track, and it really was taking all hands to pull off the wedding of Anna's dreams.

Two weeks ago, the six of them had sat at this very dining room table stuffing, addressing, sealing and stamping invitations to three hundred of the couple's close friends. The available date, November 29, was one week from today—the Sunday of Thanksgiving weekend. It wasn't ideal, since so many people went away for the holiday and traveled on that Sunday.

Because of the time crunch, the girls were under strict instructions that they could not leave Kate's house tonight until they'd each filled fifty jars.

As an incentive, Anna had offered to buy dinner for the person who finished first and helped the slow-poke of the group get up to speed.

Becca knew she might very well end up being the slowpoke tonight because her mind was elsewhere. She loved her friends, but tonight, she wanted to be a fly on the wall in the living room, where Nick was bonding with the guys.

He'd surprised her and agreed to come with her to Kate and Liam's tonight. After the arm twisting the night before last, Becca made up her mind not to push him. She couldn't think of a faster way to scare off a man than to guilt him into spending a Sunday evening with her friends.

But if the sounds coming from the living room were any indication, her friends were becoming his friends. That made her happy beyond words. Still, a fly on the wall had no use for words. So she kept her head down and her ear tuned in, trying to pick out Nick's voice among the mix of hooting, hollering and the occasional bit of hospital talk, since four of the six men were doctors.

"Who needs more wine?" Pepper hopped up and started going around the table refilling goblets with the bottle of Chianti she'd brought back from Italy.

"Becca, honey, why are you drinking that god-awful caffeine-free tea when you could be enjoying a little piece of Italian heaven. Here, let me get you a glass."

"No, thanks, Pepper. I'm good."

Pepper laughed. "How could anybody be good drinking that liquid spice ball?"

When Pepper headed off into the kitchen, Becca and Kate exchanged a look. Pepper was a sweetheart, but sometimes she could be too damn bossy for her own good. Or in tonight's circumstances, for Becca's good.

The woman was like a bloodhound—she could smell a secret two counties over. And Pepper's antennae had been up since Becca's trip to the emergency room after her bout of food poisoning. Pepper hated feeling left out. However, she was a Southern belle, and rather than ferreting out the answer she was looking for, she used techniques that involved endearment, helpfulness and graciousness—key tools of the Southern belles trade.

Tonight she would obviously not rest until Becca either drank the Chianti or served up a Pepper-approved explanation as to why she was passing on such a treat.

When she came back into the dining room, she set the glass in front of Becca and drained the rest of the bottle into it. As soon as Pepper had finished, Kate waltzed right over and swooped up the wine.

There was hierarchy at work here. Pepper was married to Kate's brother, Rob, and as the sister-in-law, Kate could get away with certain transgressions that mere mortals would never in their right minds dream of committing.

"Kate, darling, if you would like some more wine, I brought another bottle. We can open it. Granted, it's not from Italy, but I do so want Becca to try the Chianti. I don't want her to miss out."

Kate had done her part. Becca had to think fast.

"It's very sweet of you, Pepper, but I haven't felt like myself all day long. I'm afraid if I have even a taste of wine it might not settle with me. It doesn't even sound good right now. So I'd hate for you to waste it on me."

There. That was good. Only a social moron would keep pushing wine on a person who wasn't feeling well. Becca was glad to get Pepper off of her back, because she certainly couldn't tell anyone else about the babies until she told her parents.

Kate was a rare, reliable jewel, and Becca knew her secret was safe with her. Kate was more reliable than a Fort Knox vault.

"You're not pregnant, are you?" A.J. laughed at her own joke. Their friends Lily and Anna joined in the merriment because on a normal day Becca would've been voted the least likely of all the women at the table to announce she was carrying twins.

"Good one, A.J.," Becca said. "How many glasses of wine has she had tonight? I hope Shane is driving."

Then the doorbell rang.

"I'll get it." Becca stood to answer it. Kate seemed to instinctively understand that answering the door was Becca's chance to escape the inquisition. On her way, as she passed by the living room, she would also be able to glance in and see how Nick was getting along.

Nick caught her looking. She was glad, too, because even though there was a football game on the television and an abundance of testosterone in the room, he'd been in tune enough to her presence that he'd sensed her coming. Or more likely she just got lucky and happened by when he happened to be looking up.

She relished the breathless excitement, the way the mere sight of him made her stomach flip. She shot him a flirty little smile that was as much eyes as it was lips and kept right on walking to the front door.

She'd been so wrapped up in flirting with Nick, and since the usual gang was present and accounted for, she hadn't given much thought to who might be at the door.

Before Becca could actually open the door, the person on the other side let himself in. Becca found herself face-to-face with Zane Phillips, a friend of Rob's and whose own horse-breeding ranch was located about ten miles outside of Celebration. The guy was tall and rich and all kinds of gorgeous.

"Zane, hello. What a surprise. I didn't realize you were coming over."

Zane flashed her his trademark rugged, sexy smile. "Hello, Becca. I certainly am glad to see you. I had no idea that you were part of this football party or I would have joined in a lot sooner."

Last year, Zane had hosted a fund-raiser for the foundation on his ranch. At one time, Becca would have given her eyeteeth for him to ask her out. Today, as she stood there in the foyer with him acting all attentive and flirty, all she could think about was Nick.

"Come in. The guys are in the living room."

Zane lingered in the foyer. He didn't seem very worried that he was missing the game.

"How have you been?" he asked. "And why did we never go out after the fund-raiser?"

Wow. Her timing really did stink. Actually, Zane was the one with bad timing.

"If I remember correctly, it's because you had a girlfriend."

He held his index finger in the air. "You have a very good memory."

"It comes in handy sometimes."

"And, apparently, a good sense of humor, too. I don't have a girlfriend anymore. Apparently, she didn't have a very good sense of humor."

Was he about to ask her out? Right here? In the middle of Kate and Liam's foyer? Six months ago this would been something from a dream. But now Becca found herself inwardly squirming and backpedaling faster than a unicyclist poised to ride over a cliff.

"Can I get you a beer, Zane?"

Maybe she could buy herself a little time by offering him some liquid refreshment. Then Nick stepped from the living room into the foyer.

"I was just going to get myself one, Becca," Nick said. "Would you help me find the kitchen?"

Could the man—Zane someone or the other—not take a hint?

Nick knew he had no right or claim on Becca, even though she was pregnant with his babies.

Still, in his book, when a guy was late to the party and it was clear that a certain woman was there with another guy, the latecomer needed to back the hell up and stop flirting.

Was he jealous?

Was that what this foreign feeling was? Jealousy? He'd never experienced it before—or at least not like this.

Nick tried his best not to let it show as he followed Becca into the kitchen, even though Zane hadn't seemed to pick up on the subtle hint and trailed along behind them.

"How is the favor making going?"

Becca ducked her head and lowered her voice. "It would be fine if Pepper would stop pushing wine on me."

"Seriously?" he asked.

She grimaced. "Yes. I can't tell if she's just in a generous mood, wanting me to share in the wine she brought back from Italy, or if she's onto something and trying to force my hand. Know what I mean?"

Nick blew out an audible breath. "Sorry about that."

"Thanks, but it's not your fault. She can be a little bulldog when there's something she wants to know and feels like it's being kept from her."

"We can leave anytime you want," Nick said as they stepped into the kitchen.

Just like the rest of Liam and Kate's home, the kitchen was traditional and expensive-looking with its marble countertops and stainless-steel appliances. Yet, with pictures and progress reports and notes tacked to the refrigerator and silly messages and re-minders scrawled on the chalkboard that hung by the door, it still had a lived-in look that suggested this room was the heart of the Thayer family.

Liam and Kate's two girls, who had been cheering at the game Friday night, were hanging out with Lily and Cullen's brood of children, whom the couple had adopted shortly before they got married, Nick had heard. Cullen, who was chief of staff at Celebration Memorial, had been the kids' godparent before their natural parents had died in a car accident. The older kids were watching A.J. and Shane's toddler.

Everything about this group seemed to be centered around family. That concept was so foreign to Nick, but in a strange way it almost felt as if he could trust them to be a built-in support system for him and Becca—once they broke the news.

Still, the jaded, scarred part of him that had always relied on himself warned him not to be so trusting so fast. Periods of flux sometimes had people swimming for what they thought was the surface, but when it was too late they realized they were actually heading in the wrong direction.

"Aren't you having a good time?" Becca asked.

"I'm having a great time. But I don't want you to be uncomfortable."

"That's very sweet," Becca said. She touched his hand, and the urge to kiss her again had him lacing his fingers in hers.

The way she looked into his eyes made him believe that she wanted that, too. And for a moment he'd almost forgotten about Zane, who'd made a detour through the dining room to flirt with the other women, no doubt. They were married women, but the guy didn't seem to care.

For a moment Nick gave the guy the benefit of the doubt. Maybe he was just one of those men who loved women. Couldn't fault him for that. Especially since the detour seemed to indicate that he must have gotten the hint that Becca wasn't available—at least not tonight.

And then the guy made his presence known.

"Hey, what are you two conspiring about? The way you have your heads together makes me wonder if there's something I need to know."

You need to know what we're talking about is none of your business. You need to know that you should back off. You need to know that Becca obviously isn't into you—

"How about those beers, guys?" Becca said, her voice a lot perkier than it had been just moments before.

Nick held up a hand. "Thanks, but I'm good. I don't need to drink any more tonight, since I'm driving you home."

He wished he could take back that last part, but he couldn't help saying it. When would Zane finally get the hint? The guy had asked her out, and she hadn't answered; he'd noticed that the two of them had had their heads together in private conversation; and now Nick had made it very clear that he was the one taking her home.

Anyone with half a brain would catch the hint.

"I didn't even introduce you two," Becca said, suddenly all good manners and charm. "Nick, Zane is a good friend of Pepper's husband, Rob. He has been a big supporter of the Macintyre Family Foundation. He has sponsored a couple of fund-raisers for us. Zane, Nick is new in town. He's a doctor in the emergency room at Celebration Memorial. He's been here less than a month. I know I can count on you to make him feel welcome."

After a long pause, Zane extended his hand. "Welcome to Celebration, Nick. It's a great place."

As Becca got a beer out of the refrigerator, Liam entered the kitchen, carrying four empty beer bottles.

"There you are, Nick. It's halftime. Tell me more about your thoughts on the Hastings kid."

Nick watched Becca hand the bottle to Zane.

"Austin Roberts told me the boy has been in twice for chest pains over the past ten days," Nick said. "In between ER visits, he was treated by his family doctor, who diagnosed an upper respiratory infection. I heard that he was back in the ER last night. Was he tested for aortic dissection?"

Liam placed the bottles on the counter near the sink and turned back to Nick, a solemn expression on his face.

"I don't know. He's only sixteen years old. That disorder is not very common in people so young."

"Any family history of aortic dissection?"

"I couldn't tell you without his chart here in front of me, but I'll contact his pediatrician and see if he thinks tests are warranted."

"I suppose that's all we can do right now, since he has a pediatrician."

It went against protocol to question another doctor's practices and procedures, but this disorder, which caused a tear in the lining of the main artery for blood leaving the heart, wasn't common and went largely undiagnosed.

It could be spotted with medical imaging equipment and could be treated, but if undiagnosed, it could be deadly.

If Nick were his pediatrician, or if he'd been on duty last night when the boy came in again, he would've automatically ordered the tests.

Not that he didn't trust Liam to follow through, but he made a mental note to make sure somebody followed up with the boy's doctor. He just didn't want to leave anything to chance.

He'd learned the hard way that sometimes if you looked away for just a moment you didn't get a second chance to make things right. Even if the tests came back negative, he'd rather rule out the deadly condition than have the boy suffer the consequences.

Even though Nick's full attention had been trained on Liam as they discussed the case, it didn't go unnoticed that Zane was at it again.

The guy was standing much too close to Becca. He had one arm braced against the wall as he leaned into her. He saw Becca take a step back and cross her arms as she angled her body away.

After Liam, armed with four freshly opened beers, went back into the living room to rejoin the guys and watch the last half of the game, Nick was better able to hear what Zane was saying to Becca.

The guy was asking her out again. Couldn't he read her body language? It didn't take a rocket scientist to see that she wasn't interested.

Obviously, the guy wasn't very good at picking up subtle clues. Nick went over and slid his arm around Becca's waist.

"Sorry, man, she's busy."

Chapter Seven

"I'm not mad at you, Nick. I'm just confused because you keep sending me mixed messages. I get the feeling that you don't want a commitment—at least not a romantic commitment—but then when a man asks me to have dinner with him you tell him I'm busy?"

There. She'd said it. Now *almost everything* was out in the open. Except for the million-dollar question. She hoped he wouldn't make her spell it out. But on the drive back to her place from Liam and Kate's, she'd decided she was prepared to go for broke, because, really, what did she have to lose?

Him, maybe?

She didn't really have him. She was carrying his babies, and he seemed to be easing into the role of expectant father, but that didn't mean the two of them had a relationship beyond co-parenting.

"I'm sorry if I've been sending you mixed signals," he said as he steered the car into a visitors parking place in front of Becca's condo. "I guess I've been trying to figure this out myself. But spending time with you this week, and, yes, I'll admit, watching Zane make his big move, helped some things crystallize."

Becca's heart went all fluttery. Even though she knew she should tell Nick he couldn't have it both ways, when he turned to her and ran his thumb along her jawline, trailing it across her bottom lip, she met him halfway as he leaned in and covered her mouth with his.

His kiss was soft at first, transporting her to that magical place she always found herself in when she was with him.

He tasted vaguely of beer, but there was something else, something spicy and minty-cool freshening the taste. Something that tempted her to open her mouth wider and to lean in closer.

When she did, he deepened the kiss. Her whirling mind registered the velvety feel of his lips—those skilled, talented lips. God, he was just so darn good at this. So good at invading her personal space and instinctively knowing how to touch her just the way she wanted to be touched.

Becca didn't care about anything but this moment— this single moment suspended in time where nothing else mattered but the two of them and the babies growing inside of her.

"Should we go inside?" he asked, his breath whispering over her lips.

She answered him with another kiss before putting her hand on the door handle.

"Stay right there. I want to open your door for you."

"You're such a gentleman."

"I'm glad you think so, because the things I want to do to you might be considered ungentlemanly."

The thought took her breath away. "God, I hope so."

With that he let himself out of the car. The windows had begun to fog up. So she could see only the vague outline of him as he made his way around to her side.

She knew what this meant. She knew she was letting this happen again without any promises or pledges from him. And she thought of how well their bodies worked together, how he felt inside her, and that was all the promise she needed.

He helped her out of the car and put his arm around her, pulling her close and nibbling at her ear and her neck as they walked toward her front door.

"Do you know how crazy you are making me?" she asked as she took her keys out of her purse.

"How crazy? Tell me everything. How does this make you feel?"

As she unlocked the door, he positioned himself behind her, and she could feel his arousal through her coat. He moved her hair to one side to give himself better access to her neck, and the way he licked and trailed kisses made her stupid with lust.

His hands found their way inside her coat to her breasts; she inhaled sharply. If she couldn't open the door, they might just have to make love out here. He slipped his hands underneath her blouse and found her sensitive nipples. He knew just the right amount of pressure to make her want to cry out.

Thank God she was able to get the key in the lock and open the door. She pulled him inside and barely had time to shut the door when he turned her around and backed her up against the wall. She locked her hands around his neck, and he ravished her with deep kisses that blocked out everything else but him.

He slid his hands along her thigh, pausing at the crook of her knee, and drew her leg up and around him. He pushed his arousal into her, and she thrust back.

"God, Becca. Who's making who crazy now?"

She dug her fingers into the hair on the back of his head and pulled his mouth back to hers. He lifted her up so that she could encircle him with both legs, and they stayed like that kissing and thrusting, until she pulled away and said, "Let's go into the bedroom."

Before he set her down, he looked into her eyes. "Becca, I want to be here for you. I don't know if I'll be very good at it—"

"But you are, Nick. I don't understand why you can't see that."

"I have a history of messing things up when it comes to family. I was married once before, but it didn't work out, and then—"

He choked on his words, but he cleared his throat.

"I just don't have a very good track record when it comes to family. Everything I touch seems to disintegrate."

"That's not true. You are a gifted doctor. You save lives, Nick. That's sort of the opposite of making things disintegrate."

He set her down gently and took a step back, raking his hair out of his eyes and looking more intense than she'd ever seen him look.

"Do you want to talk about this?" she asked.

"Not really. Not now. Another time. But I want you to know that there is nobody else but you, and if you want to try to make this work, that's what I want, too."

She took him by the hand and led him into her bedroom, where they kissed softly, gently, for what seemed an eternity—or maybe it was only a moment. Time was suspended, until he picked her up and set her tenderly on the bed.

"I didn't realize you had a fireplace in here," he said. "I'll start a fire. I don't want you to get cold."

"Are you kidding? Here with you like this, there's no way I could get cold. Forget the fire."

He kissed her, and she felt it all the way to her toes. "Hold that thought. I'll be right back."

She watched him as he walked across the room and set logs and kindling on the fireplace's iron grate.

"There are matches on the mantel," she said. "In that little wooden box."

He picked up the matchbox and stared at it a moment before looking up at Becca.

"Are you sure this is okay? I mean, is it safe for the babies?"

"I talked to Dr. Stevens and he said it's fine. He said the only reason they classify my pregnancy *nearly normal* is because the uterus is really designed to only carry one baby. But since I'm healthy and everything seems to be fine, he said I should live as normal a life as possible within pregnancy parameters."

She was glad he asked, glad he cared about the well-being of their children. It made her want him all the more.

Minutes later the fire flared and spit tiny embers,

casting Nick in a warm glow of light and shadows. Everything about this man, from his tall, rugged build to his dark, brooding personality, set her senses on fire. The guy was a mystery, and she wanted to solve him, to get inside him and figure out what made him tick.

As he came back to her, he unbuttoned his shirt and let it fall to the floor. He unbuckled his belt and tossed it to the side. By the time he rejoined her on the bed, he was wearing only his pants.

Firelight danced across the taut muscles of his bare chest and shoulders. That's when she saw it—that single word tattooed on his left bicep in dark block letters.

Ignosces.

Was that Latin?

The first night they'd been together she hadn't noticed the date underneath the word: May 13, 1995.

"What's this?" She gently traced the word with her fingernail. "What does it mean?"

She felt him tense, maybe even pull away just a little, but she kept her hand on his arm.

He opened his mouth as if to speak but closed it before he could say a word. And then, as if thinking better of it, he said, "It means *forgive me.*"

Becca nodded, prepared to let it go at that, but he expounded.

"It's for my little brother. He died on May 13, 1995. He was only seven years old."

Becca's heart clenched. "I'm so sorry, Nick." She continued stroking his arm. "What happened?"

She knew it was a bad question to ask, even before his eyes darkened. She really wasn't trying to kill the mood. There was just so much between them that they needed to know about each other.

"That's a story for another day," he said.

Instinctively, she knew not to push him. It was the first personal detail—that and that he'd been married once before and he seemed to be convinced that everything worth loving fell apart in his hands. They were small steps. Tiny revelations she was learning about him. And if things kept going the way they were, she was confident that he would keep revealing himself to her bit by bit.

He swung his feet up onto the bed and propped himself up on one elbow. Reaching out, he smoothed a strand of hair off her forehead. His gaze was still dark, but now there was an intensity to it, and she felt herself melting like beeswax in his hands, especially when he trailed a thumb down her cheek, across her bottom lip, over the sensitive area at the base of her neck, until he reached the neckline of her sweater, where he teased the skin just below the surface.

Her mind skipped back to that first night they'd been together. He had instinctively known how to comfort her, how to please her. He'd made her feel as if she were the only woman in the world. Or at least the most adored woman in the world, and that's exactly how he was making her feel right now. Right now, in this moment, her world consisted of the two of them and the babies they'd already made. She couldn't imagine how life could be any sweeter.

His hands found their way to the bottom of her sweater and gently tugged it up and over her head, and then he made haste relieving her of her jeans, leaving her in just her bra and panties.

"Aren't you glad I stoked the fire?" he said through a lopsided smile that was more sexy than it was humorous.

"Yeah, you're good at that," she said, gazing up into his smoldering eyes. So many nights she'd thought of him, sure that she'd never see him again, never again feel his touch that seemed to instinctively know how to please her.

As if he could read her mind, his hands found her breasts, and he moved his thumb over her hard, sensitive nipple, which was aching for his touch. As he worked his magic, she found herself inhaling a ragged breath a second before a low moan escaped her lips. She didn't try to control her response; she let herself go, allowing her reaction to come spontaneously and unself-consciously.

She reached up and ran her hands over those shoulders that drove her crazy. His skin was as hot and his muscles as hard as a sheet of pressed steel. His body was smooth and strong with animal-like sexiness that had her summoning every ounce of self-control to keep from demanding that he take her right then and there. They were going to make love.

The heady realization racked Becca's body with shudders. She couldn't wait for him to do more of the same he'd done to her that first night they'd been together.

Of course, that night their lovemaking had created a baby—two babies. Right now, that seemed terribly romantic. Lying here with him naked and vulnerable, allowing him inside, past her personal barriers, there was no place to hide in the soft firelight. And that was fine because she couldn't recall ever wanting anything more.

He ran his hand down her thighs, sliding them all the way to her knees and then back up until his fingertips found their way inside the edge of her panties. Gently hooking his thumbs in the elastic, he tugged them down and slipped them off. Then he lifted her ever so slightly and removed her bra with a couple of deft movements.

It wasn't her lack of clothing that gave her pause as much as it was her emotional vulnerability. Could he read the desire in her eyes as clearly as she could read it in his? He put her at ease when he began placing gentle, unanticipated kisses on her body—on her forehead, on that ticklish spot behind her ears, trailing his way down until he'd reached the sensitive insides of her thighs.

Then he stopped, looking at her with possessive eyes. "I said I wanted to get to know you better." His voice was low and sexy. "Show me what I need to know."

He started running his hands over her, then he took her hand and moved it with his, allowing her to introduce him to her body, having her show him what she liked. This was something she'd never done during lovemaking.

He was incredibly gentle and generous. Not only did he know how to please, he seemed to give his all to every experience. Or maybe the explosiveness of his touch was a by-product of their personal chemistry.

Whatever the case, she loved everything he did. Everything he said. Everywhere he touched.

And then his tongue found its way to her center,

and he worked his magic until she cried out in pleasure that was so intense it radiated off her in waves.
Her first climax was compliments of his clever, teasing mouth, and the second time it was thanks to the
long, soft gliding strokes of his fingers.

Spellbound, she turned onto her side and braced
her hands on his strong, muscled chest, letting her
hands discover him, feeling every muscled ridge.
Then when she freed him of his pants and underwear
and took him into her hands, his head dropped back.

He groaned as she savored the hot, smooth length
of him.

Lowering her head, she swirled her tongue over
him. His whole body stiffened, and he let out a sound
that heartened and aroused her even more. With him,
she wanted to do things she'd never done before, had
never wanted to do with anyone else. She wanted him
to see her pleasure in doing them with him.

He must've known, because everything about him
was hard with arousal. And yet his hands were gentle
as he turned her over onto her back and stared lov-
ingly into her eyes.

"If you keep doing that, I won't be any good to
you. We have a lot more territory to cover."

He leaned down and kissed her softly and slowly.
"Becca, I've never seen anything more perfect than
you in my life," he said as he positioned himself over
her. "You are flawless."

His words nearly brought her to tears. No one had
ever called her flawless. No one had even remotely
thought of her that way. Or at least they hadn't told
her if they had. She'd spent so much time trying to

live up to everyone's expectations—the couple of former lovers she'd had, her family…

"You don't know how many nights I've lain awake,
thinking about this moment when we would be together again like this."

She wanted to tell him that she felt the same way,
but she was afraid that if she spoke she might break
the spell or, even worse, wake up from this lovely
dream.

Then he finally thrust into her, filling her with
his muscle and heat. She gripped his shoulders tight,
matching him thrust for thrust until she exploded in
an orgasm that seemed to last forever.

His forehead glistened with sweat and his biceps
bulged. Their gazes locked and he built a strong rhythm
that got faster and faster until his teeth clenched and
his face contorted. A long, guttural growl emanated
from his throat. Then very slowly, ever so tenderly, he
lowered his body to cover hers.

As a general rule, Nick wasn't a fan of shopping
malls, but over coffee and bagels early Monday morning before they both went to work, somehow Becca
had talked him into meeting her at the mall after he
got off work at seven that evening.

She wanted to look at baby furniture in Dallas.
After last night, she might be able to talk him into
just about anything.

He had taken a risk making love to her again—
crossing that line and making implied promises he
still, in his moments of doubt, wasn't sure he could
keep.

But damn, they were good together. In bed, they

had a chemistry that could scorch the sun. He just hoped it didn't mean that the relationship was combustible in other ways. Even that possibility didn't burn away the reality that he liked waking up beside her.

His other reason for meeting her at the mall was that he wanted to talk to her about Dr. Stevens's caution that, because they were pregnant with twins, the pregnancy was considered *nearly normal*.

Becca was healthy and Stevens had said sex was okay, but during a slow moment at work, Nick had done some research and discovered that even the slightly elevated risk associated with carrying twins warranted extra precautions as the pregnancy progressed.

He'd also picked out the best hospital in the area that specialized in high-risk births. He'd been eager to talk to her about it because he wanted her to tour the hospital to make sure she was comfortable with it, but he didn't want to alarm her any more than Dr. Stevens had. Just as he started to broach the subject, a woman who was modeling a ruby ring and necklace at the entrance to a jewelry store spoke to Becca.

"This would look lovely on you," she said, "with your fair skin and dark hair."

Becca stopped to admire the jewelry.

"Would you like to try it on?" the woman asked.

"Oh, no, that's okay," Becca said as she continued to admire the necklace. "We're in a hurry today. Maybe another time."

The way she lingered over the unusual piece belied her objections.

Nick looked at his watch. "Go ahead," he urged. "We have a few minutes."

"We still need to look at furniture," Becca said. "I know you're tired after working. I'd planned on making this quick."

"We're fine."

Becca smiled and followed the saleswoman into the store.

Once inside, the woman unhooked the ruby-studded gold chain from her neck and slipped it around Becca's neck.

"Doesn't she look exquisite wearing the necklace?"

The woman was an excellent salesperson. She was definitely working hard to earn her commission.

"She is exquisite even without the necklace," he said.

He smiled as he watched Becca's cheeks turn a pretty shade of pink. It reminded him of how color had touched her features last night as he'd made love to her in the firelight.

"Try on the ring, too." The woman took it off her finger and handed it to Becca.

"Historically, rubies have been associated with passion. They're also a symbol of romance and adventure. So, Romeo, this is a nice gift to get your sweetheart."

Yes, she was definitely working it. He had to admire her tenacity.

"Do you want the necklace?" he asked. "I'd like for you to have it."

"Oh, no, Nick, I couldn't. I mean, it's gorgeous, but it's far too expensive. I was just trying it on for fun."

Apologetically, she turned to the saleswoman. "I didn't mean to waste your time."

The woman smiled at her. "No apology needed. We're slow right now, anyway. I'm happy you tried it on."

As Becca took one last wistful glance in the mirror, the woman slipped Nick her card and mouthed, *For Christmas?*

Nick nodded. It would be a good present, he thought as he tucked the card into his pocket.

As they walked away from the store, Becca said, "I'm sorry that woman put you in an awkward position. It was sweet of you to offer to get me the necklace. But you didn't have to."

"One thing you definitely need to know about me is that it's not easy to coerce me into anything I don't want to do. I wouldn't have offered if I'd felt pressured."

"Good to know," Becca said, and a sensuous light passed between them.

He hated to potentially kill the mood. "There's something I need to talk to you about."

"Should I be worried?"

"No," he said as they entered the department store. "In fact, it should be something to ease your mind."

She slanted him a dubious look. "Okay. Why is that not comforting?"

"You haven't even heard what I have to say." They got on the escalator to the second floor, where apparently they kept the baby furniture. This was foreign territory. "After Dr. Stevens mentioned that a twin pregnancy was considered slightly high risk, I did some research."

He told her about the hospital in Dallas that specialized in high-risk births.

She frowned but didn't say anything.

"Think about it," he said. "Your obstetrician is in Dallas, and you work there. You're there almost as much as you're in Celebration. So, really, it only makes sense."

They stepped off the escalator and followed the signs to the baby department.

"What if I go into labor in the middle of the night? It would be just my luck."

"You can call me and I'll come and get you."

"I don't know if it makes sense, since Celebration Memorial is five minutes from my condo. I'm having twins, not brain surgery. I'm healthy. Do we really need to make the twenty-minute drive?"

She pointed at a crib that was adorned with a yellow checked blanket turned down over yellow flannel sheets. "What do you think? Natural wood or white for the furniture?"

"Whatever you want," he said. "Will you just agree to go for the tour? The hospital set it up for me as a professional courtesy."

"I'll think about it."

"Fair enough. The appointment isn't until December 9, but that'll be here sooner than you think."

"Becca?"

They both turned at a woman's voice behind them. Nick watched all the color drain out of Becca's cheeks when she saw her sister, Rosanna.

"What are you doing here? Are you looking at baby furniture?"

"Rosanna, hi. No, we are shopping for a baby gift."

"Oh, really? From my angle it looked like you were looking at furniture."

"Sorry to disappoint you, but we aren't." The clipped tone Becca used with her sister was foreign and far from the sweet, gentle nature that he'd come to know.

"Who's pregnant?" Rosanna was openly eyeing Becca's stomach.

"Nobody you know. Rosanna, you remember Nick, don't you?"

"Of course, the football game Friday night. Good to see you again. I have to run. If you do find yourself in the market for baby furniture, don't forget I still have Victor's stuff. It's in the attic at Mom and Dad's. I'm sure they'd be happy to get it down for you."

Becca smiled at her sister, but there was an obvious lack of warmth. "I'll keep that in mind. For future reference. See you later."

Rosanna walked in one direction. Becca and Nick headed toward the exit.

As soon as she was sure Rosanna was out of earshot, Becca turned to Nick. "What was that? Of all the people to run into right now, right here? Why her? It's as if she has radar that helps her zero in on finding me at my weakest." She put a hand on Nick's arm as if she needed to steady herself. He put his arm around her as they walked.

"Nick, I have to tell my parents. If they end up hearing the news from someone else first, they'll never forgive me. It's already going to be hard enough when they hear it from me. I just need to do it."

He reached out and took her hand. "I'll go with

you. It's all in how you present it. If you act like there's something wrong, then they'll take it badly. If we present it like the good news that it is, they'll have to be happy for us."

She scoffed and picked up a tiny pink outfit. "Obviously, you don't know my parents."

"Please, don't take this wrong, but how old are you?"

Her brows furrowed. "We're having twins, and you don't even know how old I am. We are doing things backward, aren't we?"

"We are two adults, and we are playing the cards that we've been dealt."

She gave him a one-shoulder shrug. "I guess you're right. And for the record, I'm twenty-five."

"You are a grown woman. You have your own home. You're supporting yourself. I know this will sound harsh, but your parents shouldn't get to set the rules in this circumstance."

She nodded, but she looked as if she was trying to convince herself that was true. "Do you really want to go with me? Because you don't have to."

"Of course I will. I—" A foreign feeling, that for a fleeting moment felt something like love, whooshed through him. He took a deep breath and realized it was just the protectiveness and an odd sort of possessiveness he felt for Becca. "We're in this together. Come on. I'll walk you to your car."

They'd come in separate cars, since he was meeting her after work.

Out in the parking lot, Becca said, "Before you make up your mind about going with me, I have to warn you. My parents will insist that we get married."

"That's not their decision to make."

"You're right. But they'll insist. So just be pre-pared. They like to pretend that they're terribly old-fashioned, but really they're just holier than thou. What's ironic is they've both been unhappy in their own marriage for as far back as I can remember. They've done a very good job of pretending and put-ting up a front so that everyone else thinks they have this idealistic life. They've always held themselves a little above everyone else, which I believe is just a de-fense mechanism. Rosanna got pregnant with Victor when she was fifteen. She was always the wild child and I was the good girl. My parents pretended to be the happy couple. I guess we all just fell into those roles. My parents—it's going to kill them to know that both of their daughters got pregnant outside of marriage."

More pieces of the Becca puzzle, and they ex-plained a lot. She was the good girl of the family who had probably jumped through hoops all of her life in order to win her parents' approval. Rosanna was the one who pretended not to give a damn about what anyone thought. Nick knew how that was, pre-tending not to care. Pretty soon, it became a way of life. If you grew a tough hide, no one could hurt you. But to keep people from hurting you, you had to stop letting people in, and pretty soon people just stopped trying to reach you.

"Is Victor's father involved?"

Becca shook her head. "He hasn't been around at all. Victor has never met him."

"Well, therein lies one huge difference. I plan to

be there for you and our children. Tell me when you need me, and I'll make sure I'm there."

"I'll see if they're available tomorrow evening."

Chapter Eight

"You're what?" Isabel Flannigan shrieked.

"Nick and I are pregnant with twins," Becca repeated.

"And you're getting married, Rebecca."

It was a command, not a question. And it tightened every fiber in Becca's body.

"No, we have no plans to get married, Mom."

She glanced at her father, who was sitting quietly in the striped gondola chair with his arms crossed. He was staring somewhere into the distance, and he hadn't said a word since Becca had broken the news.

"I will be there for Becca and the babies," Nick said. "They will have my full emotional and financial support."

Isabel glared at Nick.

"And are we supposed to cheer for you for owning up to your mistake?"

"Mom. These are your grandchildren. Please, don't

call them a mistake. They may have been unplanned, but they are certainly not a mistake."

Isabel continued her tirade as if she hadn't heard a word Becca had said after *Nick and I are pregnant with twins*. "Getting married is only the decent thing to do. You play, you pay, Rebecca."

Becca wanted to tell her mother that the reason she wasn't getting married was because Nick didn't love her. Not that way. But her biggest fear was being shoehorned into a loveless marriage, and because of it, she and her children and her coerced husband would end up living an unhappy life.

Just like you, Mom and Dad.

But of course she didn't say that. If she had, she would've said it in front of Nick, and the wrath she would've had to endure for embarrassing her mother in front of a stranger would've made the admonishment she'd received after breaking the news of the pregnancy look like nothing.

"With all due respect, Mrs. Flannigan, we didn't come to ask for your advice or your blessing."

Oh, good Lord. All the air whooshed out of Becca's lungs. And she wanted to hug Nick for it. He'd just succeeded in very politely and respectfully putting Isabel Flannigan in her place. How in the world had he managed that?

Oh, but wait, he wasn't finished.

"Mr. and Mrs. Flannigan, Becca and I are here out of courtesy to you. You're the grandparents of our children, and I hope that we can count on you to be supportive, but we need to establish that the way Becca and I choose to live our lives and how we raise our children is our decision."

Isabel opened her mouth as if she were going to say something but decided better. That was a first.

"Of course it's your decision," said Patrick Flannigan. It was the first indication that he'd heard a single word spoken this evening. "I just hope you understand this comes as a shock. It's the last thing we expected from Rebecca. We always thought she would take a more traditional path. And, young man, we met you for the first time five days ago. We don't know anything about you. So why don't we start with…how long have you known our daughter?"

Nick and Rebecca looked at each other. *If ever there was a chance that he could read her mind, please, let it be now.* Surely he would know that they didn't need to know about the one-night stand. But just in case—

"We met at the hospital, the night of Victor's accident."

"Let the man speak for himself, Rebecca," her mother said.

She hated how a single comment from her mother could make her feel fourteen years old. She braced herself for her parents to do the math and, from the sum of the equation, figure out she'd gotten pregnant that night.

Instead, her mother insisted, "Why were you at the hospital the night of Victor's accident?"

"I'm an emergency medicine doctor," Nick said. "Becca had some questions about her nephew's condition, and I was happy to answer them. We had dinner, and the rest is history."

Yes. Perfect. Becca held her breath for a moment,

waiting for them to catch on, but if they knew, they didn't mention it.

Thank you. Becca glanced at Nick again and there was that subtle, sensual bond that connected them like a thread.

He understood her. At that moment she thought she might possibly be in love for the first time in her life.

After Isabel and Patrick Flannigan were satisfied with the grilling that they had given Nick, Isabel said, "Then I suppose you and Rebecca will be doing double duty on Thanksgiving. I'm sure you want to see your parents, too."

As much as Becca hated to admit it, it was a good question. Nick always seemed to skirt the issue when family came up. She was curious to know more about his folks. She knew his younger brother had passed away much too early, but she had no idea if he had other siblings.

"My mother is no longer living," Nick said in a very matter-of-fact tone. "My father lives in Florida. So, no, I won't see him for Thanksgiving."

"Did you invite him for the holiday?"

"I'm sure he has to work."

"Couldn't he make time?"

"Mom, really? Don't you think you've interrogated Nick enough for tonight?"

Isabel pinned Becca with a withering glare. "Rebecca, this man is the father of our grandchildren. I don't think it's out of line to ask a few questions to get to know him.

"Have you broken the news about the twins to him yet?" she pressed.

"No, not yet. We wanted to share it with you and Mr. Flannigan first."

Ooh! Brownie points. Nice touch, Nick.

To Becca's surprise, Isabel's face softened.

"Since you have no family in town, we will set a place for you at our table."

Becca blinked. Nick didn't know this, but this was a huge gesture on her mother's part. She guarded her holidays zealously. They were for family only. In fact, her brother Mark's wife, Beth, had not been invited until after she and Mark were engaged. It seemed that Nick had managed to skip a couple of steps. Or maybe babies trumped marriage? Who knew what logic Isabel applied.

"That's a very gracious offer," Nick said. "But I'm scheduled to work Thursday."

The silence was deafening.

"But I'm scheduled for the early shift this week. How about if I come over after I get off work?"

"Nick, you'll be exhausted. Mom, he works twelve-hour shifts. I'm sure he doesn't want to come after work."

"Don't be ridiculous, Rebecca. It's Thanksgiving. It's when families get together. And it will be as good a time as any for the two of you to announce the pregnancy and any other plans you might come up with between now and then."

Tuesday evening after leaving her parents' house, Becca was certain of two things: first, Nick had managed the impossible—he had basically charmed her mother into submission—and second, she was falling in love with Nick. He'd walked that fine line between saying the right things and not kowtowing.

Since Nick had agreed to endure Thanksgiving Flannigan-style, she'd given him some space Wednesday night. He had to work the 7:00 a.m. to 7:00 p.m. shift. He was sure to be exhausted.

But Becca would've been lying to herself if she didn't admit she'd been a little disappointed when he hadn't called last night. Of course, she hadn't called him, either—hence the giving him space part. But it was the first day that had gone by since they'd received the results of the pregnancy test that they hadn't at least texted.

On Thursday morning, she picked up her phone, brought up his number and sent him a message:

Happy Thanksgiving! Looking forward to seeing you tonight.

She stared at the screen expectantly for a moment, tamping down the hope that he would text her right back.

But he didn't.

She swallowed her disappointment. He was working. He'd been there since before she'd even gotten out of bed. She needed to cut him some slack.

Mandatory family dinners were never easy to get through. They usually involved at least thirty relatives. Of course, there were her mother's judgmental comments and her sister's temperamental prickliness. Someone always had too much to drink and ended up saying or doing something that offended someone else.

For the most part, it was like a three-ring circus.

Her aunts and uncles were generally pleasant, for the most part. Mark and Beth were nice and Becca tried to stick with them or at least fly under the radar until she'd helped wash, dry and put away the last dish, and she could take her leave until the next time.

What was it like to be part of a family that wasn't quite so dysfunctional?

As she took the pumpkin pies she'd prepared from scratch out of the oven, she vowed when her daughters were born she would do everything in her power to foster a good relationship with them. Daughters? Well, that was a Freudian slip if she'd ever heard one. She had no idea what the sex of her babies would be—if they were fraternal or identical—and, yes, when it came right down to it, she simply wanted healthy children, whatever the sex. Still, deep inside she knew she'd love to have a couple of little girls with whom she could have a good relationship and do all of the things she wished she and her mother could have done and shared.

How had her relationship with her mother ended up getting so off track? All she had ever done was try to please her mother, try to make her see that she was worthy of her love. In all fairness, her mother loved her in her own quirky way. But she always seemed to disapprove. It was her mother's approval she'd always been trying to earn. No matter what she did or how hard she tried, she never seemed to measure up.

As Becca carried the trays with her homemade pies to her car, she vowed to never make her children feel as if they had to earn her approval.

The first thing her mother said to her when she

arrived at the house at four o'clock was "You're late, Rebecca."

"It's four o'clock, mother. We won't serve dinner until seven-thirty."

"Well, since I gave the staff Thanksgiving Day off, it would've been nice for you to offer to help."

Of course, she was being sarcastic. She didn't have staff. Isabel Flannigan prided herself on being a homemaker—and a darn good one at that, if you were giving credit where credit was due. Besides, she probably wouldn't have been able to find somebody to measure up to her standards if she could have had staff. And then there was the problem of finding someone who actually had the hide of steel to withstand her mother's scrutiny on an hourly basis. Becca couldn't even imagine such a person existed.

"Why didn't you ask me to come earlier? I'm not very good at reading minds. Where is Rosanna? Is she here yet?"

"Oh, heavens, no. I want this to be a pleasant day. She and I would simply be at each other's throats. I told her and Victor to arrive around six o'clock."

So that was the secret, huh? If you made Isabel miserable enough, you were released from family obligation. Her sister was smarter than her mother gave her credit for.

"Well, then, she gets to do the cleanup," Becca said. "Just because she's hard to get along with doesn't mean she gets a vacation."

"Oh, Rebecca, stop saying nasty things about your sister. Do you hear yourself?"

No, Mom, I can't seem to hear myself over the echo of your negativity.

That's what Rosanna would have said, and the two of them would've gotten into a sparring match that would've lasted until Rosanna left in tears or their mother ended up going upstairs with a *sick head-ache*. Becca, on the other hand, swallowed her words, sat down at the kitchen table and started peeling the sweet potatoes.

She'd rather cook than clean up, anyway. And with Nick here, she'd have a good reason to leave the cleanup to Rosanna. Becca's stomach gave a nervous turn when she remembered running into Rosanna at the mall. Of course, there was the little matter of the little white lie she'd told when Rosanna had been quizzing her about why she was browsing in the baby department. There would be hell to pay for that one.

For a moment Becca contemplated pulling Rosanna aside and sharing the news with her before she and Nick told the rest of the family. But as quickly as the idea presented itself, Becca decided against it. She wanted to keep today as uncomplicated as possible. Despite how her parents had mandated that she and Nick announce their news to the rest of the family today, they were onboard with it. It made sense. The next time the entire family would be together would be Christmas.

She wanted to share the news with her friends. Since Celebration was such a small town, if she did that, a family member was bound to find out. She wouldn't want to receive news like that secondhand. So this was a do unto others as she would hope that they would do for her sort of decision. But Rosanna could be such a loose cannon, if Becca tried to ap-pease her, she might end up spilling the beans before

Becca and Nick had a chance to make the announcement. Faced with the potential fallout of that and her sister's inevitable protests that Becca had lied to her, Becca was better prepared to deal with Rosanna.

All she had to say to her sister about that day at the mall was she didn't want to tell her about the babies until she and Nick had told Mom and Dad.

Becca was surprised how fast time flew. She'd been busy in the kitchen all afternoon—even if her mother had insisted that she stay seated. It was amazing what could be accomplished at the kitchen table. Now it was seven-fifteen, and Victor had been enlisted by his grandmother to round up the crew and instruct them to wash their hands and be at their respective places at the table—there were place cards for the assigned seating, and Victor had a list and was to help them find their way. His chest was puffed out with the importance of this job that allowed him to tell the adults what to do, for a change, rather than being bossed by the adults.

As her mother placed the turkey on the serving tray, Becca was anxiously aware that Nick had not yet arrived.

An unsettled wave of apprehension washed over her. What if he'd changed his mind? What if he wasn't coming?

That was a ridiculous thought. Had Nick let her down yet?

No. But after Tuesday night's interrogation, she really wouldn't blame him if he decided to skip the Flannigan's annual turkey brawl.

Come on, Becca. Buck up. He had to work until seven. Maybe something came up.

Like a better offer.

No. That was decidedly not the man she'd fallen in love with. He'd been her rock, her touchstone. While she knew she was capable of breaking the news of the pregnancy to her family, she had liked the idea of him standing beside her, helping her set the tone, when they made the announcement.

As the parade of side dishes, dinner rolls and condiments started to roll toward the table, Becca slipped off to check her phone. Just in case.

Her heart nearly stopped when she saw the text from Nick.

Sorry for the late notice. I have an emergency and I can't get away from the hospital. Will try to stop by later if it's not too late. Please give your parents my regrets. Happy Thanksgiving.

Chapter Nine

Nick steered his car onto the Flannigans' paved circular driveway and parked behind a dark Toyota Prius.

After work, he'd gone home to take a quick shower and trade his scrubs for a pair of black pants and a button-down. He swapped out the Harley for the Jeep before going to Thanksgiving dinner. He'd done it for Becca's sake more than anything. After meeting Isabel and Patrick and informing them that their daughter was having his babies, he'd come away with the impression that they'd like him even less if he showed up on a bike.

He wasn't trying to impress them or win them over. Her mother had already proven she could be a handful, and Nick simply didn't want to add fuel to the fire.

That was all right. He was in a good mood. He always was after he saved someone's life.

He grabbed the bottle of merlot he'd bought for the occasion and headed up the porch steps that led to the front door of the two-story brick home.

This was the home where Becca had grown up.

Before he reached the porch, he wondered which window had been hers and how many boys might have stood below it and tossed pebbles to get her attention.

The gas coach lamps glowed, and other ambient lighting lit up the lush, well-landscaped yard that still looked remarkably green despite the unseasonably cold temperatures. The redbrick Colonial wasn't a mansion by any means, but it certainly wasn't a shack.

It was a nice upper-middle class abode that any family would be lucky to call home. It was a far cry from the places he'd lived as a child as he'd shuffled back and forth between his parents' places. They were usually leased apartments in a part of town where rent was *affordable*. His parents' divorce had not only torn apart the family, but it had also ruined both of them financially.

On the porch, Nick could see through the illuminated windows into the dining room, where a crowd was gathered around the table enjoying dessert.

Maybe he should've texted Becca before he came, but he was already so late that he'd been in a hurry to get there. Now it seemed pointless to text from the front porch.

He rang the doorbell and heard the sound of running feet and a couple *I'll get its*—a herd of children, no doubt, racing to answer the door.

He was right. When the door opened, a small crowd of kids clustered around the threshold.

"Who are you?" asked a boy who may have been six or seven years old. His nose was covered with freckles, and he was missing his two front teeth.

Nick shifted his weight from one foot to the other. "I'm Nick. Who are you?"

"My mom says I can't talk to strangers," said the boy, who was obviously the spokesperson for the munchkins.

"Probably a good idea," Nick said. "Would you please go get Becca so I can talk to her?"

"He's here to see Becca?" a little blonde girl asked. "How come he's not at his house having Thanksgiving?"

"Because he's here to see Becca," the freckle-faced boy said, in that way older and usually self-designated wiser kids talked down to younger kids.

"He's right," Nick said. "I'm supposed to come over and have Thanksgiving with Becca. Right here in this house with you."

The little girl ducked back behind the door.

The freckled kid assessed him for a moment before bellowing, *"Beccaaaaa!"*

He drew out the *aaaaa* until a startled-looking Becca came to the door.

"Oh! Nick. It's you." Her face brightened. "You're here. How long have you been standing there?"

"Not long. They were just telling me that they're not allowed to talk to strangers."

Becca laughed. "Right. Well, uh, thanks, Jesse. This is Nick. He's my friend. It's okay to invite him in."

Becca ruffled the kid's sandy-brown hair.

"You can come in," Jesse said, stepping back. "But I don't think we have any turkey left. We have Brussels sprouts, though."

"What are you talking about, Jesse? We still have some turkey."

As Nick stepped into the foyer, the kid frowned at Becca and then put his finger to his lips and made a shushing noise. "I'm taking that home. Auntie Bel said I could take it home. He can have the *Brussels sprouts*."

"Jesse, you need to share. Nick just got off work, and I'm sure he's hungry. Believe me, there will be plenty of turkey for you and everyone else to take home if Nick has some. It's cold outside. Please, move out of the way so he can come in."

Either Jesse was easily convinced or he lost interest, because the next thing Nick knew the boy and his wolf pack had run off, leaving him gloriously alone in the foyer with Becca.

"Hi," he said, leaning in a little bit.

"Hi," she repeated, meeting him halfway. "I'm glad to see you."

He kissed her, and suddenly her lips were the only thing in the world he craved. He was lost in the taste of her cranberry-and-spice lips until he heard giggles coming from around the corner.

"See!" Jesse said victoriously. "I told you if we left they'd kiss." This was uproariously funny to the brood, who were holding their stomachs and throwing back their small heads in laughter. Then when Jesse started chanting, *"Kissing! Kissing!"* his band of mini minions began following him around the house reciting in unison.

"That's embarrassing. Sorry. Welcome to Thanksgiving with the Flannigans. You can run now and save yourself."

"That's all right. I'm up for it."

Becca leaned in and planted one more kiss on his lips. "Come on in, but don't say I didn't warn you."

Of course, the house looked the same, but it had a decidedly different air with all the rooms lit up and the sound of people chatting and laughing. Good smells filled the air, and Nick's stomach rumbled in appreciation.

Becca paused outside the dining room. "I was afraid you wouldn't be able to make it."

"I'm sorry about that," he said. "We had an emergency. This boy who was in the ER twice before with chest pains was back today."

Becca grimaced. "Poor kid. And on Thanksgiving, too."

"I confirmed a diagnosis of aortic dissection. He had a tear in the lining of the main artery for blood leaving the heart. If we hadn't caught it, he could've died."

"Nick. You saved his life."

He gave a quick nod. "Do you think that earns me a beer?"

Becca gave him a hug and then looked up at him. "You can have whatever you want."

He liked the way she felt in his arms. It felt like coming home. Or he imagined it did. It was unlike any home he'd ever known.

A large man with a red face turned the corner of the dining room and nearly ran into them. "Hey, you two. Knock that off. No wonder the kids are running around here chanting about kissing."

His tone suggested he was joking. Nonetheless, Nick stepped away from Becca.

"Uncle Don," Becca said. "I want you to meet Nick Ciotti. Nick, this is my uncle Don."

Nick shook the man's hand. "Is this the boyfriend your mother was telling us about?" Don said.

Becca sputtered a bit. "You know how Mom is."

"She mentioned that there might be wedding bells in the future. She's a good catch, man. Don't let her get away."

Nick wasn't quite sure what to say. So he simply nodded in what he hoped was a noncommittal way.

The collar of his shirt suddenly felt tight, despite the fact that it was open. It was a little warm in the house, despite the nearly freezing temperatures outside.

He was probably coming down off the adrenaline rush brought on by the fast pace of the day. Plus, he was hungry, and he really could use that beer.

"Uncle Don, Nick was just telling me he saved a boy's life today. He's an ER doctor at the hospital, and he's just coming from work."

Becca definitely had a talent for steering an uncomfortable conversation in a different direction.

"Is that so? Well, it'll be good to have a doctor in the family. Good job, Becs. I need to run in *here* for a minute." He gestured toward a room off the hallway that led to the living room. "I'll catch up with you lovebirds a little later."

After Don disappeared, Becca made an exasperated face at Nick. "I warned you."

"And that you did." He hadn't expected so much

pressure. He hoped her family wouldn't turn into an angry mob after they broke the news about the pregnancy.

He was about to ask her if she really thought tonight was a good night to tell them and suggest that maybe they should do it in smaller groups, when Isabel found them.

"Nick, how lovely to see you." She leaned in and offered her cheek. "I was afraid you wouldn't be able to join us."

"I'm sorry I'm late, Mrs. Flannigan. I got tied up at work."

Isabel cocked her head to the right, but her posture was still impeccable. "Nothing serious, I hope."

As Don passed by again, he said, "He saved a kid's life tonight."

Isabel's eyes flew open wide. "You did? And on Thanksgiving. Oh, Nick, I'll bet the family is so very thankful for you today. We have a hero, right here in our midst."

Nick waved her off and tried to tell her it was nothing, really. "It was all in a day's work."

But Isabel wasn't listening. She was already leading the way into the dining room, where at least twenty people were crowded around the large formal table talking and eating. A cornucopia resided at the center of the table. Along the back wall was an ornate wooden buffet that housed a fancy silver coffee service, complete with creamer and sugar bowl situated on a large, gleaming tray. At least a half dozen pies of various types were positioned on either side.

"Please, come into the dining room and sit down. Victor, move so Nick can sit down and eat." The skinny teenage boy cast a moody glance over his left shoulder, but he obediently got up from the table.

"Sit down right there, Nick. Becca will bring you a place setting and fix you a plate."

"Really, I don't want to put you out. If you've already put the food away, I'll just have a beer or coffee. Or whatever you have handy."

"Nonsense. It's Thanksgiving. On Thanksgiving you will eat turkey and all the trimmings. Now, sit down. Becca, don't just stand there. Go get his food."

Nick slanted Becca a glance, worried that she might be bristling over her mother's directives. But she didn't seem bothered. She was already on her way out of the room.

He could see others through the doorway that led to the kitchen and still more people sitting in the living room, where Nick and Becca had sat with Isabel and Patrick two nights ago.

After Nick's mom had died, it was just him and his dad. Caiden was gone, and his dad wasn't close with his extended family. There had been no holidays with grandparents or aunts, uncles and cousins.

A gathering of the boisterous Flannigan clan was a little overwhelming. To say the least.

Especially when Don said in his booming voice, "Hey, everyone, this is Nick, Becca's boyfriend. He saved a kid's life tonight. That's why he's late to Thanksgiving."

Sounds of awed admiration echoed through the room. Things like this were bright spots, but they really were just part of a day's work. He forgot how it must sound when civilians heard about lives being saved. Especially when they were young.

As he waited for Becca to return, he fielded questions about the procedure. He was careful to keep the details general enough so as not to violate the boy's privacy. But then again, as cool as people who weren't in the business may have thought hospital talk was, it didn't take long before the average person's eyes started glazing over.

Soon enough, most everyone returned to their own conversations. A few talked to Nick, asking him about himself and how he and Becca met and how long they'd been dating. Until finally Becca presented Nick with a frosty mug of beer and a heaping plate of food.

He'd barely finished his meal when Patrick entered the room. "Nick, you're here."

He offered his hand, and Nick stood before he shook it.

"You might as well remain standing," Patrick instructed him. "Now is as good a time as any to share your news with the family. People are going to start leaving pretty soon, and we don't want anyone left out."

As Isabel herded the others into the dining room or at least within earshot, Nick glanced around the table.

Working in the emergency room, he was used to dealing with blood and guts and some of the strangest and typically scary things a layperson could imagine. Nothing much fazed him.

Except for the Flannigans.

He found the lot of them terrifying.

This was some serious family togetherness. They were a unit. A clan. They were in each other's business, and the elders definitely ran the show, dictating when everyone should jump and exactly how high.

Comparatively, Nick was a lone wolf. He preferred to ride a motorcycle, and no one gave him the hairy eyeball. If he wanted a tattoo, he didn't need to ask permission. If he chose to, he could eat a plateful of candy corn for his Thanksgiving dinner. Although, he had to admit that the dinner was delicious. It was perfect. Like a Norman Rockwell scene or a cover of the *Saturday Evening Post*.

Now it was suddenly crystal clear why Becca had hesitated to tell her family about the pregnancy. He wasn't so sure he wanted to announce this rather personal piece of news to the family.

"Is everyone here?" Isabel hollered. "Nick and Becca have an announcement for the entire family."

"You're getting married, aren't you?" Don said. "I knew it. I called it."

"No, Uncle Don," Becca said. "We're going to have a baby. Twins, actually."

Virtual crickets chirped in the dining room.

Everyone had been stunned.

Stunned silent.

Becca couldn't remember this ever happening. Not even when Rosanna had gotten pregnant. Of course, Becca had been eleven years old at the time and she couldn't recall her parents making such a cavalier announcement. But she figured everyone would know sooner or later. At least this way they seemed supportive.

Becca tried to avoid looking at Rosanna, but guilt must've made her glance over. Her sister was sitting there with a smug smirk on her face. Becca was holding her breath, hoping against hope that Rosanna would not bring up running into her and Nick in the baby department.

Aunt Millie was the first to speak. "So this means you're getting married, right?"

Becca could feel Nick withdrawing under all the pressure.

"Actually, we have no plans for that, right now."

It surprised Becca how much it hurt to say those words, more than she'd expected. And she had to admit that she was disappointed when Nick didn't speak up and say something that vaguely hinted that marriage wasn't out of the question.

Just because she was falling in love with him didn't mean the feeling was mutual. And the only thing worse than not being married to the father of your child was to be married to a man who didn't love you.

One person could not bring all the love to a marriage. She'd learned that through her parents.

"We're working on that," Isabel said without a trace of teasing in her tone. "We'll have them walking down the aisle before next Thanksgiving. Just watch."

Obviously, she wasn't joking. Becca wanted to melt into a puddle and disappear through the fine cracks in the mahogany floorboards.

Suddenly, Nick stood. "It's nice to meet you," he said to no one in particular. "Thank you for letting me share your Thanksgiving, but I really should be going."

"You haven't had your pie yet," said Aunt Millie.

Nick smiled at her, but Becca could see the weariness in his eyes and around the corners of his mouth. "Everything was so delicious, I'm stuffed. I couldn't eat another bite, but thank you."

Meeting the entire family like this, under these circumstances, had been a lot to swallow. She didn't blame him for wanting to leave.

"Get yourself a piece to take home with you," Aunt Mille said. "Your bride-to-be made all those pies. You don't want to miss out."

In the time that it took Nick to say his thank-yous and good-nights, someone had wrapped up an entire pie, and Aunt Millie was thrusting it at him. Resigned, he graciously accepted it.

Becca walked with him outside to his car. The temperatures felt as if they'd dipped down below the freezing mark. The weathercasters had warned they would experience the first freezing temperatures of the season tonight. So the chill in the air wasn't solely emanating from Nick.

"That must've been overwhelming for you," she said.

"Just a little bit." He unlocked the car and placed the pie in the backseat.

"It was overwhelming for me, and I've known most of those people all my life."

All he did was smile, but it didn't reach his eyes, and he looked absolutely rung out.

Even so, he hugged her good-night.

While she was in his arms, she breathed in the scent of him, wanting to saturate her senses with it so she could memorize it. Because right now things between them felt fragile and fleeting.

She loved her family in spite of their quirks. Heck, they *were* their quirks. That's what made them unique. They were big and loud and overbearing and brassy, nosy and bossy. God, they could have their own version of the Seven Dwarfs. Although right now, she'd be divested of her role as goody-goody.

She would no longer be thought of as the good girl of the family. It was about time.

Because tonight she'd come to some realizations of her own. Not everyone found her family endearing. And her mother—that bit about making sure she and Nick walked down the aisle before next Thanksgiving—that was inexcusable.

"It's been a long, long day," Nick said. "I need to go. I'll talk to you tomorrow."

"Tomorrow I'm going to be tied up with the tree lighting in the park," she said. "But I hope you'll stop by. It really is pretty. It's a nice way to kick off the holidays."

He didn't say one way or the other if he'd be there tomorrow night, but he did give her a peck on the lips before he got in his car and drove away. And that was something.

Wasn't it?

Chapter Ten

After Nick left, Becca went back inside her parents' house.

She walked into the kitchen, where her mother was directing the cleanup process.

"Mom, I need to talk to you. Can we please go in the other room?"

"Not now, Rebecca. We need to get this kitchen cleaned up. In fact, there is a whole rack of wineglasses over there that need to be dried and put away. You can sit down while you help. Go do that."

"Mom. The wineglasses will wait. You and I need to have a talk right now. Please, come in the other room, unless you want me to say what I have to say in front of everybody here."

She'd never challenged her mom like this. For the second time that night you could've heard a pin drop, everyone was so taken aback. Even Rosanna. She'd lost her smirk and was watching this showdown unfold with wide eyes.

Isabel glared at Becca for a moment. But then she put down her dish towel, untied her apron and patted her perfect lacquered hair into place.

"If you insist, Rebecca. But make it quick."

The next day, Becca decided to give Nick some space. It wasn't hard, since the foundation tree-lighting ceremony had kept her running all day. Now, as time drew closer for them to flip the switch on the tree and for everybody to *oooh* and *ahhh* and clap their appreciation, everything switched into high gear.

The tree lighting was becoming a nice annual tradition that the entire population of Celebration looked forward to every year. And every year it was getting more and more involved.

The foundation sponsored the event, but this year, they'd added a fund-raising element to benefit the foundation. There was a booth selling Christmas trees, a Christmas shop with ornaments and stockings and other holiday decorations, and a table that encouraged people to think about year-end in giving.

Since this was their first year trying their hand at fund-raising, Becca had been in charge of coordinating the volunteers, in addition to hiring the tree decorator, arranging all the permits and concessions, the carolers and the entertainment.

The prancing reindeer from Miss Jeannie's School of Dance were performing in the gazebo right now. An a cappella group dressed in period costume were singing carols over by the tree. Someone had tracked her down to tell her no one had shown up to man the roasted chestnut booth, so they had to pull somebody from the kettle corn and hot spiced cider stations to fill in until the chestnut roaster arrived.

She had just put out that fire when her neighbor Mrs. Cavett, who she'd appointed as a volunteer for the holiday shop in a moment of weakness, sidled up next to her.

"Lovely event, Becca sweetheart. But you know, honey, next year you really should organize better. It's only proper to provide dinner for the volunteers or at least snacks. I'm starving. It was such a bother to have to take our breaks in rotation. You know, if we had food, we could eat right there while we worked. Happy volunteers make for happy sales."

Becca had a fleeting image of Mrs. Cavett and Mrs. Milton huddled around a platter of shrimp cocktail and ignoring the customers while they gorged.

"I'm sorry you're hungry, Mrs. Cavett. I should have recommended that you eat dinner before you came. I didn't even think about snacks, since the shifts are only two hours long."

Mrs. Cavett *tsked*. Then she took a hold of Becca's upper arm as if for emphasis.

"Sweetheart, the mark of a good hostess is to always feed your guests or, in this case, your volunteers."

"The only problem is this is a fund-raiser. We didn't really have a budget for volunteer snacks. But I do appreciate your input. And, hey, maybe next year we can organize a committee to get food donations or maybe the volunteers could each bring some finger food. May I count on you to coordinate the volunteer treats for us next year?"

"Becca, darling, you don't burden your volunteers by asking them to bring food."

She could see this conversation was going nowhere fast. She'd have better luck arranging a Radio City Music Hall gig for Miss Jeannie's dancing reindeer than trying to get Mrs. Cavett to see things her way. Becca swallowed her indignation.

"Thank you for your input, Mrs. Cavett. I'll pass along your helpful notes to next year's committee."

Of course, she was the sole member of next year's committee.

Becca was thrilled to see Mrs. Milton barreling toward them…looking and sounding like a rampant reindeer who had broken loose from Santa's sleigh, in her brown muumuu and jingle bell necklace, complete with matching earrings.

Even before she arrived, it was clear that Mrs. Milton was coming over to join the criticism choir. Becca knew she'd better disengage now before the two women had her cornered.

"Hi, Mrs. Milton. I'm sorry, but I have to run. I have to get over to the stage to make sure everything is in order for the tree lighting."

As she walked away, Becca wondered who was manning the holiday shop, but she knew if she went back to ask she'd never get away.

Instead, she detoured over to the concession area and bought a bottle of water. It was the first moment she'd had since lunch to stop and take a break, and she was tired. She was scanning the crowd to see if she could spot Nick, when she saw Kate, who seemed to have the same idea as she did, only with hot chocolate.

"Someday we are going to hire someone else to

handle this shindig so we can go Black Friday shopping," said Kate.

"Right. Whose brilliant idea was this to do the tree lighting on the day after Thanksgiving?" Becca smiled. "Oh, yeah, her name is Kate Thayer. She's worse than the Grinch who stole Christmas."

"I hear she's fabulous," Kate said. "A true visionary."

Becca rolled her eyes and laughed.

"I haven't had a chance to talk to you all day," Kate said. "How did Thanksgiving with your parents go?"

Becca rubbed her hands over her eyes and sighed. "Which do you want to hear about first? The part where Aunt Millie tried to force-feed Nick pumpkin pie? The one where my mom announced to everyone that she would make sure Nick and I got married before next Thanksgiving? Or the grand finale where I told off my mother?"

Kate's jaw dropped. "And why didn't you invite me to Thanksgiving? This is like Thanksgiving dinner theater. All we had was a boring dinner with turkey and stuffing. Although, the dessert Liam and I shared was particularly delicious this year, if you know what I mean."

Kate waggled her eyebrows.

"And I'm the one who ends up pregnant with twins."

Kate shrugged, and for a moment Becca thought she glimpsed a hint of sadness in her eyes.

"Are you okay?" Becca asked.

"I'm fine. We have about ten minutes before we have to head over to the stage. I want to hear everything. Especially the part about you telling your mother off. I never thought I'd live to see the day that happened.

I'd ask if you'd been drinking, but I already know the answer to that. What happened?"

Becca squeezed her eyes shut for a moment, trying to erase the memory of the bad scene.

She gave Kate the basic rundown.

"…and after we went upstairs, I told her I didn't appreciate the way she kept insisting that Nick and I were getting married. And my mother kept insisting she'd done nothing wrong. And I told her she needed to stop this constant interference because I'm twenty-five years old and she just needs to stop."

"Get out." Kate's eyes were huge, and she'd had her hand over her mouth the entire time Becca had been telling the story. Kate knew Isabel, and she also understood that Becca's confronting her basically amounted to World War Three.

"Do you know what my mother had the nerve to say?"

Kate shook her head. "I have no idea. I'm terrified of your mother. I can't believe you lived to tell the story."

Becca nodded.

"She said my life *needed* a little more interference from somebody with better sense than I had, since I'd gone and gotten myself pregnant."

Kate winced. "Oh, honey, I'm sorry. That's really out of line."

Becca lifted her chin a notch. "It is. As of right now, we're not speaking. But after the numbness wore off, I realized I've been letting her get away with stunts like that my entire life. I've always thought if I just kept my mouth shut, if I did everything right, she'd love me—"

Becca's voice broke. She cleared her throat.

"But I don't think she knows how to love, Kate. Last night was an epiphany. All these years I've been thinking there was something wrong with me. Well, it's not me, and I'm tired of her making me feel like I'm not good enough to earn her love."

Becca felt her eyes start to well, and she swiped at the tears. The realization had been a weight lifted off her shoulders, but with the burden gone, the heaviness had been replaced by a strange sort of emptiness.

Kate put her hand on Becca's arm and gave it a squeeze.

"Dare I ask, how did Nick handle everything?"

Becca shrugged. "I don't know. He left before my mom and I had it out. I haven't talked to him today. He seemed pretty overwhelmed by everything last night. He just got sort of quiet. I told him I'd be here. Told him that he could meet me for the tree lighting if he wanted to. I haven't heard from him."

"Well, that's because he just walked up."

Becca's breath hitched in her chest.

Kate pointed with her head. "He's right over there with Liam and Jake. I'm pretty sure they're waiting for us to finish what we're doing here so we can join them for the tree lighting."

There he was. Standing there with the entire Sunday night football crew, looking as if he'd always been one of them.

Becca glanced at her phone. He hadn't texted her. But he was here. He probably hadn't texted her for the same reason she didn't text him when he was at work. She had a job to do, and he respected that she didn't have time to be on her phone.

It was actually a courtesy.

After all, he was here tonight. If he hadn't wanted to see her, he could've stayed home or at least avoided her friends... But they had become his friends, too.

Becca checked in with the people from the mayor's office, who were on the podium where the mayor would address the citizens of Celebration before pulling the lever that would officially light the Christmas tree for this season. They were all set. She pointed out the area at the right-hand corner of the stage and told them that's where she'd be if they needed anything.

Then she took a deep breath and went down to join her friends. And Nick.

"There you are," he said. "I was beginning to think you stood me up."

He greeted her with a kiss, and everything seemed fine. She was so relieved she wanted to cry.

"I'm glad you're here."

He put his arm around her, and she snuggled into the warmth of him. She couldn't think of any place else she'd rather be than right here with him.

"And two cups for Becca and Nick?" Pepper asked.

"Hey, Pepper. What's going on?" Becca asked.

"Rob and I would like to buy everyone a cup of hot mulled wine. We need to toast the holidays."

"Oh, that's so nice of you. Nick? Would you like some wine?"

"Sounds great, thanks."

"Okay, one each for Becca and Nick."

Becca held up her hand. "None for me, thanks."

"Come on, Becca," said Pepper. "Don't be a party pooper. We need to have a group toast."

"I'll toast with my water. I'm working."

Pepper squinted at Becca. "Kate's working, but she's having wine. When did you become such a teetotaler? You've never turned down a glass of wine—until lately. What's going on with you? Are you pregnant? You are, aren't you?"

"Pepper..." Becca said, unsure of how to answer. After all, they'd told her family. Their friends would find out soon enough. Why not now?

Becca glanced up at Nick, worried that two nights of pregnancy announcements might send him over the edge. But he gave her his lopsided smile and a barely perceptible shrug.

"And what if she is?" he said to Pepper.

Pepper's jaw dropped. "Are you saying what I think you're saying?"

Becca looked at Nick again, fortified by what she saw in his eyes.

"Yes," Becca said.

Pepper unleashed an earsplitting squeal, and then she threw her arms around Becca's neck. "I knew it! I knew it. I knew it. I knew it. Oh, I am so happy for you two."

"So, you've been baiting me with the wine, haven't you?" Becca asked.

Pepper shot her a sly smile. *"Maaaybe."*

"How in the world did you know?" Becca asked.

Kate was a vault. There was no way she'd betray Becca's confidence. That was one of the few constants in the world she could count on.

Pepper shrugged. "Just intuition, I guess."

Becca didn't believe her, and Pepper must've seen it in her eyes—or maybe it was more of that intuition she was claiming to possess.

"Okay, I'll confess I overheard you and Kate talking about it at the office after you got so sick with the food poisoning. After you recovered, I guess I was a little jealous, because I wanted to celebrate with you, too."

"Pepper, I'm sorry. We had to tell my family before we told anyone else."

"I totally understand," Pepper said. "And I am totally going to throw you the best baby shower this town has ever seen."

Nick was quiet. Of course, nobody could get a word in edgewise when Pepper was excited about something. But Becca was learning that Nick tended to stand back and take things in. He had to process them.

As they stood in the glow of the lighted Christmas tree, Nick standing behind her with his arms around her, holding her close, a calming peace settled over her. Last night, after Nick had left her parents' house, things had been so uncertain between them, she'd feared she might never know this peace again. But she'd trusted her instincts, and she'd given him room to think, to process everything.

He'd come back to her.

Of course, they hadn't talked about her family and everything that had transpired last night. She wasn't going to bring it up tonight. Especially after they said goodbye to their friends and went over to the Christmas tree booth and chose a tree together.

As Nick carried it to her car for her, she caught herself pretending that they were a real family. Because maybe they could be…someday.

Right now, theirs might not be the traditional

situation she wished it would be, but it was one of those situations where she had a choice: the glass could be half empty, or it could be half full.

It was her choice, and she chose half full.

So many good things had happened lately. They had been blessed with not one, but two children. The babies had survived the food poisoning. Nick had come back into her life. She had to trust that everything would be okay.

Maybe if she kept repeating the positive over and over, like a mantra, she could will him to love her enough to make it all true.

Chapter Eleven

"I can't believe Jake and Anna's wedding is tomorrow," Becca said as she unlocked her front door and flipped on the foyer light.

Nick nodded and bent down to pet Priscilla, who had met them at the door.

Tonight's rehearsal dinner and tomorrow's wedding were the last of what seemed like an endless succession of events that had followed one after the other since Thanksgiving at her parents'. It's not that he wasn't glad to be part of the festivities and the celebrations surrounding his new friends' wedding. He was glad everything would be slowing down pretty soon.

At the risk of sounding like a Scrooge, after telling her parents about the babies on Tuesday, telling her extended family at Thanksgiving dinner, telling their friends about the babies at the tree-lighting ceremony on Friday and going to Jake and Anna's rehearsal dinner tonight, Nick was looking forward to getting back to work, where everything didn't feel so out of control.

Truth be told, he was a little weary, feeling as if he was living someone else's life. Because three months ago, if you had asked him what he'd be doing for the holidays, it wouldn't have been any of the events that had been on his social calendar lately.

He'd volunteered to work tomorrow night, but somehow, despite a good number of the hospital's staff attending the wedding, they'd scheduled him off for the night. Becca was in the wedding, so he would've been just as happy working and giving someone else a chance to go, but Jake and Anna wouldn't hear of it. Nick had begun to feel like a miscreant protesting to the contrary.

He followed Becca into the living room. The dog padded along behind him.

The Christmas tree they'd purchased last night was sitting in a stand in the corner. Becca kicked off her high heels. She looked gorgeous in her black cocktail dress. Nick especially enjoyed the view of her curvy little backside when she bent down and plugged something into the wall.

The tree lit up. Nick blinked in surprise, taking it all in. It didn't have any ornaments, but it shone bright with tiny colorful lights.

"Did you put the tree in the stand?" he asked.

"Not all by myself. Kate helped me. You should've seen the two of us. We were like Laverne and Shirley. I'm surprised we didn't end up putting the trunk through the window. But we eventually got it upright and into the stand."

He frowned. "Should you be lifting things like

that, even with somebody else's help? You should've called me."

"Nick, I'm pregnant, not an invalid. I'm fine. The babies are fine. Thank you for being concerned. And just so you don't feel as if you're missing out, I bought some ornaments we can hang on the tree together."

She held up a red sphere that was decorated with a delicate gold pattern. "I got these for us today. I was hoping you'd want to help me decorate the tree. That's why I went ahead and put the lights on. Because you have to do that first before you can put on any of the other decorations."

"I think you need to slow down a little, Becca. Don't wear yourself out."

"I'm fine. I promise I'm listening to my body."

It had been a long time since he'd bothered with a tree. When he was married to Delilah, they'd spent two Christmases together. She'd badgered him until they'd gotten a tree. He didn't blame her for wanting one. Most people observed that tradition. Hell, most people celebrated traditions.

He glanced at his watch. It was nearly ten o'clock. "I'd love to, but could we wait until next week? There's been so much going on, and we still have the wedding tomorrow."

Disappointment flashed in Becca's eyes, but she recovered quickly, smiling at him. "Of course. We've had a lot going on this week. I'm sure you're exhausted."

Now he was beginning to feel like the Grinch.

"How about if we hang a few tonight and the rest next week? Is that a fair compromise?" he asked.

Her face lit up. "I think it's the perfect compromise."

She planted a whisper-soft kiss on his lips and handed him the ornament.

"Hang it anywhere on the tree you'd like."

She turned on some Christmas music.

Christmas music? It's not even December yet.

He contemplated teasing her about it, but she disappeared into the kitchen before he could.

Instead, he turned to find a place on the tree for the ornament.

Out of nowhere, a memory swam from the murky recesses of his subconscious. He remembered how his mother waited patiently until the day after Thanksgiving to play holiday tunes. But only because she and his father had come to that agreement. If his dad had had it his way, there would never have been any Christmas music until the week before the holiday. On the flip side of that coin, his mother would've started torturing them with "Frosty the Snowman" and his ilk as soon as the first chill cooled the air.

In a sense, it was their own compromise. Nick hadn't thought about it in years. It was a happy time, before they'd stopped working together and everything had gone so terribly wrong.

Becca returned a moment later with a bottle of wine and one glass and a mug of something in her other hand.

"You know, it's an honor to get to hang the first ornament," she said as she poured the wine. "So consider yourself honored."

She handed him the glass of wine.

"Mark, Rosanna and I used to fight over who got to hang this Santa ornament that had been in our family for as far back as I can remember. My mom used to keep track of whose year it was to hang it. One year she swore it was Mark's turn, but Rosanna kept insisting that Mark had hung it the year before and it was her turn. She tried to grab it away from Mark and ended up knocking it out of his hand. It smashed into tiny pieces, and that was the end of Santa. Isabel made Rosanna clean up the pieces and then sit on the couch. She didn't get to help decorate the tree that year."

"She didn't punish your brother?"

Becca shook her head. "No, because in her eyes, he hadn't done anything wrong. Rosanna killed Santa. I don't think either of them has forgiven the other."

"So for the most part, you are like the Switzerland of your family. You seem to be a pretty calming influence on everyone."

Becca shrugged. "Somebody has to be. If not, either we'd not be speaking to each other, or we'd be living our life in constant turmoil."

She grimaced.

"What's wrong?"

"Actually, my mother and I are in a bit of a tiff right now."

"What happened?"

Becca took a deep breath, staring off into the distance for a moment. "After you left Thursday, I told her she was out of line for pushing the issue of us getting married. I'm sorry she did that."

Nick waved her off. "Don't worry about it. I think she was just a little overzealous. No hard feelings on my part. So don't let it put you in a bad place with your mother. Go back to being Switzerland."

"We will get past it. I'll just give her a little bit of

space right now. Speaking of parents, when do you want to tell your father about the babies?"

He hadn't even thought about it. Well, he'd thought about it, but he hadn't come to any conclusion. They'd been on the go so much that he hadn't had a chance to think much beyond Thanksgiving dinners and tree lightings and weddings.

"I don't know, Becca."

He hadn't meant for the words to come out quite so sharp. But they had, and Becca was frowning.

"I'm sorry about that," he said. "I haven't seen my father in years. So there's a little more to it than calling him up and telling him he's going to be a grandfather."

Becca nodded.

"What would you think of inviting him to come for Christmas? We could tell him about the babies together and in person."

Nick took a long sip of his wine, weighing his words before he spoke. But all he could come up with was "I don't know."

She put a hand on his arm. "Remember what you said to me. It's all in how you set the tone. And could you think of a better Christmas gift to give somebody than to tell him he's going to be a grandfather?"

The guy hadn't been a particularly great father. Nick wasn't sure how his dad would react to being a grandfather. *The stubborn old coot.*

Becca must have mistaken his shrug for an *I'll think about it.*

"If this is something you want to do, we need to book his airfare soon. It could be our Christmas present to him."

Nick held up a hand. "Whoa, wait there. I don't even know if he would come. I'm guessing he still works." Nick shrugged again. "That's how little I know about him."

Becca was looking at him. She wasn't exactly frowning, but her brows were knit, and those gorgeous full lips were pursed.

"I know you probably think that's crazy," he said. "But that's just the way things are between him and me. I don't like it. But he hasn't seemed too bothered by it all these years, either."

"Don't you think now is as good a time as any to initiate a peace offering It's Christmas, Nick."

After all these years he'd never considered the logistics of being the one to extend the olive branch. Sure, there'd been times when he'd wondered what it would be like to see his old man again after all of these years, but that was usually where it stopped. He couldn't envision himself reaching out to make the first move toward reconciliation. Not when there was a very high chance that his father would reject him all over again.

"Yeah. I don't know about that, Becca. It's really not as easy as simply setting the tone. It's complicated."

"Nick, what could have happened that was so horrible that you can't put it behind you? What did he do to you?"

"It wasn't what he did to me. Well, I mean, if you don't count the way he abandoned my mother and me."

Becca watched him expectantly, as if certain he would continue. But the truth was he didn't know how to explain. He didn't know where to start. He wanted to tell her to not push him. That he and his dad weren't like her and her family. But he knew that would sting. It would hurt her, and it would only make him feel worse.

Still, he heard himself talking before he realized what he was doing.

"When I was fourteen, I went on a cruise with my family. My parents were arguing about something, I don't even know what. But they sent my brother, Caiden, and me down to the pool while they worked things out. My mom told me to look after my brother, but I was distracted, and flirting with a girl. Caiden kept pestering me. 'Hey, Nicky, look at this! Hey, Nicky, watch me! Hey, Nicky, are you gonna kiss that girl?' I got mad at him, and I told him to go away. I just wanted him to go away for a few minutes and leave me alone. Ten minutes later, a swimmer pulled my little brother out of the deep end of the pool. He drowned. I was supposed to take care of him, but I didn't. He drowned because of my carelessness. When my parents found out, for a split second, I saw this look in my mom's eyes. I knew she blamed me even though she never said a word. She blamed me. It was my fault."

Becca reached out and took Nick's hand.

"I'm so sorry, Nick. That must've been horrific."

Her words hung in the air between them, heavy and still.

"But you were only fourteen years old," she said. "Who puts that kind of responsibility on the shoulders of a kid?"

Nick shook his head. "I was old enough to know

better. I did know better. He couldn't swim. But I never thought he'd go near the deep end of the pool."

Nick still had nightmares of them pulling his brother out of the water. Twenty-one years later, and the image was still burned into his brain as if it happened yesterday.

"How long after your brother's accident did your parents divorce?"

Nick leaned forward, bracing his elbows on his knees, studying the grain in the hardwood floors. The song on the stereo changed to "Silent Night."

How long had it been?

"Five, six months, maybe? I think they tried to make it work for me or maybe out of habit or obligation. In so many ways it seemed like they split the moment they found out about Caiden. My dad ended up moving out. I came home from school one day, and he was gone. My mom was a shadow of herself. She just went through the motions. She didn't cry. She didn't talk much. A year later she died. An aneurism. It was as if all her grief had bottled up inside her and exploded. God, I've never told anyone this before."

"Not even your ex-wife?"

"Delilah and I were married for less than two years. She was too busy complaining about how many hours I was away from home to worry about something like this."

They sat there quietly for a while. He felt her gaze on him, but he couldn't look at her. He didn't want to see the pity in her eyes.

Pity had been one of the worst things he'd had to deal with after they returned home, and all the neighbors found out.

Whispers and pity.

Their family is never going to be the same.

Oh, that poor Ciotti boy.

He was never really sure if they were talking about him or his brother. It had to be Caiden, because he knew he didn't deserve any pity.

"Nick, it wasn't your fault. You have to stop blaming yourself. And most of all, you need to forgive yourself. You were just a kid."

It was all just one more thing that made him feel out of control of his life—babies on the way, a new town that had already sucked him into a way of living he wasn't used to. But he should like it. He should love being part of something bigger than himself. He should welcome a reason to step outside of himself. He knew that.

This was Becca's life. She was at the center of it all. Heart and soul and lifeblood. She thrived in the midst of friends and community and even family, no matter how dysfunctional she thought hers was.

Here he was, trying to be part of it, part of her life. But, really, he was standing on the outside looking in.

It seemed so much bigger than him. It was all coming at him so fast. When it came down to it, could he really give her what she needed to be happy? He wished he could. He wanted to. But she deserved better. Was it fair to her to hold on to her if he couldn't give her all that?

He knew he could sit there all night banging his head against the proverbial wall and telling himself this life should be what he wanted, that he should feel lucky, but he just wanted to run.

He set his wineglass on the coffee table and stood up.

"Look, it's late," he said. "I need to go into the hospital tomorrow and check on some things before the wedding. I need to go."

The next evening, Nick sat in the ballroom at Regency Cypress Plantation and Botanical Gardens waiting for the wedding to start.

Since Becca had been tied up with bridesmaid duties all day and he'd had to take care of a few matters at the hospital, Becca had ridden to the Regency Cypress with Kate. He'd met her there.

In the midst of the rush of all the festivities, Nick hadn't had a chance to get Anna and Jake a wedding present. So, before the wedding he'd swung by the mall to pick up a gift. While he was there, he'd found his way back to the jewelry store where Becca had tried on the ruby necklace. He'd gotten it for her.

He wasn't much of a shopper. So, he figured he might as well pick up the necklace for her Christmas present.

The only other time he'd bought jewelry for a woman was when he'd purchased Delilah's wedding ring. Since they'd eloped, there'd been no engagement ring. Just functional, plain gold his-and-hers bands.

Shortly after the wedding, Delilah had taken to purchasing her own jewelry. That way, she told him, he didn't have to worry about it, and she got exactly what she wanted. She always made sure she got exactly what she wanted.

Sitting here, alone in a sea of people, Nick wondered if the necklace was a good idea. Did buying jewelry for a woman send the wrong message?

It was just a necklace. It wasn't as if he'd bought her a ring.

The string quartet began playing a classical tune that Nick recognized but couldn't name—maybe "Ode to Joy" or that one by Pachelbel, maybe something else. It was pleasant, and for the first time in days—perhaps even since he and Becca had reconnected and he'd learned he was going to be a father—he sat back and took a deep breath.

Liam was one of Jake's groomsmen. He and Jake's three brothers, whom Nick had met briefly at the rehearsal dinner last night, stepped out and took their places beside Jake at the front of the ballroom.

He'd have to remind himself to rib Liam about cleaning up well and about making him miss the football game tonight.

The musical ensemble shifted into another familiar but unidentifiable piece, and a couple of tiny girls in white dresses with deep red sashes tottered down the aisle carrying baskets that were nearly as big as they were and scattering handfuls of flower petals.

One decided to stop midway along the journey to the altar, blinking at the people all around her. She looked as if she was about ready to burst into tears, but the other little girl, who looked as if she might be a year or two older, walked back and took her by the hand and restarted her journey.

The guests *awwed* and *cooed* at the adorableness. Nick stewed in the thought that weddings as a general rule were daunting.

After seeing his parents' marriage go up in flames and failing at his own attempt, he'd probably stop midway to the altar and question what he was doing, too.

Becca was the first bridesmaid to walk down the aisle.

She looked beautiful in the clingy red dress that hugged her in all the right places. She caught his eye as she marched past and smiled. He smiled back. An unexpected warmth started in his solar plexus and radiated outward. What was it about this woman? She had his mind performing a one-eighty every time he saw her. Just a minute ago, he'd been thinking how he wasn't cut out for marriage, that he couldn't be a family man or be part of a close-knit community. Yet every time he set eyes on her, something inside him wanted to recalibrate his life compass and see if it might point to a different true north.

Anna was a beautiful bride as she walked down the aisle on her father's arm. And when Jake swiped at a tear as his father-in-law gave Anna's hand to him, Nick had to admit he couldn't remember seeing anyone look as happy.

The minister called the dearly beloved together and said a few words about guests being fortunate to witness the joining of these two souls.

"I only wish Jake's father and mother could be here today," said the minister. "Jake, your father was a good friend of mine, and I know both of your parents are here in spirit. I know they're thrilled that these two are being joined in holy matrimony, since they knew Anna practically all of her life, too.

"On this Thanksgiving weekend, I urge everyone to hold loved ones close. If there's someone you haven't talked to, call them."

Nick thought of his father. He really did owe it to him to reach out to him and tell him about the babies. Becca's words about forgiving himself rang in his head.

He knew it was true.

He watched the kind, smart, beautiful woman who was carrying his children. He wondered for a moment if there was something wrong with him.

Because surely, if he couldn't love her, he didn't deserve love. She was right, he needed to forgive himself before he could move on and love anyone else.

The first step to forgiveness started with contacting his father.

"I have a surprise for you," Nick said after he put a basket of garlic bread on the table and took his place across from Becca.

"Dinner and a surprise?" she asked.

Nick had already surprised her by calling her this morning and asking if he could cook dinner for her tonight. Apparently, spaghetti and homemade meatballs was his specialty, and he wanted to make it for her.

Here they sat, in his tiny studio apartment, a single white taper candle lit between them, with delicious food on the table and the smell of garlic and Italian seasoning hanging in the air.

"How would you like to meet my father?" Nick asked.

"What? When? I'd love to meet him. Did you call him?"

Nick nodded and smiled.

"And?" she demanded. "Tell me everything."

Nick braced his elbows on the table and laced his fingers together. "The more I thought about it, the more I realized you were right. I owed it to him to tell him about the babies."

She waited a moment for him to continue, but when he didn't, she said, "How did that go?"

A look of tenderness passed over Nick's face. It was an expression she hadn't seen before, and she was a little mesmerized.

"Better than I expected," he said. "It was a little strained at first. I mean, it's been sixteen years since we last talked. I can't believe he still has the same phone number. But he does. He said it was good to hear from me. That he thought about me often and wondered where I was."

Becca had to wonder why the man hadn't tried to get in touch with his son. Surely he didn't blame Nick for what happened to Caiden. But people had their own quirks and ways of dealing with heartbreak.

"I asked him to come. Told him I'd send him a ticket. He wants to meet you. The only thing is, he's flying in the day we are supposed to tour the Dallas hospital."

Becca held up her hands. "That's okay. We can reschedule."

Nick shook his head. "No need. He lands in the evening. We can go to the airport after the tour and pick him up. Would you be up to having dinner with us?"

"Of course, I'd love to. Thank you."

Becca's first thought was *Nick is introducing me to his father.* But then the voice of reason set in. He hadn't seen the man in sixteen years.

"But are you sure you don't want to meet with him first? So the two of you can have some time alone to catch up? I could meet you for dessert or maybe lunch the next day? Is he staying with you?"

Nick glanced around the room. "No. I'm pretty picky about who I share a bed with. I made a reservation for him at the Celebration Inn."

She thought about how he'd been right there with her to break the news about the babies to her parents. Even though Nick had already told his father, she wondered if maybe he wanted her there for a little reinforcement during the first meeting.

She reached out and took his hand. "Nick, I'm so happy for you. It has to be a good sign that he's willing to come and see you."

Nick shrugged. "At least it's a step in the right direction."

On the day of the hospital tour when Becca's phone rang she thought Nick was calling to say that he'd arrived and was waiting outside her office to pick her up for the drive to the hospital.

She picked up her phone with one hand and answered the call as she closed out of the computer file that she'd been working on with the other.

"Becca, it's Nick. I'm sorry to do this at the last minute, but can you meet me at Southwestern Medical Center? I had a hectic morning. We were pretty busy, and then a reporter showed up wanting to interview me for an article about aortic dissection. I should have asked her to reschedule, but I didn't and it ended up going a lot longer than I expected. If I pick you up, we'll be late."

Becca closed the folder on her desk and glanced at her watch. "No problem. I'll meet you there at four.

Unless you want to reschedule, or you know, I could just have the babies at Celebration Memorial. That would be easier on everyone. Lots of healthy twins are born there every day, Nick."

"Unless an emergency happened, and they couldn't give you the treatment that you'd need."

She loved the way he got all protective and puffed up when it came to making sure she got the very best OB care possible, but was this specialty hospital really necessary?

"Nick, think about it," she said. "What would happen if there was an emergency? Couldn't they just put me in an ambulance and send me to Southwestern Medical Center?"

He was quiet on the other end of the line, and for a moment she thought they'd been disconnected.

"Nick?"

"Yep."

She was beginning to see a pattern: when he got stressed, he became very uncommunicative.

"Look," she said, "I understand that you're busy, but taking this tour seems like a lot today with your dad coming in. Let's make him our priority and reschedule."

"My children are my priority—"

"They're mine, too, Nick. I hope you're not questioning that. I'm just trying to keep things in perspective."

"The tour was arranged as a professional courtesy," he said, as if he hadn't heard her. "I'm not going to ask for a reschedule at this late date."

Fine. Got it.

His *children* were his priority. He'd made that exceedingly clear. Good grief, this guy could run hot and cold. One minute he was talking about introducing her to his father—and she thought that just maybe he might feel something for her, too. And the next minute there were reality checks like this that shifted everything into perspective and reminded her that she shouldn't let her heart get carried away. Even though it already had.

"Okay," she said. "I'll meet you at Southwestern at four o'clock."

Five minutes later, as Becca was waiting at the elevator to leave the office, Kate appeared with her purse on her arm.

"Fancy meeting you here," Kate said. "Is Nick here to pick you up for the appointment?"

Becca took a deep breath. "No. I'm meeting him there. Some things came up at the hospital, and if he picks me up, we'll be late. Where are you off to?"

"I have an appointment with the superintendent of schools to talk about the foundation funding Get Lost In A Book Week. Are you okay? You seem a little rattled."

Becca shrugged. "Nick's father is arriving tonight. I'm sensing that he might be a little nervous about that, though he won't admit it."

It was either nerves, or Nick was pulling away. Or maybe she was superimposing her own anxiety onto Nick. The only thing she knew for sure was that she would be glad when the hospital tour was over. Maybe then she'd have more clarity about whether or not she was comfortable delivering at Southwestern Medical Center. Nick was a doctor. She knew she should trust him, but not at the expense of going against her own instincts. And for some reason her instincts were telling her she wanted to have the babies closer to home.

"He said it's been a long time since he and his father have communicated, right?"

Becca nodded. Nick had been increasingly hot and cold since Thanksgiving and the string of festivities in between.

"Sometimes he's hard to read, and other times I worry that I am reading too much into our relationship."

Kate's brows knit together. "He acted fine at the tree lighting, and he was attentive at the wedding. From my perspective, you two looked like a couple. A cute couple, as a matter of fact. And now he's introducing you to his father. Of course, I'm not you, but it looks to me like you have yourself a boyfriend."

Becca rolled her eyes at her friend. "A boyfriend. What does that even mean?"

What did it mean? She would certainly like to know.

"I never took you for somebody who needed to slap a label on a relationship," Kate said.

"I'm not looking for a label. But I am looking for answers."

She gazed at her friend. If there was anyone in the world Becca could confide in, it was Kate. The elevator arrived, and the two stepped inside.

As soon as the doors shut, Becca said, "I could really fall for this guy, Kate. I guess I'm just protecting my heart."

Kate's expression turned tender. "Could fall for the guy or *have fallen* for the guy? I'm guessing the latter."

Becca shrugged, not ready to say the words out

loud. Maybe she wasn't even ready to admit it to herself. So she changed the subject.

"Maybe it would be a good idea for me to let him meet with his father alone tonight. I mean, they haven't seen each other in years. Maybe I should give them a little time? What would you do?"

They stepped off the interior elevator and walked together across the lobby toward the lift that would take them to the parking garage.

"Did you ask him if that's what he wanted?" Kate asked.

"I did."

"What did he say?"

"He wants me to come with him."

"Well, there you go. Let him make that call. Unless you're the one who is having doubts."

"Me? Not a chance. I was the one who urged him to call his dad and tell him about the babies. I wanted to pay for part of his ticket as a Christmas present from the two of us, but when I asked him about it, he skirted the issue."

Kate grimaced. "Do you want me to be honest?"

"Always."

"Don't make an issue where there's not one."

"I'm not making an issue of it. I just thought he might wait so we could tell him together. I thought we were bringing him here to tell him about the babies, but Nick told him on the phone when he talked to him…"

"Are you disappointed that he told him without you?"

"No. Well, sort of, I guess…but that's selfish. I know that, and I wouldn't admit it to anybody but you. I guess I thought it would be similar to when we told my parents together."

The truth was, he had gone with her as moral support—not because they were the happy, loving couple giddy about sharing joyous news. Things were different with his dad. Realistically, Nick probably needed an opener, a reason for calling his dad. When you haven't spoken with somebody in nearly two decades, *hello, how have you been?* doesn't always get it. *You're going to be a grandfather* does a lot better cutting through the minutia.

"I'm a big girl. I understand why he did what he did. Now I guess this trip is more about the two of them, and that's great."

"But his dad wants to meet you. Or Nick wants to introduce you."

"Right. He does. Or so Nick said. But since he's already told him we're expecting, this trip is more about them healing their relationship and making things right between them. I'm all for that. It has to happen before anything else can be right. He's only here for two nights. I just don't want to cut into their time."

Kate smiled at her. "You're going with him. Be glad about it, and everything will be fine."

Kate hugged Becca.

"I don't mean to give you a hard time. I just wish you'd stop giving yourself such a hard time."

In the car, Becca grappled with her feelings. Kate was right. She was always so logical. Becca needed to stop reading more into this than was really there. She needed to ignore the hollow feeling that wanted to consume her. In fact, when she felt too empty and off-kilter, she knew that's when she needed to erase her mental Etch A Sketch and focus on the positive.

As she drove to meet Nick, though, she should've been focusing on the car to her right. If she had been, maybe she would've been able to stop before it ran the stop sign and hit her car.

Chapter Twelve

By the time Nick got the news that Becca had been in an accident, he was already at Southwestern Medical Center in Dallas, waiting for her, wondering why she was late when she was usually early.

Kate had called him and told him she'd been in a fender bender. She'd witnessed the accident. Apparently, a teenager had been texting and ran a stop sign and hit the right fender of Becca's Honda. The boy hadn't been going very fast, but as a precaution, Becca had been transported by ambulance to Southwestern Medical Center, where she'd been examined.

Even though Kate had assured Nick that the accident wasn't serious, as he waited, Nick was in a numb haze.

Thank God for air bags and seat belts.

Several hours later, after the doctor had released

Becca and assured him that she and the babies were fine, he'd insisted on driving her home. Kate had put her car back in the parking garage. He told Becca he'd drive her to work tomorrow and they'd make arrangements to take her car into the body shop to be fixed. But on the way home from the hospital, realization set in. If he'd picked up Becca as he'd promised, rather than being so consumed with talking to that damn reporter, this would've never happened. He could've gotten her and his children killed by not following through. She hadn't even wanted to go on the blasted tour. This would've never happened if he hadn't been so focused on himself and so insistent on not inconveniencing his colleague at Southwestern Medical Center.

He felt Becca's gaze on him, but he kept his eyes glued to the road, not wanting to have a wreck be the cause of Becca being in two accidents in one day.

Wouldn't that just be par for his course?

In his life, tragedy seemed to appear in pairs. His brother had died and his parents divorced. Delilah had divorced him and married his best friend. Because he didn't pick Becca up, she'd gotten into that accident. He'd be damned if he was going to look away even for a second and endanger her again. He drove with extraordinary care to keep the pattern from repeating itself today.

He didn't expect life to be strife-free. Ups and downs were a part of the package. The down times made the good times better.

But the rough times in his life—the times that had produced the worst despair, Caiden's death, his parents' divorce, Delilah sleeping with his friend—

it all could've been prevented if he'd just done the right thing.

Now the right thing seemed that Becca and the babies would be better off without him. He'd provide support, of course, but he really was starting to believe he would be of more service to them if he focused on his job and didn't try to have much of a personal life.

He'd said it before, he was married to his work, and medicine was a jealous spouse. The ER seemed to be the place where he did the most good and wreaked the least amount of havoc.

"I keep waiting for you to tease me about the lengths I'd go to to get out of that hospital tour," Becca said.

He nodded, and he thought he smiled—he meant to—but he kept his eyes pinned to the road. The town had put up the decorations the day after the tree-lighting ceremony. Now all of downtown Celebration was decked out in its yuletide finest.

"Did your dad's plane get in?"

"It did."

He'd texted him that there'd been an emergency, apologized and told him he'd meet him later at the inn. He purposely left the details vague because he didn't want to worry him. His dad had sounded genuinely delighted when he told him he was going to be a grandfather. Another part of him didn't want to start off this potential reconciliation with the thoughts *so you ruined this relationship, too* wedged in between them like the proverbial elephant in the room.

"Nick?"

"Hmm?"

"Did he take a cab to the inn?"

"Yes. I would assume so."

Nick glanced at the clock on the dashboard. It was close to eight o'clock. It was getting a little late for dinner, but he'd get over to the Celebration Inn as soon as he could. As soon as he got Becca settled at home.

"Are you still going to go see him?"

"Yes."

Becca was quiet for a few beats.

"Would you like to see him alone tonight? I'm eager to meet him, but I haven't been able to shake the feeling that maybe it would be best if the two of you met by yourselves first."

"Sure."

"Nick, talk to me." Becca reached out and put her hand on his arm.

"About what?"

"We could start with why you're being so quiet. You've barely said a word since you got to the hospital. The words you have uttered have been all but monosyllabic. Are you mad at me? Because you know the accident wasn't my fault. It was an accident."

He pulled up to a red light, rolled to a slow, gentle stop before looking over at her.

"Of course it's not your fault. That kid ran a stop sign."

The light turned green, and he trained his attention on the road again.

They rode in silence until they got to Becca's condominium complex. Nick parked, got out and walked around to Becca's door, intending to open it, but she'd already let herself out of the car and had started walking toward the door.

Oh, boy.

"Becca, wait."

He caught up with her at the door. She was fishing her keys out of her purse.

He suddenly didn't know what to say. He could tell she was upset. Hell, he was upset—not with her, but it had just been one of those days.

With the accident and the fear of losing his children compounded with seeing his father again, which was dredging up all kinds of unwelcome memories, he was starting to feel a little claustrophobic.

And the burning question kept raging through his head: What if she had died? What if they hadn't gotten so lucky and she had died? Like his brother and his mom—

He shook away the thoughts. He couldn't let himself go down that slippery slope. Because once he started, he might not be able to pull himself out.

The attending on duty in the Southwestern ER who had examined Becca had given her the green light. She'd said she felt fine—no bumps and bruises. She'd only been a little shaken, as most people were when they were involved in a minor accident.

Nick knew the best thing he could do for both of them was to give her a chance to rest and him a chance to gather his wits—and he still had to go see his father. Since he was in town for only two nights, Nick couldn't very well bring him here and then blow him off.

Becca had gotten the door unlocked. The porch

light wasn't on and she'd had to use her phone as a flashlight.

He could've helped her instead of standing there with his hands in his pockets, but she was so capable, so strong—so better off without him.

He took a step back. She took a step inside. Priscilla ran around in circles as she barked a greeting. When Becca turned to look at him, hurt, anger, confusion—probably all of that and more—clouded those beautiful blue eyes.

He should hug her.

He wanted to hug her.

Why couldn't he move toward her? What the hell was wrong with him? He had no idea, which proved that it would be best for both of them for him to clear his head before he did something irreparably stupid.

"Get some sleep," he said.

She shook her head and closed the door, leaving him standing there in the dark.

The last time Nick had seen his dad, the two of them had exchanged words. In his junior year of high school after his mom had died, and Nick had gone to live with his father, Nick had admittedly been a little hard to handle.

Ronnie Ciotti had been a tough customer. Blue-collar from his crew cut to his work boots, Ronnie had been an electrical worker, a union man, a wiry guy with a fierce temper who played by the rules and expected no less from his smart-ass son.

After Nick's parents had divorced, Ronnie hadn't come around much. Back in the day, Nick had taken it personally, on behalf of himself and his mom. But now with the clarity that hindsight offered and the perspective that came from maturity, he realized the divorce must have been just as hard on his father as it had been on his mother.

Ronnie Ciotti didn't like to lose. From this vantage point, it must've been damn difficult to lose his entire family the way he had.

This afternoon, Nick had glimpsed a similar feeling when for several excruciating moments he hadn't known Becca's condition after Kate had called him to tell him about the accident. She wouldn't have told him the worst of it over the phone.

The sad thing was, he'd prepared himself for the bottom to fall out of everything. He'd braced himself for that sickeningly familiar feeling of having someone he loved ripped away from him, having his heart torn right out of his chest and thrown on the floor. When it didn't happen, when he'd realized Becca and the babies were fine—and he was so grateful they were—he also realized he didn't want to render himself so vulnerable.

He'd make a terrible father, anyway. If he kept his distance, he could provide for them without actively screwing up their lives.

Over the years, he'd managed to keep from getting involved. Now he knew why. When you opened yourself to love—especially with someone like Becca—you opened yourself to potential pain and loss. That realization made him want to retreat back into his world of emergency medicine, where he was good at what he did, where he could fix people but not have to get involved. In the emergency room he had control over most things—not all things, but he was removed from the things that were out of his control, the losses faced by other people at the cruel hands of fate.

Nick walked into the lobby of the inn and looked around for his father. He'd texted him as he was leaving Becca's, saying he'd be there within ten minutes. It was after eight-thirty now. If the guy hadn't gotten himself something to eat, he must be starving by now.

"Welcome to the Celebration Inn," said a perky redhead who was manning the desk. "Are you staying with us tonight?"

"I'm meeting someone."

Nick had no idea what he was walking into, if his dad still had the same volatile temperament, or if he'd mellowed over the years. It was just nerves on Nick's part, he knew it. The knot in his stomach was testament to that. Besides, would the guy have come all the way from Florida to Texas just to have words with him? He could've done that over the phone; he could've hung up on him. Nick reminded himself his dad had been agreeable.

Maybe time had mellowed him.

The front desk clerk motioned toward an adjacent doorway. "You might want to check the sitting area."

When Nick entered the room, he caught a glimpse of someone sitting in a chair in the corner reading a newspaper and sipping a cup of something that Nick assumed was coffee. The room smelled as if someone had just brewed a pot.

"Dad?"

The guy looked up and smiled, and it reached all the way to his dark eyes. He looked a little older, and he'd gone a little soft around the middle. There was more gray than brown in his close-cropped curly hair, but Nick could see back through the years to the man he hadn't talked to in nearly two decades.

Ronnie stood and offered his hand. Nick shook it.

"Son, it's good to see you."

"You, too. Thanks for coming all this way. Are you hungry?"

Ronnie nodded. "I could eat a bite. But where is your lady? Isn't she coming with us?"

Nick glanced around the quaint sitting room, at the white wicker furniture that looked more decorative than comfortable despite the bright floral-patterned pillows that covered the seats and backs.

He was suddenly exhausted and couldn't bear the thought of having to explain the accident. Becca and the babies were fine. He and his dad had so many other things to discuss.

"She couldn't make it tonight," he said. "Maybe tomorrow, though. We'll see. We'd better get going. Celebration rolls up the sidewalks at ten o'clock. Are you up for walking? The place I have in mind is just down the street."

"I've been sitting so much today, a walk would do me some good."

The inn was located right across from Central Park. As they walked out the front doors toward the restaurant, the lit Christmas tree caught Nick's eye. His thoughts tumbled back to the night of the tree-lighting ceremony and how right Becca had felt in his arms and how happy their friends had been learning the news.

Everyone seemed to be taking the news well, actually—not that it should matter if anyone didn't. It wasn't anybody's business but his and Becca's. Why was it, though, that Nick still couldn't seem to wrap his mind around parenthood and fatherhood? What was wrong with him? But the even bigger question was, how come every time he allowed himself to get close to someone, tragedy struck?

He was a scientist. He wasn't superstitious. But sometimes you just had to look at the writing on the wall.

The accident was his fault. He shouldn't have insisted that they go to Southwestern. The fact that Becca and the babies had escaped unscathed was making him think that maybe they'd be better off if he took a more hands-off approach.

Maybe he just needed some space to think and to figure things out. But first, he needed to catch up with his dad.

"That's a nice Christmas tree over there in the park," Ronnie said. His deep voice was a little gravellier than it used to be. He hoped his dad had kicked the cigarette habit. He hadn't smelled like smoke, the way he used to—Ronnie's aftershave had always mixed with the smell of cigarette smoke, creating a close, almost suffocating calling card that had permeated their whole apartment.

"Yeah, this is a nice, close-knit little town. The residents take a lot of pride in doing things like that. In fact, the foundation that Becca works for was instrumental in organizing the tree lighting. The whole town turned out for it."

Ronnie nodded. "That Becca of yours sounds like quite a woman. I hope I get to meet her while I'm here. I don't know when I'll make it back for a visit.

Then again, maybe the two of you could come and visit me in Florida."

Nick's first thought was *maybe after the babies were born*, but he didn't know what their situation would be. But things seemed to be going well with his father, and Nick was hesitant to introduce any bit of negativity.

Instead of answering, Nick gave a noncommittal nod. By that time, they'd reached Taco's, Nick's favorite restaurant in downtown Celebration.

Nick approached the hostess stand. "Are you still seating for dinner?"

The blond smiled at him as she gathered up two menus. "Yes sir, we are happy to seat people until 10:00 p.m. I have a table available for you. Please, follow me."

The place wasn't very busy, so they'd no more than settled in when the server came over and took their drink orders—cold draft beer for both of them. Then they were both quiet as they perused the menu.

Taco's was located near the square, and it was his default restaurant when his refrigerator was bare or he was short on time and needed to pick up something quickly—which was most of the time.

He ordered the chicken enchilada platter. His dad, the same. It struck Nick as a little odd that Ronnie, who had always been so full of strong opinions and my-way-or-the-highway stances, seemed to be deferring to his son. It was only beer and enchiladas, but Nick couldn't remember a time when the guy he'd always butted heads with deferred to anyone.

With their orders placed and the cold mugs of beer

in hand, the two of them began the slow, cautious journey of catching up.

Of course, they'd both been busy. Ronnie was still working, even though he'd moved from San Antonio to Florida. He'd wanted a change of scenery—a new start.

"It's really good to see you, son. You've done a good job. Really made something of yourself. You're my idea of a self-made man."

Nick didn't know about that. He made a good salary and he saved a good portion of it, but he certainly wasn't Rockefeller rich. That was his idea of a self-made man. But he could see why he might think that. He took a lot of pride in not asking anyone for help. He liked his job. Did he like his life?

Until he'd met Becca and moved to Celebration, he hadn't really had a life outside of work. Maybe that's one of the things that was plaguing him, making him question what should be the best thing that had ever happened to him.

The truth was Nick thrived on change in work environments, but personally, in much the same way that he always returned to the chicken enchilada platter at Taco's, he found comfort in the sameness of his personal life.

Becca stirred things up. Not in a malicious way, more like holding up a mirror so that he could see his life reflected back at him. It had thrown him out of his comfort zone and into chaos.

But the truth was, if not for her, he probably wouldn't be sitting here with his father right now. They were both stubborn men. Who knew if either of them would've ever made the first move toward reconciliation if not for Becca.

You have to forgive yourself before you can move on.

The comfort of sameness was an illusion. It was also a bandit that robbed you of time and relationships you might never recover.

You have to forgive yourself...

"What happened, Nicky?" Ronnie asked.

The question threw Nick, because the last time he could remember his father calling him Nicky was before Caiden died.

"Why have we not spoken in all these years?"

A silent growl of defensiveness wanted to pop off something smart-assed and hard-edged. But he wasn't seventeen years old anymore.

Ronnie must've mistaken his silence for blame, because he said, "Whatever it is that I did to you—it's been so damn long ago that I don't even remember—I'm sorry."

Nick hardly recognized the man sitting across the table from him. His father was apologizing?

Apologizing. And it sounded as if he was willing to shoulder the brunt of the blame. That wasn't right.

"It was my fault. I should never have taken my eyes off Caiden. If I'd done what I was supposed to do, he'd still be alive and I'm sure our lives would've all turned out differently. Mom might still be here—or at least I'd like to think she would, because the two of you probably wouldn't have gotten a divorce—"

Ronnie held up his hand. "I loved your mother. I don't want you to ever think that I didn't. But our marriage had been in trouble for a long time. We just worked hard to hide it from you and Caiden. The cruise was supposed to get our relationship back on track. But it didn't."

"Well, it might have if Caiden hadn't died. And that's my fault."

Ronnie stared at Nick for several beats. "Son, I know you blamed yourself after everything happened. I even lied to myself and thought that the reason you needed to get away was because losing your brother was just too painful. It was hard on all of us. But one thing I know right now, sitting here with you, is that I made a mistake letting you go away with so much guilt in your heart. If anyone was to blame, it was your mother and me for allowing you to shoulder the responsibility of your brother. You were just a kid. And you need to know your mother and I never blamed you."

Nick's instinct was to throw up the shutters. To clam up and retreat deep inside where he didn't have to deal with these feelings. He'd spent a good portion of his life burying them because they were simply too painful to deal with.

"Of course you blamed me. It was my fault. I was the one to blame, and I will carry that with me for the rest of my life."

Ronnie slapped his hand down on the table. "Well, you're not the only one who has been carrying this guilt with you. How do you think it feels to know if I hadn't been fighting with my wife that day my younger son wouldn't be dead and I wouldn't have ruined your life and driven you away from me? If I hadn't been fighting with your mother, all of our lives might've turned out different."

Strangely, there was an odd comfort…well, maybe not comfort, but it was reassuring to see that his fiery father hadn't completely changed. No, it wasn't comfort. It was a completely new perspective on guilt to which Nick had always thought he owned the exclusive rights.

It was an eye-opener.

He had no idea his dad had been shouldering the burden of blame, too. For the first time since he could remember, he and his father saw eye to eye on something.

But what was he supposed to do with that? It certainly wasn't something he wanted to share a fist bump of solidarity over. They both felt guilty. They both blamed themselves. Arguing over who was guiltier or the bigger schmuck or the worst human being alive wouldn't change anything. It wouldn't bring back Caiden or Mom. It certainly wouldn't give them back the lost years. Nick didn't know what to say.

"You know, your mom and I didn't just lose one son that day." His dad's voice was softer now. "We lost you, too. You were gone long before you left home. And it's taken me all these years to realize that. But after you called me and told me I was going to be a grandfather, it was as if you'd given me back my life. That day last week when I heard your voice, it was as if you'd offered me a new start."

Ronnie paused. Nick wondered if he was waiting for Nick to object or to throw something back at him. But words jumbled and knotted in the back of Nick's throat. He couldn't have said anything, even if he'd known what to say.

"I had to take sick days to come here and see you, but when I heard your voice, I knew I would rather get fired—hell, I would rather die—than waste the chance to make things right with my boy. You and your kids and Becca, if she'll allow me, are the only family I have. Son, I screwed up with your mom. I didn't man up because I was too busy wallowing in my own sadness to let her lean on me. She was the love of my life, and I just let her walk out the door. I let you walk out the door. I was such a self-centered jackass. If I could change one thing in my life, I would go back and make sure your mother knew how much I loved her. And I'd make sure you know how much I regret losing the past sixteen years with you. I hope you know how sorry I am."

Ronnie's voice broke. A tear trailed down his cheek. It cut Nick to the bone because he couldn't remember a single time in his life when he'd seen his father cry.

Not at Caiden's funeral.

Not at his wife's funeral.

Certainly not the day Nick had left home to join the marines.

Or maybe it was the simple act of his father apologizing that was melting the ice that had formed in Nick's heart all these years.

He slid a napkin across the table toward his father. It must've embarrassed him, because the older man said, "Yeah, hey, sorry about this. I'll be right back."

As Ronnie stood up and started to walk away, Nick said, "Dad, I'll make a deal with you. If you forgive me, I'll forgive you. And then we both have to forgive ourselves."

Ronnie stared at Nick for what seemed an eternity. Then he offered a solemn nod before he turned and walked toward the restrooms in the back of the restaurant.

Chapter Thirteen

Someone was knocking at the door. In fact, Priscilla, the corgi, was going crazy barking and turning in circles as she tried her best to herd Becca off the sofa and into the foyer. It was ten o'clock at night and whoever it was wasn't just knocking, he or she was being rather insistent.

If Priscilla didn't wake the neighbors, her uninvited guest would. Becca rolled her eyes as she thought about the upbraiding she was sure to get from Mrs. Milton and Mrs. Cavett.

But soon enough annoyance gave way to an anxious hopefulness that left her a little queasy as her stomach twisted and plummeted. Maybe Nick had come back to apologize.

As quick as the glimmer of hope appeared, Becca squashed it. She was tired of these ups and downs.

Tired of feeling as if she was walking on eggshells around him. Tired of trying so hard to do everything right. *Dammit.*

"Priscilla, please, be quiet. You're a good watchdog, but I can take it from here."

As if she understood perfectly, Priscilla dropped into a submissive stance—front paws down, corgi butt in the air—and uttered a quieter sound that was more embarrassed yodel than fierce watchdog bark.

"Good girl." Becca bent to give the little dog an appreciative stroke. She was in no hurry to get to the door. If it was Nick, he could stew for a minute. If he didn't want to be with her and his children, they would be better off on their own.

She glanced at the Christmas tree, which was adorned with only the lights Becca had installed and the two ornaments they'd hung—one each. She couldn't even get him to commit to decorating the tree—probably too domestic for him. Not enough emergency room blood and guts. Much too boring and long-term, seeing how she liked to leave up the tree until Epiphany.

She wasn't going to force him to do anything he didn't want to do. If he couldn't come to this relationship table willingly, she sure as shoot fire was not going to beg him.

After the Thanksgiving incident with her mother, whom she still hadn't heard from, and after Nick had gone all stoic and standoffish, Becca had realized she was done earning people's love.

Done.

Finito.

It was a matter of self-preservation.

She took a moment to gather her thoughts as she slowly made her way to the door. She flipped on the porch light—only so she could get a clear look out the peephole.

One could never be too cautious.

Ha! She should've thought of that before she let herself fall for a guy who had no desire to settle down with a wife and children. With a guy who withdrew to inner Siberia every time life got a little messy.

Well, you know what, Nick? Life is messy. It can be messy and ugly and unpredictable. People had accidents, and when they survived you were supposed to love them and count your blessings. You weren't supposed to retreat and push them away.

But if he wanted to back away, that was fine. She wasn't going to chase him and try to convince him that he needed her, that she was worth loving. All her life she'd been the good girl, and all it had gotten her was the expectation that her sole purpose in this life was to please other people.

She was prepared to say those words to him. In fact, she hoped he'd come by so she could tell him everything she'd been thinking since he'd so unceremoniously dropped her off at home after the accident.

However, when she looked out the peephole, it wasn't Nick. It was her mother and Rosanna.

The disappointment that it wasn't Nick was nearly crushing. Becca hated herself for it. She breathed through the sting and hit the mental *save* button on the memo to Nick in her brain.

That's what it was. It wasn't that she wanted to see him so much as she'd wanted the chance to tell him exactly what was on her mind.

Her mother knocked again, or at least Becca assumed it was her mother, because she'd been the one closer to the door. Rosanna had been standing a safe distance behind her.

"Rebecca, are you in there?" her mother called. "Please, open the door."

Please?

Had Isabel Flannigan actually ended a sentence with the word *please*?

That was a good sign. Or at least Becca hoped it was a good sign. She'd been through so much today with the accident and Nick going emotionally AWOL, she simply didn't have the energy to go to battle with her mother.

Isabel started pounding again, and Becca jerked open the door, bracing herself for her mother to unleash a tirade about how it was cold outside and Becca had left her standing there. Instead, Isabel threw her arms around her daughter and started sobbing.

"Mom."

"Rebecca, I heard you were in an accident. Why on earth didn't you call me?"

This was weird for three reasons—probably even more, but right now Becca was too taken aback to count—1) she and her mother hadn't spoken since Thanksgiving; 2) Isabel *never* made the first move toward reconciliation; and 3) her mother considered any physical displays of affection vulgar.

Yet here she was, practically squeezing the stuffing out of her.

"Are you okay, Rebecca? Colleen Carlton's daughter works at Southwestern Medical Center, and Colleen called me to ask if you were okay. Of course,

I had no idea that you'd even been in an accident. I didn't know what to say. She had to fill me in based on what her daughter had told me."

Oh. Okay. Here we go.

Still caught in her mother's embrace, Becca exchanged a look with her sister. To her surprise, it was more concern than the usual disdain.

"But that doesn't matter. You're here, and you're okay." Isabel pulled back, still holding Becca at arm's length, and assessed her daughter.

The sight of her mother standing there with tears streaming down her face, holding on to her as if she were afraid she'd float out into the ether if she let go, liquefied the hard stance Becca had been prepared to take with her mother.

"Mom, I'm fine. Please, don't cry."

"Good luck getting her to listen," Rosanna said. "I was telling her that the whole way over."

Again, Becca braced for Hurricane Isabel to unleash her fury, but this time on Rosanna. Again, she refrained.

"Accidents happen so fast." Isabel's voice was barely a whisper. "If I'd lost you today without being able to talk to you and mend this rift, and I'd never gotten the chance to tell you I'm sorry and I love you, I don't think I could've gone on."

"Mom, I told you. I'm fine. Really, I am. Everything is fine. I'm not mad at you. Please, don't be upset."

So much for the new hard-hearted Becca.

She could stand up for herself, but she didn't have to be mean and heartless. Her mother was so upset, and Becca couldn't bear to see her that way.

"Come in, please," Becca said. "Rosanna, will you please shut the door?"

Her sister, who was also curiously subdued tonight, nodded and did as Becca had asked.

She walked arm in arm with their mother into the living room.

The three of them sat for a moment, looking at each other.

"I'm sorry I didn't call you," Becca said. "I was fine, and I didn't want to worry you."

Isabel drew in a deep breath. "No, I suspect you didn't call me because you were mad at me. And I don't blame you."

She paused and swallowed so hard, Becca could hear her mother's throat working.

"You were right, Rebecca. What I did at Thanksgiving dinner was out of line. I not only embarrassed you and Nick, I embarrassed myself. I hope you will be able to forgive me."

Nick's *ignosces* tattoo flashed in Becca's mind.

Forgive me.

The memory of how his hard bicep felt under her fingers, as she'd traced the letters, made her shudder. She blinked away the thought.

"Are you okay?" Isabel asked.

"I am. I'm touched by what you said. As far as I'm concerned, we can put it behind us as long as you realize, Mom, we may not always see eye to eye, but as long as we respect each other, we will be fine. And what I mean by respect is you can't browbeat me into doing things your way."

Isabel straightened in her chair. Her chin lifted a couple of notches in a guarded stance that had Becca bracing for her to go on the defensive. Becca was so tired of fighting. So tired of trying to please everyone that she almost did a double take when her mother said, "I'll behave myself. I promise. And I'd like to apologize to Nick. When can the two of you come for dinner?"

Becca took care not to let her face give away what she was really feeling. Because she didn't know if there would be another family dinner with Nick, but she didn't have to explain that to anyone. At least not right now.

When Nick had learned that his father would be visiting, he'd arranged to take off the whole time he was in Celebration.

When he'd told Cullen Dunlevy why he wanted the time off, Cullen had been generous, telling him to take all the time he needed. Actually, he needed only two nights because he'd been late getting to him last night due to the circumstances of the day.

The morning after their dinner, Nick met his father for breakfast. Afterward, they'd met Cece Harrison, the guide who was giving them a tour of Celebration, sharing some of the lesser known history of the area. The woman who tended the front desk at the Celebration Inn had arranged the tour for them. She'd promised that Cece, who was also a staff writer for the *Dallas Journal of Business and Development*, was not only a friend, but also a knowledgeable local historian. She highly recommended her.

Cece didn't disappoint. She was perky and pretty and everything a person looking to learn more about the town might hope for.

She even tried to flirt a little with Nick, which caused Ronnie to elbow him good-naturedly. But that only made Nick's mind drift back to Becca. Ronnie said, "Don't waste your efforts on him. He's in love."

And he was.

Just like that, Nick knew it. But he had no idea what to do about it.

Cece smiled and cooed about how romantic it was to see someone so much in love and how she wished that someday she'd find someone who was just as smitten with her.

Ronnie joked about applying for the job. It was all good-natured and harmless, since he was old enough to be her father.

"Where's this lucky lady today?" Cece asked.

Both she and Ronnie turned expectant eyes on Nick.

"She's at work." He hoped. He really should've called her to make sure she was okay. But the tour was moving on.

They learned that Celebration was founded in the mid-nineteenth century and had been settled by the Rice family. They stopped in front of the sprawling Victorian mansion that overlooked the east side of the park.

"This was the home of the Rice family," Cece said. "They decided to name the town Celebration because, after months and months of searching, the family had finally found a place to call home, and, of course, this was a great cause for *celebration*."

As Cece and Ronnie joked about her play on words, Nick was struck by how the whole town seemed to be all about family.

The thought of a man sacrificing everything to give his family a safe place to call home made Nick ache with a vast emptiness. What was wrong with him that he couldn't man up for Becca?

He had to admit that his panic over her accident really was just an excuse. It was selfish justification: if he didn't get attached, then he wouldn't hurt those he loved, and in turn he couldn't get hurt himself.

Was he really that weak?

Weren't things with his father so much better than he ever could have hoped for? It was a fresh start for both of them, and it never would've happened if he hadn't taken a chance.

Ronnie was laughing at something that Cece had said, but Nick had missed it, and he didn't want to ask her to repeat herself. His mind was wandering too much to concentrate on the tour.

"There's something I need to take care of," Nick said. "Would you excuse me?"

"Everything okay?" Ronnie asked.

"I hope so," he said. "I'll let you know when I see you tonight at dinner."

Becca should've told Nick no instead of betraying the new stronger, tougher, I'm-tired-of-beating-myself-up-to-win-your-love woman she'd become.

But here she was parking her car in front of Bentleys across the street from the hospital.

Of course she would go to him. Her office was in Dallas and his was right here.

God, would she never learn?

Of course, if she'd told him no the first time instead

of spending the night with him, they wouldn't be meeting to have this conversation.

Of course, he'd been cryptic about why he wanted to meet her today. Since he hadn't indicated otherwise, she was going to assume that this meeting was goodbye.

Well, goodbye to any notion of them being a couple or a traditional family. The thought made her heart hurt, but they might as well establish things now. Because the longer they dragged them out, the harder it would be to separate herself.

She'd already let herself fall in love with him, and look where that had gotten her.

As she got out of the car, she squared her shoulders. This would be the last time she would accommodate him. And she intended to tell him that when she saw him.

Her heart felt hollow and fragile. Her eyes burned with the threat of tears that she would not let fall. She couldn't, because if she started crying now, she might not stop.

She couldn't let him see her that way. She knew him well enough to believe he wasn't a cruel man who would take pleasure in watching her suffer.

No, this was more a case of not humiliating herself in front of a man who didn't want her. It was as plain and simple as that. The man she'd fallen in love with didn't love her back. He didn't want her.

That reminder dried up any threat of falling tears. It would be her mantra when she was feeling weak. Her pillar if she felt as if she was starting to fall.

As she pulled open the door to the restaurant, she had another sinking spell. Her mind skipped back to *that night*. That fateful night when she'd accommodated Rosanna's demand for space, and she'd come over to Bentleys to get out of the way.

She'd fallen for him the minute she'd laid eyes on him, and all common sense had gone out the window.

Why had she agreed to meet him here?

As she approached the hostess stand, she reminded herself that it was too late now. She was here—*ohhh*…and there he was sitting at the same booth they'd shared that night.

She took back the benefit of the doubt that she'd afforded him. Because choosing that table just seemed cruel.

When he'd called and asked if she could meet him there, she'd assumed that he was asking for his convenience. So he could get back to the hospital fast.

Now she wasn't sure.

In fact, she wasn't sure of anything except that she should've insisted on him meeting her halfway between Dallas and Celebration. In the future, when they had to see each other for a matter that had to do with their children, she would make sure that they split the difference the same way they would split everything else—expenses, holidays with the kids…

"I see the person I'm meeting," Becca said to the hostess, taking care to smile and temper her voice so as not to misdirect her frustrations.

When Nick saw her, he stood, offering a half smile.

Damn him for being so good-looking and so cool about the situation. Especially when she was falling apart inside. She swallowed the lump in her throat, determined to not let him see just how hard this was for her.

When she reached the booth, there was an awkward moment where neither of them seemed to know what to do. For a split second, she actually thought he might lean in and kiss her. But that was just wishful thinking.

She ducked her head and slid into the booth. He did the same.

"How are you?" he asked.

"I'm fine, Nick. How are you? How's your dad?"

Yes, that was the key. Keep it light. Make him believe she really was fine. Maybe if she pretended long enough, she really would be.

"My dad is— He's great. We've had some good talks. Can't thank you enough for pushing me to get in touch with him."

Pushing him?

Is that how she'd come across? Pushy? She cringed inwardly, but she was careful to not let it show. Or at least she hoped she didn't. She certainly hadn't realized she'd pushed him.

"Nick, I'm sorry if you ever felt like I pushed you. I was never trying to force you into anything. That was never my intention."

"I guess that didn't really come out the way I meant it to. You never made me feel pushed. But your encouragement did help me do the right thing in contacting my dad."

Nick looked down at his hands for a moment. They were resting on the table, big, capable hands that knew just how to touch her. She would miss those hands.

"He and I both agreed that we were idiots for going so long without talking to each other. You were right,

Becca. He never did blame me. In fact, all these years he's blamed himself. He's been carrying the burden around as long as I have, and we both agreed to set it down and move forward. We both missed so much."

"That's great, Nick. I really am happy for you. For both of you. I'm sorry I didn't get a chance to meet your father. When did he leave?"

"He's still here. He's taking a walking tour of Celebration. The woman who runs the inn set it up for him."

"Oh, you should be with him. Instead of here with me. This could've waited."

Nick raked his hand through his hair. It seemed like a nervous gesture, and it reminded Becca that she'd gotten carried away there for a moment. God, he did have that effect on her, didn't he?

"Actually, no, this couldn't wait."

"Oh."

Becca smoothed her skirt over her knees. If she'd known she was having lunch with him today, she would've worn something different. Not that there was anything wrong with her navy merino wool skirt. It was just a little plain. A no-nonsense outfit that had suited her mood this morning when she'd woken up. And, okay, it was one of the few pieces of clothing in her closet that she could still fit into.

No, if she'd known that today was the day she'd officially get dumped, she would've worn something a little more inspired. Something that made a man look twice—think twice before letting her go. But who was she trying to fool? This was who she was when no one was looking and she liked that person, even if he didn't. She sat up a little straighter, squared her shoulders.

There wasn't a thing in the world wrong with that version of Becca.

"Becca—"

Before he could get to the point, the server walked up to the table. "Hi, I'm Kathy. I'll be taking care of you today. May I tell you about some of our specials?"

She didn't wait for them to answer—really, it was a rhetorical question—and began rattling off the list from memory.

They quickly placed their order—a Reuben sandwich for him and a cup of clam chowder for her. She didn't have much of an appetite right now, but she was afraid that not ordering would've given off a hostile vibe. And there she was worrying about what he thought.

Forever the people pleaser.

No. No, she wasn't. She'd ordered the soup to make herself feel more comfortable. If she didn't feel like eating it, she wouldn't.

"So, what was it that was so important that you're letting it cut into your visit with your dad?"

He nodded and looked at her a little bit too long. Maybe he was weighing his words. Probably. Obviously, this wasn't easy for either of them.

"Two things, actually. I have something for you. But first, the thing that can't wait—Becca, I acted like a total jerk yesterday, and I'm sorry. You didn't deserve that. The accident wasn't your fault."

The old Becca would've told him it was okay. She would've immediately tried to set his mind to rest, but he *had* acted like a jerk, and it wasn't acceptable.

"I needed you, Nick, and you shut me out. I appreciate your apology, but whether or not we're together, we're going to be in each other's lives. We're going to have to communicate and get along for the sake of our kids. You can't just go inward and refuse to talk to me."

He reached out and covered her hand with his.

"I know. Believe me, I know. I came from a home where my parents' lack of communication and constant bickering shattered our lives. And I know it's been an issue with your family, too."

His hand was still on hers, and it was wreaking all kinds of havoc with her emotions. Since she was the one who had brought up the fact that they needed to communicate if they were going to have a healthy co-parenting relationship, she knew what she had to say.

She drew her hand away, trying not to imagine that he looked a little bothered by it.

"Nick, I have to be honest with you. I have feelings for you. I have since that night that we sat right here and… I guess I fell in love with you that night, but—"

"Becca—"

"No, Nick, let me finish."

His eyes held so much tenderness that she had to look away because her own eyes were starting to fill with tears.

She wasn't going to cry.

She wasn't.

She couldn't.

Oh, God. She was.

"Look, you can't do this—" she said, but her voice broke, and she couldn't get the rest of the words out.

All she had to say was that he couldn't keep doing

this—he couldn't keep touching her like this, and, for that matter, he really shouldn't look at her that way, either—but how could you set boundaries and parameters on the way someone looked at another person?

She hadn't really noticed, but maybe that was just his face. His gorgeous, perfect face. Maybe that was how he looked at everyone, and she'd simply misunderstood and read way too much into it.

Touching, on the other hand—now, that was a clear boundary.

She took a deep breath, gathering herself to lay down the no-touching law, when Nick suddenly stood up.

Where was he—

He was kneeling in front of her. And the tears were still rolling down her cheeks.

She just needed to get a hold of herself.

What the heck was he doing?

Oh, God. What was that? A Christmas ornament? Why was he kneeling in front of her with a Christmas ornament?

"Becca, I got you that ruby necklace you tried on in the jewelry store."

Okay, but you're holding a Christmas ornament?

Oh, wait, maybe he took the necklace back.

"I wanted to give it to you for Christmas. But somehow it just didn't feel *right*."

"You really don't have to tell me this, Nick. It's an expensive piece of jewelry. That saleswoman put us in an awkward position."

"Actually, I found something else I wanted to give you instead."

He held up the Christmas ornament.

Becca's heart sank. Not because of the gift—it was pretty. She couldn't see it very well because of how he was holding it, but it looked as if it had a scene of a town—maybe a Currier and Ives Christmas scene. It was probably lovely, but did he really have to give it to her this way? Everyone in the restaurant was looking at them.

Becca swiped at her tears.

"I know I've probably done more things wrong than I've done right," Nick said. "I mean, we haven't even finished decorating the tree."

"It's okay, really," Becca said.

"I've never been very good at relationships. But one thing that I have done right is to realize that I love you."

Becca blinked, and her heart lurched. Had she heard him right? Surely not.

"You are the best thing that's ever happened to me, Becca. Will you give me a chance? Will you please give *us* a chance?" He turned the ornament around. *Our First Christmas* was spelled out in ornate gold lettering.

Becca's mouth dropped open as realization settled over her.

Then she saw that there was something else— something small and shiny tied to the ornament with a red ribbon.

"Nothing in the world would make me happier than if you'd be my wife. You and the babies and I, we could be a family."

He looked as if he was holding his breath as he untied the ribbon that held the ring.

As the cymbal monkey started up in her chest, she hadn't realized that she'd been holding her breath, too.

"Yes!" she said breathlessly. "Yes, Nick, there's nothing that I'd rather do than be your wife."

As he slipped the traditional round diamond on her finger, it winked and glittered in the afternoon light streaming in through the large, leaded glass windows, and everyone at the tables around them broke into applause.

Epilogue

On Christmas Eve, Becca's father walked her down the aisle of the Celebration Chapel. On her journey, she took a moment to look at everyone who had gathered for the happiest day of her life.

When her gaze landed on Nick, who was standing amid the red and white poinsettias that decorated the altar, smiling at her with so much love in his eyes, she knew without a doubt that she was the luckiest woman in the world.

And when the minister asked, "Who gives this woman in marriage?" her father said a resolute, "Her mother and I do."

The words made Becca's breath hitch.

Then her father lifted the blusher on her veil and planted a kiss on her cheek before placing her hand in Nick's.

Her sister, Rosanna, was her maid of honor. She looked stunning in her close-fitting red velvet dress. She gently took Becca's bouquet of red roses, while Kate, who was her bridesmaid, straightened the train of Becca's dress so that it lay perfectly, showing off the traditional line of the silk-and-lace ball-gown-style dress.

Since they'd planned the wedding in short order, Becca had allowed Rosanna and Kate to choose their own dresses. The only mandates Becca gave were the dresses had to complement each other, and they had to be in the same color family as the ruby necklace that Nick had given her. Becca was wearing it as her *something new*.

The wedding dress was her something old. It was her mother's. A seamstress had worked her magic to alter the dress to accommodate Becca's growing baby bump, and even if Becca had had years to plan and have a dress custom made, it would've been exactly like the shimmering lace-and-silk ball gown her mother had worn when she'd married Becca's father.

Isabel had a lot of quirks, but she also had impeccable, timeless taste.

Kate had lent her a pair of diamond earrings that were the perfect understated complement to the more ornate ruby necklace. And her something blue? It was her garter, hidden beneath the yards and yards of material that made up her voluminous skirt.

Nick's father was his best man. He'd been able to get additional time off from work, and he stood next to Nick looking handsome in a traditional black tux. Liam served as a groomsman.

Becca heard a sniffle in the front row and turned to see her mother brushing away a tear. Isabel had been remarkably cooperative over the past two weeks as they'd planned the wedding in warp speed. Her mother mouthed a silent *I love you*. Becca blew her a kiss, and with that, she turned to her husband-to-be.

As Nick reached out and took her hands, she looked into his dark brown eyes and saw her future: they would love each other for better or worse, richer or poorer; in good times and in bad.

They'd already been through so much and had found love on the other side. She couldn't wait to start their life together.

Her heart beat an anxious staccato, but it was a far cry from the frantic cymbal monkey who seemed to have gotten lost shortly after Nick had proposed. The eager excitement made her breath catch, and it was the best feeling Becca could imagine.

Nick was the love of her life. She had a feeling he would always give her butterflies. That's how much she loved this man.

Together, they would be a family.

A family.

The only place she wanted to be was in the arms of the handsome man standing in front of her.

She'd loved him from the moment she'd first set eyes on him. In fact, in some form or another, she'd been searching for him her entire life. Now she'd finally found him.

She knew, without a shadow of a doubt, that there was no place in the world that she would rather be than right here, proclaiming her love for him in front of God and the entire world. And when a single tear rolled out of the corner of Nick's eye as he said his vows, she knew that they both had found their happily-ever-after.

* * * * *

'Do it,' she said, pointing to the floor. 'The full down-on-bended-knee thing.'

'Seriously?' he said, dark brows raised.

'Yes,' she said imperiously. He grinned. 'Okay.'

The tall, denim-clad hunk obediently knelt down on one knee, took her right hand in both of his and looked up into her face. 'Andie, will you do me the honour of becoming my fake fiancée?' he intoned, in that deep, so-sexy voice.

Looking down at his roughly handsome face, Andie didn't know whether to laugh or cry. 'Yes, I accept your proposal,' she said, in a voice that wasn't quite steady.

Dominic squeezed her hand hard as relief flooded his face. He got up from bended knee, and for a moment she thought he might kiss her…

GIFT-WRAPPED
IN HER
WEDDING DRESS

BY
KANDY SHEPHERD

All rights reserved including the right of reproduction in whole or in part in any form. This edition is published by arrangement with Harlequin Books S.A.

This is a work of fiction. Names, characters, places, locations and incidents are purely fictional and bear no relationship to any real life individuals, living or dead, or to any actual places, business establishments, locations, events or incidents. Any resemblance is entirely coincidental.

This book is sold subject to the condition that it shall not, by way of trade or otherwise, be lent, resold, hired out or otherwise circulated without the prior consent of the publisher in any form of binding or cover other than that in which it is published and without a similar condition including this condition being imposed on the subsequent purchaser.

® and ™ are trademarks owned and used by the trademark owner and/or its licensee. Trademarks marked with ® are registered with the United Kingdom Patent Office and/or the Office for Harmonisation in the Internal Market and in other countries.

Published in Great Britain 2015
by Mills & Boon, an imprint of Harlequin (UK) Limited,
Eton House, 18-24 Paradise Road, Richmond, Surrey, TW9 1SR

© 2015 Kandy Shepherd

ISBN: 978-0-263-25182-1

23-1115

Harlequin (UK) Limited's policy is to use papers that are natural, renewable and recyclable products and made from wood grown in sustainable forests. The logging and manufacturing processes conform to the legal environmental regulations of the country of origin.

Printed and bound in Spain
by CPI, Barcelona

Kandy Shepherd swapped a career as a magazine editor for a life writing romance. She lives on a small farm in the Blue Mountains near Sydney, Australia, with her husband, daughter and lots of pets. She believes in love at first sight and real-life romance—they worked for her! Kandy loves to hear from her readers. Visit her at www.kandyshepherd.com.

To all my Christmas magazine colleagues,
in particular Helen, Adriana and Jane—
the magic of the season lives on!

CHAPTER ONE

So HE'D GOT on the wrong side of the media. Again. Dominic's words, twisted out of all recognition, were all over newspapers, television and social media.

Billionaire businessman Dominic Hunt refuses to sleep out with other CEOs in charity event for homeless.

Dominic slammed his fist on his desk so hard the pain juddered all the way up his arm. He hadn't *refused* to support the charity in their Christmas appeal, just refused the invitation to publicly bed down for the night in a cardboard box on the forecourt of the Sydney Opera House. His donation to the worthy cause had been significant—but anonymous. *Why wasn't that enough?*

He buried his head in his hands. For a harrowing time in his life there had been no choice for him but to sleep rough for real, a cardboard box his only bed. He couldn't go there again—not even for a charity stunt, no matter how worthy. There could be no explanation—he would not share the secrets of his past. *Ever.*

With a sick feeling of dread he continued to read on-screen the highlights of the recent flurry of negative press about him and his company, thoughtfully compiled in a report by his Director of Marketing.

Predictably, the reporters had then gone on to rehash his well-known aversion to Christmas. Again he'd been misquoted. It was true he loathed the whole idea of celebrating Christmas. But not for the reasons the media had so fancifully contrived. Not because he was a *Scrooge.* How he hated that label and the erroneous aspersions that he didn't ever give to charity. Despaired that he was included in a round-up of Australia's Multi-Million-Dollar Misers. *It couldn't be further from the truth.*

He strongly believed that giving money to worthy causes should be conducted in private—not for public acclaim. But this time he couldn't ignore the name-calling and innuendo. He was near to closing a game-changing deal on a joint venture with a family-owned American corporation run by a man with a strict moral code that included obvious displays of philanthropy.

Dominic could not be seen to be a Scrooge. He had to publicly prove that he was not a miser. But he did not want to reveal the extent of his charitable support because to do so would blow away the smokescreen he had carefully constructed over his past.

He'd been in a bind. Until his marketing director had suggested he would attract positive press if he opened his harbourside home for a lavish fund-raising event for charity. 'Get your name in the newspaper for the right reasons,' he had been advised.

Dominic hated the idea of his privacy being invaded but he had reluctantly agreed. He wanted the joint venture to happen. If a party was what it took, he was prepared to put his qualms aside and commit to it.

The party would be too big an event for it to be organised in-house. His marketing people had got outside companies involved. Trouble was the three so-called 'party planners' he'd been sent so far had been incompetent and he'd shown them the door within minutes of meeting. Now there was a fourth. He glanced down at the eye-catching card on the desk in front of him. Andrea Newman from a company called Party Queens—*No party too big or too small* the card boasted.

Party Queens. It was an interesting choice for a business name. Not nearly as stitched up as the other companies that had pitched for this business. But did it have the gravitas required? After all, this event could be the deciding factor in a deal that would extend his business interests internationally.

He glanced at his watch. This morning he was working from his home office. Ms Newman was due to meet with him right now, here at his house where the party was to take place. Despite the attention-grabbing name of the business, he had no reason to expect Party Planner Number Four to be any more impressive than the other three he'd sent packing. But he would give her twenty minutes—that was only fair and he made a point of always being fair.

On cue, the doorbell rang. Punctuality, at least, was a point in Andrea Newman's favour. He headed down the wide marble stairs to the front door.

His first impression of the woman who stood on his porch was that she was attractive, not in a conventionally pretty way but something rather more interesting—an angular face framed by a tangle of streaked blonde hair, a wide generous mouth, unusual green eyes. So attractive he found himself looking at her for a moment longer than was required to sum up a possible contractor. And the almost imperceptible curve of her mouth let him know she'd noticed.

'Good morning, Mr Hunt—Andie Newman from Party Queens,' she said. 'Thank you for the pass code that got me through the gate. Your security is formidable, like an eastern suburbs fortress.' Was that a hint of challenge underscoring her warm, husky voice? If so, he wasn't going to bite.

'The pass code expires after one use, Ms Newman,' he said, not attempting to hide a note of warning. The three party planners before her were never going to get a new pass code. But none of them had been remotely like her—in looks or manner.

She was tall and wore a boldly patterned skirt of some silky fine fabric that fell below her knees in uneven layers, topped by a snug-fitting rust-coloured jacket and high heeled shoes that laced all the way up her calf. A soft leather satchel was slung casually across her shoulder. She presented as smart but more unconventional than the corporate dark suits and rigid briefcases of the other three—whose ideas had been as pedestrian as their appearances.

'Andie,' she replied and started to say something else about his security system. But, as she did, a sudden gust of balmy spring breeze whipped up her skirt, revealing long slender legs and a tantalising hint of red underwear. Dominic tried to do the gentlemanly thing and look elsewhere—difficult when she was standing so near to him and her legs were so attention-worthy.

'Oh,' she gasped, and fought with the skirt to hold it down, but no sooner did she get the front of the skirt in place, the back whipped upwards and she had to twist around to hold it down. The back view of her legs was equally as impressive as the front. He balled his hands into fists by his sides so he did not give into the temptation to help her with the flyaway fabric.

She flushed high on elegant cheekbones, blonde hair tousled around her face, and laughed a husky, uninhibited laugh as she battled to preserve her modesty. The breeze died down as quickly as it had sprung up and her skirt floated back into place. Still, he noticed she continued to keep it in check with a hand on her thigh.

'That's made a wonderful first impression, hasn't it?' she said, looking up at him with a rueful smile. For a long moment their eyes connected and he was the first to look away. *She was beautiful*.

As she spoke, the breeze gave a final last sigh that ruffled her hair across her face. Dominic wasn't a fanciful man, but it seemed as though the wind was ushering her into his house.

'There are worse ways of making an impression,' he said gruffly. 'I'm interested to see what you follow up with.'

Andie wasn't sure what to reply. She stood at the threshold of Dominic Hunt's multi-million-dollar mansion and knew for the first time in her career she was in serious danger of losing the professional cool in which she took such pride.

Not because of the incident with the wind and her skirt. Or because she was awestruck by the magnificence of the house and the postcard-worthy panorama of Sydney Harbour that stretched out in front of it. No. It was the man who towered above her who was making her feel so inordinately flustered. Too tongue-tied to come back with a quick quip or clever retort.

'Th…thank you,' she managed to stutter as she pushed the breeze-swept hair back from across her face.

During her career as a stylist for both magazines and advertising agencies, and now as a party planner, she had acquired the reputation of being able to manage difficult people. Which was why her two partners in their fledgling business had voted for her to be the one to deal with Dominic Hunt. Party Queens desperately needed a high-profile booking like this to help them get established. Winning it was now on her shoulders.

She had come to his mansion forewarned that he could be a demanding client. The gossip was that he had been scathing to three other planners from other companies much bigger than theirs before giving them the boot. Then there was his wider reputation as a Scrooge—a man who did not share his multitude of money with others less fortunate. He was everything she did not admire in a person.

Despite that, she been blithely confident Dominic Hunt wouldn't be more than she could handle. Until he had answered that door. Her reaction to him had her stupefied.

She had seen the photos, watched the interviews of the billionaire businessman, had recognised he was good-looking in a dark, brooding way. But no amount of research had prepared her for the pulse-raising reality of this man—tall, broad-shouldered, powerful muscles apparent even in his sleek tailored grey suit. He wasn't pretty-boy handsome. Not with that strong jaw, the crooked nose that looked as though it had been broken by a viciously aimed punch, the full, sensual mouth with the faded white scar on the corner, the spiky black hair. And then there was the almost palpable emanation of power.

She had to call on every bit of her professional savvy to ignore the warm flush that rose up her neck and onto her cheeks, the way her heart thudded into unwilling awareness of Dominic Hunt, not as a client but as a man.

She could not allow that to happen. This job was too important to her and her friends in their new business. *Anyway, dark and brooding wasn't her type*. Her ideal man was sensitive and sunny-natured, like her first lost love, for whom she felt she would always grieve.

She extended her hand, willing it to stay steady, and forced a smile. 'Mr Hunt, let's start again. Andie Newman from Party Queens.'

His grip in return was firm and warm and he nodded acknowledgement of her greeting. If a mere handshake could send shivers of awareness through her, she could be in trouble here.

Keep it businesslike. She took a deep breath, tilted back her head to meet his gaze full-on. 'I believe I'm the fourth party planner you've seen and I don't want there to be a fifth. I should be the person to plan your event.'

If he was surprised at her boldness, it didn't show in his scrutiny; his grey eyes remained cool and assessing.

'You'd better come inside and convince me why that should be the case,' he said. Even his voice was attractive—deep and measured and utterly masculine.

'I welcome the opportunity,' she said in the most confident voice she could muster.

She followed him into the entrance hall of the restored nineteen-twenties house, all dark stained wood floors and cream marble. A grand central marble staircase with wrought-iron balustrades split into two sides to climb to the next floor. This wasn't the first grand home she'd been in during the course of her work but it was so impressive she had to suppress an impulse to gawk.

'Wow,' she said, looking around her, forgetting all about how disconcerted Dominic Hunt made her feel. 'The staircase. It's amazing. I can just see a choir there, with a chorister on each step greeting your guests with Christmas carols as they step into the house.' Her thoughts raced ahead of her. Choristers' robes in red and white? Each chorister holding a scrolled parchment printed with the words to the carol? What about the music? A string quartet? A harpsichord?

'What do you mean?' he said, breaking into her reverie.

Andie blinked to bring herself back to earth and turned to look up at him. She smiled. 'Sorry. I'm getting ahead of myself. It was just an idea. Of course I realise I still need to convince you I'm the right person for your job.'

'I meant about the Christmas carols.'

So he would be that kind of pernickety client, pressing her for details before they'd even decided on the bigger picture. Did she need to spell out the message of 'Deck the Halls with Boughs of Holly'?

She shook her head in a don't-worry-about-it way. 'It was just a top-of-mind thought. But a choir would be an amazing use of the staircase. Maybe a children's choir. Get your guests into the Christmas spirit straight away, without being too cheesy about it.'

'It isn't going to be a Christmas party.' He virtually spat the word *Christmas*.

'But a party in December? I thought—'

He frowned and she could see where his reputation came from as his thick brows drew together and his eyes darkened. 'Truth be told, I don't want a party here at all. But it's a necessary evil—necessary to my business, that is.'

'Really?' she said, struggling not to jump in and say the wrong thing. A client who didn't actually want a party? This she hadn't anticipated. Her certainty that she knew how to handle this situation—this man—started to seep away.

She gritted her teeth, forced her voice to sound as conciliatory as possible. 'I understood from your brief that you wanted a big event benefiting a charity in the weeks leading up to Christmas on a date that will give you maximum publicity.'

'All that,' he said. 'Except it's not to be a Christmas party. Just a party that happens to be held around that time.'

Difficult and demanding didn't begin to describe this. But had she been guilty of assuming December translated into Christmas? Had it actually stated that in the brief? She didn't think she'd misread it.

She drew in a calming breath. 'There seems to have been a misunderstanding and I apologise for that,' she said. 'I have the official briefing from your marketing department here.' She patted her satchel. 'But I'd rather hear your thoughts, your ideas for the event in your own words.

A successful party plan comes from the heart. Can we sit down and discuss this?'

He looked pointedly at his watch. Her heart sank to the level of the first lacing on her shoes. She did not want to be the fourth party planner he fired before she'd even started her pitch. 'I'll give you ten minutes,' he said.

He led her into a living room that ran across the entire front of the house and looked out to the blue waters of the harbour and its icons of the Sydney Harbour Bridge and the Opera House. Glass doors opened out to a large terrace. *A perfect summer party terrace.*

Immediately she recognised the work of one of Sydney's most fashionable high-end interior designers—a guy who only worked with budgets that started with six zeros after them. The room worked neutral tones and metallics in a nod to the art deco era of the original house. The result was masculine but very, very stylish.

What an awesome space for a party. But she forced thoughts of the party out of her head. She had ten minutes to win this business. Ten minutes to convince Dominic Hunt she was the one he needed.

CHAPTER TWO

DOMINIC SAT ANDIE NEWMAN down on the higher of the two sofas that faced each other over the marble coffee table—the sofa he usually chose to give himself the advantage. He had no need to impress her with his greater height and bulk—she was tall, but he was so much taller than her even as he sat on the lower seat. Besides, the way she positioned herself with shoulders back and spine straight made him think she wouldn't let herself be intimidated by him or by anyone else. *Think again.* The way she crossed and uncrossed those long legs revealed she was more nervous than she cared to let on.

He leaned back in his sofa, pulled out her business card from the inside breast pocket of his suit jacket and held it between finger and thumb. 'Tell me about Party Queens. This seems like a very new, shiny card.'

'Brand new. We've only been in business for three months.'

'We?'

'My two business partners, Eliza Dunne and Gemma Harper. We all worked on a magazine together before we started our own business.'

He narrowed his eyes. 'Now you're "party queens"?' He used his fingers to enclose the two words with quote marks. 'I don't see the connection.'

'We always were party queens—even when we were working on the magazine.' He quirked an eyebrow and she paused. He noticed she quirked an eyebrow too, in unconscious imitation of his action. 'Not in that way.' She tried to backtrack, then smiled. 'Well, maybe somewhat in that way. Between us we've certainly done our share of partying. But then you have to actually enjoy a party to organise one; don't you agree?'

'It's not something I've given thought to,' he said. Business-wise, it could be a point either for her or against her.

Parties had never been high on his agenda—even after his money had opened so many doors for him. Whether he'd been sleeping rough in an abandoned building project in the most dangerous part of Brisbane or hobnobbing with decision makers in Sydney, he'd felt he'd never quite fitted in. So he did the minimum socialising required for his business. 'You were a journalist?' he asked, more than a little intrigued by her.

She shook her head. 'My background is in interior design but when a glitch in the economy meant the company I worked for went bust, I ended up as an interiors editor on a lifestyle magazine. I put together shoots for interiors and products and I loved it. Eliza and Gemma worked on the same magazine, Gemma as the food editor and Eliza on the publishing side. Six months ago we were told out of the blue that the magazine was closing and we had all lost our jobs.'

'That must have been a shock,' he said.

When he'd first started selling real estate at the age of eighteen he'd lived in terror he'd lose his job. Underlying all his success was always still that fear—which was why he was so driven to keep his business growing and thriving. Without money, without a home, he could slide back into being Nick Hunt of 'no fixed abode' rather than Dominic Hunt of Vaucluse, one of the most exclusive addresses in Australia.

'It shouldn't have come as a shock,' she said. 'Magazines close all the time in publishing—it's an occupational hazard. But when it actually happened, when *again* one minute I had a job and the next I didn't, it was…soul-destroying.'

'I'm sorry,' he said.

She shrugged. 'I soon picked myself up.'

He narrowed his eyes. 'It's quite a jump from a magazine job to a party planning business.' Her lack of relevant experience could mean Party Planner Number Four would go the way of the other three. He was surprised at how disappointed that made him feel.

'It might seem that way, but hear me out,' she said, a determined glint in her eye. If one of the other planners had said that, he would have looked pointedly at his watch. This one, he was prepared to listen to—he was actually interested in her story.

'We had to clear our desks immediately and were marched out of the offices by security guards. Shell-shocked, we all retired to a café and thought about what we'd do. The magazine's deputy editor asked could we organise her sister's eighteenth birthday party. At first we said no, thinking she was joking. But then we thought about it. A big magazine shoot that involves themes and food and props is quite a production. We'd also sometimes organise magazine functions for advertisers. We realised that between us we knew a heck of a lot about planning parties.'

'As opposed to enjoying them,' he said.

'That's right,' she said with a smile that seemed reminiscent of past parties enjoyed. 'Between the three of us we had so many skills we could utilise.'

'Can you elaborate on that?'

She held up a slender index finger, her nails tipped with orange polish. 'One, I'm the ideas and visuals person—creative, great with themes and props and highly organised with follow-through.' A second finger went up.

'Two, Gemma trained as a chef and is an amazing food person—food is one of the most important aspects of a good party, whether cooking it yourself or knowing which chefs to engage.'

She had a little trouble getting the third finger to stay straight and swapped it to her pinkie. 'Then, three, Eliza has her head completely around finances and contracts and sales and is also quite the wine buff.'

'So you decided to go into business together?' Her entrepreneurial spirit appealed to him.

She shook her head so her large multi-hoop gold earrings clinked. 'Not then. Not yet. We agreed to do the eighteenth party while we looked for other jobs and freelanced for magazines and ad agencies.'

'How did it work out?' He thought about his eighteenth birthday. It had gone totally unmarked by any celebration —except his own jubilation that he was legally an adult and could never now be recalled to the hell his home had become. It had also marked the age he could be tried as an adult if he had skated too close to the law—though by that time his street-fighting days were behind him.

'There were a few glitches, of course, but overall it was a great success. The girl went to a posh private school and both girls and parents loved the girly shoe theme we organised. One eighteenth led to another and soon we had other parents clamouring for us to do their kids' parties.'

'Is there much money in parties for kids?' He didn't have to ask all these questions but he was curious. Curious about her as much as anything.

Her eyebrows rose. 'You're kidding, right? We're talking wealthy families on the eastern suburbs and north shore. We're talking one-upmanship.' He enjoyed the play of expressions across her face, the way she gesticulated with her hands as she spoke. 'Heck, we've done a four-year-old's party on a budget of thousands.'

'All that money for a four-year-old?' He didn't have anything to do with kids except through his anonymous charity work. Had given up on his dream he would ever have children of his own. In fact, he was totally out of touch with family life.

'You'd better believe it,' she said.

He was warming to Andie Newman—how could any red-blooded male not?—but he wanted to ensure she was experienced enough to make his event work. All eyes would be on it as up until now he'd been notoriously private. If he threw a party, it had better be a good party. Better than good.

'So when did you actually go into business?'

'We were asked to do more and more parties. Grown-up parties too. Thirtieths and fortieths, even a ninetieth. It snowballed. Yet we still saw it as a stopgap thing although people suggested we make it a full-time business.'

'A very high percentage of small businesses go bust in the first year,' he couldn't help but warn.

She pulled a face that told him she didn't take offence. 'We were very aware of that. Eliza is the profit and loss spreadsheet maven. But then a public relations company I worked freelance for asked us to do corporate parties and product launches. The work was rolling in. We began to think we should make it official and form our own company.'

'A brave move.' He'd made brave moves in his time—and most of them had paid off. He gave her credit for initiative.

She leaned forward towards him. This close he could appreciate how lovely her eyes were. He didn't think he had ever before met anyone with genuine green eyes. 'We've leased premises in the industrial area of Alexandria and we're firing. But I have to be honest with you—we haven't done anything with potentially such a profile as your party.

We want it. We need it. And because we want it to so much we'll pull out every stop to make it a success.'

Party Planner Number Four clocked up more credit for her honesty. He tapped the card on the edge of his hand. 'You've got the enthusiasm; do you have the expertise? Can you assure me you can do my job and do it superlatively well?'

Those remarkable green eyes were unblinking. 'Yes. Absolutely. Undoubtedly. There might only be three of us, but between us we have a zillion contacts in Sydney—chefs, decorators, florists, musicians, waiting staff. If we can't do it ourselves we can pull in the right people who can. And none of us is afraid of the hard work a party this size would entail. We would welcome the challenge.'

He realised she was now sitting on the edge of the sofa, her hands clasped together and her foot crossed over her ankle was jiggling. She really did want this job—wanted it badly.

Dominic hadn't got where he was without a fine-tuned instinct for people. Instincts honed first on the streets where trusting the wrong person could have been fatal and then in the cut-throat business of high-end real estate and property development. His antennae were telling him Andie Newman would be able to deliver—and that he would enjoy working with her.

Trouble was, while he thought she might be the right person for the job, he found her very attractive and would like to ask her out. And he couldn't do both. He *never* dated staff or suppliers. He'd made that mistake with his ex-wife—he would not make it again. Hire Andie Newman and he was more than halfway convinced he would get a good party planner. Not hire her and he could ask her on a date. But he needed this event to work—and for that the planning had to be in the best possible hands. He was torn.

'I like your enthusiasm,' he said. 'But I'd be taking

a risk by working with a company that is in many ways still…unproven.'

Her voice rose marginally—she probably didn't notice but to him it betrayed her anxiety to impress. 'We have a file overflowing with references from happy clients. But before you come to any decisions let's talk about what you're expecting from us. The worst thing that can happen is for a client to get an unhappy surprise because we've got the brief wrong.'

She pulled out a folder from her satchel. He liked that it echoed the design of her business card. That showed an attention to detail. The chaos of his early life had made him appreciate planning and order. He recognised his company logo on the printout page she took from the folder and quickly perused.

'So tell me,' she said, when she'd finished reading it. 'I'm puzzled. Despite this briefing document stating the party is to be "A high-profile Christmas event to attract favourable publicity for Dominic Hunt" you still insist it's not to reference Christmas in any way. Which is correct?'

Andie regretted the words almost as soon as they'd escaped from her mouth. She hadn't meant to confront Dominic Hunt or put him on the spot. Certainly she hadn't wanted to get him offside. But the briefing had been ambiguous and she felt she had to clarify it if she was to secure this job for Party Queens.

She needed their business to succeed—never again did she want to be at the mercy of the whims of a corporate employer. To have a job one day and then suddenly not the next day was too traumatising after that huge personal change of direction she'd had forced upon her five years ago. But she could have put her question with more subtlety.

He didn't reply. The silence that hung between them became more uncomfortable by the second. His face tightened with an emotion she couldn't read. Anger? Sorrow? Regret? Whatever it was, the effect was so powerful she had to force herself not to reach over and put her hand on his arm to comfort him, maybe even hug him. And that would be a mistake. Even more of a mistake than her ill-advised question had been.

She cringed that she had somehow prompted the unleashing of thoughts that were so obviously painful for him. Then braced herself to be booted out on to the same scrapheap as the three party planners who had preceded her.

Finally he spoke, as if the words were being dragged out of him. 'The brief was incorrect. Christmas has some… difficult memories attached to it for me. I don't celebrate the season. Please just leave it at that.' For a long moment his gaze held hers and she saw the anguish recede.

Andie realised she had been holding her breath and she let it out with a slow sigh of relief, amazed he hadn't shown her the door.

'Of…of course,' she murmured, almost gagging with gratitude that she was to be given a second chance. And she couldn't deny that she wanted that chance. Not just for the job but—she could not deny it—the opportunity to see more of this undoubtedly interesting man.

There was something deeper here, some private pain, that she did not understand. But it would be bad-mannered prying to ask any further questions.

She didn't know much about his personal life. Just that he was considered a catch—rich, handsome, successful. *Though not her type, of course.* He lived here alone, she understood, in this street in Vaucluse where house prices started in the double digit millions. Wasn't there a bitter divorce in his background—an aggrieved ex-wife, a public battle for ownership of the house? She'd have to look it up. If she were to win this job—and she understood that it was still a big *if*—she needed to get a grasp on how this man ticked.

'Okay, so that's sorted—no Christmas,' she said, aiming to sound briskly efficient without any nod to the anguish she had read at the back of his eyes. 'Now I know what you *don't* want for your party, let's talk about what you *do* want. I'd like to hear in your words what you expect from this party. Then I can give you my ideas based on your thoughts.'

The party proposals she had hoped to discuss had been based on Christmas; she would have to do some rapid thinking.

Dominic Hunt got up from the sofa and started to pace. He was so tall, his shoulders so broad, he dominated even the large, high-ceilinged room. Andie found herself wondering about his obviously once broken nose—who had thrown the first punch? She got up, not to pace alongside him but to be closer to his level. She did not feel intimidated by him but she could see how he could be intimidating.

'The other planners babbled on about how important it was to invite A-list and B-list celebrities to get publicity. I don't give a damn about celebrities and I can't see how that's the right kind of publicity.'

Andie paused, not sure what to say, only knowing she had to be careful not to *babble on*. 'I can organise the party, but the guest list is up to you and your people.'

He stopped his pacing, stepped closer. 'But do you agree with me?'

Was this a test question? Answer incorrectly and that scrapheap beckoned? As always, she could only be honest. 'I do agree with you. It's my understanding that this party is aimed at…at image repair.'

'You mean repair to my image as a miserly Scrooge who hoards all his money for himself?'

She swallowed a gasp at the bitterness of his words, then looked up at him to see not the anger she expected but a kind of manly bewilderment that surprised her.

'I mightn't have put it quite like that, but yes," she said. 'You do have that reputation and I understand you want to demonstrate it's not so. And yes, I think the presence of a whole lot of freeloading so-called celebrities who run the gamut from the A to the Z list and have nothing to do with the charities you want to be seen to be supporting might not help. But you *are* more likely to get coverage in the social pages if they attend.'

He frowned. 'Is there such a thing as a Z-list celebrity?'

She laughed. 'If there isn't, there should be. Maybe I made it up.'

'You did say you were creative,' he said. He smiled— the first real smile she'd seen from him. It transformed his face, like the sun coming out from behind a dark storm cloud, unleashing an unexpected charm. Her heartbeat tripped into double time like it had the first moment she'd seen him. Why? Why this inexplicable reaction to a man she should dislike for his meanness and greed?

She made a show of looking around her to disguise her consternation. Tamed the sudden shakiness in her voice into a businesslike tone. 'How many magazines or life-style programmes have featured this house?' she asked.

'None. They never will,' he said.

'Good,' she said. 'The house is both magnificent and unknown. I reckon even your neighbours would be will-ing to cough up a sizeable donation just to see inside.' In her mind's eye she could see the house transformed into a glittering party paradise. 'The era of the house is nine-teen-twenties, right?'

'Yes,' he said. 'It was originally built for a wealthy wool merchant.'

She thought some more. 'Why not an extravagant

Great Gatsby twenties-style party with a silver and white theme—that gives a nod to the festive season—and a strictly curated guest list? Guests would have to dress in silver or white. Or both. Make it very exclusive, an invitation to be sought after. The phones of Sydney's social set would be set humming to see who got one or not.' Her eyes half shut as her mind bombarded her with images. 'Maybe a masked party. Yes. Amazing silver and white masks. Bejewelled and befeathered. Fabulous masks that could be auctioned off at some stage for your chosen charity.'

'Auctioned?'

Her eyes flew open and she had to orientate herself back into the reality of the empty room that she had just been envisioning filled with elegant partygoers. Sometimes when her creativity was firing she felt almost in a trance. Then it was her turn to frown. How could a Sydney billionaire be such a party innocent?

Even she, who didn't move in the circles of society that attended lavish fund-raising functions, knew about the auctions. The competitive bidding could probably be seen as the same kind of one-upmanship as the spending of thousands on a toddler's party. 'I believe it's usual to have a fund-raising auction at these occasions. Not just the masks, of course. Other donated items. Something really big to up the amount of dollars for your charity.' She paused. 'You're a property developer, aren't you?'

He nodded. 'Among other interests.'

'Maybe you could donate an apartment? There'd be some frenzied bidding for that from people hoping for a bargain. And you would look generous.'

His mouth turned down in an expression of distaste. 'I'm not sure that's in keeping with the image I want to… to reinvent.'

Privately she agreed with him—why couldn't people just donate without expecting a lavish party in return? But she kept her views to herself. Creating those lavish parties was her job now.

'That's up to you and your people. The guest list and the auction, I mean. But the party? That's my domain. Do you like the idea of the twenties theme to suit the house?' In her heart she still longed for the choristers on the staircase. Maybe it would have to be a jazz band on the steps. That could work. Not quite the same romanticism and spirit as Christmas, but it would be a spectacular way to greet guests.

'I like it,' he said slowly.

She forced herself not to panic, not to bombard him with a multitude of alternatives. 'If not that idea, I have lots of others. I would welcome the opportunity to present them to you.'

He glanced at his watch and she realised she had been there for much longer than the ten-minute pitch he'd allowed. Surely that was a good sign.

'I'll schedule in another meeting with you tomorrow afternoon,' he said.

'You mean a second interview?' she asked, fingers crossed behind her back.

'No. A brainstorming session. You've got the job, Ms Newman.'

It was only as, jubilant, she made her way to the door—conscious of his eyes on her back—that she wondered at the presence of a note of regret in Dominic Hunt's voice.

CHAPTER THREE

TRY AS SHE MIGHT, Andie couldn't get excited about the nineteen-twenties theme she had envisaged for Dominic Hunt's party. It would be lavish and glamorous and she would enjoy every moment of planning such a visually splendid event. Such a party would be a spangled feather in Party Queens' cap. But it seemed somehow *wrong*.

The feeling niggled at her. How could something so extravagant, so limited to those who could afford the substantial donation that would be the cost of entrance make Dominic Hunt look less miserly? Even if he offered an apartment for auction—and there was no such thing as a cheap apartment in Sydney—and raised a lot of money, wouldn't it be a wealthy person who benefited? Might he appear to be a Scrooge hanging out with other rich people who might or might not also be Scrooges? Somehow, it reeked of…well, there was no other word but hypocrisy.

It wasn't her place to be critical—the media-attention-grabbing party was his marketing people's idea. Her job was to plan the party and make it as memorable and spectacular as possible. But she resolved to bring up her reservations in the brainstorming meeting with him. *If she dared.*

She knew it would be a fine line to tread—she did not want to risk losing the job for Party Queens—but she felt she had to give her opinion. After that she would just keep her mouth shut and concentrate on making his event the most memorable on the December social calendar.

She dressed with care for the meeting, which was again at his Vaucluse mansion. *An outfit that posed no danger of showing off her underwear.* Slim white trousers, a white top, a string of outsize turquoise beads, silver sandals that strapped around her ankles. At the magazine she'd made friends with the fashion editor and still had access to sample sales and special deals. She felt her wardrobe could hold its own in whatever company she found herself in— even on millionaire row.

'I didn't risk wearing that skirt,' she blurted out to Dominic Hunt as he let her into the house. 'Even though there doesn't appear to be any wind about.'

Mentally she slammed her hand against her forehead. What a dumb top-of-mind remark to make to a client. But he still made her nervous. Try as she might, she couldn't shake that ever-present awareness of how attractive he was.

His eyes flickered momentarily to her legs. 'Shame,' he said in that deep, testosterone-edged voice that thrilled through her.

Was he flirting with her?

'It…it was a lovely skirt,' she said. 'Just…just rather badly behaved.' How much had he seen when her skirt had flown up over her thighs?

'I liked it very much,' he said.

'The prettiness of its fabric or my skirt's bad behaviour?'

She held his cool grey gaze for a second longer than she should.

'Both,' he said.

She took a deep breath and tilted her chin upward. 'I'll take that as a compliment,' she said with a smile she hoped radiated aplomb. 'Thank you, Mr Hunt.'

'Dominic,' he said.

'Dominic,' she repeated, liking the sound of his name on her lips. 'And thank you again for this opportunity to plan your party.' *Bring it back to business.*

In truth, she would have liked to tell him how good he looked in his superbly tailored dark suit and dark shirt but she knew her voice would come out all choked up. Because it wasn't the Italian elegance of his suit that she found herself admiring. It was the powerful, perfectly proportioned male body that inhabited it. And she didn't want to reveal even a hint of that. *He was a client.*

He nodded in acknowledgement of her words. 'Come through to the back,' he said. 'You can see how the rooms might work for the party.'

She followed him through where the grand staircase split—a choir really would be amazing ranged on the steps—over pristine marble floors to a high-ceilinged room so large their footsteps echoed as they walked into the centre of it. Furnished minimally in shades of white, it looked ready for a high-end photo shoot. Arched windows and a wall of folding doors opened through to an elegant art deco style swimming pool and then to a formal garden planted with palm trees and rows of budding blue agapanthus.

For a long moment Andie simply absorbed the splendour of the room. 'What a magnificent space,' she said finally. 'Was it originally a ballroom?'

'Yes. Apparently the wool merchant liked to entertain in grand style. But it wasn't suited for modern living, which is why I opened it up through to the terrace when I remodelled the house.'

'You did an awesome job,' she said. In her mind's eye she could see flappers in glittering dresses trimmed with feathers and fringing, and men in dapper suits doing the Charleston. Then had to blink, not sure if she was imagining what the room had once been or how she'd like it to be for Dominic's party.

'The people who work for me did an excellent job,' he said.

'As an interior designer I give them full marks,' she said. She had gone to university with Dominic's designer. She just might get in touch with him, seeking inside gossip into what made Dominic Hunt tick.

She looked around her. 'Where's the kitchen? Gemma will shoot me if I go back without reporting to her on the cooking facilities.'

'Through here.'

Andie followed him through to an adjoining vast state-of-the-art kitchen, gleaming in white marble and stainless steel. The style was sleek and modern but paid homage to the vintage of the house. She breathed out a sigh of relief and pleasure. A kitchen like this would make catering for hundreds of guests so much easier. Not that the food was her department. Gemma kept that under her control. 'It's a superb kitchen. Do you cook?'

Was Dominic the kind of guy who ate out every night and whose refrigerator contained only cartons of beer? Or the kind who excelled at cooking and liked to show off his skills to a breathlessly admiring female audience?

'I can look after myself,' he said shortly. 'That includes cooking.'

That figured. After yesterday's meeting she had done some research into Dominic Hunt—though there wasn't much information dating back further than a few years. Along with his comments about celebrating Christmas being a waste of space, he'd also been quoted as saying he would never marry again. From the media accounts, his marriage in his mid-twenties had been short, tumultuous and public, thanks to his ex-wife's penchant for spilling the details to the gossip columns.

'The kitchen and its position will be perfect for the caterers,' she said. 'Gemma will be delighted.'

'Good,' he said.

'You must love this house.' She could not help a wistful note from edging her voice. As an interior designer she knew only too well how much the remodelling would have cost. Never in a million years would she live in a house like this. He was only a few years older than her—thirty-two to her twenty-eight—yet it was as if they came from different planets.

He shrugged those impressively broad shoulders. 'It's a spectacular house. But it's just a house. I never get attached to places.'

Or people?

Her online research had showed him snapped by paparazzi with a number of long-legged beauties—but no woman more than once or twice. *What did it matter to her?*

She patted her satchel. *Back to business.* 'I've come prepared for brainstorming,' she said. 'Have you had any thoughts about the nineteen-twenties theme I suggested?'

'I've thought,' he said. He paused. 'I've thought about it a lot.'

His tone of voice didn't give her cause for confidence. 'You…like it? You don't like it? Because if you don't I have lots of other ideas that would work as well. I—'

He put up his right hand to halt her—large, well sculpted, with knuckles that looked as if they'd sustained scrapes over the years. His well-spoken accent and obvious wealth suggested injuries sustained from boxing or rugby at a private school; the tightly leashed power in those muscles, that strong jaw, gave thought to injuries sustained in something perhaps more visceral.

'It's a wonderful idea for a party,' he said. 'Perfect for this house. Kudos to you, Ms Party Queen.'

'Thank you.' She made a mock curtsy and was pleased when he smiled. *How handsome he was without that scowl.* 'However, is that a "but" I hear coming on?'

He pivoted on his heel so he faced out to the pool, gleaming blue and pristine in the afternoon sun of a late-spring day in mid-November. His back view was impressive, broad shoulders tapering to a tight, muscular rear end. Then he turned back to face her. 'It's more than one "but",' he said. 'The party, the guest list, the—'

'The pointlessness of it all?' she ventured.

He furrowed his brow. 'What makes you say that?'

She found herself twisting the turquoise beads on her necklace between her finger and thumb. Her business partners would be furious with her if she lost Party Queens this high-profile job because she said what she *wanted* to say rather than what she *should* say.

'This party is all about improving your image, right? To make a statement that you're not the…the Scrooge people think you are.'

The fierce scowl was back. 'I'd rather you didn't use the word Scrooge.'

'Okay,' she said immediately. But she would find it difficult to stop *thinking* it. 'I'll try again: that you're not a…a person lacking in the spirit of giving.'

'That doesn't sound much better.' She couldn't have imagined his scowl could have got any darker but it did. 'The party is meant to be a public display of something I would rather be kept private.'

'So…you give privately to charity?'

'Of course I do but it's not your or anyone else's business.'

Personally, she would be glad if he wasn't as tight-fisted as his reputation decreed. But this was about more than what she felt. She could not back down. 'If that's how you feel, tell me again why you're doing this.'

He paused. 'If I share with you the reason why I agreed to holding this party, it's not to leave this room.'

'Of course,' she said. A party planner had to be dis-

creet. It was astounding what family secrets got aired in
the planning of a party. She leaned closer, close enough
to notice that he must be a twice-a-day-shave guy. *Lots of
testosterone, all right.*

'I've got a big joint venture in the United States on
the point of being signed. My potential business partner,
Walter Burton, is the head of a family company and he is
committed to public displays of philanthropy. It would go
better with me if I was seen to be the same.'

Andie made a motion with her fingers of zipping her
lips shut. 'I…I understand,' she said. Disappointment
shafted through her. *So he really was a Scrooge.*

She'd found herself wanting Dominic to be someone
better than he was reputed to be. But the party, while pur-
porting to be a charity event, was simply a smart business
ploy. More about greed than good-heartedness.

'Now you can see why it's so important,' he said.

Should she say what she thought? The scrapheap of dis-
carded party planners beckoned again. She could imagine
her silver-sandal-clad foot kicking feebly from the top of
it and hoped it would be a soft landing.

She took a deep steadying breath. 'Cynical journalists
might have a field-day with the hypocrisy of a Scrooge—
sorry!—trying to turn over a new gilded leaf in such an
obvious and staged way.'

To her surprise, something like relief relaxed the tense
lines of his face. 'That's what I thought too.'

'You…you did?'

'I could see the whole thing backfiring and me no better off in terms of reputation. Possibly worse.'

If she didn't stop twisting her necklace it would break
and scatter her beads all over the marble floor. 'So—help
me out here. We're back to you not wanting a party?'

*She'd talked him out of the big, glitzy event Party
Queens really needed.* Andie cringed at the prospect of

the combined wrath of Gemma and Eliza when she went back to their headquarters with the contract that was sitting in her satchel waiting for his signature still unsigned.

'You know I don't.' *Thank heaven.* 'But maybe a different kind of event,' he said.

'Like…handing over a giant facsimile cheque to a charity?' Which would be doing her right out of a job.

'Where's the good PR in that?'

'In fact it could look even more cynical than the party.'

'Correct.'

He paced a few long strides away from her and then back. 'I'm good at turning one dollar into lots of dollars. That's my skill. Not planning parties. But surely I can get the kind of publicity my marketing department wants, impress my prospective business partner and actually help some less advantaged people along the way?'

She resisted the urge to high-five him. 'To tell you the truth, I couldn't sleep last night for thinking that exact same thing.' *Was it wise to have admitted that?*

'Me too,' he said. 'I tossed and turned all night.'

A sudden vision of him in a huge billionaire's bed, all tangled in the sheets wearing nothing but…well nothing but a billionaire's birthday suit, flashed through her mind and sizzled through her body. *Not my type. Not my type.* She had to repeat it like a mantra.

She willed her heartbeat to slow and hoped he took the flush on her cheekbones for enthusiasm. 'So we're singing from the same hymn sheet. Did you have any thoughts on solving your dilemma?'

'That's where you come in; you're the party expert.'

She hesitated. 'During my sleepless night, I did think of something. But you might not like it.'

'Try me,' he said, eyes narrowed.

'It's out of the ball park,' she warned.

'I'm all for that,' he said.

She flung up her hands in front of her face to act as a shield. 'It…it involves Christmas.'

He blanched under the smooth olive of his tan. 'I told you—'

His mouth set in a grim line, his hands balled into fists by his sides. Should she leave well enough alone? After all, he had said the festive season had difficult associations for him. 'What is it that you hate so much about Christmas?' she asked. She'd always been one to dive straight into the deep end.

'I don't *hate* Christmas.' He cursed under his breath. 'I'm misquoted once and the media repeat it over and over.'

'But—'

He put up his hand to halt her. 'I don't have to justify anything to you. But let me give you three good reasons why I don't choose to celebrate Christmas and all the razzmatazz that goes with it.'

'Fire away,' she said, thinking it wasn't appropriate for her to counter with three things she adored about the festive season. This wasn't a debate. It was a business brainstorming.

'First—the weather is all wrong,' he said. 'It's hot when it should be cold. A *proper* Christmas is a northern hemisphere Christmas—snow, not sand.'

Not true, she thought. For a born-and-bred Australian like her, Christmas was all about the long, hot sticky days of summer. Cicadas chirruping in the warm air as the family walked to a midnight church service. Lunch outdoors, preferably around a pool or at the beach. Then it struck her—Dominic had a distinct trace of an English accent. That might explain his aversion to festivities Down Under style. But something still didn't seem quite right. His words sounded…too practised, as if he'd recited them a hundred times before.

He continued, warming to his point as she wondered

about the subtext to his spiel. 'Then there's the fact that the whole thing is over-commercialised to the point of being ludicrous. I saw Christmas stuff festooning the shops in September.'

She almost expected him to snarl a Scrooge-like *Bah! Humbug!* but he obviously restrained himself.

'You have a point,' she said. 'And carols piped through shopping malls in October? So annoying.'

'Quite right,' he said. 'This whole obsession with extended Christmas celebrations, it…it…makes people who don't celebrate it—for one reason or another—feel…feel excluded.'

His words faltered and he looked away in the direction of the pool but not before she'd seen the bleakness in his eyes. She realised those last words hadn't been rehearsed. That he might be regretting them. Again she had that inane urge to comfort him—without knowing why he needed comforting.

She knew she had to take this carefully. 'Yes,' she said slowly. 'I know what you mean.' That first Christmas without Anthony had been the bleakest imaginable. And each year after she had thought about him and the emptiness in her heart he had left behind him. But she would not share that with this man; it was far too personal. And nothing to do with the general discussion about Christmas.

His mouth twisted. 'Do you?'

She forced her voice to sound cheerful and impersonal. Her ongoing sadness over Anthony was deeply private. 'Not me personally. I love Christmas. I'm lucky enough to come from a big family—one of five kids. I have two older brothers and a sister and a younger sister. Christmas with our extended family was always—still is—a special time of the year. But my parents knew that wasn't the case for everyone. Every year we shared our celebration with children who weren't as fortunate as we were.'

'Charity cases, you mean,' he said, his voice hard-edged with something she couldn't identify.

'In the truest sense of the word,' she said. 'We didn't query them being there. It meant more kids to play with on Christmas Day. It didn't even enter our heads that there would be fewer presents for us so they could have presents too. Two of them moved in with us as long-term foster kids. When I say I'm from five, I really mean from seven. Only that's too confusing to explain.'

He gave a sound that seemed a cross between a grunt and a cynical snort.

She shrugged, inexplicably hurt by his reaction. 'You might think it goody-two-shoes-ish but that's the way my family are, and I love them for it,' she said, her voice stiff and more than a touch defensive.

'Not at all,' he said. 'I think it…it sounds wonderful. You were very lucky to grow up in a family like that.' With the implication being he hadn't?

'I know, and I'm thankful. And my parents' strong sense of community didn't do us any harm. In fact those Christmas Days my family shared with others got me thinking. It was what kept me up last night. I had an idea.'

'Fire away,' he said.

She channelled all her optimism and enthusiasm to make her voice sound convincing to Sydney's most notorious Scrooge. 'Wouldn't it be wonderful if you opened this beautiful home on Christmas Day for a big lunch party for children and families who do it hard on Christmas Day? Not as a gimmick. Not as a stunt. As a genuine act of hospitality and sharing the true spirit of Christmas.'

CHAPTER FOUR

DOMINIC STARED AT Andie in disbelief. Hadn't she heard a word he'd said about his views on Christmas? She looked up at him, her eyes bright with enthusiasm but backlit by wariness. 'Please, just consider my proposal,' she said. 'That's all I ask.' He could easily fire her for straying so far from the brief and she must know it—yet that didn't stop her. Her tenacity was to be admired.

Maybe she had a point. No matter what she or anyone else thought, he was not a Scrooge or a hypocrite. To make a holiday that could never be happy for him happy for others had genuine appeal. He was aware Christmas *was* a special time for a huge percentage of the population. It was just too painful for him to want to do anything but lock himself away with a bottle of bourbon from Christmas Eve to Boxing Day.

Deep from within, he dredged memories of his first Christmas away from home. Aged seventeen, he'd been living in an underground car park beneath an abandoned shopping centre project. His companions had been a ragtag collection of other runaways, addicts, criminals and people who'd lost all hope of a better life. Someone had stolen a branch of a pine tree from somewhere and decorated it with scavenged scraps of glittery paper. They'd all stood around it and sung carols with varying degrees of sobriety. Only he had stood aloof.

Now, he reached out to where Andie was twisting her

necklace so tightly it was in danger of snapping. Gently, he disengaged her hand and freed the string of beads. Fought the temptation to hold her hand for any longer than was necessary—slender and warm in his own much bigger hand. Today her nails were painted turquoise. And, as he'd noticed the day before, her fingers were free of any rings.

'Your idea could have merit,' he said, stepping back from her. Back from her beautiful interesting face, her intelligent eyes, the subtle spicy-sweet scent of her. 'Come and sit outside by the pool and we can talk it over.'

Her face flushed with relief at his response and he realised again what spunk it had taken for her to propose something so radical. He was grateful to whoever had sent Party Planner Number Four his way. Andie was gorgeous, smart and not the slightest in awe of him and his money, which was refreshing. His only regret was that he could not both employ her and date her.

He hadn't told the complete truth about why he'd been unable to sleep the night before. Thoughts of her had been churning through his head as much as concerns about the party. He had never felt so instantly attracted to a woman. Ever. If they had met under other circumstances he would have asked her out by now.

'I really think it could work,' she said as she walked with him through the doors and out to the pool area.

For a heart-halting second he thought Andie had tuned into his private thoughts—that she thought dating her could work. *Never.* He'd met his ex-wife, Tara, when she'd worked for his company, with disastrous consequences. The whole marriage had, in fact, been disastrous—based on lies and deception. He wouldn't make that mistake again—even for this intriguing woman.

But of course Andie was talking about her party proposal in businesslike tones. 'You could generate the right kind of publicity—both for your potential business partner and in general,' she said as he settled her into one of the white outdoor armchairs that had cost a small fortune because of its vintage styling.

'While at the same time directly benefiting people who do it tough on the so-called Big Day,' he said as he took the chair next to her.

'Exactly,' she said with her wide, generous smile. When she smiled like that it made him want to make her do it again, just for the pleasure of seeing her face light up. *Not a good idea.*

Her chair was in the shade of one of the mature palm trees he'd had helicoptered in for the landscaping but the sun was dancing off the aqua surface of the pool. He was disappointed when she reached into her satchel, pulled out a pair of tortoiseshell-rimmed sunglasses and donned them against the glare. They looked 'vintage' too. In fact, in her white clothes and turquoise necklace, she looked as if she belonged here.

'In principal, I don't mind your idea,' he said. 'In fact I find it more acceptable than the other.'

Her smile was edged with relief. 'I can't tell you how pleased that makes me.'

'Would the lunch have to be on actual Christmas Day?' he said.

'You could hold it on Christmas Eve or the week leading up to Christmas. In terms of organisation, that would be easier. But none of those peripheral days is as lonely and miserable as Christmas Day can be if you're one…one of the excluded ones,' she said. 'My foster sister told me that.'

The way she was looking at him, even with those too-perceptive green eyes shaded from his view, made him think she was beginning to suspect he had a deeply personal reason for his anti-Christmas stance.

He'd only ever shared that reason with one woman— Melody, the girl who'd first captivated, then shredded, his teenage heart back in that car park squat. By the time Christmas had loomed in the first year of his marriage to Tara, he'd known he'd never be sharing secrets with her. But there was something disarming about Andie that seemed to invite confidences—something he had to stand guard against. She might not be what she seemed—and he had learned the painful lesson not to trust his first impressions when it came to beautiful women.

'I guess any other day doesn't have the same impact,' he reluctantly agreed, not sure he would be able to face the festivities. Did he actually have to be present on the day? Might it not be enough to provide the house and the meal? No. To achieve his goal, he knew his presence would be necessary. Much as he would hate every minute of it.

'Maybe your marketing people will have other ideas,' she said. 'But I think opening your home on the actual December twenty-five to give people who really need it a slap-up feast would be a marvellous antidote to your Scrooge…sorry, *miser*…I mean *cheap* reputation.' She pulled a face. 'Sorry. I didn't actually mean any of those things.'

Why did it sting so much more coming from her? 'Of course you did. So does everyone else. People who have no idea of what and where I might give without wanting any fanfare.' The main reason he wanted to secure the joint venture was to ensure his big project in Brisbane would continue to be funded long after his lifetime.

She looked shamefaced. 'I'm sorry.'

He hated that people like Andie thought he was stingy. Any remaining reservations he might hold about the party had to go. He needed to take action before this unfair reputation become so deeply entrenched he'd never free himself from it. 'Let's hope the seasonal name-calling eases if I go ahead with the lunch.'

She held up a finger in warning. 'It wouldn't appease everyone. Those cynical journalists might not be easily swayed.'

He scowled. 'I can't please everyone.' But he found himself, irrationally, wanting to please *her*.

'It might help if you followed through with a visible, ongoing relationship with a charity. If the media could see…could see…'

Her eyes narrowed in concentration. He waited for the end of her sentence but it wasn't forthcoming. 'See what?'

'Sorry,' she said, shaking her head as if bringing herself back to earth. 'My thoughts tend to run faster than my words sometimes when I'm deep in the creative zone.'

'I get it,' he said, though he wasn't sure what the hell being in the creative zone meant.

'I meant your critics might relent if they could see your gesture was genuine.'

He scowled. 'But it *will* be genuine.'

'You know it and I know it but they might see it as just another publicity gimmick.' Her eyes narrowed again and he gave her time to think. 'What if you didn't actually seek publicity for this day? You know—no invitations or press releases. Let the details leak. Tantalise the media.'

'For a designer, you seem to know a lot about publicity,' he said.

She shrugged. 'When you work in magazines you pick up a lot about both seeking and giving publicity. But your marketing people would have their own ideas, I'm sure.'

'I should talk it over with them,' he said.

'As it's only six weeks until Christmas, and this would be a big event to pull together, may I suggest there's not a lot of discussion time left?'

'You're right. I know. But it's a big deal.' So much bigger for him personally than she realised.

'You're seriously considering going ahead with it?'

He so much preferred it to the Z-list celebrity party. 'Yes. Let's do it.'

She clapped her hands together. 'I'm so glad. We can make it a real dream-come-true for your guests.'

'What about you and your business partners? You'd have to work on Christmas Day.'

'Speaking for me, I'd be fine with working. True spirit of Christmas and all that. I'll have to speak to Gemma and Eliza, but I think they'd be behind it too.' Securing Dominic Hunt's business for Party Queens was too important for them to refuse.

'What about caterers and so on?' he asked.

'The hospitality industry works three hundred and sixty-five days a year. It shouldn't be a problem. There are also people who don't celebrate Christmas as part of their culture who are very happy to work—especially for holiday pay rates. You don't have to worry about all that—that's our job.'

'And the guests? How would we recruit them?' He was about to say he could talk to people in Brisbane, where he was heavily involved in a homeless charity, but stopped himself. That was too connected to the secret part of his life he had no desire to share.

'I know the perfect person to help—my older sister, Hannah, is a social worker. She would know exactly which charities to liaise with. I think she would be excited to be involved.'

It was her. *Andie*. He would not be considering this direction if it wasn't for her. The big glitzy party had seemed so wrong. She made him see what could be right.

'Could we set up a meeting with your sister?' he asked.

'I can do better than that,' she said with a triumphant toss of her head that set her oversized earrings swaying. 'Every Wednesday night is open house dinner at my parents' house. Whoever of my siblings can make it comes.

Sometimes grandparents and cousins too. I know Hannah will be there tonight and I'm planning to go too. Why don't you come along?'

'To your family dinner?' His first thought was to say no. Nothing much intimidated him—but meeting people's families was near the top of the list.

'Family is an elastic term for the Newmans. Friends, waifs and strays are always welcome at the table.'

What category would he be placed under? His memory of being a real-life stray made him wince. Friend? Strictly speaking, if circumstances were different, he'd want to be more than friends with Andie. Would connecting with her family create an intimacy he might later come to regret?

He looked down at his watch. Thought about his plan to return to the office.

'We need to get things moving,' she prompted.

'I would like to meet your sister tonight.'

Her wide smile lit her eyes. 'I have a really good feeling about this.'

'Do you always go on your feelings?' he asked.

She took off her sunglasses so he was treated to the directness of her gaze. 'All the time. Don't you?'

If he acted on his feelings he would be insisting they go to dinner, just the two of them. He would be taking her in his arms. Tasting her lovely mouth. Touching. Exploring. *But that wouldn't happen.*

He trusted his instincts when it came to business. But trusting his feelings when it came to women had only led to bitterness, betrayal and the kind of pain he never wanted to expose himself to again.

No to feeling. *Yes* to pleasant relationships that mutually fulfilled desires and were efficiently terminated before emotions ever became part of it. And with none of the complications that came with still having to work with that person. Besides, he suspected the short-term liaison that was all he had to offer would not be acceptable to Andie. She had *for ever* written all over her.

Now it was her turn to look at her watch. 'I'll call my mother to confirm you'll be joining us for dinner. How about I swing by and pick you up at around six?'

He thought about his four o'clock meeting. 'That's early for dinner.'

'Not when there are kids involved.'

'Kids?'

'I have a niece and two nephews. One of the nephews belongs to Hannah. He will almost certainly be there, along with his cousins.'

Dominic wasn't sure exactly what he was letting himself in for. One thing was for certain—he couldn't have seen himself going to a family dinner with any of Party Planners Numbers One to Three. And he suspected he might be in for more than one surprise from gorgeous Party Planner Number Four.

Andie got up from the chair. Smoothed down her white trousers. They were nothing as revealing as her flyaway skirt but made no secret of her slender shape.

'By the way, I'm apologising in advance for my car.'

He frowned. 'Why apologise?'

'I glimpsed your awesome sports car in the garage as I came in yesterday. You might find my hand-me-down hatchback a bit of a comedown.'

He frowned. 'I didn't come into this world behind the wheel of an expensive European sports car. I'm sure your hatchback will be perfectly fine.'

Just how did she see him? His public image—Scrooge, miser, rich guy—was so at odds with the person he knew himself to be. That he wanted her to know. But he could not reveal himself to her without uncovering secrets he would rather leave buried deep in his past.

CHAPTER FIVE

DOMINIC HAD FACED down some fears in his time. But the prospect of being paraded before Andie's large family ranked as one of the most fearsome. As Andie pulled up her hatchback—old but in good condition and nothing to be ashamed of—in front of her parents' home in the northern suburb of Willoughby, sweat prickled on his forehead and his hands felt clammy. How the hell had he got himself into this?

She turned off the engine, took out the keys, unclipped her seat belt and smoothed down the legs of her sleek, very sexy leather trousers. But she made no effort to get out of the car. She turned her head towards him. 'Before we go inside to meet my family I… I need to tell you something first. Something…something about me.'

Why did she look so serious, sombre even? 'Sure, fire away,' he said.

'I've told them you're a client. That there is absolutely nothing personal between us.'

'Of course,' he said.

Strange how at the same time he could be relieved and yet offended by her categorical denial that there ever could be anything *personal* between them.

Now a hint of a smile crept to the corners of her mouth. 'The thing is…they won't believe me. You're good-looking, you're smart and you're personable.'

'That's nice of you to say that,' he said. He noticed she hadn't added that he was rich to his list of attributes.

'You know it's true,' she said. 'My family are determined I should have a man in my life and have become the most inveterate of matchmakers. I expect they'll pounce on you. It could get embarrassing.'

'You're single?' He welcomed the excuse to ask.

'Yes. I…I've been single for a long time. Oh, I date. But I haven't found anyone special since…since…' She twisted right around in the car seat to fully face him. She clasped her hands together on her lap, then started to twist them without seeming to realise she was doing it. 'You need to know this before we go inside.' The hint of a smile had completely dissipated.

'If you think so,' he said. She was twenty-eight and single. What was the big deal here?

'I met Anthony on my first day of university. We were inseparable from the word go. There was no doubt we would spend our lives together.'

Dominic braced himself for the story of a nasty break-up. Infidelity? Betrayal? A jerk in disguise as a nice guy? He was prepared to make polite noises in response. He knew all about betrayal. But a *quid pro quo* exchange over relationships gone wrong was not something he ever wanted to waste time on with Andie or anyone else.

'It ended?' he said, making a terse contribution only because it was expected.

'He died.'

Two words stated so baldly but with such a wealth of pain behind them. Dominic felt as if he'd been punched in the chest. Nothing he said could be an adequate response. 'Andie, I'm sorry,' was all he could manage.

'It was five years ago. He was twenty-three. He…he went out for an early-morning surf and didn't come back.' He could hear the effort it took for her to keep her tone even.

He knew about people who didn't come back. Good-byes left unsaid. Personal tragedy. That particular kind of pain. 'Did he…? Did you—?'

'He…he washed up two days later.' She closed her eyes as if against an unbearable image.

'What happened?' He didn't want her to think he was interrogating her on something so sensitive, but he wanted to find out.

'Head injury. An accident. The doctors couldn't be sure exactly how it happened. A rock? His board? A sandbank? We'll never know.'

'Thank you for telling me.' He felt unable to say anything else.

'Better for you to know than not to know when you're about to meet the family. Just in case someone says something that might put you on the spot.'

She heaved a sigh that seemed to signal she had said what she felt she had to say and that there would be no further confidences. Why should there be? *He was just a client.* Something prompted him to want to ask—was she over the loss? Had she moved on? But it was not his place. Client and contractor—that was all they could be to each other. Besides, could anyone *ever* get over loss like that?

'You needed to be in the picture.' She went to open her door. 'Now, let's go in—Hannah is looking forward to meeting you. As I predicted, she's very excited about getting involved.'

Her family's home was a comfortable older-style house set in a chaotic garden in a suburb where values had rocketed in recent years. In the car on the way over, Andie had told him she had lived in this house since she was a baby. All her siblings had. He envied her that certainty, that security.

'Hellooo!' she called ahead of her. 'We're here.'

He followed her down a wide hallway, the walls crammed with framed photographs. They ranged from old-fashioned sepia wedding photos, dating from pre-Second World War, to posed studio shots of cherubic babies. Again he found himself envying her—he had only a handful of family photos to cherish.

At a quick glance he found two of Andie—one in a green checked school uniform with her hair in plaits and that familiar grin showing off a gap in her front teeth; another as a teenager in a flowing pink formal dress. A third caught his eye—an older Andie in a bikini, arm in arm with a tall blond guy in board shorts who was looking down at her with open adoration. The same guy was with her in the next photo, only this time they were playing guitars and singing together. Dominic couldn't bear to do more than glance at them, aware of the tragedy that had followed.

Just before they reached the end of the corridor, Andie stopped and took a step towards him. She stood so close he breathed in her scent—something vaguely oriental, warm and sensual. She leaned up to whisper into his ear and her hair tickled his neck. He had to close his eyes to force himself from reacting to her closeness.

'The clan can be a bit overwhelming *en masse*,' she said. 'I won't introduce you to everyone by name; it would be unfair to expect you to remember all of them. My mother is Jennifer, my father is Ray. Hannah's husband is Paul.'

'I appreciate that,' he said, tugging at his collar that suddenly seemed too tight. As an only child, he'd always found meeting other people's families intimidating.

Andie gave him a reassuring smile. 'With the Newman family, what you see is what you get. They're all good people who will take you as they find you. We might even get some volunteers to help on Christmas Day out of this.'

The corridor opened out into a spacious open-plan family room. At some time in the last twenty years the parents had obviously added a new extension. It looked dated now but solid—warm and comfortable and welcoming. Delicious aromas emanated from the farmhouse-style kitchen in the northern corner. He sniffed and Andie smiled. 'My mother's lasagne—wait until you taste it.'

She announced him with an encompassing wave of her arm. 'Everyone, this is Dominic. He's a very important new client so please make him welcome. And yes, I know he's gorgeous but it's strictly business between us.'

That was met with laughter and a chorus of 'Hi, Dominic!' and 'Welcome!' Andie then briefly explained to them about the party and Hannah's likely role in it.

There were so many of them. Andie's introduction had guaranteed all eyes were on him. About ten people, including kids, were ranged around the room, sitting in comfortable -looking sofas or around a large trestle table.

Each face came into focus as the adults greeted him with warm smiles. It wasn't difficult to tell who was related—Andie's smile was a strong family marker that originated with her father, a tall, thin man with a vigorous handshake. Her mother's smile was different but equally welcoming as she headed his way from the kitchen, wiping her hands on her apron before she greeted him. Three young children playing on the floor looked up, then kept on playing with their toys. A big black dog with a greying muzzle, lying stretched out near the kids, lifted his head, then thumped his tail in greeting.

Andie's sister Hannah and her husband, Paul, paused in their job of setting the large trestle table to say hello. His experience with social workers in his past had been good—a social worker had pretty much saved his life—and he was not disappointed by Hannah's kind eyes in a gentle face.

'I straight away know of several families who are facing a very grim Christmas indeed,' she said. 'Your generous gesture would make an immense difference to them.'

Andie caught his eye and smiled. Instinctively, he knew she had steered him in the right direction towards her sister. If all Andie's ideas for his party were as good as this one, he could face the Christmas Day he dreaded with more confidence than he might have expected.

Andie's policy of glaring down any family member who dared to even hint at dating possibilities with Dominic was working. Except for her younger sister, Bea, who could not resist hissing, 'He's hot,' at any opportunity, from passing the salad to refilling her water glass. Then, when Andie didn't bite, Bea added, 'If you don't want him, hand him over to me.' Thankfully, Dominic remained oblivious to the whispered exchanges.

Her family had, unwittingly or not, sat Dominic in the same place at the table where Anthony had sat at these gatherings. *Andie and Ant—always together.* She doubted it was on purpose. Dominic needed to sit between Hannah and her and so it had just happened.

In the years since he'd died, no man had come anywhere near to replacing Anthony in her heart. How could they? Anthony and she had been two halves of the same soul, she sometimes thought. Maybe she would never be able to love anyone else. *But she was lonely.* The kind of loneliness that work, friends, family could not displace.

In the months after Anthony's death her parents had left Anthony's customary seat empty out of respect. Unable to bear the emptiness that emphasised his absence, she had stopped coming to the family dinners until her mother had realised the pain it was causing. From then on, one of her brothers always occupied Anthony's chair.

Now she told herself she was okay with Dominic sitting there. He was only a client, with no claim to any place in her heart. Bringing him along tonight had worked out well—one of those spur-of-the-moment decisions she mightn't have made if she'd given it more thought.

Dominic and Hannah had spent a lot of time talking— but he'd managed to chat with everyone else there too. They were obviously charmed by him. That was okay too. *She* was charmed by him. Tonight she was seeing a side of him, as he interacted with her family, that she might never have seen in everyday business dealings.

Her sister was right. *Dominic was hot.* And Andie was only too aware of it. She was surprised at the fierce urge of possessiveness that swept over her at the thought of 'handing over' Dominic to anyone else. Her sister could find her own hot guy.

Even at the dinner table, when her back was angled away from him to talk to her brother on her other side, she was aware of Dominic. His scent had already become familiar—citrus-sharp yet warm and very masculine. Her ears were tuned into the sound of his voice—no matter where he was in the room. Her body was on constant alert to that attraction, which had been instant and only continued to grow with further contact. On their way in, in the corridor, when she'd drawn close to whisper so her family would not overhear, she'd felt light-headed from the proximity to him.

It had been five years now since Anthony had gone— the same length of time they'd been together. She would never forget him but that terrible grief and anguish she had felt at first had eventually mellowed to a grudging acceptance. She realised she had stopped dreaming about him.

People talked about once-in-a-lifetime love. She'd thought she'd found it at the age of eighteen—and a cruel fate had snatched him away from her. Was there to be only one great love for her?

Deep in her heart, she didn't want to believe that. Surely there would be someone for her again? She didn't want to be alone. One day she wanted marriage, a family. She'd been looking for someone like Anthony—and had been constantly disappointed in the men she'd gone out with. But was it a mistake to keep on looking for a man like her teenage soulmate?

Thoughts of Dominic were constantly invading her mind. He was so different from Anthony there could be no comparison. Anthony had been blond and lean, laidback and funny, always quick with a joke, creative and musical. From what she knew of Dominic, he was quite the opposite. She'd dismissed him as not for her. But her body's reaction kept contradicting her mind's stonewalling. How could she be so certain he was Mr Wrong?

Dessert was being served—spring berries and homemade vanilla bean ice cream—and she turned to Dominic at the precise moment he turned to her. Their eyes connected and held and she knew without the need for words that he was happy with her decision to bring him here.

'Your family is wonderful,' he said in a low undertone.

'I think so,' she said, pleased. 'What about you? Do you come from a large family?'

A shadow darkened his eyes. He shook his head. 'Only child.'

She smiled. 'We must seem overwhelming.'

'In a good way,' he said. 'You're very lucky.'

'I know.' Of course she and her siblings had had the usual squabbles and disagreements throughout their childhood and adolescence. She, as number four, had had to fight for her place. But as adults they all got on as friends as well as brothers and sisters. She couldn't have got through the loss of Anthony without her family's support.

'The kids are cute,' he said. 'So well behaved.'

Her nephews, Timothy and Will, and her niece, Caitlin,

were together down the other end of the table under the watchful eye of their grandmother. 'They're really good kids,' she agreed. 'I adore them.'

'Little Timothy seems quite…delicate,' Dominic said, obviously choosing his words carefully. 'But I notice his older cousin looks after him.'

A wave of sadness for Hannah and Paul's little son overwhelmed her. 'They're actually the same age,' she said. 'Both five years old. Timothy just looks as though he's three.'

'I guess I don't know much about kids,' Dominic said, shifting uncomfortably in his chair.

She lowered her voice. 'Sadly, little Timothy has some kind of rare growth disorder, an endocrine imbalance. That's why he's so small.'

Dominic answered in a lowered voice. 'Can it be treated?'

'Only with a new treatment that isn't yet subsidised by the public health system. Even for private treatment, he's on a waiting list.' It was the reason why she drove an old car, why Bea had moved back home to save on rent, why the whole family was pulling together to raise the exorbitant amount of money required for tiny Timothy's private treatment.

But she would not tell Dominic that. While she might be wildly attracted to him, she still had no reason to think he was other than the Scrooge of his reputation. A man who had to be forced into a public display of charity to broker a multi-million-dollar business deal. Not for one moment did she want him to think she might be angling for financial help for Timothy.

'It's all under control,' she said as she passed him a bowl of raspberries.

'I'm glad to hear that,' he said, helping himself to the berries and then the ice cream. 'Thank you for inviting

me tonight and for introducing me to Hannah. The next
step is for you and your business partners to come in to
my headquarters for a meeting with my marketing people.
Can the three of you make it on Friday?'

CHAPTER SIX

ANDIE AND HER two business partners, Gemma and Eliza, settled themselves in a small waiting room off the main reception area of Dominic's very plush offices in Circular Quay. She and her fellow Party Queens had just come out of the Friday meeting with Dominic, his marketing people and senior executives in the boardroom and were waiting for Dominic to hear his feedback.

Situated on Sydney Cove, at the northern end of the CBD, the area was not just one of the most popular harbourside tourist precincts in Sydney—it was also home to the most prestigious office buildings. Even in this small room, floor-to-ceiling glass walls gave a magnificent close view of the Sydney Harbour Bridge and a luxury cruise liner in dock.

Andie couldn't help thinking the office was an ideal habitat for a billionaire Scrooge. Then she backtracked on the thought. That might not be fair. He hated the term and she felt vaguely disloyal even thinking it. Dominic was now totally committed to the Christmas Day feast for underprivileged families and had just approved a more than generous budget. She was beginning to wonder if his protestation that he was *not* a Scrooge had some truth in it. And then there was his gift to her mother to consider.

As she pondered the significance of that, she realised her thoughts had been filled with nothing much but Dominic since the day she'd met him. Last night he had even invaded her dreams—in a very passionate encounter that made her blush at the hazy dream memory of it. *Did he kiss like that in real life?*

It was with an effort that she forced her thoughts back to business.

'How do you guys think it went?' she asked the other two. 'My vote is for really well.' She felt jubilant and buoyant—Dominic's team had embraced her idea with more enthusiasm than she could ever have anticipated.

'Considering the meeting was meant to go from ten to eleven and here it is, nearly midday, yes, I think you could say that,' said Eliza with a big smile splitting her face.

'Of course that could have had something to do with Gemma's superb macadamia shortbread and those delectable fruit mince pies,' said Andie.

'Yes,' said Gemma with a pleased smile. 'I thought I could describe until I was blue in the face what I wanted to serve for the lunch, but they'd only know by tasting it.'

Party Queens' foodie partner had not only come up with a detailed menu for Dominic's Christmas Day lunch, but she'd also brought along freshly baked samples of items from her proposed menus. At the end of the meeting only a few crumbs had remained on the boardroom's fine china plates. Andie had caught Dominic's eye as he finished his second pastry and knew it had been an inspired idea. The Christmas star shaped serviettes she had brought along had also worked to keep the meeting focused on the theme of traditional with a twist.

'I think they were all-round impressed,' said Eliza. 'We three worked our collective socks off to get our presentations so detailed and professional in such a short time. Andie, all the images and samples you prepared to show the decorations and table settings looked amazing—I got excited at how fabulous it's going to look.'

'I loved the idea of the goody bags for all the guests too,' said Gemma. 'You really thought of everything.'

'While we're doing some mutual backslapping I'm giving yours a hearty slap, Eliza,' said Andie. 'Their finance guy couldn't fault your detailed costings and timelines.'

Eliza rubbed her hands together in exaggerated glee. 'And I'm sure we're going to get more party bookings from them. One of the senior marketing people mentioned her daughter was getting married next year and asked me did we do weddings.'

'Well done, Party Queens,' said Andie. 'Now that the contract is signed and the basic plan approved I feel I can relax.' Her partners had no idea of how tight it had been to get Dominic across the line for the change from glitz and glamour to more humble with heart.

She and her two friends discreetly high-fived each other. The room was somewhat of a goldfish bowl and none of them wanted to look less than professional to any of Dominic's staff who might be walking by.

Eliza leaned in to within whispering distance of Andie and Gemma. 'Dominic Hunt was a surprise,' she said in an undertone. 'I thought he'd be arrogant and overbearing. Instead, I found myself actually liking him.'

'Me too,' said Gemma. 'Not to mention he's so handsome. I could hardly keep my eyes off him. And that voice.' She mimed a shiver of delight.

'But *he* couldn't keep his eyes off Andie,' said Eliza. 'You'd be wasting your time there, Gemma.'

Had he? Been unable to keep his eyes off her? Andie's Dominic radar had been on full alert all through the meeting. Again she'd that uncanny experience of knowing exactly where he was in the room even when her back was turned. Of hearing his voice through the chatter of others. She'd caught his eye one too many times to feel comfortable. Especially with the remnants of that dream lingering in her mind. She'd had to force herself not to let her gaze linger on his mouth.

'Really, Andie?' said Gemma. 'Has he asked you out?'

'Nothing like that,' Andie said.

Eliza nodded thoughtfully. 'But you like him. Not in the way I liked him. I mean you *really* like him.'

Andie had no intention of admitting anything to anyone. She forced her voice to sound cool, impartial—though she doubted she would fool shrewd Eliza. 'Like you, I was surprised at how easy he is to get on with and how professional he is—even earlier this week when I switched the whole concept of his party into something he had never envisaged.' That overwhelming attraction was just physical—nothing more.

'And you totally didn't get how hot he was?' said Gemma. 'Don't expect me to believe that for one moment.'

Eliza rolled her eyes at Andie. 'I know what's coming next. *He's not your type.* How many times have I heard you say that when you either refuse a date or dump a guy before you've even had a chance to get to know him?'

Andie paused. 'Maybe that's true. Maybe that's why I'm still single. I'm beginning to wonder if I really know what *is* my type now.'

Her friendships with Gemma and Eliza dated from after she'd lost Anthony. They'd been sympathetic, but never really got why she had been so determined to try and find another man cast in the same mould as her first love. That her first love had been so perfect she'd felt her best chance of happiness would be with someone like Anthony.

Trouble was, they'd broken the mould when they'd made Anthony. Maybe she just hadn't been ready. Maybe she'd been subconsciously avoiding any man who might challenge her. Or might force her to look at why she'd put her heart on hold for so long. *Dominic would be a challenge in every way.* The thought both excited and scared her.

Eliza shook her head. 'It's irrelevant anyway,' she said. 'It would be most unwise for you to start anything with Dominic Hunt. His party is a big, important job for us and we don't have much time to organise it. It could get very messy if you started dating the client. Especially when I've never known you to stay with anyone for more than two weeks.'

'In my eagerness to get you fixed up with a handsome rich guy, I hadn't thought of that,' said Gemma. 'Imagine if you broke up with the billionaire client right in the middle of the countdown to the event. Could get awkward.'

'It's not going to happen, girls,' Andie said. 'I won't lie and say I don't think he's really attractive. But that's as far as it goes.' Thinking of last night's very intimate dream, she crossed her fingers behind her back.

'This is a huge party for us to pull together so quickly. We've got other jobs to get sorted as well. I can't afford to get…distracted.' How she actually stopped herself from getting distracted by Dominic was another matter altogether.

'I agree,' said Eliza. 'Eyes off the client. Okay?'

Andie smiled. 'I'll try,' she said. 'Seriously, though, it's really important for Dominic that this party works. He's got a lot riding on it. And it's really important for us. As you say, Eliza, more work could come from this. Not just weddings and private parties. But why not his company's business functions too? We have to think big.'

Gemma giggled. 'Big? Mr Hunt is way too big for me anyway. He's so tall. And all those muscles. His face is handsome but kind of tough too, don't you think?'

'Shh,' hissed Eliza, putting her finger to her lips. 'He's coming.'

Andie screwed up her eyes for a moment. How mortifying if he'd caught them gossiping about him. She'd been just about to say he wasn't too big for her to handle.

Along with the other two, she looked up and straightened her shoulders as Dominic strode towards them. In his dark charcoal suit he looked every inch the billionaire businessman. And, yes, very big.

She caught her breath at how handsome he looked. At the same time she caught his eye. And got the distinct impression that, of the three women in the room, she was the only one he really saw.

Did Andie get more and more beautiful every time he saw her? Dominic wondered. Or was it just the more he got to know her, the more he liked and admired her?

He had been impressed by her engaging and professional manner in the boardroom—the more so because he was aware she'd had such a short time to prepare her presentation. Her two business partners had been impressive too. It took a lot to win over his hard-nosed marketing people but, as a team, Party Queens had bowled them over.

The three women got up from their seats as he approached. Andie, tall and elegant in a deceptively simple caramel-coloured short dress—businesslike but with a snug fit that showed off her curves. Her sensational legs seemed to go on for ever to end in sky-high leopard-skin-print stilettos. He got it. She wanted to look businesslike but also let it be known who was the creative mind behind Party Queens. It worked.

Gemma—shorter, curvier, with auburn hair—and sophisticated, dark-haired Eliza were strikingly attractive too. They had a glint in their eyes and humour in their smiles that made him believe they could enjoy a party as well as plan them. But, in his eyes, Andie outshone them. Would any other woman ever be able to beat her? It was disturbing that a woman who he had known for such a short time could have made such an impression on him.

He addressed all three, while being hyper aware of

Andie as he did so. Her hair pulled back in a loose knot that fell in soft tendrils around her face, her mouth slicked with coral gloss, those remarkable green eyes. 'As I'm sure you're aware,' he began, 'my marketing team is delighted at both the concept for the party and the way you plan to implement the concept to the timeline. They're confident the event will meet and exceed the target we've set for reputation management and positive media engagement.'

It sounded like jargon and he knew it. But how else could he translate the only real aim of the party: to make him look less the penny-pincher and more the philanthropist?

'We're very pleased to be working with such a professional team,' said Eliza, the business brains of the partnership. But all three were business savvy in their own way, he'd realised through the meeting.

'Thank you,' he said. He glanced at his watch. 'The meeting ran so late it's almost lunchtime. I'm extending an invitation to lunch for all of you,' he said. 'Not that restaurants around here, excellent as they are, could match the standard of your cooking, Gemma.'

'Thank you,' said Gemma, looking pleased. 'But I'm afraid I have an appointment elsewhere.'

'Me too, and I'm running late,' said Eliza. 'But we couldn't possibly let you lunch alone, Mr Hunt, could we, Andie?'

Andie flushed high on those elegant cheekbones. 'Of course not. I'd be delighted to join Dominic for lunch.'

Her chin tilted upwards and he imagined her friends might later be berated for landing her in this on her own. Not that he minded. The other women were delightful, but lunch one-on-one with Andie was his preferred option.

'There are a few details of the plan I need to finalise with Dominic anyway,' she said to her friends.

Dominic shook hands with Gemma and Eliza and they

headed towards the elevators. He turned to Andie. 'Thank you for coming to lunch with me,' he said.

She smiled. 'Be warned, I'm starving. I was up at the crack of dawn finalising those mood boards for the presentation.'

'They were brilliant. There's only one thing I'd like to see changed. I didn't want to mention it in the meeting as it's my personal opinion and I didn't want to have to debate it.'

She frowned, puzzled rather than worried, he thought. 'Yes?'

He put his full authority behind his voice—he would not explain his reasons. Ever. 'The Christmas tree. The big one you have planned for next to the staircase. I don't want it.'

'Sure,' she said, obviously still puzzled. 'I thought it would be wonderful to have the tree where it's the first thing the guests see, but I totally understand if you don't want it there. We can put the Christmas tree elsewhere. The living room. Even in the area near where we'll be eating. Wherever you suggest.'

He hadn't expected this to be easy—he knew everyone would expect to see a decorated tree on Christmas Day. 'You misunderstood me. I mean I don't want a Christmas tree anywhere. No tree at all in my house.'

She paused. He could almost see her internal debate reflected in the slight crease between her eyebrows, the barely visible pursing of her lips. But then she obviously thought it was not worth the battle. 'Okay,' she said with a shrug of her slender shoulders. 'No tree.'

'Thank you,' he said, relieved he wasn't going to have to further assert his authority. At this time of year, Christmas trees were appearing all over the place. He avoided them when he could. But he would never have a tree in his home—a constant reminder of the pain and loss and guilt associated with the festive season.

They walked together to the elevator. When it arrived, there were two other people in it. They got out two floors below. Then Dominic was alone in the confined space of the elevator, aware of Andie's closeness, her warm scent. What was it? Sandalwood? Something exotic and sensual. He had the craziest impulse to hold her closer so he could nuzzle into the softness of her throat, the better to breathe it in.

He clenched his fists beside him and moved as far as he could away from her so his shoulder hit the wall of the elevator. That would be insanity. And probably not the best timing when he'd just quashed her Christmas tree display.

But she wouldn't be Andie if she didn't persevere. 'Not even miniature trees on the lunch table?' she asked.

'No trees,' he said.

She sighed. 'Okay, the client has spoken. No Christmas tree.'

The elevator came to the ground floor. He lightly placed his hand at the small of her back to steer her in the direction of the best exit for the restaurant. Bad idea. Touching Andie even in this casual manner just made him want to touch her more.

'But you're happy with the rest of the plan?' she said as they walked side by side towards the restaurant, dodging the busy Sydney lunchtime crush as they did.

'Very happy. Except you can totally discard the marketing director's suggestion I dress up as Santa Claus.'

She laughed. 'Did you notice I wrote it down but didn't take the suggestion any further?' Her eyes narrowed as she looked him up and down in mock inspection. 'Though it's actually a nice idea. If you change your mind—'

'No,' he said.

'That's what I thought,' she said, that delightful smile dancing around the corners of her mouth.

'You know it's been a stretch for me to agree to a Christmas party at all. You won't ever see me as Santa.'

'What if the marketing director himself could be convinced to play Santa Claus?' she said thoughtfully. 'He volunteered to help out on the day.'

'This whole party thing was Rob Cratchit's idea so that might be most appropriate. Take it as an order from his boss.'

'I'll send him an email and say it's your suggestion,' she said with a wicked grin. 'He's quite well padded and would make a wonderful Santa—no pillow down the front of his jacket required.'

'Don't mention that in the email or all hell will break loose,' he said.

'Don't worry; I can be subtle when I want to,' she said, that grin still dancing in her eyes as they neared the restaurant.

In Dominic's experience, some restaurants were sited well and had a good fit-out; others had excellent food. In this case, his favourite place to eat near the office had both—a spectacular site on the top of a heritage listed building right near the water and a superlative menu.

There had been no need to book—a table was always there for him when he wanted one, no matter how long the waiting list for bookings.

An attentive waiter settled Andie into a seat facing the view of Sydney Harbour. 'I've always wanted to eat at this restaurant,' she said, looking around her.

'Maybe we should have our meetings here in future?'

'Good idea,' she said. 'Though I'll have to do a detailed site inspection of your house very soon. We could fit in a meeting then, perhaps?'

'I might not be able to be there,' he said. 'I have a series of appointments in other states over the next two weeks. Any meetings with you might have to be via the Internet.'

Was that disappointment he saw cloud her eyes. 'That's a shame. I—'

'My assistant will help you with access and the security code,' he said. He wished he could cancel some of the meetings, but that was not possible. Perhaps it was for the best. The more time he spent with Andie, the more he wanted to break his rules and ask her on a date. But those rules were there for good reason.

'As you know, we have a tight timeline to work to,' she said. 'The more we get done early the better, to allow for the inevitable last-minute dramas.'

'I have every confidence in you that it will go to plan.'

'Me too,' she said with another of those endearing grins. 'I've organised so many Christmas room sets and table settings for magazine and advertising clients. You have to get creative to come up with something different each year. This is easier in a way.'

'But surely there must be a continuity?' he asked, curious even though Christmas was his least favourite topic of conversation.

'Some people don't want to go past traditional red and green and that's okay,' she said. 'I've done an entire room themed purple and the client was delighted. Silver and gold is always popular in Australia, when Christmas is likely to be sweltering—it seems to feel cooler somehow. But—'

The waiter came to take their orders. They'd been too busy talking to look at the menu. Quickly they discussed their favourites before they ordered: barramundi with prawns and asparagus for him; tandoori roasted ocean trout with cucumber salsa for her and an heirloom tomato salad to share. They each passed on wine and chose mineral water. 'Because it's a working day,' they both said at the exact time and laughed. *It felt like a date.* He could not let his thoughts stray that way. Because he liked the idea too much.

'You haven't explained the continuity of Christmas,' he said, bringing the conversation back to the party.

'It's nothing to do with the baubles and the tinsel and everything to do with the feeling,' she said with obvious enthusiasm. 'Anticipation, delight, joy. For some it's about religious observance, spirituality and new life; others about sharing and generosity. If you can get people feeling the emotion, then it doesn't really matter if the tree is decorated in pink and purple or red and green.'

How about misery and fear and pain? Those were his memories of Christmas. 'I see your point,' he said.

'I intend to make sure your party is richly imbued with that kind of Christmas spirit. Hannah told me some of the kids who will be coming would be unlikely to have a celebration meal or a present and certainly not both if it wasn't for your generosity.'

'I met with Hannah yesterday; she mentioned how important it will be for the families we're inviting. She seems to think the party will do a powerful lot of good. Your sister told me how special Christmas is in your family.' It was an effort for him to speak about Christmas in a normal tone of voice. But he seemed to be succeeding.

'Oh, yes,' said Andie. 'Heaven help anyone who might want to celebrate it with their in-laws or anywhere else but my parents' house.'

'Your mother's a marvellous cook.'

'True, but Christmas is well and truly my dad's day. My mother is allowed to do the baking and she does that months in advance. On the day, he cooks a traditional meal—turkey, ham, roast beef, the lot. He's got favourite recipes he's refined over the years and no one would dare suggest anything different.'

Did she realise how lucky she was? How envious he felt when he thought about how empty his life had been of the kind of family love she'd been gifted with. He'd used to think he could start his own family, his own traditions, but his ex-wife had disabused him of that particular dream. It involved trust and trust was not a thing that came easily to him. Not when it came to women. 'I can't imagine you would want to change a tradition.'

'If truth be told, we'd be furious if he wanted to change one little thing,' she said, her voice warm with affection for her father. *She knew.*

He could see where she got her confidence from—that rock-solid security of a loving, supportive family. But now he knew she'd been tempered by tragedy too. He wanted to know more about how she had dealt with the loss of her boyfriend. But not until it was appropriate to ask.

'What about you, Dominic—did you celebrate Christmas with your family?' she asked.

This never got easier—which was why he chose not to revisit it too often. 'My parents died when I was eleven,' he said.

'Oh, I'm so sorry,' she said with warm compassion in her eyes. 'What a tragedy.' She paused. 'You were so young, an only child…who looked after you?'

'We lived in England, in a village in Norfolk. My father was English, my mother Australian. My mother's sister was staying with us at the time my parents died. She took me straight back with her to Australia.' It was difficult to keep his voice matter of fact, not to betray the pain the memories evoked, even after all this time.

'What? Just wrenched you away from your home?' She paused. 'I'm sorry. That wasn't my call to say that. You were lucky you had family. Did your aunt have children?'

'No, it was just the two of us,' he said and left it at that. There was so much more he could say about the toxic relationship with his aunt but that was part of his past he'd rather was left buried.

Wrenched. That was how it had been. Away from everything familiar. Away from his grandparents, whom he didn't see again until he had the wherewithal to get himself back to the UK as an adult. Away from the dog he'd adored. Desperately lonely and not allowed to grieve, thrust back down in Brisbane, in the intense heat, straight into the strategic battleground that was high school in a foreign country. To a woman who had no idea how to love a child, though she had tried in her own warped way.

'I'd prefer not to talk about it,' he said. 'I'm all grown up now and don't angst about the past.' Except when it was dark and lonely and he couldn't sleep and he wondered if he was fated to live alone without love.

'I understand,' she said. But how could she?

She paused to leave a silence he did not feel able to fill.

'Talking about my family,' she finally said, 'you're my mother's new number one favourite person.'

Touched by not only her words but her effort to draw him in some way into her family circle, he smiled. 'And why is that?'

'Seriously, she really liked you at dinner on Wednesday night. But then, when you had flowers delivered the next day, she was over the moon. Especially at the note that said she cooked the best lasagne you'd ever tasted.'

'I'm glad she liked them. And it was true about the lasagne.' Home-made anything was rarely on the menu for him so he had appreciated it.

'How did you know pink was her favourite colour in flowers?'

'I noticed the flowers she'd planted in her garden.'

'But you only saw the garden so briefly.'

'I'm observant,' he said.

'But the icing on the cake was the voucher for dinner for two at their local bistro.'

'She mentioned she liked their food when we were talking,' he said.

'You're a thoughtful guy, aren't you?' she said, tilting her head to the side.

'Some don't think so,' he said, unable to keep the bitterness from his voice.

She lowered her voice to barely a whisper so he had to lean across the table to hear her, so close their heads were touching. Anyone who was watching would think they *were* on a date.

She placed her hand on his arm in a gesture of comfort which touched him. 'Don't worry. The party should change all that. I really liked Rob's idea that no media would be invited to the party. That journalists would have to volunteer to help on the day if they wanted to see what it was all about.'

'And no photographers allowed, to preserve our guests' privacy. I liked that too.'

'I really have a good feeling about it,' she said. She lifted her hand off his arm and he felt bereft of her touch.

He nodded. If it were up to him, if he didn't *have* to go ahead with the party, he'd cancel it at a moment's notice. Maybe there was a touch of Scrooge in him after all.

But he didn't want Andie to think that of him. Not for a moment.

He hadn't proved to be a good judge of women. His errors in judgement went right back to his aunt—he'd loved her when she was his fun auntie from Australia. She'd turned out to be a very different person. Then there'd been Melody—sweet, doomed Melody. At seventeen he'd been a man in body but a boy still in heart. He'd been gutted at her betrayal, too damn wet behind the ears to realise a teenage boy's love could never be enough for an addict. Then how could he have been sucked in by Tara? His ex-wife was a redhead like Melody, tiny and delicate. But her frail exterior hid an avaricious, dishonest heart and she had lied to him about something so fundamental to their marriage that he could never forgive her.

Now there was Andie. He didn't trust his feelings when he'd made such disastrous calls before. *'What you see is what you get,'* she'd said about her family.

Could he trust himself to judge that Andie was what she appeared to be?

He reined in his errant thoughts—he only needed to trust Andie to deliver him the party he needed to improve his public image. Anything personal was not going to happen.

CHAPTER SEVEN

'ANDIE, I NEED to see you.' Dominic's voice on her smartphone was harsh in its urgency. It was eight a.m. and Andie had not been expecting a call from him. He'd been away more than a week on business and she'd mainly communicated with him by text and email—and only then if it was something that needed his approval for the party. The last time she'd seen him was the Friday they'd had lunch together. The strictly business lunch that had somehow felt more like a date. But she couldn't let herself think like that.

'Sure,' she said. 'I just have to—'

'Now. Please. Where do you live?'

Startled at his tone, she gave him the address of the apartment in a converted warehouse in the inner western suburb of Newtown she shared with two old schoolfriends. Her friends had both already left for work. Andie had planned on a day finalising prop hire and purchase for Dominic's party before she started work for a tuxedo-and-tiara-themed twenty-first birthday party.

She quickly changed into skinny denim jeans and a simple loose-knit cream top that laced with leather ties at the neckline. Decided on her favourite leopard-print stilettos over flats. And make-up. And her favourite sandalwood and jasmine perfume. What the heck—her heart was racing at the thought of seeing him. She didn't want to seem as though she were trying too hard—but then again she didn't want to be caught out in sweats.

When Dominic arrived she was shocked to see he didn't look *his* sartorial best. In fact he looked downright dishevelled. His black hair seemed as if he'd used his fingers for a comb and his dark stubble was one step away from a beard. He was wearing black jeans, a dark grey T-shirt and had a black leather jacket slung over his shoulders. Immediately he owned the high-ceilinged room, a space that overwhelmed men of lesser stature, with the casual athleticism of his stance, the power of his body with its air of tightly coiled energy.

'Are you alone?' he asked.

'Yes,' she said. *Yes!*

Her first thought was that he looked hotter than ever—so hot she had to catch her breath. This Dominic set her pulse racing even more than executive Dominic in his made-to-measure Italian suits.

Her second thought was that he seemed stressed—his mouth set in a grim line, his eyes red-rimmed and darkly shadowed. 'Are you okay?' she asked.

'I've come straight from the airport. I just flew in from Perth.' Perth was on the other side of Australia—a six-hour flight. 'I cut short my trip.'

'But are you okay?' She forced her voice to sound calm and measured, not wanting him to realise how she was reacting to his untamed good looks. Her heart thudded with awareness that they were alone in the apartment.

With the kind of friendly working relationship they had now established, it would be quite in order to greet him with a light kiss on his beard-roughened cheek. But she wouldn't dare. She might not be able to resist sliding her mouth across his cheek to his mouth and turning it into a very different kind of kiss. And that wouldn't do.

'I'm fine. I've just…been presented with…with a dilemma,' Dominic said.

'Coffee might help,' she said.

'Please.'

'Breakfast? I have—'

'Just coffee.'

But Andie knew that sometimes men who said they didn't want anything to eat needed food. And that their mood could improve immeasurably when they ate something. Not that she'd been in the habit of sharing breakfast with a man. Not since… She forced her mind back to the present and away from memories of breakfasts with Anthony on a sun-soaked veranda. Her memories of him were lit with sunshine and happiness.

Dominic dragged out a chair and slumped down at her kitchen table while she prepared him coffee. *Why was he here?* She turned to see him with his elbows on the tabletop, resting his head on his hands. Tired? Defeated? Something seemed to have put a massive dent in his usual self-assured confidence.

She slid a mug of coffee in front of him. 'I assumed black but here's frothed milk and sugar if you want.'

'Black is what I need,' he said. He put both hands around the mug and took it to his mouth.

Without a word, she put a thick chunk of fresh fruit bread, studded with figs and apricots, from her favourite baker in King Street in front of him. Then a dish of cream cheese and a knife. 'Food might help,' she said.

He put down his coffee, gave her a weary imitation of his usual glower and went to pick up the bread. 'Let me,' she said and spread it with cream cheese.

What was it about this man that made her want to comfort and care for him? He was a thirty-two-year-old billionaire, for heaven's sake. Tough, self-sufficient. Wealthier than she could even begin to imagine. And yet she sometimes detected an air of vulnerability about him that wrenched at her. A sense of something broken. But it was not up to her to try and fix him. He ate the fruit bread in two bites. 'More?' she asked.

He nodded. 'It's good,' he said.

Andie had to be honest with herself. She wanted to comfort him, yes. She enjoyed his company. But it was more than that. She couldn't deny that compelling physical attraction. He sat at her kitchen table, his leather jacket slung on the back of the chair. His tanned arms were sculpted with muscle, his T-shirt moulded ripped pecs and abs. With his rough-hewn face, he looked so utterly *male*.

Desire, so long unfamiliar, thrilled through her. She wanted to kiss him and feel those strong arms around her, his hands on her body. *She wanted more than kisses.* What was it about this not-my-type man who had aroused her interest from the moment she'd first met him?

When he'd eaten two more slices of fruit bread, he pushed his plate away and leaned back in his seat. His sigh was weary and heartfelt. 'Thank you,' he said. 'I didn't realise I was hungry.'

She slipped into the chair opposite him and nursed her own cooling cup of coffee to stop the impulse to reach over and take his hand. 'Are you able to tell me about your dilemma?' she asked, genuinely concerned.

He raked his hands through his hair. 'My ex-wife is causing trouble. Again.'

In her research into Dominic, Andie had seen photos of Tara Hunt—she still went by his name—a petite, pale-skinned redhead in designer clothes and an over-abundance of jewellery.

'I'm sorry,' she said, deciding on caution in her reaction. 'Do you want to tell me about it?' Was that why he wanted to see her? To cry on her shoulder about his ex-wife? Dominic didn't seem like a crying-on-shoulders kind of guy.

He went to drink more coffee, to find his mug was

nearly empty. He drained the last drops. 'You make good coffee,' he said appreciatively.

'I worked as a barista when I was a student,' she said.

She and Anthony had both worked in hospitality, saving for vacation backpacker trips to Indonesia and Thailand. It seemed so long ago now, those days when she took it for granted they had a long, happy future stretched out ahead of them. They'd been saving for a trip to Eastern Europe when he'd died.

She took Dominic's mug from him, got up, refilled it, brought it back to the table and sat down again. He drank from it and put it down.

Dominic leaned across the table to bring him closer to her. 'Can I trust you, Andie?' he asked in that deep, resonant voice. His intense grey gaze met hers and held it.

'Of course,' she said without hesitation.

He sat back in his chair. 'I know you're friends with journalists, so I have to be sure what I might talk to you about today won't go any further.' The way he said it didn't sound offensive; in fact it made her feel privileged that he would consider her trustworthy. Not to mention curious about what he might reveal.

'I assure you, you can trust me,' she said.

'Thank you,' he said. 'Tara found out about my impending deal with Walter Burton and is doing her best to derail it.'

Andie frowned. 'How can she do that?'

'Before I married Tara, she worked for my company in the accounts department. She made it her business to find out everything she could about the way I ran things. I didn't know, but once I started dating her she used that knowledge to make trouble, hiding behind the shield of our relationship. None of my staff dared tell me.'

'Not good,' Andie said, wanting to express in no uncertain terms what she thought of his ex, yet not wanting to get into a bitching session about her.

'You're right about that,' he said. 'It's why I now never date employees.'

His gaze met hers again and held it for a long moment. Was there a message in there for her? If she wasn't a contractor, would he ask her out? If she hadn't promised her partners to stay away from him, would she suggest a date?

'That policy makes…sense,' she said. What about after Christmas, when she and Dominic would no longer be connected by business? Could they date then? A sudden yearning for that to happen surprised her with its intensity. *She wanted him.*

'It gets worse,' he continued. 'A former employee started his own business in competition with me—' Andie went to protest but Dominic put up his hand. 'It happens; that's legit,' he said. 'But what happened afterwards wasn't. After our marriage broke up, Tara used her knowledge of how my company worked to help him.'

Andie couldn't help her gasp of outrage. 'Did her…her betrayal work?'

'She gave him the information. That didn't mean he knew how to use it. But now I've just discovered she's working with him in a last-minute rival bid for the joint venture with Walter Burton.'

Andie shook her head in disbelief. 'Why?' Her research had shown her Tara Hunt had ended up with a massive divorce settlement from Dominic. Per day of their short marriage, she had walked away with an incredible number of dollars.

Dominic shrugged. 'Revenge. Spite. Who knows what else?'

'Surely Walter Burton won't be swayed by that kind of underhand behaviour?'

'Traditional values are important to Walter Burton. We

know that. That's why we're holding the party to negate the popular opinion of me as a Scrooge.'

'So what does your ex-wife have to do with the deal?'

Dominic sighed, a great weary sigh that made Andie want to put comforting arms around him. She'd sensed from the get-go he was a private person. He obviously hated talking about this. Once more, she wondered why he had chosen to.

He drew those dark brows together in a scowl. 'Again she's raked over the coals of our disastrous marriage and talked to her media buddies. Now she's claiming I was unfaithful—which is a big fat lie. According to her, I'm a womaniser, a player and a complete and utter bastard. She dragged out my old quote that I will never marry again and claims it's because I'm incapable of settling with one woman. It's on one of the big Internet gossip sites and will be all over the weekend newspapers.' He cursed under his breath.

Andie could see the shadow of old hurts on his face. He had once loved his ex enough to marry her. A betrayal like this must be painful, no matter how much time had elapsed. She had no such angst behind her. She knew Anthony had been loyal to her, as she had been to him. *First love.* Sometimes she wondered if they might have grown apart if he'd lived. Some of their friends who had dated as teenagers had split when they got older. But she dismissed those thoughts as disloyal to his memory.

Andie shook her head at Dominic's revelations about his ex—it got worse and worse. 'That's horrible—but can't you just ignore it?'

'I would ignore it, but she's made sure Walter Burton has seen all her spurious allegations set out as truth.'

Andie frowned. 'Surely your personal life is none of Mr Burton's business? Especially when it's not true.' She believed Dominic implicitly—why, she wasn't completely sure. Trust went both ways.

'He might think it's true. The *"bed-hopping billionaire"*,' the article calls me.' Dominic growled with wounded outrage. 'That might be enough for Burton to reconsider doing business with me.'

Andie had to put her hand over her mouth to hide her smile at the description.

But Dominic noticed and scowled. 'I know it sounds ludicrous, but to a moralistic family man like Walter Burton it makes me sound immoral and not the kind of guy he wants to do business with.'

'Why do you care so much about the deal with Mr Burton? If you have to pretend to be someone you're not, how can it be worth it?'

'You mean I should pretend *not* to be a bed-hopping billionaire?'

'You must admit the headline has a certain ring to it,' Andie said, losing her battle to keep a straight face.

That forced a reluctant grin from him. 'A tag like that might be very difficult to live down.'

'Is…is it true? Are you a bed-hopping guy?' She held her breath for his reply.

'No. Of course I've had girlfriends since my divorce. Serial monogamy, I think they call it. But nothing like what this scurrilous interview with my ex claims.'

Andie let out her breath on a sigh of relief. 'But do you actually need to pursue this deal if it's becoming so difficult? You're already very wealthy.'

Dominic's mouth set in a grim line. 'I'm not going to bore you with my personal history. But home life with my aunt was less than ideal. I finished high school and got out. I'd tried to run away before and she'd dragged me back. This time she let me go. I ended up homeless, living in a squat. At seventeen I saw inexplicably awful things a boy that age should never see. I never again want to be without money and have nowhere to live. That's all I intend to say about that.' He nodded to her. 'And I trust you not to repeat it.'

'Of course,' she said, rocked by his revelations, aching to know more. *Dominic Hunt was a street kid?* Not boring. There was so much more about his life than he was saying. She thought again about his scarred knuckles and broken nose. There had been nothing about his past in her online trawling. She hoped he might tell her more. It seemed he was far more complex than he appeared. Which only made him more attractive.

'My best friend and first business partner, Jake Marlow, is also in with me on this,' he said. 'He wants it as much as I do, for his own reasons I'm not at liberty to share.'

'Okay,' she said slowly. 'So we're working on the party to negate the Scr...uh...the other reputation, to get Mr Burton on board. What do you intend to do about the bed-hopper one?'

'When Burton contacted me I told him that it was all scuttlebutt and I was engaged to be married.'

She couldn't help a gasp. 'You're engaged?' She felt suddenly stricken. 'Engaged to who?'

'I'm not engaged. I'm not even dating anyone.'

'Then why...?' she said.

He groaned. 'Panic. Fear. Survival. A gut reaction like I used to have back in that squat. When you woke up, terrified, in your cardboard box to find some older guy burrowing through your backpack and you told him you had nothing worth stealing even though there was five dollars folded tiny between your toes in your sock. If that money was stolen, you didn't eat.'

'So you lied to Mr Burton?'

'As I said, a panic reaction. But it gets worse.' Again he raked his fingers through his hair. 'Burton said he was flying in to Sydney in two weeks' time to meet with both me and the other guy. He wants to be introduced to my fiancée.'

Andie paused, stunned at what Dominic had done, appalled that he had lied. 'What will you do?'

Again he leaned towards her over the table. 'I want you to be my fiancée, Andie.'

CHAPTER EIGHT

DOMINIC WATCHED ANDIE'S reactions flit across her face—shock and indignation followed by disappointment. In him? He braced himself—certain she was going to say *no*.

'Are you serious?' she finally said, her hands flat down on the table in front of her.

'Very,' he said, gritting his teeth. He'd been an idiot to get himself into a mess like this. *Panic*. He shouldn't have given in to panic in that phone call with Walter Burton. He hadn't let panic or fear rule him for a long time.

Andie tilted her head to one side and frowned. 'You want me to *marry* you? We hardly know each other.'

Marriage? Who was talking about marriage? 'No. Just to *pretend*—' Whatever he said wasn't going to sound good. 'Pretend to be my fiancée. Until after the Christmas party.'

Andie shook her head in disbelief. 'To pretend to be engaged to you? To lie? No! I can't believe you asked me to…to even think of such a thing. I'm a party planner, not a…a…the type of person who would agree to that.'

She looked at him as though she'd never seen him before. And that maybe she didn't like what she saw. Dominic swallowed hard—he didn't like the feeling her expression gave him. She pushed herself up from the chair and walked away from the table, her body rigid with disapproval. He was very aware she wanted to distance herself from him. He didn't like that either. It had seemed so intimate, drinking coffee and eating breakfast at her table. And he *had* liked that.

He swivelled in his chair to face her. 'It was a stupid thing to do, I know that,' he said. He had spent the entire flight back from Perth regretting his impulsive action. 'But it's done.'

She turned around, glared at him. 'Then I suggest you undo it.'

'By admitting I lied?'

She shrugged. 'Tell Mr Burton your fiancée dumped you.'

'As if that would fly.'

'You think it's beyond belief that a woman would ever dump you?'

'I didn't say that.' Though it was true. Since it had ended with Melody, he had always been the one to end a relationship. 'It would seem too…sudden.'

'Just like the sudden engagement?'

'It wouldn't denote…stability.'

'You're right about that.' She crossed her arms in front of her chest—totally unaware that the action pushed up her breasts into an enticing cleavage in the V-necked top she wore. 'It's a crazy idea.'

'I'm not denying that,' he growled. He didn't need to have his mistake pointed out to him. 'But I'm asking you to help me out.'

'Why me? Find someone else. I'm sure there would be no shortage of candidates.'

'But it makes sense for my fiancée to be you.' He could be doggedly persistent when he wanted to be.

He unfolded himself from the too-small chair at the kitchen table. Most chairs were too small for him. He took a step towards her, only for her to take a step back from him. 'Andie. Please.'

Her hair had fallen across her face and she tossed it back. 'Why? We're just client and contractor.'

'Is that all it is between us?'

'Of course it is.' But she wouldn't meet his gaze and he felt triumphant. *So she felt it too.* That attraction that had flashed between them from the get-go.

'When I opened the door to the beautiful woman with the misbehaving skirt—' that got a grudging smile from her '—I thought it could be more than just a business arrangement. But you know now why I don't date anyone hired by the company.'

'And Party Queens has a policy of not mixing business with…with pleasure.' Her voice got huskier on the last words.

He looked her direct in the face, pinning her with his gaze. 'If it ever happened, it would be pleasure all the way, Andie, I think we both know that.' She hadn't quite cleared her face of a wisp of flyaway hair. He reached down and gently smoothed it back behind her ear.

She trembled under his touch. A blush travelled up her throat to stain her cheeks. 'I've never even thought about it, the…the *pleasure,* I mean,' she said.

She wouldn't blush like that if she hadn't. Or flutter her hands to the leather laces of her neckline. *Now who was lying?*

She took a deep breath and he tried to keep his gaze from the resulting further exposure of her cleavage. 'I don't want to be involved in this mad scheme in any way,' she said. 'Except to add your pretend fiancée—when you find one—to the Christmas party guest list.'

'I'm afraid you're already involved.'

She frowned. 'What do you mean?'

Dominic took the few steps necessary back to his chair and took out his smartphone from the inside pocket of his leather jacket. He scrolled through, then handed it to Andie.

She stared at the screen. 'But this is me. *Us*.'

The photo she was staring at was of him and her at a restaurant table. They were leaning towards each other, looking into each other's faces, Andie's hand on his arm.

'At the restaurant in Circular Quay, the day of the Friday meeting,' she said.

'Yes,' he said. The business lunch that had felt like a date. In this photo, it *looked* like a date.

She shook her head, bewildered. 'Who took it?'

'Some opportunistic person with a smartphone, I expect. Maybe a trouble-making friend of Tara's. Who knows?'

She looked back down at the screen, did some scrolling of her own. He waited for her to notice the words that accompanied the image on the gossip site.

Her eyes widened in horror. 'Did you see this?' She read out the heading. '"*Is This the Bed-Hopping Billionaire's New Conquest?*"' She swore under her breath—the first time he had heard her do so.

'I'm sorry. Of course I had no idea this was happening. But, in light of it, you can see why it makes sense that my fake fiancée should be you.'

She shook her head. 'No. It doesn't make any sense. That was a business lunch. Not the…the romantic rendezvous it appears to be in the picture.'

'You know that. I know that. But the way they've cropped the photo, that's exactly what it seems. Announce an engagement and suddenly the picture would make a whole lot of sense. Good sense.'

Her green eyes narrowed. 'This photo doesn't bother me. It will blow over. We're both single. Who even cares?' He'd been stunned to see the expression in his eyes as he'd looked into her face in the photo. It had looked as if he wanted to have her for dessert. Had she noticed? No wonder the gossip site had drawn a conclusion of romantic intrigue.

'If you're so indifferent, why not help me out?' he said. 'Be my fake fiancée, just until after Christmas.'

'Christmas is nearly a month away. Twenty-five days, to be precise. For twenty-five days I'd have to pretend to be your fiancée?'

'So you're considering it? Because we've already been "outed", so to speak, it wouldn't come out of the blue. It would be believable.'

'Huh! We've only known each other for two weeks. Who would believe it?'

'People get married on less acquaintance,' he said.

'Not people like me,' she said.

'You don't think anyone would believe you could be smitten by me in that time? I think I'm offended.'

'Of course not,' she said. 'I…I believe many women would be smitten by you. You're handsome, intelligent—'

'And personable, yes, you said. Though I bet you don't think I'm so personable right now.'

She glared at him, though there was a lilt to the corners of her mouth that made it seem like she might want to smile. 'You could be right about that.'

'Now to you—gorgeous, sexy, smart Andie Newman.' Her blush deepened as he sounded each adjective. 'People would certainly believe I could be instantly smitten with such a woman,' he said. 'In fact they'd think I was clever getting a ring on your finger so quickly.'

That flustered her. 'Th…thank you. I…I'm flattered. But it wouldn't seem authentic. We'd have to pretend so much. It would be such deception.'

With any other woman, he'd be waiting for her to ask: *What's in it for me?* Not Andie. He doubted the thought of a reward for her participation had even entered her head. He would have to entice her with an offer she couldn't refuse. And save the big gun to sway her from her final refusal.

'So you're going to say "yes"?'

She shook her head vehemently. 'No. I'm not. It wouldn't be right.'

'What's the harm? You'd be helping me out.'

She spun on her heel away from him and he faced her back view, her tensely hunched shoulders, for a long moment before she turned back to confront him. 'Can't you see it makes a mockery of…of a man and a woman committing to each other? To spending their lives together in a loving union? That's what getting engaged is all about. Not sealing a business deal.'

He closed his eyes at the emotion in her voice, the blurring of her words with choking pain. Under his breath he cursed fluently. Because, from any moral point of view, she was absolutely right.

'Were you engaged to…to Anthony?' he asked.

Her eyes when she lifted them to him glistened with the sheen of unshed tears. 'Not officially. But we had our future planned, even the names of our kids chosen. That's why I know promising to marry someone isn't something you do lightly. And not…not for a scam. Do you understand?'

Of course he did. He'd once been idealistic about love and marriage and sharing his life with that one special woman. But he couldn't admit it. Or that he'd become cynical that that kind of love would ever exist for him. Too much rode on this deal. Including his integrity.

'But this isn't really getting engaged,' he said. 'It's just …a limited agreement.'

Slowly she shook her head. 'I can't help you,' she said. 'Sorry.'

Dominic braced himself. He'd had to be ruthless at times to get where he'd got. To overcome the disadvantages of his youth. *To win.*

'What if by agreeing to be my fake fiancée you were helping someone else?' he said.

She frowned. 'Like who? Helping Walter Burton to make even more billions? I honestly can't say I like the sound of that guy, linking business to people's private lives. He sounds like a hypocrite, for one thing—you know, rich men and eyes of needles and all that. I'm not lying for him.'

'Not Walter Burton. I mean your nephew Timothy.' The little boy was his big gun.

'What do you mean, Timothy?'

Dominic fired his shot. 'Agree to be my fake fiancée and I will pay for all of Timothy's medical treatment—both immediate and ongoing. No limits. Hannah tells me there's a clinic in the United States that's at the forefront of research into treatment for his condition.'

Andie stared at him. 'You've spoken to Hannah? You've told Hannah about this? That you'll pay for Timothy if I agree to—'

He put up his hand. 'Not true.'

'But you—'

'I met with Hannah the day after the dinner with your family to talk about her helping me recruit the families for the party. At that meeting—out of interest—I asked her to tell me more about Timothy. She told me about the American treatment. I offered *then* to pay all the treatment—airfares and accommodation included.'

The colour rushed back into Andie's cheeks. 'That… that was extraordinarily generous of you. What did Hannah say?'

'She refused.'

'Of course she would. She hardly knows you. A Newman wouldn't accept charity. Although I might have tried to convince her.'

'Maybe you could convince her now. If Hannah thought

I was going to be part of the family—her brother-in-law, in fact—she could hardly refuse to accept, could she? And isn't it the sooner the better for Timothy's treatment?'

Andie stared at Dominic for a very long moment, too shocked to speak. 'Th…that's coercion. Coercion of the most insidious kind,' she finally managed to choke out.

A whole lot more words she couldn't express also tumbled around in her brain. Ruthless. Conniving. Heartless. And yet…he'd offered to help Timothy well before the fake fiancée thing. *Not a Scrooge after all*. She'd thought she'd been getting to know him—but Dominic Hunt was more of a mystery to her than ever.

He drew his dark brows together. 'Coercion? I wouldn't go that far. But I did offer to help Timothy without any strings attached. Hannah refused. This way, she might accept. And your nephew will get the help he needs. I see it as a win-win scenario.'

Andie realised she was twisting the leather thronging that laced together the front of her top and stopped it. Nothing in her life had equipped her to make this kind of decision. 'You're really putting me on the spot here. Asking me to lie and be someone I'm not—'

'Someone you're not? How does that work? You'd still be Andie.'

She found it difficult to meet his direct, confronting gaze. Those observant grey eyes seemed to see more than she wanted him to. 'You're asking me to pretend to be… to pretend to be a woman in love. When…when I'm not.' She'd only ever been in love once—and she didn't want to trawl back in her memories to try and relive that feeling—love lost hurt way too much. She did have feelings for Dominic beyond the employer/contractor relationship—but they were more of the other 'l' word—lust rather than love.

His eyes seemed to darken. 'I suppose I am.'

'And you too,' she said. 'You would have to pretend to be in love with…with me. And it would have to look darn authentic to be convincing.'

This was why she was prevaricating. As soon as he'd mentioned Timothy, she knew she would have little choice but to agree. If it had been any other blackmailing billionaire she would probably have said "yes" straight away—living a lie for a month would be worth it for Timothy to get the treatment her family's combined resources couldn't afford.

But not *this* man. How could she blithely *pretend* to be in love with a man she wanted as much as she wanted him? It would be some kind of torture.

'I see,' he said. Had he seriously not thought this through?

'We would be playing with big emotions, here, Dominic. And other people would be affected too. My family thinks you hung the moon. They'd be delighted if we dated—a sudden engagement would both shock and worry them. At some stage I would have to introduce you to Anthony's parents—they would be happy for me and want to meet you.'

'I see where you're going,' he said, raking his hand through his hair once more in a gesture that was becoming familiar.

She narrowed her eyes. 'And yet…would it all be worth it for Hannah to accept your help for Timothy?' She put up her hand to stop him from replying. 'I'm thinking out loud here.'

'And helping me achieve something I really want.'

There must be something more behind his drive to get this American deal. She hoped she'd discover it one day, sooner rather than later. It might help her understand him.

'You've backed me into a corner here, Dominic, and I can't say I appreciate it. How can I say "no" to such an incredible opportunity for Timothy?'

'Does that mean your answer is "yes"?'

She tilted her chin upwards—determined not to capitulate too readily to something about which she still had serious doubts. 'That's an unusual way to put it, Dominic—rather like you've made me a genuine proposal.'

Dominic pulled a face but it didn't dull the glint of triumph in his eyes. He thought he'd won. But she was determined to get something out of this deal for herself too.

Andie had no doubt if she asked for recompense—money, gifts—he'd give it to her. Dominic was getting what he wanted. Timothy would be getting what he so desperately needed. But what about *her*?

She wasn't interested in jewellery or fancy shopping. What she wanted was *him*. She wanted to kiss him, she wanted to hold him and she very much wanted to make love with him. Not for fake—for real.

There was a very good chance this arrangement would end in tears—her tears. But if she agreed to a fake engagement with this man, who attracted her like no other, she wanted what a fiancée might be expected to have—*him*. She thought, with a little shiver of desire, about what he'd said: *pleasure all the way.* She would be fine with that.

'Would it help if I made it sound like a genuine proposal?' he said, obviously bemused.

That hurt. Because the way he spoke made it sound as if there was no way he would ever make a genuine proposal to her. Not that she wanted that—heck, she hardly knew the guy. But it put her on warning. *Let's be honest,* she thought. She wanted him in her bed. But she also wanted to make darn sure she didn't get hurt. This was just a business deal to him—nothing personal involved.

'Do it,' she said, pointing to the floor. 'The full down-on-bended-knee thing.'

'Seriously?' he said, dark brows raised.

'Yes,' she said imperiously.

He grinned. 'Okay.'

The tall, black denim-clad hunk obediently knelt down on one knee, took her left hand in both of his and looked up into her face. 'Andie, will you do me the honour of becoming my fake fiancée?' he intoned in that deep, so-sexy voice.

Looking down at his roughly handsome face, Andie didn't know whether to laugh or cry. 'Yes, I accept your proposal,' she said in a voice that wasn't quite steady.

Dominic squeezed her hand hard as relief flooded his face. He got up from bended knee and for a moment she thought he might kiss her.

'But there are conditions,' she said, pulling away and letting go of his hand.

CHAPTER NINE

ANDIE ALMOST LAUGHED out loud at Dominic's perplexed expression. He was most likely used to calling the shots—in both business and his relationships. 'Conditions?' he asked.

'Yes, conditions,' she said firmly. 'Come on over to the sofa and I'll run through the list with you. I need to sit down; these heels aren't good for pacing in.' The polished concrete floor was all about looks rather than comfort.

'Do I have any choice about these "conditions"?' he grumbled.

'I think you'll see the sense in them,' she said. This was not going to go all his way. There was danger in this game she'd been coerced into playing and she wanted to make sure she and her loved ones were not going to get hurt by it.

She led him over to the red leather modular sofa in the living area. The apartment in an old converted factory warehouse was owned by one of her roommates and had been furnished stylishly with Andie's help. She flopped down on the sofa, kicked off the leopard stilettos that landed in an animal print clash on the zebra-patterned floor rug, and patted the seat next to her.

As Dominic sat down, his muscular thighs brushed against hers and she caught her breath until he settled at a not-quite-touching distance from her, his arm resting on the back of the sofa behind her. She had to close her eyes momentarily to deal with the rush of awareness from his already familiar scent, the sheer maleness of him in such close proximity.

'I'm interested to hear what you say,' he said, angling his powerful body towards her. He must work out a lot to have a chest like that. She couldn't help but wonder what it would feel like to splay her hands against those hard muscles, to press her body against his.

But it appeared he was having no such sensual thoughts about *her.* She noticed he gave a surreptitious glance to his watch.

'Hey, no continually checking on the clock,' she said. 'You have to give time to an engagement. Especially a make-believe one, if we're to make it believable. Not to mention your fake fiancée just might feel a tad insulted.'

She made her voice light but she meant every word of it. She had agreed to play her role in this charade and was now committed to making it work.

'Fair enough,' he said with a lazy half-smile. 'Is that one of your conditions?'

'Not one on its own as such, but it will fit into the others.'

'Okay, hit me with the conditions.' He feinted a boxer's defence that made her smile.

'Condition Number One,' she said, holding up the index finger of her left hand. 'Hannah never knows the truth—not now, not ever—that our engagement is a sham,' she said. 'In fact, none of my family is *ever* to know the truth.'

'Good strategy,' said Dominic. 'In fact, I'd extend that. *No one* should ever know. Both business partners and friends.'

'Agreed,' she said. It would be difficult to go through with this without confiding in a friend but it had to be that way. *No one must know how deeply attracted she was to him.* She didn't want anyone's pity when she and Dominic went their separate ways.

'Otherwise, the fallout from people discovering they'd been deceived could be considerable,' he said. 'What's next?'

She held up her middle finger. 'Condition Number Two—a plausible story. We need to explain why we got engaged so quickly. So start thinking…'

'Couldn't we just have fallen for each other straight away?'

Andie was taken aback. She hadn't expected anything that romantic from Dominic Hunt. 'You mean like "love at first sight"?'

'Exactly.'

'Would that be believable?'

He shook his head in mock indignation. 'Again you continue to insult me…'

'I didn't mean…' She'd certainly felt *something* for him at first sight. Sitting next to him on this sofa, she was feeling it all over again. But it wasn't *love*—she knew only too well what it was like to love. To love and to lose the man she loved in such a cruel way. Truth be told, she wasn't sure she wanted to love again. It hurt too much to lose that love.

'I don't like the lying aspect of this any more than you do,' he said. He removed his arm from the back of the sofa so he could lean closer to her, both hands resting on his knees. 'Why not stick to the truth as much as possible? You came to organise my party. I was instantly smitten, wooed you and won you.'

'And I was a complete walkover,' she said dryly.

'So we change it—you made me work very hard to win you.'

'In two weeks—and you away for one of them?' she said. 'Good in principle. But we might have to fudge the timeline a little.'

'It can happen,' he said. 'Love at first sight, I mean. My

parents…apparently they fell for each other on day one and were married within mere months of meeting. Or so my aunt told me.'

His eyes darkened and she remembered he'd only been eleven years old when left an orphan. If she'd lost her parents at that age, her world would have collapsed around her—as no doubt his had. But he was obviously trying to revive a happy memory of his parents.

'How lovely—a real-life romance. Did they meet in Australia or England?'

'London. They were both schoolteachers; my mother was living in England. She came to his school as a temporary mathematics teacher; he taught chemistry.'

Andie decided not to risk a feeble joke about their meeting being explosive. Not when the parents' love story had ended in tragedy. 'No wonder you're clever then, with such smart parents.'

'Yes,' he said, making the word sound like an end-of-story punctuation mark. She knew only too well what it was like not to want to pursue a conversation about a lost loved one.

'So we have a precedent for love at first sight in your family,' she said. 'I…I fell for Anthony straight away too. So for both of us an…an instant attraction—if not *love*—could be feasible.' Instant and ongoing for her—but he was not to know that.

That Dominic had talked about his parents surprised her. For her, thinking about Anthony—as always—brought a tug of pain to her heart but this time also a reminder of the insincerity of this venture with Dominic. She knew what real commitment should feel like. But for Timothy to get that vital treatment she was prepared to compromise on her principles.

'Love at first sight it is,' he said.

'*Attraction* at first sight,' she corrected him.

'Surely it would had to have led to love for us to get engaged,' he said.

'True,' she conceded. He tossed around concepts of love and commitment as if they were concepts with which to barter, not deep, abiding emotions between two people who cared enough about each other to pledge a lifetime together. *Till death us do part.* She could never think of that part of a marriage ceremony without breaking down. She shouldn't be thinking of it now.

'Next condition?' he said.

She skipped her ring finger, which she had trouble keeping upright, and went straight for her pinkie. 'Condition Number Three: no dating other people—for the duration of the engagement, that is.'

'I'm on board with that one,' he said without hesitation.

'Me too,' she said. She hadn't even thought about any man but Dominic since the moment she'd met him, so that was not likely to be a hardship.

He sat here next to her in jeans and T-shirt like a regular thirty-two-year-old guy—not a secretive billionaire who had involved her in a scheme to deceive family and friends to help him make even more money. If he were just your everyday handsome hunk she would make her interest in him known. But her attraction went beyond his good looks and muscles to the complex man she sensed below his confident exterior. She had seen only intriguing hints of those hidden depths—she wanted to discover more.

Andie's thumb went up next. 'Resolution Number Four: I dump you, not the other way around. When this comes to an end, that is.'

'Agreed—and I'll be a gentleman about it. But I ask you not to sell your story. I don't want to wake up one morning to the headline *"My Six Weeks with Scrooge".*'

He could actually *joke* about being a Scrooge—Dominic had come a long way.

'Of course,' she said. 'I promise not to say *"I Hopped Out of the Billionaire's Bed"* either. Seriously, I would never talk to the media. You can be reassured of that.'

'No tacky headlines, just a simple civilised break-up to be handled by you,' he said.

They both fell silent for a moment. Did he feel stricken by the same melancholy she did at the thought of the imagined break-up of a fake engagement? And she couldn't help thinking she'd like a chance to hop *into* his bed before she hopped *out* of it.

'On to Condition Number Five,' she said, holding up all five fingers as she could not make her ring finger stand on its own. 'We have to get to know each other. So we don't get caught out on stuff we would be expected to know about each other if we were truly…committing to a life together.'

How different this fake relationship would be to a real relationship—getting to know each other over shared experiences, shared laughter, shared tears, long lazy mornings in bed…

Dominic sank down further into the sofa, his broad shoulders hunched inward. 'Yup.' It was more a grunt than a word.

'You don't sound keen to converse?'

'What sort of things?' he said with obvious reluctance. Not for the first time, she had a sense of secrets deeply held.

'For one thing, I need to know more about your marriage and how it ended.' And more about his time on the streets. And about that broken nose and scarred knuckles. And why he had let people believe he was a Scrooge when he so obviously wasn't. Strictly speaking, she probably didn't *need* to know all that about him for a fake engagement. Fact was, she *wanted* to know it.

'I guess I can talk to you about my marriage,' he said,

still not sounding convinced. 'But there are things about my life that I would rather remain private.'

What things? 'Just so long as I'm not made a fool of at some stage down the track by not knowing something a real fiancée would have known.'

'Fine,' he grunted in a response that didn't give her much confidence. She ached to know more about him. And yet there was that shadow she sensed. She wouldn't push for simple curiosity's sake.

'As far as I'm concerned, my life's pretty much an open book,' she said, in an effort to encourage him to open up about his life—or past, to be more specific. 'Just ask what you need to know about me and I'll do my best to answer honestly.'

Was any person's life truly an open book? Like anyone else, she had doubts and anxieties and dumb things she'd done that she'd regretted, but nothing lurked that she thought could hinder an engagement. No one would criticise her for finding love again after five years. In truth, she knew they would be glad for her. So would Anthony.

She remembered one day, lying together on the beach. *'I would die if I lost you,'* she'd said to Anthony.

'Don't say that,' he'd said. *'If anything happened to me, I'd want you to find another guy. But why are we talking like this? We're both going to live until we're a hundred.'*

'Why not schedule in a question-and-answer session?' Dominic said.

She pulled her thoughts back to the present. 'Good idea,' she said. 'Excellent idea, in fact.'

Dominic rolled his eyes in response.

'Oh,' she said. 'You weren't serious. I…I was.'

'No, you're right. I guess there's no room for spontaneity in a fake engagement.' It was a wonder he could get the words out when his tongue was so firmly in his cheek. 'A question-and-answer session it is. At a time to be determined.'

'Good idea,' she said, feeling disconcerted. Was all this just a game to him?

'Are there any more conditions to come?' he asked. 'You're all out of fingers on one hand, by the way.'

'There is one more very important condition to come—and may I remind you I do have ten fingers—but first I want to hear if there's anything you want to add.'

She actually had two more conditions, but the final condition she could not share with him: *that she could not fall for him.* She couldn't deal with the fallout in terms of pain if she were foolish enough to let down the guard on her heart.

Andie's beautiful green eyes had sparkled with good humour in spite of the awkward position he had put her into. *Coerced* her into. But now her eyes seemed to dim and Dominic wondered if she was being completely honest about being an 'open book'.

Ironically, he already knew more about Andie, the fake fiancée, than he'd known about Tara when he'd got engaged to her for real. His ex-wife had kept her true nature under wraps until well after she'd got the wedding band on her finger. *What you see is what you get.* He so wanted to believe that about Andie.

'My condition? You have to wear a ring,' he said. 'I want to get you an engagement ring straight away. Today. Once Tara sees that she'll know it's serious. And the press will too. Not to mention a symbol for when we meet with Walter Burton.'

She shrugged. 'Okay, you get me a ring.'

'You don't want to choose it yourself?' He was taken aback. Tara had been so avaricious about jewellery.

'No. I would find it…sad. Distressing. The day I choose

my engagement ring is the day I get engaged for real. To me, the ring should be a symbol of a true commitment, not a...a prop for a charade. But I agree—I should wear one as a visible sign of commitment.'

'I'll organise it then,' he said. He had no idea why he should be disappointed at her lack of enthusiasm. She was absolutely right—the ring would be a prop. But it would also play a role in keeping it believable. 'What size ring do you wear?'

'I haven't a clue,' she said. She held up her right hand to show the collection of tiny fine silver rings on her slender fingers. Her nails were painted cream today. 'I bought these at a market and just tried them on until I found rings that fitted.' She slid off the ring from the third finger of her right hand. 'This should do the trick.' She handed it to him. It was still warm with her body heat and he held it on his palm for a moment before pocketing it.

'What style of engagement ring would you like?' he asked.

Again she shrugged. 'You choose. It's honestly not important to me.'

A hefty carat solitaire diamond would be appropriate— one that would give her a good resale value when she went to sell it after this was all over.

'Did you choose your ex-wife's engagement ring?' Andie asked.

He scowled at the reminder that he had once got engaged for real.

Andie pulled one of her endearing faces. 'Sorry. I guess that's a sensitive issue. I know we'll come to all that in our question-and-answer session. I'm just curious.'

'She chose it herself. All I had to do was pay for it.' That alone should have alerted him to what the marriage was all about—giving her access to his money and the lifestyle it bought.

'That wasn't very…romantic,' Andie said.

'There was nothing romantic about my marriage. Shall I tell you about it now and get all that out of the way?'

'If you feel comfortable with it,' she said.

'Comfortable is never a word I would relate to that time of my life,' he said. 'It was a series of mistakes.'

'If you're ready to tell me, I'm ready to listen.' He thought about how Andie had read his mood so accurately earlier this morning—giving him breakfast when he hadn't even been aware himself that he was hungry. She was thoughtful. And kind. Kindness wasn't an attribute he had much encountered in the women he had met.

'The first mistake I made with Tara was that she reminded me of someone else—a girl I'd met when I was living in the squat. Someone frail and sweet with similar colouring—someone I'd wanted to care for and look after.' It still hurt to think of Melody. Andie didn't need to know about her.

'And the second mistake?' Andie asked, seeming to understand he didn't want to speak further about Melody. She leaned forward as if she didn't want to miss a word.

'I believed her when she said she wanted children.'

'You wanted children?'

'As soon as possible. Tara said she did too.'

Andie frowned. 'But she didn't?'

Even now, bitterness rose in his throat. 'After we'd been married a year and nothing had happened, I suggested we see a doctor. Tara put it off and put it off. I thought it was because she didn't want to admit to failure. It was quite by accident that I discovered all the time I thought we'd been trying to conceive, she'd been on the contraceptive pill.'

Andie screwed up her face in an expression of disbelief and distaste. 'That's unbelievable.'

'When I confronted her, she laughed.' He relived the horror of discovering his ex-wife's treachery and the reali-

sation she didn't have it in her to love. Not him. Certainly
not a child. Fortunately, she hadn't been clever enough to
understand the sub-clauses in the pre-nuptial agreement
and divorce had been relatively straightforward.

'You had a lucky escape,' Andie said.

'That's why I never want to marry again. How could I
ever trust another woman after that?'

'I understand you would feel that way,' she said. 'But
not every woman would be like her. Me...my sisters, my
friends. I don't know anyone who would behave with such
dishonesty. Don't write off all women because of one.'

Trouble was, his wealth attracted women like Tara.

He was about to try and explain that to Andie when her
phone started to sound out a bar of classical music.

She got up from the sofa and headed for the kitchen
countertop to pick it up. 'Gemma,' she mouthed to him.
'I'd better take it.'

He nodded, grateful for the reprieve. Tara's treachery had got him into this fake engagement scenario with
Andie, who was being such a good sport about the whole
thing. He did not want to waste another word, or indeed
thought, on his ex. Again, he thanked whatever providence
had sent Andie into his life—Andie who was the opposite
of Tara in every way.

He couldn't help but overhear Andie as she chatted to
Gemma. 'Yes, yes, I saw it. We were having lunch after
the meeting that Friday. Yes, it does look romantic. No, I
didn't know anyone took a photo.'

Andie waved him over to her. 'Shall I tell her?' she
mouthed.

He gave her the thumbs-up. 'Yes,' he mouthed back
as he got up. There was no intention of keeping this 'engagement' secret. He walked over closer to Andie, who
was standing there in bare feet, looking more beautiful in
jeans than any other woman would look in a ball gown.

'Actually, Gemma, I…haven't been completely honest with you. I…uh…we…well, Dominic and I hit it off from the moment we first saw each other.'

Andie looked to Dominic and he nodded—she was doing well.

She listened to Gemma, then spoke again. 'Yes. We are…romantically involved. In fact…well…we're engaged.' She held the phone out from her ear and even Dominic could hear the excited squeals coming from Gemma.

When the squeals had subsided, Andie spoke again. 'Yes. It is sudden. I know that. But…well…you see I've learned that you have to grab your chance at happiness when you can. I…I've had it snatched away from me before.' She paused as she listened. 'Yes, that's it. I didn't want to wait. Neither did he. Gemma, I'd appreciate it if you didn't tell anyone just yet. Eliza? Well, okay, you can tell Eliza. I'd just like to tell my family first. What was that? Yes, I'll tell him.' She shut down her phone.

'So it's out,' he said.

'Yes,' she said. 'No denying it now.'

'What did Gemma ask you to tell me?'

She looked up at him. 'That she hoped you knew what a lucky guy you are to…to catch me.'

He looked down at her. 'I know very well how lucky I am. You're wonderful in every way and I appreciate what you're doing to help me.'

For a long moment he looked down into her face—still, serious, even sombre without her usual animated expression. Her eyes were full of something he couldn't put a name to. But not, he hoped, regret.

'Thank you, Andie.'

He stepped closer. For a long moment her gaze met his and held it. He saw wariness but he also saw the stirrings of what he could only read as invitation. To kiss his pretend fiancée would probably be a mistake. But it was a mistake he badly wanted to make.

He lifted his hand to her face, brushed first the smooth skin of her cheek and then the warm softness of her lips with the back of his knuckles. She stilled. Her lips parted under his touch and he could feel the tremor that ran through her body. He dropped his hand to her shoulder, then dipped his head and claimed her mouth in a firm gentle kiss. She murmured her surprise and pleasure as she kissed him back.

CHAPTER TEN

DOMINIC WAS KISSING her and it was more wonderful than Andie ever could have imagined. His firm, sensuous mouth was sure and certain on hers and she welcomed the intimate caress, the nudging of his tongue against the seam of her lips as she opened her mouth to his. His beard growth scratched her face but it was a pleasurable kind of pain. *The man knew how to kiss.*

But as he kissed her and she kissed him back she was shocked by the sudden explosion of chemistry between them that turned something gentle into something urgent and demanding. She wound her arms around his neck to bring him closer in a wild tangle of tongues and lips as she pressed herself against his hard muscular chest. He tasted of coffee and hot male and desire. Passion this instant, this insistent was a surprise.

But it was too soon.

She knew she wanted him. But she hadn't realised until now just how *much* she wanted him. And how careful she would have to be to guard her heart. Because these thrilling kisses told her that intimate contact with Dominic Hunt might just become an addiction she would find very difficult to live without. To him, this pretend engagement was a business ploy that might also develop into an entertaining game on the side. *She did not want to be a fake fiancée with benefits.*

When it came down to it, while she had dated over the

last few years, her only serious relationship had been with a boy who had adored her, and whom she had loved with all her heart. Not a man like Dominic, who had sworn off marriage and viewed commitment so lightly he could pretend to be engaged. Her common sense urged her to stop but her body wanted more, more, more of him.

With a great effort she broke away from the kiss. Her heart was pounding in triple time, her breath coming in painful gasps. She took a deep steadying breath. And then another.

'That…that was a great start on Condition Number Six,' she managed to choke out.

Dominic towered over her; his breath came in ragged gasps. He looked so darkly sensual, her heart seemed to flip right over in her chest. 'What?' he demanded. 'Stopping when we'd just started?'

'No. I…I mean the actual kiss.'

He put his hand on her shoulder, lightly stroking her in a caress that ignited shivers of delight all through her.

'So tell me about your sixth condition,' he said, his deep voice with a broken edge to it as he struggled to control his breathing.

'Condition Number Six is that we…we have to look the part.'

He frowned. 'And that means…?'

'I mean we have to act like a genuine couple. To seem to other people as if we're…we're crazy about each other. Because it would have to be…something very powerful between us for us to get engaged so quickly. In…real life, I mean.'

She found it difficult to meet his eyes. 'I was going to say we needed to get physical. And we just did…get physical. So we…uh…know that there's chemistry between us. And that…that it works.'

He dropped his hand from her shoulder to tilt her chin

upwards with his finger so she was forced to meet his gaze. 'There was never any doubt about that.'

His words thrummed through her body. That sexual attraction had been there for her the first time she'd met him. *Had he felt it too?*

'So the sixth condition is somewhat superfluous,' she said, her voice racing as she tried to ignore the hunger for him his kiss had ignited. 'I think we might be okay, there. You know, holding hands, arms around each other. Appropriate Public Displays of Affection.' It was an effort to force herself to sound matter of fact.

'This just got to be my favourite of all your conditions,' he said slowly, his eyes narrowing in a way she found incredibly sexy. 'Shall we practise some more?'

Her traitorous body wrestled down her hopelessly outmatched common sense. 'Why not?' she murmured, desperate to be in his arms again. He pulled her close and their body contact made her aware he wanted her as much as she wanted him. She sighed as she pressed her mouth to his.

Then her phone sang out its ringtone of a piano sonata. 'Leave it,' growled Dominic.

She ignored the musical tone until it stopped. But it had brought her back to reality. There was nothing she wanted more than to take Dominic by the hand and lead him up the stairs to her bedroom. She intended to have him before this contract between them came to an end.

But that intuition she usually trusted screamed at her that to make love with him on the first day of their fake engagement would be a mistake. It would change the dynamic of their relationship to something she did not feel confident of being able to handle.

No sooner had the ringtone stopped than it started again.

Andie untangled herself from Dominic's embrace and

stepped right back from him, back from the seductive reach of his muscular arms.

'I…I have to take this,' she said.

She answered the phone but had to rest against the kitchen countertop to support knees that had gone shaky and weak. Dominic leaned back against the wall opposite her and crossed his arms against his powerful chest. His muscles flexed as he did so and she had to force herself to concentrate on the phone call.

'Yes, Eliza, it's true. I know—it must have been a surprise to you. A party?' Andie looked up to Dominic and shook her head. He nodded. She spoke to Eliza. 'No. We don't want an engagement party. Yes, I know we're party queens and it's what we do.' She rolled her eyes at Dominic and, to her relief, he smiled. 'The Christmas party is more than enough to handle at the moment,' she said to Eliza.

We. She and Dominic were a couple now. A fake couple. It would take some getting used to. So would handling the physical attraction between them.

'The wedding?' Eliza's question about the timing of the wedding flustered her. 'We…we…uh…next year some time. Yes, I know next year is only next month. The wedding won't be next month, that's for sure.' *The* wedding— wouldn't a loved-up fiancée have said *our* wedding?

She finished the call to Eliza and realised her hands were clammy. 'This is not going to be easy,' she said to Dominic.

'I never thought it would be,' he said. Was there a double meaning there?

'I have no experience in this kind of deception. The first thing Eliza asked me was when are we getting married. She put me on the spot. I…I struggled to find an answer.'

He nodded slowly. 'I suggest we say we've decided on a long engagement. That we're committed but want to use the engagement time to get to know each other better.'

'That sounds good,' she said.

The deceptive words came so easily to him while she was so flustered she could scarcely think. She realised how hopelessly mismatched they were: he was more experienced, wealthier, from a completely different background. And so willing to lie.

And yet... That kiss had only confirmed how much she wanted him.

Her phone rang out again. 'Why do I get the feeling this phone will go all day long?' she said, a note of irritation underscoring her voice. She looked on the caller ID. 'It's my fashion editor friend, Karen. I knew Gemma wouldn't be able to stop at Eliza,' she told Dominic as she answered it.

The first part of the conversation was pretty much a repeat of the conversation she'd had with Gemma. But then Karen asked should she start scouting around for her wedding dress. Karen hunted down bargain-priced clothes for her; of course she'd want to help her with a wedding. 'My wedding dress? We...uh...haven't set a date for the wedding yet. Yes, I suppose it's never too early to think about the dress. Simple? Vintage inspired? Gorgeous shoes?' She laughed and hoped Karen didn't pick up on the shrill edge to her laughter. 'You know my taste only too well, Karen. A veil? A modest lace veil? Okay. Yes. I'll leave it to you. Thank you.'

'Your friends move fast,' Dominic said when she'd disconnected the call.

'They're so thrilled for me. After...after...well, you know. My past.' Her past of genuine love, unsullied by lies and deception.

'Of course,' he said.

She couldn't bring herself to say anything about the kisses they'd shared. It wasn't the kind of thing she found easy to talk about. Neither, it appeared, did he.

He glanced down at his watch. The action drew her attention to his hands. She noticed again how attractive they were, with long strong fingers. And thought how she would like to feel them on her body. Stroking. Caressing. Exploring. *She had to stop this.*

'I know I'm breaking the terms of one of your conditions,' he said. 'But I do have to get to the office. There are cancelled meetings in other states to reschedule and staff who need to talk to me.'

'And I've got to finalise the furniture hire for the Christmas party. With two hundred people for lunch, we need more tables and chairs. It's sobering, to have all those families in need on Christmas Day.'

'Hannah assures me it's the tip of a tragic iceberg,' said Dominic.

They both paused for a long moment before she spoke. 'I also have to work on a tiaras-and-tuxedos-themed twenty-first party. Ironic, isn't it, after what we've just been saying?' But organising parties was her job and brought not only employment to her and her partners but also the caterers, the waiting staff and everyone else involved.

'I didn't think twenty-first parties were important any more, with eighteen the legal age of adulthood,' Dominic said.

'They're still very popular. This lovely girl turning twenty-one still lives at home with her parents and has three more years of university still ahead of her to become a veterinarian. I have to organise tiaras for her dogs.'

'Wh…what?' he spluttered. 'Did you say you're putting a tiara on a *dog*?'

'Her dogs are very important to her; they'll be honoured guests at the party.'

He scowled. 'I like dogs but that's ridiculous.'

'We're getting more and more bookings for dog parties.

A doggy birthday boy or girl invites their doggy friends. They're quite a thing. And getting as competitive as the kids' parties. Of course it's a learning curve for a party planner—considering doggy bathroom habits, for one thing.'

'That is the stupidest—'

Andie put up her hand. 'Don't be too quick to judge. The doggy parties are really about making the humans happy—I doubt the dogs could care less. Frivolity can be fun. Eliza and I have laid bets on how many boys will arrive wearing tiaras to the vet student's twenty-first.'

She had to smile at his bah-humbug expression.

'By the time I was twenty-one, I had established a career in real estate and had my first million in sight.'

That interested her. 'I'd love to know about—'

He cut her off. 'Let's save that for the question-and-answer session, shall we?'

'Which will start…?'

'This afternoon. Can you come to my place?'

'Sure. It doesn't hurt to visit the party site as many times as I can.'

'Only this time you'll be coming to collect your engagement ring.'

'Of…of course.' She had forgotten about that. In a way, she dreaded it. 'And to find out more about you, fake fiancé. We have to be really well briefed to face my family tomorrow evening.'

She and Anthony had joked that by the time they'd paid off their student loans all they'd be able to afford for an engagement ring would be a ring pull from a can of soft drink. The ring pull would have had so much more meaning than this cynical exercise.

She felt suddenly subdued at the thought of deceiving her family. Her friends were used to the ups and downs of dating. A few weeks down the track, they'd take a broken engagement in their stride. If those kisses were anything to go by, she might be more than a tad upset when her time with Dominic came to an end. She pummelled back down to somewhere deep inside her the shred of hope that perhaps something real could happen between them after the engagement charade was done.

'When will you tell your parents?' Dominic asked.

'Today. They'd be hurt beyond belief if they found out from someone else.'

'And you'll talk to Hannah about Timothy?'

'At the family dinner. We should speak to her and Paul together.'

'I hope she won't be too difficult to convince. I really want to help that little boy.'

'I know,' she said, thinking of how grateful her family would be to him. How glad she was she'd agreed to all this for her tiny nephew's sake. But what about Dominic's family? This shouldn't be all about hers. 'What about your aunt? Do we need to tell her?'

The shutters came slamming down. 'No. She's out of the picture.'

The way he said it let her know not to ask more. Not now anyway.

Dominic shrugged on his leather jacket in preparation to go. She stared, dumbstruck, feasting her eyes on him. *He was so hot.* She still felt awkward after their passionate kissing session. Should she reach up and kiss him on the cheek?

While she was making up her mind, he pulled her close for a brief, exciting kiss on her mouth. She doubted there could be any other type of kiss but exciting from Dominic. 'Happy to fulfil Condition Number Six at any time,' he said, very seriously.

She smiled, the tension between them immediately dissipated. But she wasn't ready to say goodbye just yet.

'Before you go...' She picked up her smartphone again. 'The first thing my friends who don't know you will want to see is a photo of my surprise new fiancé.'

He ran his hand over his unshaven chin. 'Like this? Can't it wait?'

'I like your face like that. It's hot. No need to shave on my behalf.' Without thinking, she put her fingers up to her cheek, where there was probably stubble rash. *His kiss had felt so good.*

'If you say so,' he said, looking pleased.

'Just lean against the door there,' she said. 'Look cool.'

He slouched against the door and sent her a smouldering look. The wave of want that crashed through her made her nearly drop the phone. 'Do I look *cool*?' he said in a self-mocking tone. 'I thought you liked *hot*?'

'You know exactly what I mean.' She was discovering a light-hearted side to Dominic she liked very much.

Their gazes met and they both burst into laughter. He looked even more gorgeous when he laughed, perfect teeth white in his tanned face, and she immediately captured a few more images of him. Who would recognise this good-humoured hunk in jeans and leather jacket as the billionaire Scrooge of legend?

'What about a selfie of us together?' she asked. 'In the interests of authenticity,' she hastily added.

Bad idea. She stood next to him, aware of every centimetre of body contact, and held her phone out in front of them. She felt more self-conscious than she could ever remember feeling. He pulled her in so their faces were close together. She smiled and clicked, and as she clicked again he kissed her on the cheek.

'That will be cute,' she said.

'Another?' he asked. This time he kissed her on the mouth. *Click. Click. Click.* And then she forgot to click.

After he had left, Andie spent more minutes than she should scrolling through the photos on her phone. *No one would know they were faking it.*

CHAPTER ELEVEN

DOMINIC NOW KNEW more about diamond engagement rings than even a guy who was genuinely engaged to be married needed to know. He'd thought he could just march into Sydney's most exclusive jewellery store and hand over an investment-sized price for a big chunk of diamond. Not so.

The sales guy—rather, *executive consultant*—who had greeted him and ushered him into a private room had taken the purchase very seriously. He'd hit Dominic with a barrage of questions. It was unfortunate that the lady was unable to be there because it was very important the ring would suit her personality. What were the lady's favourite colours? What style of clothes did she favour? Her colouring?

'Were you able to answer the questions?' Andie asked, her lips curving into her delightful smile.

She had just arrived at his house. After she'd taken some measurements in the old ballroom, he had taken her out to sit in the white Hollywood-style chairs by the pool. Again, she looked as if she belonged. She wore a natural-coloured linen dress with her hair piled up and a scarf twisted and tied right from the base of her neck to the top of her head. It could have looked drab and old-fashioned but, on her, with her vintage sunglasses and orange lipstick, it looked just right.

Last time she'd been there he'd been so caught up with her he hadn't thought to ask her would she like a drink.

He didn't want a live-in housekeeper—he valued his privacy too much—but his daily housekeeper had been this morning and the refrigerator was well stocked. He'd carried a selection of cool drinks out to the poolside table between their two chairs.

'You're finding this story amusing, aren't you?' he said, picking up his iced tea.

She took off her sunglasses. 'Absolutely. I had no idea the rigmarole involved in buying an engagement ring.'

'Me neither. I thought I'd just march in, point out a diamond ring and pay for it.' This was a first for him.

'Me too,' said Andie. 'I thought that's what guys did when they bought a ring.'

'Oh, no. First of all, I'd done completely the wrong thing in not having you with me. He was too discreet to ask where you were, so I didn't have to come up with a creative story to explain your absence.'

'One less lie required anyway,' she said with a twist of her lovely mouth. 'Go on with the story—I'm fascinated.'

'Apparently, the done thing is to have a bespoke ring—like the business suits I have made to measure.'

'A bespoke ring? Who knew?' she said, her eyes dancing.

'Instead, I had to choose from their ready-to-wear couture pieces.'

'I had no idea such a thing existed,' she said with obvious delight. *Her smile.* It made him feel what he'd thought he'd never feel again, made him want what he'd thought he'd never want.

'You should have been there,' he said. 'You would have had fun.' He'd spent the entire time in the jewellery store wishing she'd been by his side. He could imagine her suppressing giggles as the consultant had run through his over-the-top sales pitch.

'Perhaps,' she said, but her eyes dimmed. 'You know

my reasons for not wanting to get involved in the purchase. Anyway, what did you tell them about my—' she made quote marks in the air with her fingers '—"personal style"? That must have put you on the spot?'

'I told the consultant about your misbehaving skirt—only I didn't call it that, of course. I told him about your shoes that laced up your calves. I told him about your turquoise necklace and your outsized earrings. I told him about your leopard-print shoes and your white trousers.'

Andie's eyes widened. 'You remember all that about what I wear?'

'I did say I was observant,' he said.

Ask him to remember what Party Planners Numbers One to Three had been wearing for their interviews and he would scarcely recall it. But he remembered every detail about her since that errant breeze at his front door had blown Andie into his life.

At the jewellery store, once he'd relaxed into the conversation with the consultant, Dominic had also told him how Andie was smart and creative and a touch unconventional and had the most beautiful smile and a husky, engaging laugh. 'This is a lucky lady,' the guy had said. 'You must love her very much.'

That had thrown Dominic. 'Yes,' he'd muttered. *Love* could not enter into this. He did not want Andie to get hurt. And hurt wasn't on his personal agenda either. He didn't think he had it in him to love. To give love you had to be loved—and genuine love was not something that had been part of his life.

'So… I'm curious,' said Andie. What kind of ring did you—did I—end up with?'

'Not the classic solitaire I would have chosen. The guy said you'd find it boring.'

'Of course I wouldn't have found it boring,' she said not very convincingly.

'Why do I not believe you?' he said.

'Stop teasing me and show me the darn ring,' she said.

Dominic took out the small, leather, case from his inside suit jacket pocket. 'I hope you like it,' he said. *He wanted her to like it.* He didn't know why it was suddenly so important that she did.

He opened the case and held it out for Andie to see. Her eyes widened and she caught her breath. 'It...it's exquisite,' she said.

'Is it something you think you could wear?' he asked.

'Oh, yes,' she said. 'I love it.'

'It's called a halo set ring,' he said. 'The ring of little diamonds that surround the big central diamond is the halo. And the very narrow split band—again set with small diamonds—is apparently very fashionable.'

'That diamond is enormous,' she said, drawing back. 'I'd be nervous to wear it.'

'I got it well insured,' he said.

'Good,' she said. 'If I lost it, I'd be paying you back for the rest of my life and probably still be in debt.'

'The ring is yours, Andie.'

'I know, for the duration,' she said. 'I promise to look after it.' She crossed her heart.

'You misunderstand. The ring is yours to keep after... after all this has come to an end.'

She frowned and shook her head vehemently. 'No. That wasn't part of the deal. Timothy's treatment was the deal. I give this ring back to you when...when I dump you.'

'We'll see about that,' he said, not wanting to get into an argument with her. As far as he was concerned, this ring was *hers*. She could keep it or sell it or give it away— he never wanted it back. 'Now, shouldn't I be getting that diamond on your finger?'

He was surprised to find his hand wasn't steady as he took the ring out of its hinged case. It glittered and sparkled as the afternoon sunlight danced off the multi-cut facets of the diamonds. 'Hold out your hand,' he said.

'No', she said, again shaking her head. 'Give it to me and I'll put it on myself. This isn't a real engagement and I don't want to jinx myself. When I get engaged for real, my real fiancé will put my ring on my wedding finger.'

Again, Dominic felt disappointed. Against all reason. He wanted to put the ring on her finger. But he understood why he shouldn't. He felt a pang of regret that he most likely would never again be anyone's 'real fiancé'—and a pang of what he recognised as envy for the man who would win Andie's heart for real.

He put the ring back in its case. 'You do want to get married one day?'

He wasn't sure if she was still in love with the memory of her first boyfriend—and that no man would be able to live up to that frozen-in-time ideal. Melody had been his first love—but he certainly held no romanticised memories of her.

'Of course I do. I want to get married and have a family. I...I... It took me a long time to get over the loss of my dreams of a life with Anthony. I couldn't see myself with anyone but him. But that was five years ago. Now... I think I'm ready to move on.'

Dominic had to clear his throat to speak. 'Okay, I see your point. Better put on the ring yourself,' he said.

Tentatively, she lifted the ring from where it nestled in the velvet lining of its case. 'I'm terrified I'll drop it and it will fall into the pool.' She laughed nervously as she slid it on to the third finger of her left hand. 'There—it's on.' She held out her hand, fingers splayed to better display the ring. 'It's a perfect fit,' she said. 'You did well.'

'It looks good on you,' he said.

'That sales guy knew his stuff,' she said. 'I can't stop looking at it. It's the most beautiful ring I've ever seen.'

She looked up at him. 'I still have my doubts about the wisdom of this charade. But I will enjoy wearing this magnificent piece of jewellery. Thank you for choosing something so perfect.'

'Thank you for helping me out with this crazy scheme,' he said. The scheme that had seemed crazy the moment he'd proposed it and which got crazier and crazier as it went along. But it was important he sealed that deal with Walter Burton. And was it such a bad thing to have to spend so much time with Andie?

Andie took a deep breath to try and clear her head of the conflicting emotions aroused by wearing the exquisite ring that sat so perfectly on her finger. *The ring pull would have been so much more valuable.* This enormous diamond with its many surrounding tiny diamonds symbolised not love and commitment but the you-scratch-my-back-and-I'll-scratch-yours deal between her and Dominic.

Still, she couldn't help wondering how he could have chosen a ring so absolutely *her*.

'I've been thinking about our getting-to-know-each-other session,' she said. 'Why don't we each ask the other three questions?'

'Short and to the point,' he said with obvious relief.

'Or longer, as needs might be. I want to be the best fake fiancée I can. No way do I want to be caught out on something important I should know about you. I didn't like the feeling this morning when I froze as Karen questioned me about our wedding plans.'

Dominic drank from his iced tea. To give himself time to think? Or plan evasive action? 'I see where you're going. Let's see if we can make it work.'

Andie settled back in the chair. She didn't know whether to be disappointed or relieved there was a small table between her and Dominic. She would not be averse to his thigh nudged against hers—at the same time, it would undoubtedly be distracting. 'Okay. I'll start. My Question Number One is: How did you get from street kid to billionaire?'

Dominic took his time to put his glass back down on the table. 'Before I reply, let's get one thing straight.' His gaze was direct. 'My answers are for you and you alone. What I tell you is to go no further.'

'Agreed,' she said, meeting his gaze full-on. 'Can we get another thing straight? You can trust me.'

'Just so long as we know where we stand.'

'I'm surprised you're not making me sign a contract.' She said the words half in jest but the expression that flashed across his face in response made her pause. She sat forward in her seat. 'You thought about a contract, didn't you?'

With Dominic back in his immaculate dark business suit, clean-shaven, hair perfectly groomed, she didn't feel as confident with him as she had this morning.

'I did think of a contract and quickly dismissed it,' he said. 'I do trust you, Andie.'

Surely he must be aware that she would not jeopardise Timothy's treatment in any way? 'I'm glad to hear that, Dominic, because this won't work if we don't trust each other—it goes both ways. Let's start. C'mon—answer my question.'

He still didn't answer. She waited, aware of the palm leaves above rustling in the same slight breeze that ruffled the aquamarine surface of the pool, the distant barking of a neighbour's dog.

'You know I hate this?' he said finally.

'I kind of get that,' she said. 'But I couldn't "marry" a man whose past remained a dark secret to me.'

Even after the question-and-answer session, she suspected big chunks of his past might remain a secret from her. Maybe from anyone.

He dragged in a deep breath as if to prepare himself for something unpleasant. 'As I have already mentioned, at age seventeen, I was homeless. I was living in an underground car park on the site of an abandoned shopping centre project in one of the roughest areas of Brisbane. The buildings had only got to the foundation stage. The car park was…well, you can imagine what an underground car park that had never been completed was like. It was a labyrinth of unfinished service areas and elevator shafts. No lights, pools of water whenever it rained, riddled with rats and cockroaches.'

'And human vermin too, I'll bet.' Andie shuddered. 'What a scary place for a teenager to be living—and dangerous.'

He had come from such a dark place. She could gush with sympathy and pity. But she knew instinctively that was not what he wanted to hear. Show how deeply moved she was at the thought of seventeen-year-old Dominic living such a perilous life and he would clam up. And she wanted to hear more.

Dominic's eyes assumed a dark, faraway look as though he was going back somewhere in his mind he had no desire to revisit. 'It was dangerous and smelly and seemed like hell. But it was also somewhere safer to sleep than on the actual streets. Darkness meant shadows you could hide in, and feel safe even if it was only an illusion of safety.'

She reached out and took the glass from his hand; he seemed unaware he was gripping it so tightly he might break it. 'Your home life must have been kind of hellish too for you to have preferred that over living with your aunt.'

'Hell? You could say that.' The grim set of his mouth let her know that no more would be forthcoming on that subject.

'Your life on the streets must have been…terrifying.'

'I toughened up pretty quick. One thing I had in my favour was I was big—the same height I am now and strong from playing football at school. It was a rough-around-the-edges kind of school, and I'd had my share of sorting out bullies there.' He raised his fists into a fighting position in a gesture she thought was unconscious.

So scratch the elite private school. She realised now that Dominic was a self-made man. And his story of triumph over adversity fascinated her. 'So you could defend yourself against thugs and…and predators.'

Her heart went out to him. At seventeen she'd had all the security of a loving family and comfortable home. But she knew first-hand from her foster sisters that not all young people were that fortunate. It seemed that the young Dominic had started off with loving parents and a secure life but had spiralled downwards from then on. What the heck was wrong with the aunt to have let that happen?

She reached over the table and trailed her fingers across his scarred knuckles. 'That's how you got these?' It was amazing the familiarity a fake engagement allowed.

'I got in a lot of fights,' he said.

'And this?' She traced the fine scar at the side of his mouth.

'Another fight,' he said.

She dropped her hands to her sides, again overwhelmed by that urge to comfort him. 'You were angry and frightened.'

He shifted uncomfortably in his seat. 'All that.'

'But then you ended up with this.' She waved her hand to encompass the immaculate art deco pool, the expensively landscaped gardens, the superb house. It was an oasis of beauty and luxury.

'My fighting brought me to the attention of the police. I was charged with assault,' he said bluntly.

She'd thought his tough exterior was for real—had sensed the undercurrents of suppressed rage.

'Believe me, the other guy deserved it,' he said with an expression of grim satisfaction. 'He was drug-dealing scum.'

'What happened? With the police, I mean.' He'd been seventeen—still a kid. All she'd been fighting at that age was schoolgirl drama.

'I got lucky. The first piece of luck was that I was under eighteen and not charged as an adult. The second piece of luck was I was referred to a government social worker— Jim, his name was. Poor man, having to deal with the sullen, unhappy kid I was then couldn't have been easy. Jim was truly one of the good guys—still is. He won my confidence and got me away from that squat, to the guidance of another social worker friend of his down the Queensland Gold Coast.'

'Sun, surf and sand,' she said. She knew it sounded flippant but Dominic would not want her to pity his young self.

'And a booming real estate market. The social worker down there was a good guy too. He got me a job as a gofer in a real estate agency. I was paid a pittance but it was a start and I liked it there. To cut a long story short, I was soon promoted to the sales team. I discovered I was good at selling the lifestyle dream, not just the number of bedrooms and bathrooms. I became adept at gauging what was important to the client.'

'Because you were observant,' she said. And tough and resilient and utterly admirable.

'That's important. Especially when I realised the role the woman played in a residential sale. Win her over and you more than likely closed the sale.'

Andie could see how those good looks, along with intuition and charm and the toughness to back it up, could have accelerated him ahead. 'Fascinating. And incredible how you've kept all the details away from the public. Surely people must have tried to research you, would have wanted to know your story?'

'As a juvenile, my record is sealed. I've never spoken about it. It's a time of my life I want well behind me. Without Jim the social worker, I might have gone the other way.'

'You mean you could have ended up as a violent thug or a drug dealer? I don't believe that for a second.'

He shrugged those broad street-fighter shoulders. 'I appreciate your faith in me. But, like so many of my fellow runaways, I could so easily have ended up...broken.'

Andie struggled to find an answer to that. 'It...it's a testament to your strength of character that you didn't.'

'If you say,' he said. But he looked pleased. 'Once I'd made enough money to have my own place and a car—nowhere as good as your hatchback, I might add—I started university part-time. I got lucky again.'

'You passed with honours?' She hadn't seen a university degree anywhere in her research on him but there was no harm in asking.

'No. I soon realised I knew more about making money and how business operated than some of the teachers in my commerce degree. I dropped out after eighteen months. But in a statistics class I met Jake Marlow. He was a brilliant, misunderstood geek. Socially, I still considered myself an outcast. We became friends.'

'And business partners, you said.' He was four years older than she was, and yet had lived a lifetime more. And had overcome terrible odds to get where he had.

'He was playing with the concept of ground-breaking online business software tools but no bank would loan him the money to develop them. I was riding high on commissions. We set up a partnership. I put in the money he needed. I could smell my first million.'

'Let me guess—it was an amazing success?'

'That software is used by thousands of businesses around the world to manage their digital workflow. We made a lot of money very quickly. Jake is still developing successful new software.' His obvious pride in his friend warmed his words.

'And you're still business partners.'

He nodded. 'The success of our venture gave me the investment dollars I needed to also spin off into my own separate business developing undervalued homemaker centres. We call them bulky goods centres—furnishing, white goods, electricals.'

'I guess the Gold Coast got too small for you.' That part she'd been able to research.

'I moved to Sydney. You know the rest.'

In silence she drank her mineral water with lime, he finished his iced tea. He'd given her a lot to think about. Was that anger that had driven him resolved? Or could it still be bubbling under the surface, ready to erupt?

He angled himself to look more directly at her. 'Now it's your turn to answer my question, Andie,' he said. 'How did you get over the death of your...of Anthony?'

She hadn't been expecting that and it hit her hard. But he'd dug deep. She had to too. 'I... I don't know that I will ever be able to forget the shock of it. One minute he was there, the next minute gone. I... I was as good as a widow, before I'd had the chance to be a bride.'

Dominic nodded, as if he understood. Of course he'd lost his parents.

'We were staying the weekend at his parents' beach house at Whale Beach. Ant got up very early, left a note to say he'd gone surfing, kissed me—I was asleep but awake enough to know he was going out—and then he was gone. Of course I blamed myself for not going with him. Then I was angry he'd gone out by himself.'

'Understandably,' he said and she thought again how he

seemed to see more than other people. She had no deep, dark secrets. But, if she did, she felt he'd burrow down to them without her even realising it.

'After Anthony died, I became terrified of the sea. I hated the waves—blamed them for taking him from me, which I know was all kinds of irrational. Then one day I went to the beach by myself and sat on the sand. I remember hugging my knees as I watched a teenage boy, tall and blond like Anthony, ride a wave all the way into the shore, saw the exultation on his face, the sheer joy he felt at being one with the wave.'

'If this is bringing back hurtful memories, you don't have to go any further.'

'I'm okay… When someone close dies, you look for a sign from them—I learned I wasn't alone in that when I had counselling. That boy on his board was like a message from Anthony. He died doing something he truly loved. I ran into the surf and felt somehow connected to him. It was a healing experience, a turning point in my recovery from grief.'

'That's a powerful story,' Dominic said.

'The point of it is, it's five years since he died and of course I've moved on. Anyone who might wonder if my past could affect our fake future can be assured of that. Anthony was part of my youth; we grew up together. In some ways I'm the person I am because of those happy years behind me. But I want happy years ahead of me too. I've dated. I just haven't met the right person.'

For the first time she wondered if she could feel more for Dominic than physical attraction. For a boy who had been through what he had and yet come through as the kind of man who offered to pay for a little boy's medical treatment? Who was more willing to open his house to disadvantaged people than celebrities? There was so much more to Dominic than she ever could have imagined—and the more she found out about him the more she liked about him.

And then there were those kisses she had not been able to stop thinking about—and yearning for more.

'I appreciate you telling me,' he said.

She poured herself another long, cool mineral water. Offered to pour one for Dominic, but he declined.

'On to my next question,' she said. 'It's about your family. Do you have family other than your aunt? My mother will certainly want to know because she's already writing the guest list for the wedding.'

'You told your mother about the engagement?'

'She couldn't be more delighted. In fact...well...she got quite tearful.' Andie had never felt more hypocritical than the moment she realised her mother was crying tears of joy for her.

'That's a relief,' he said.

'You could put it that way. I didn't realise quite how concerned they were about me being...lonely. Not that I am lonely, by the way—I have really good friends.' But it was not the same as having a special someone.

'I'm beginning to see that,' he said. 'I'm surprised we've been able to have this long a conversation without your phone going off.'

'That's because I switched it off,' she said. 'There'll probably be a million messages when I switch it back on.'

'So your mother didn't question our...haste?'

'No. And any guilt I felt about pulling the wool over her eyes I forced firmly to the back of my mind. Timothy getting the treatment he needs is way more important to my family than me finding a man.' She looked at him. 'So now—the guest list, your family?'

'My aunt and my mother were the only family each other had. So there is no Australian family.'

'Your aunt has...has passed away?' There was something awkward here that she didn't feel comfortable probing. But they were—supposedly—planning to get married. It made sense for her to know something of his family.

'She's in the best of residential care, paid for by me. That's all I want to say about her.'

'Okay,' she said, shaken by the closed look on his face.

'I have family in the UK but no one close since my grandparents died.'

'So no guests from your side of the family for our imaginary wedding?'

'That's right. And I consider the subject closed. In fact, I've had a gutful of talking about this stuff.'

'Me too,' she said. Hearing about his difficult youth, remembering her early loss was making her feel down. 'I reckon we know enough about each other now to be able to field any questions that are thrown at us. After all, we're not pretending to have known each other for long.'

She got up from her chair, walked to the edge of the pool, knelt at the edge and swished her hand through the water. 'This is such a nice pool. Do you use it much?'

'Most days I swim,' he said, standing behind her. 'There's a gym at the back of the cabana too.'

She imagined him working out in his gym, then plunging into the pool, muscles pumped, spearing through the water in not many clothes, maybe in *no* clothes.

Stop it!

She got up, wishing she could dive in right now to cool herself down. 'Do you like my idea to hire some lifeguards so the guests can swim on Christmas Day?'

'It's a good one.'

'And you're okay with putting a new swimsuit and towel in each of the children's goody bags? Hannah pointed out that some of the kids might not have a swimsuit.'

'I meant to talk to you about that,' he said. Surely he wasn't going to query the cost of the kids' gifts? She would be intensely disappointed if he did. 'I want to buy each of the adults a new swimsuit too; they might not have one either,' he said. 'I don't want anyone feeling excluded for any reason we can avoid.'

She looked up at him. 'You're not really a Scrooge, are you?'

'No,' he said.

'I don't think people are going to be calling you that for much longer. Certainly not if I've got anything to do with it.'

'But not a word about my past.'

'That's understood,' she said, making a my-lips-are-sealed zipping motion over her mouth. 'Though I think you might find people would admire you for having overcome it.'

The alarm on her watch buzzed. 'I'm running late,' she said. 'I didn't realise we'd been talking for so long.'

'You have an appointment? I was going to suggest dinner.'

'No can do, I'm afraid.' Her first impulse was to cancel her plans, to jump at the opportunity to be with Dominic. But she would not put her life on hold for the fake engagement.

'I have a hot date with a group of girlfriends. It's our first Tuesday of the month movie club. We see a movie and then go to dinner. We're supposed to discuss the movie but we mainly catch up on the gossip.' She held out her hand, where the diamond flashed on the third finger of her left hand. 'I suspect this baby is going to be the main topic of conversation.'

She made to go but, before she could, Dominic had pulled her close for a kiss that left not a scrap of lipstick on her mouth and her hair falling out of its knot.

It was the kind of kiss she could get used to.

CHAPTER TWELVE

ANDIE SAT AT her desk in the Party Queens' headquarters. 'Headquarters' was rather a grand term for their premises. It comprised an industrial kitchen where Gemma could do her thing; a workroom used for making props; a storage area; and an area loosely termed an office, where she and her two partners squeezed in their desks.

To say they were frantically busy would be an understatement. The weeks leading up to Christmas and New Year were the busiest time of the year for established party planners. For a new company like Party Queens to be so busy was gratifying. But it was the months after the end of the long Aussie summer vacation they had to worry about for advance bookings. Business brain, Eliza, was very good at reminding them of that.

Andie's top priority was Dominic's Christmas party. Actually, it was no longer just his party. As his fiancée, she had officially become co-host. But that didn't mean she wasn't flat-out with other bookings, including a Christmas Eve party for the parents of their first eighteenth party girl. Andie wanted to pull out all the stops for the people who'd given Party Queens their very first job. And then there was the business of being Dominic's fake fiancée—almost a job on its own.

Andie had been 'engaged' to Dominic for ten days and so far so good. She'd been amazed that no one had seriously queried the speed at which she had met, fallen in love with and agreed to marry a man she had known for less than a month.

The swooning sighs of 'love at first sight' and 'how romantic' from her girlfriends she understood, not so much the delight from her pragmatic father and the tears of joy from her mother. She hardly knew Dominic and yet they were prepared to believe she would commit her life to him?

Of course it was because her family and friends had been worried about her, wanted her to be happy, had been concerned she had grieved for Anthony for too long.

'Your dad and I are pleased for you, sweetheart, we really are,' her mother had said. 'We were worried you were so fearful about loving someone again in case you lost them, that you wouldn't let yourself fall in love again,' she'd continued. 'But Dominic is so strong, so right for you; I guess he just broke through those barriers you'd spent so long putting up. And I understand you didn't want to waste time when you knew what it was like to have a future snatched away from you.'

Really? She'd put up *barriers*? She'd just been trying to find someone worthy of stepping into Anthony's shoes. Now she'd found a man who had big boots of his own and would never walk in another man's shadow. *But he wasn't really hers.*

'You put us off the scent by telling us Dominic wasn't your type,' Gemma had said accusingly. Gemma, who was already showing her ideas for a fabulous wedding cake she planned to bake and decorate for her when the time came. Andie felt bad going through images of multi-tiered pastel creations with Gemma, knowing the cake was never going to happen.

Condition Number One, that she and Dominic didn't *ever* tell *anyone* about the deception, seemed now like a very good idea. To hear that their engagement had been a cold-blooded business arrangement was never going to go down well with all these people wishing them well.

At last Wednesday's family dinner, Dominic had been joyfully welcomed into the Newman family. 'I'm glad you saw sense about how hot he was,' her sister Bea had said, hugging her. 'And as for that amazing rock on your finger… Does Dominic have a brother? No? Well, can you find me someone just like him, please?'

But every bit of deception was all worth it for Timothy. After the family dinner, Andie and Dominic had drawn Hannah and Paul aside. Now that Dominic was to be part of the family—or so they thought—her sister and her husband didn't take much convincing to accept Dominic's offer of paying all Timothy's medical expenses.

Dominic's only condition was that they kept him posted on their tiny son's progress. 'Of course we will,' Hannah had said, 'but Andie will keep you updated and you'll see Timothy at family functions. You'll always be an important part of his life.' And the little boy had more chance of a better life, thanks to Dominic's generosity.

Later, Hannah had hugged her sister tight. 'You've got yourself a good man, Andie, a very, very good man.'

'I know,' said Andie, choked up and cringing inside. She was going to have to come up with an excellent reason to explain why she 'dumped' Dominic when his need for the fake engagement was over.

There had only been one awkward moment at the dinner. Her parents wanted to put an announcement of the engagement in the newspaper. 'Old-fashioned, I know, but it's the right thing to do,' her mother had said.

She'd then wanted to know what Dominic's middle name was for the announcement. Apparently full names were required, Andrea Jane Newman was engaged to Dominic *who*?

She had looked at Dominic, eyes widened by panic.

She should have known that detail about the man she was supposedly going to marry.

Dominic had quickly stepped in. 'I've kept quiet about my middle name because I don't like it very much,' he'd said. 'It's Hugo. Dominic Hugo Hunt.'

Of course everyone had greeted that announcement with cries of how much they loved the name Hugo. 'You could call your first son Hugo,' Bea had suggested.

That was when Andie had decided it was time to go home. She felt so low at deceiving everyone, she felt she could slink out of the house at ankle level. If it wasn't for Timothy, she would slide that outsize diamond off her finger and put an end to this whole deception.

Dominic had laughed the baby comment off—and made no further mention of it. He'd wanted a baby with his first wife—how did he feel about children now?

Her family was now expecting babies from her and Dominic. She had not anticipated having to handle that expectation. But of course, since then, the image of a dear little boy with black spiky hair and grey eyes kept popping into her mind. A little boy who would be fiercely loved and never have to face the hardships his father had endured.

She banished the bordering on insane thoughts to the area of her brain reserved for impossible dreams. Instead, she concentrated on confirming the delivery date of two hundred and ten—the ten for contingencies—small red-and-white-striped hand-knitted Christmas stockings for Dominic's party. They would sit in the centre of each place setting and contain all the cutlery required by that person for the meal.

She had decided on a simple red-and-white theme, aimed squarely at pleasing children as well as the inner child of the adults. Tables would be set up in the ballroom for a sit-down meal served from a buffet. She wanted it to be as magical and memorable as a Christmas lunch in the home of a billionaire should be—but without being intimidating.

Gemma had planned fabulous cakes, shaped and frosted like an outsize white candle and actually containing a tea light, to be the centrepiece of each table. Whimsical Santa-themed cupcakes would sit at each place with the name of the guest piped on the top. There would be glass bowls of candy canes and masses of Australian Christmas bush with its tiny red flowers as well as bowls of fat red cherries.

Andie would have loved to handle all the decorations herself but it was too big a job. She'd hired one of her favourite stylists to coordinate all the decorations. Jeremy was highly creative and she trusted his skills implicitly. And, importantly, he'd been happy to work on Christmas Day.

She'd been careful not to discuss anything too 'Christmassy' with Dominic, aware of his feelings about the festive season. He still hadn't shared with her just why he hated it so much; she wondered if he ever would. There was some deep pain there, going right back to his childhood, she suspected.

The alarm on her computer flashed a warning at her the same time the alarm on her watch buzzed. Not that she needed any prompts to alert her that she was seeing Dominic this evening.

He had been in meetings with Walter Burton all afternoon. Andie was to join them for dinner. At her suggestion, the meal was to be at Dominic's house. Andie felt that a man like Walter might prefer to experience home-style hospitality; he must be sick of hotels and restaurants. Not that Dominic's house was exactly the epitome of cosy, but it was elegant and beautiful and completely lacking in any brash, vulgar display of wealth.

A table set on the terrace at the front of the house facing the harbour. A chef to prepare the meal. A skilled waiter to serve them. All organised by Party Queens with a menu devised by Gemma. Eliza had, as a matter of course, checked with Walter's personal assistant as to the tycoon's personal dietary requirements.

Then there would be Andie, on her best fiancée behaviour. After all, Mr Burton's preference for doing business with a married man was the reason behind the fake engagement.

Not that she had any problem pretending to be an attentive fiancée. That part of the role came only too easily. Her heartbeat accelerated just at the thought of seeing Dominic this evening. He'd been away in different states on business and she'd only seen him a few times since the family dinner. She checked her watch again. There was plenty of time to get home to Newtown and then over to Vaucluse before the guest of honour arrived.

Dominic had been in Queensland on business and only flown back into Sydney last night. He'd met Walter Burton from a very early flight from the US this morning. After an afternoon of satisfactory meetings, Dominic had taken him back to his hotel. The American businessman would then make his own way to Vaucluse for the crucial dinner with Dominic and Andie.

As soon as he let himself in through the front door of the house Dominic sensed a difference. There was a subtle air of expectation, of warmth. The chef and his assistant were in the kitchen and, if enticing aromas had anything to do with it, dinner was under way. Arrangements of exotic orchids were discreetly arranged throughout the house. That was thanks to Andie.

It was all thanks to Andie. He would have felt uncomfortable hosting Walter Burton in his house if it weren't for her. He would have taken him to an upscale restaurant, which would have been nice but not the same. The older man had been very pleased at the thought of being invited to Dominic's home.

And now here she was, heading towards him from the terrace at the eastern end of the house where they would dine. He caught his breath at how beautiful she looked in a body-hugging cream top and matching long skirt that wrapped across the front and revealed, as she walked, tantalising glimpses of long slender legs and high heeled ankle-strap sandals. Her hair was up, but tousled strands fell around her face. Her only jewellery was her engagement ring. With her simple elegance, again she looked as if she belonged in this house.

'You're home,' she said in that husky voice, already so familiar.

Home. That was the difference in his house this evening. *Andie's presence made it a home.* And he had not felt he'd had a real home for a long time.

But Andie and her team were temporary hired help—she the lead actress in a play put on for the benefit of a visiting businessman. *This was all just for show.*

Because of Walter Burton, because there were strangers in the house, they had to play their roles—he the doting fiancé and she his betrothed.

Andie came close, smiling, raised her face for his kiss. Was that too for show? Or because she was genuinely glad to see him? At the touch of her lips, hunger for her instantly ignited. He closed his eyes as he breathed in her sweet, spicy scent, not wanting to let her go.

A waiter passed by on his way to the outdoor terrace, with a tray of wine glasses.

'I've missed you,' Andie murmured. For the waiter's benefit or for Dominic's? She sounded convincing but he couldn't be sure.

'Me too—missed you, I mean,' he said stiffly, self-consciously.

That was the trouble with this deception he had initiated. It was only too easy to get caught between a false intimacy and an intimacy that could possibly be real. Or could it? He broke away from her, stepped back.

'Is this another misbehaving skirt?' he asked.

He resisted the urge to run his hand over the curve of her hip. It would be an appropriate action for a fiancé but stepping over the boundaries of his agreement with Andie. Kisses were okay—their public displays of affection had to look authentic. Caresses of a more intimate nature, on the other hand, were *not* okay.

She laughed. 'No breeze tonight so we'll never know.' She lowered her voice. 'Is there anything else you need to brief me about before Mr Burton arrives? I've read through the background information you gave me. I think I'm up to speed on what a fiancée interested in her future husband's work would most likely know.'

'Good,' he said. 'I have every faith you won't let me down. If you're not sure of anything, just keep quiet and I'll cover for you. Not that I think I'll have to do that.'

'Fingers crossed I do you proud,' she said.

Walter Burton arrived punctually—Dominic would have been surprised if he hadn't. The more time he spent with his prospective joint venture partner, the more impressed he was by his acumen and professionalism. *He really wanted this deal.*

Andie greeted the older man with warmth and charm. Straight away he could see Walter was impressed.

She led him to the front terrace where the elegantly set round table—the right size for a friendly yet business orientated meal—had been placed against a backdrop of Sydney Harbour, sparkling blue in the light of the long summer evening. As they edged towards the longest day on December the twenty-second, it did not get dark until after nine p.m.

Christmas should be cold and dark and frosty. He pushed the painful thought away. Dwelling on the past was not appropriate here, not when an important deal hung in the balance.

Andie was immediately taken with Walter Burton. In his mid-sixties and of chunky build, his silver hair and close-trimmed silver beard gave him an avuncular appearance. His pale blue eyes actually sparkled and she had to keep reminding herself that he could not be as genial as he appeared and be such a successful tycoon.

But his attitude to philanthropy was the reason she was here, organising the party, pretending to be Dominic's betrothed. He espoused the view that making as much money as you could was a fine aim—so long as you remembered to share it with those who had less. 'It's a social responsibility,' he said.

Dominic had done nothing but agree with him. There was not a trace of Scrooge in anything he said. Andie had begun to believe the tag was purely a media invention.

Walter—he insisted she drop the 'Mr Burton'—seemed genuinely keen to hear all the details of the Christmas party. He was particularly interested when she told him Dominic had actively sought to dampen press interest. That had, as intended, flamed media interest. They already had two journalists volunteer to help out on that day—quite an achievement considering most people wanted to spend it with their families or close friends.

Several times during the meal, Andie squeezed Dominic's hand under the table—as a private signal that she thought the evening was going well. His smile in return let her know he thought so too. The fiancée fraud appeared to be doing the trick.

The waiter had just cleared the main course when Walter sat back in his chair, relaxed, well fed and praising the excellent food. Andie felt she and Dominic could also finally relax from the knife-edge of tension required to impress the American without revealing the truth of their relationship.

So Walter's next conversational gambit seemed to come from out of the blue. 'Of course you understand the plight of your Christmas Day guests, Dominic, as you've come from Struggle Street yourself,' he said. 'Yet you do your utmost to hide it.'

Dominic seemed shocked into silence. Andie watched in alarm as he blanched under his tan and gripped the edge of the table so his knuckles showed white. 'I'm not sure what you mean,' he said at last.

Walter's shrewd eyes narrowed. 'You've covered your tracks well, but I have a policy of never doing business with someone I haven't fully researched. I know about young Nick Hunt and the trouble he got into.'

Dominic seemed to go even paler. 'You mean the assault charge? Even though it never went to court. Even though I was a juvenile and there should be no record of it. How did you—?'

'Never mind how I found out. But I also discovered how much Dominic Hunt has given back to the world in which he had to fight to survive.' Walter looked to Andie. 'I guess you don't know about this, my dear.'

'Dominic has told me about his past,' she said cautiously. She sat at the edge of her seat, feeling trapped by uncertainty, terrified of saying the wrong thing, not wanting to reveal her ignorance of anything important. 'I also know how very generous he is.'

'Generous to the point that he funds a centre to help troubled young people in Brisbane.' Andie couldn't help a gasp of surprise that revealed her total lack of knowledge. 'He hasn't told you about his Underground Help Centre?' Walter didn't wait for her to answer. 'It provides safe emergency accommodation, health care, counselling, rehab—all funded by your fiancé. Altogether a most admirable venture.'

Why had Dominic let everyone think he was a Scrooge?

'You've done your research well, Walter,' Dominic said. 'Yes, I haven't yet told Andie about the centre. I wanted to take her to Brisbane and show her the work we do there.'

'I'll look forward to that, darling,' she said, not having to fake her admiration for him.

Dominic addressed both her and Walter. 'When I started to make serious money, I bought the abandoned shopping centre site where I'd sought refuge as a troubled runaway and redeveloped it. But part of the site was always going to be for the Underground Help Centre that I founded. I recruited Jim, the social worker who had helped me, to head it up for me.'

Andie felt she would burst with pride in him. Pride and something even more heartfelt. He must hate having to reveal himself like this.

Walter leaned towards Dominic. 'You're a self-made man and I admire that,' he said. 'You're sharing the wealth you acquired by your own hard work and initiative and I admire that too. What I don't understand, Dominic, is why you keep all this such a big secret. There's nothing to be ashamed of in having pulled yourself up by your bootstraps.'

'I'm not ashamed of anything I've done,' Dominic said. 'But I didn't want my past to affect my future success. Especially, I didn't want it to rub off on my business partner, Jake Marlow.'

Andie felt as if she was floundering. Dominic had briefed her on business aspects she might be expected to know about tonight, but nothing about this. She could only do what she felt was right. Without hesitation, she reached out and took his hand so they stood united.

'People can be very judgemental,' she said to Walter. 'And the media seem to be particularly unfair to Dominic. I'm incredibly proud of him and support his reasons for wanting to keep what he does in Brisbane private. To talk about that terrible time is to relive it, over and over again. From what Dominic has told me, living it once would be more than enough for anyone.'

Dominic squeezed her hand back, hard, and his eyes were warm with gratitude. Gratitude and perhaps—just perhaps—something more? 'I can't stop the nightmares of being back there,' he said. 'But I can avoid talking about it and bringing those times back to life.'

Andie angled herself to face Walter full-on. She was finding it difficult to keep her voice steady. 'If people knew about the centre they'd find out about his living rough and the assault charge. People who don't know him might judge him unfairly. At the same time, I'd love more people to know how generous and kind he actually is and—' She'd probably said enough.

Walter chuckled. 'Another thing he's done right is his choice of fiancée.'

Dominic reached over to kiss her lightly on the lips. 'I concur, Walter,' he said. Was it part of the act or did he really mean it?

'Th…thank you,' stuttered Andie. She added Walter to the list of people who would be disappointed when she dumped Dominic.

'I'm afraid I can't say the same for your choice of first wife,' Walter said.

Dominic visibly tensed. 'What do you mean?'

'I met with her and your former employee this morning. He's an impressive guy, though not someone I feel I want to do business with. But your ex-wife made it clear she would do anything—and I stress *anything*—to seal the deal. She suggested that to me—happily married for more than forty years and who has never even looked at another woman.'

Dominic made a sound of utter disgust but nothing more. Andie thought more of him that he didn't say anything to disparage Tara, appalling though her behaviour had been. Dominic had more dignity.

'The upshot of this is, Dominic, that you are exactly the kind of guy I want to do business with. You and your delightful wife-to-be. You make a great team.'

Dominic reached over to take Andie's hand again. 'Thank you, Walter. Thank you from us both.'

Andie smiled with lips that were aching from all her false smiles and nodded her thanks. The fake engagement had done exactly what it was intended to. She should be jubilant for Dominic's sake. But that also meant there would soon be no need to carry on with it. And that made her feel miserable. *She wasn't doing a very good job of guarding her heart.*

When Andie said goodnight to Dominic, she clung to him for a moment longer than was necessary. Playing wife-to-be for the evening had made her start to wish a real relationship with Dominic could perhaps one day be on the cards.

Perhaps it was a good thing she wouldn't see Dominic again until Christmas Eve. He had to fly out to Minneapolis to finalise details with Walter, leaving her to handle the countdown to the Christmas party. And trying not to think too much about what had to happen after Christmas, when her 'engagement' would come to an end.

CHAPTER THIRTEEN

It was midday on Christmas Eve and as Andie pushed open the door into Dominic's house she felt as if she was stepping into a nightmare. The staircase railings were decorated as elegantly as she'd hoped, with tiny lights and white silk cord. The wreath on the door was superb. But dominating the marble entrance hall was an enormous Christmas tree, beautifully decorated with baubles and ornaments and winking with tiny lights. She stared at it in shocked disbelief. *What the heck was that doing there?*

When she said it out loud she didn't say *heck* and she didn't say it quietly.

Her stylist Jeremy's assistant had been rearranging baubles on the lower branches of the tree. She jumped at Andie's outburst and a silver bauble smashed on to the marble floor. Calmly, very calmly, Andie asked the girl where Jeremy was. The girl scuttled out to get him.

Throughout all the Christmas party arrangements, through all the fake fiancée dramas, Andie had kept her cool. Now she was in serious danger of losing it. She had planned this party in meticulous detail. Of all the things that could go wrong, it would have to be this—Dominic would think she had deliberately defied his specific demand. And she didn't want him thinking badly of her.

Jeremy came into the room with a swathe of wide red ribbons draped over his outstretched arm. Andie recognised them as the ones to be looped and tied into extravagant bows on the back of the two hundred chairs in the ballroom.

She had to grit her teeth to stop herself from exploding. 'Why is there a Christmas tree in here?' Her heart was racing with such panic she had to put her hand on her chest to try and slow it.

'Because this entrance space cried out for one. How can you have a Christmas party without a tree?' Jeremy said. 'I thought you'd made a mistake and left it off the brief. Doesn't it look fabulous?'

'It does indeed look fabulous. Except the client specifically said *no tree*.' She could hear her voice rising and took a deep breath to calm herself.

How had she let this happen? Maybe she should have written *NO CHRISTMAS TREE* in bold capitals on every page of the briefing document. She'd arrived here very early this morning to let the decorating crew in and to receive final deliveries of the extra furniture. Jeremy had assured her that all was on track. And it was—except for this darn tree.

'But why?' asked Jeremy. 'It seems crazy not to have a tree.'

Crazy? Maybe. She had no idea why—because Dominic, for all his talk with Walter Burton over dinner that night that had seemed so genuine, still refused to let her in on the events in his past he held so tightly to himself. He'd drip-fed some of the details but she felt there was something major linked to Christmas he would not share. It made her feel excluded—put firmly in her place as no one important in his life. And she wanted to be important to him. She swallowed hard. *Had she really just admitted that to herself?*

'The client actually has a thing against Christmas trees,' she said. 'You might even call it a phobia. For heaven's sake, Jeremy, why didn't you call me before you put this up?' Her mouth was dry and her hands felt clammy at the thought of Dominic's reaction if he saw the tree.

'I'm sorry,' said Jeremy, crestfallen. 'You didn't specify not to include a tree in the decorations. I was just using my initiative.'

On other jobs she'd worked with Jeremy she'd told him to think for himself and not bother her with constant calls, so she couldn't be *too* cranky with him. Creative people could be tricky to manage—and Jeremy's work was superb. The tree was, in fact, perfect for the spot where he'd placed it.

She took a step back to fully appraise its impact. The tree looked spectacular, dressed in silver with highlights of red, in keeping with her overall colour scheme. She sighed her pleasure at its magnificence. This perfect tree would make a breathtaking first impression for the guests tomorrow. To the children it would seem to be the entrance to a magical world. It spoke of tradition, of hope, of generosity. Everything they were trying to achieve with this party. It would make Dominic look good.

The beautiful tree was beginning to work its magic on her. Surely it would on Dominic too? He'd come such a long way since that first day, when he'd been so vehemently anti everything Christmas. *Christmas was not Christmas without a tree*.

She took a series of deep, calming breaths. Dominic should at least have the chance to see the tree in place. To see how wonderful it looked there. Maybe the sight of this tree would go some way towards healing those hidden deep wounds he refused to acknowledge.

She turned to Jeremy, the decision firm in her mind. 'We'll leave it. You've done such a good job on the tree, it would be a real shame to have to take it down.'

'What about the client?'

'He's a client but he's also my fiancé.' The lie threatened to choke her but she was getting more adept at spinning falsehoods. 'Leave him to me. In the meantime, let me give you a hand with placing the final few ornaments on the lower branches,' she said. She was wearing work clothes—jeans, sneakers and a loose white shirt. She rolled up her sleeves and picked up an exquisite glass angel. Her hand wasn't quite steady—if only she was as confident as she had tried to appear.

Dominic was due back in to Sydney early this evening. *What if he hated the tree?* Surely he wouldn't. He seemed so happy with everything else she'd done for the party; surely he would fall in love with the tree.

But it would take a Christmas miracle for him to fall in love with *her*.

She longed for that miracle. Because she couldn't deny it to herself any longer—she had developed feelings for him.

Dominic had managed to get an earlier flight out of Minneapolis to connect with a non-stop flight to Sydney from Los Angeles. Nonetheless, it was a total flight of more than twenty hours. Despite the comfort of first class, he was tired and anxious to get away from the snow and ice of Minnesota and home to sunny Sydney. A bitterly cold Christmas wasn't quite as he'd remembered it to be.

Overriding everything else, he wanted to get home to Andie. He had thought about her non-stop the whole trip, wished she'd been with him. Next time, he'd promised Walter, he'd bring Andie with him.

As the car he'd taken from the airport pulled up in front of his house, his spirits lifted at the thought of seeing her. He hadn't been able to get through to her phone, so he'd called Party Queens. Eliza had told him she was actually at his house in Vaucluse, working on the decorations for the party.

On the spur of the moment, he'd decided not to let her know he'd got in early. It might be better to surprise her. He reckoned if she didn't know he was coming, she wouldn't have time to put on her fake fiancée front. Her first reaction to him would give him more of a clue of her real feelings towards him.

Because while he was away he had missed her so intensely, he'd been forced to face *his* real feelings towards *her*. He was falling in love with her. Not only was he falling in love with her; he realised he had never had feelings of such intensity about a woman.

Melody had been his first love—and sweet, damaged Melody had loved him back to the extent she was capable of love. But it hadn't been enough. That assault charge had happened because he had been protecting her. Protecting her from a guy assaulting her in an alley not far from the takeaway food shop where he'd worked in the kitchen in return for food and a few dollars cash in hand.

But the guy had been her dealer—and possibly her pimp. Melody had squealed at Dominic to leave the guy alone. She'd shrieked at him that she knew what she was doing; she didn't need protecting. Dominic had ignored her, had pulled the creep off her, smashed his fist into the guy's face. Then the dealer's mates had shown up and Dominic had copped a beating too. But, although younger than the low-lifes, he'd been bigger, stronger and inflicted more damage. The cops had taken him in, while the others had disappeared into the dark corners that were their natural habitat. And Melody had gone with them without a backward glance, leaving him with a shattered heart as well as a broken nose. He'd never seen her again.

Of course Melody hadn't been her real name. He'd been too naïve to realise that at the time. Later, when he'd set up the Underground Help Centre, he'd tried to find her but without any luck. He liked to think she was living a safe happy life somewhere but the reality was likely to be less cosy than that.

Then there'd been Tara—the next woman to have betrayed him. The least thought he gave to his ex-wife the better.

But Andie. Andie was different. He felt his heart, frosted over for so long, warm when he thought about her. *What you saw was what you got.* Not only smart and beautiful, but loyal and loving. He'd told her more about his past than he'd ever told anyone. He could be himself with her, not have to pretend, be Nick as well as Dominic. Be not the billionaire but the man. Their relationship could be real. *He could spend his life with Andie.*

And he wanted to tell her just that.

The scent of pine needles assaulted his senses even before he put his key in his front door. The sharp resin smell instantly revived memories of that Christmas Eve when he'd been eleven years old and the happy part of his childhood had come to its terrible end. Christmas trees were the thing he most hated about Christmas.

The smell made him nauseous, started a headache throbbing in his temples. Andie must be using pine in some of the decorations. It would have to go. He couldn't have it in the house.

He pushed the door silently open—only to recoil at what he saw.

There was a Christmas tree in his house. A whopping great Christmas tree, taking up half his entrance hallway and rising high above the banisters of the staircase.

What the hell? He had told Andie in no uncertain terms there was to be no Christmas tree—anywhere. He gritted his teeth and fisted his hands by his sides. *How could she be so insensitive?*

There was a team of people working on the tree and its myriad glitzy ornaments. Including Andie. He'd never thought she could be complicit in this defiance of his wishes. He felt let down. *Betrayed.*

She turned. Froze. Her eyes widened with shock and alarm when she saw him. A glass ornament slid from her hands and smashed on the floor but she scarcely seemed to notice.

'What part of "no Christmas tree" did you not get, Andie?'

She got up from her kneeling position and took a step towards him, put up her hands as if to ward off his anger. The people she was with scuttled out of the room, leaving them alone. But he bet they were eavesdropping somewhere nearby. The thought made him even more livid.

'Dominic, I'm sorry. I know you said no tree.'

'You're damn right I did.'

'It was a mistake. The tree was never meant to be here. There were some…some crossed lines. I wasn't expecting it either. But then I saw it and it's so beautiful and looks so right here. I thought you might…appreciate it, might see how right it is and want to keep it.'

He could feel the veins standing out on his neck, his hands clenched so tight they hurt. 'I don't see it as beautiful.'

Her face flushed. She would read that as an insult to her skills. He was beyond caring. 'Why? Why do you hate Christmas trees?' she said. 'Why this…this irrational dislike of Christmas?'

Irrational? He gritted his teeth. 'That's none of your concern.'

'But I want it to be. I thought I could help you. I—'

'You thought wrong.'

Now her hands were clenched and she was glaring at him. 'Why won't you share it with me—what makes you hurt so much at this time of year? Why do I have to guess? Why do I have to tiptoe around you?' Her voice rose with each question as it seemed her every frustration and doubt rushed to the surface.

Dominic was furious. How dared she put him through this…this humiliation?

'Don't forget your place,' he said coldly. 'I employ you.' With each word he made a stabbing motion with his finger to emphasise the words. 'Get rid of the tree. Now.'

He hated the stricken look on Andie's face, knowing he had put it there. But if she cared about him at all she never would have allowed that tree to enter his house. He could barely stand to look at her.

For a long moment she didn't say anything. 'Yes,' she said finally, her voice a dull echo of its usual husky charm. 'Yes, sir,' she added.

In a way he appreciated the defiance of the hissed 'sir'. But he was tired and jet-lagged and grumpy and burning with all the pain and loss he associated with Christmas— and Christmas trees in particular. Above all, he was disappointed in her that she thought so little of his wishes that she would defy him.

His house was festooned with festive paraphernalia. Everywhere he looked, it glittered and shone, mocking him. He'd been talked into this damn party against his wishes. *He hated Christmas.* He uttered a long string of curses worthy of Scrooge.

'I'm going upstairs. Make sure this tree is gone when I come back down. And all your people as well.' He glared in the general direction of the door through which her team had fled.

She met his glare, chin tilted upwards. 'It will take some time to dismantle the tree,' she said. 'But I assure you I will get rid of every last stray needle so you will never know it was there.' She sounded as though she spoke through gritted teeth. 'However, I will need all my crew to help me. We have to be here for at least a few more hours. We still have to finish filling the goody bags and setting the tables.' She glared at him. 'This is *your* party. And you know as well as I do that it must go on. To prove you're not the Scrooge people think you are.'

Some part of him wanted to cross the expanse of floor between them and hug her close. To tell her that of course he understood. That he found it almost impossible to talk about the damage of his childhood. To knuckle down and help her adorn his house for the party tomorrow. But the habits of Christmases past were hard to break.

So was the habit of closing himself off from love. Letting himself love Andie would only end in disappointment and pain, like it had with every other relationship. For her as well as himself. *It seemed he was incapable of love.*

'Text me when you're done,' he said.

He stomped up the stairs to his study. And the bottle of bourbon that waited there.

Andie felt humiliated, angry and upset. How dared Dominic speak to her like that? *'Don't forget your place.'* His harsh words had stabbed into her heart.

Jeremy poked his head around the door that connected through to the living room. She beckoned him to come in. She forced her voice to sound businesslike, refused to let even a hint of a tear burr her tone. 'I told you he wouldn't be happy with the tree.' Her effort at a joke fell very flat.

'Don't worry about it,' Jeremy said, putting a comforting hand on her shoulder. 'We'll get rid of this tree quicksmart. No matter your man is in a mood. The show has to go on. You've got two hundred people here for lunch tomorrow.'

'Thanks, Jeremy,' she said. 'Dominic has just got off a long flight. He's not himself.' But her excuses for him sounded lame even to her own ears.

Was that angry man glaring at her with his fists clenched at his sides the true Dominic? She'd known the anger was there bubbling below the surface, was beginning to understand the reasons for it. But she'd thought that anger that had driven him to violence was in his past. How could she possibly have thought she'd fallen in love with him? She didn't even know the man.

'What do you suggest we do with the tree?' Jeremy asked. 'There are no returns on cut trees.'

Andie's thoughts raced. 'We've got a Christmas Eve party happening elsewhere tonight. The clients have put up a scrappy old artificial tree that looks dreadful. We'll get this delivered to them with the compliments of Party Queens. Keep whatever ornaments you can use here; the rest we'll send with the tree. Let's call a courier truck now.'

Seething, she set to work dismantling the beautiful tree. As she did so, she felt as if she were dismantling all her hopes and dreams for love with Dominic. The diamond ring felt like a heavy burden on her finger, weighted by its duplicity and hypocrisy. While he'd stood there insulting her, she'd felt like taking the ring off and hurling it at him. If it had hit him and drawn blood she would have been glad. His words had been so harsh they felt like they'd drawn blood from her heart.

But of course she couldn't have thrown her ring at him while there were other people in the house. She would be professional right to the end. After all, wasn't she known for her skill at dealing with difficult people?

In spite of that, she'd had her fill of this particular difficult man. He'd got what he wanted from her in terms of his American deal. She'd got what her family needed for Timothy. Both sides of the bargain fulfilled. He'd been her employer, her fake fiancé—she'd liked to think they'd become friends of a sort. She'd wanted more—but that was obviously not to be. She'd stick it out for the Christmas lunch. Then she'd be out of here and out of his life.

The crew worked efficiently and well. When they were done and the tree was gone she waved them goodbye and wished them a Merry Christmas. But not before asking them to please not repeat what they might have heard today. Talk of Dominic's outburst could do serious damage to the rehabilitation of his Scrooge image.

By the time they had all gone it was early evening. She stood and massaged the small of her back where it ached. She would let Dominic know she was done and going home. But she had no intention of texting him as he'd asked. Not asked. *Demanded.* She had things to say that had to be said in person.

CHAPTER FOURTEEN

WITH A HEAVY HEART—wounded hearts *hurt*—Andie made her way up the stylishly decorated staircase, its tiny lights discreetly winking. She hadn't been up here before, as this part of the house was off-limits for the party. When she thought of it, she actually had no idea where Dominic could be.

The first two doors opened to two fashionably furnished empty bedrooms. The third bedroom was obviously his—a vast bed with immaculate stone-coloured linens, arched windows that opened to a sweeping view of the harbour. But he wasn't there.

Then she noticed a door ajar to what seemed like a study.

There was no response to her knock, so she pushed it open. The blinds were drawn. Dominic lay sprawled asleep on a large chesterfield sofa. The dull light of a tall, arching floor lamp pooled on him and seemed to put him in the spotlight.

His black lace-up business shoes lay haphazardly at the end of the sofa. He had taken off his jacket and removed his tie. The top buttons of his shirt were undone to reveal an expanse of bare, well-muscled chest her traitorous libido could not help but appreciate as it rose and fell in his sleep.

His right arm fell to the floor near a bottle of bourbon. Andie picked it up. The bottle was nearly full, with probably no more than a glassful gone. Not enough for him to be drunk—more likely collapsed into the sleep of utter exhaustion. She put the bottle on the desk.

There was a swivel-footed captain's chair near the sofa with a padded leather seat. She sat on the edge of it and watched Dominic as he slept. Darn it, but that wounded heart of hers beat faster as she feasted her eyes on his face, which had become so familiar. So…so—she nearly let herself think *so beloved*. But that couldn't be.

She swallowed hard at the lump that rose in her throat. Why on earth had she let herself fall for a man who was so difficult, so damaged, so completely opposite to the man who had made her so happy in the past?

Dominic's hair stood up in spikes. He obviously hadn't shaved since he'd left Minneapolis and his beard was in that stubble stage she found so incredibly sexy. She hadn't realised how long and thick his eyelashes were. His mouth was slightly parted. She longed to lean over and kiss it. She sighed. There would be no more kissing of this man.

He moaned in his sleep and she could see rapid eye movement behind his lids as if he were being tortured by bad dreams. She could not help but reach out to stroke his furrowed forehead. He returned to more restful sleep. Then his eyes flickered open. Suddenly he sat up, startling her. He looked around, disorientated, eyes glazed with sleep. He focused on her.

'Andie,' he breathed. 'You're here.' He gave a huge sigh, took her hand and kissed it. 'I didn't think I'd ever see you again.'

He didn't deserve to, she thought. But her resolve was weakening.

'Are you okay?' she said, trying to ignore the shivers of pleasure that ran up her arm from his kiss. He had been rude and hurtful to her.

'I've just had a horrible dream,' he said.

'What kind of dream?'

'A nightmare. I was in a cemetery and saw my own headstone.'

She shook her head. 'No, Dominic—I don't want to hear this.' The day of Anthony's funeral had been the worst day of her life. When she'd had to accept she'd never see him again. She couldn't bear to think of Dominic buried under a headstone.

But he continued in a dramatic tone she didn't think was appropriate for such a gruesome topic. 'It said: 'Here lies Dominic—they called him Scrooge'. And I think it was Christmas Day.'

Not so gruesome after all. She couldn't help a smile.

'You think my nightmare was funny?' he said, affronted.

'I'm sure it was scary at the time. But you'll never be called Scrooge again. Not after tomorrow. I…I'm sorry about what I said earlier. About your…your Scroogeness, I mean.'

He slammed the hand that wasn't holding hers against his forehead. 'The Christmas tree. I'm sorry, Andie. That was unforgivable. Pay your crew a bonus to make up for it, will you, and bill it to me.'

Did he think everything could be solved by throwing money at it?

'I'm also sorry about the tree, Dominic. It was an honest mistake. It's all gone now.'

Maybe she'd been in the wrong too, to imagine he might like the tree when he'd been so vehement about not having one in the house. But she hadn't been wrong about expecting better behaviour from him.

He shuddered. 'It was a shock. The smell of it. The sight of it. Brought back bad memories.'

She shifted in her seat but did not let go of his hand. 'Do you think it might be time to tell me why Christmas trees upset you so much? Because I didn't like seeing that anger. Especially not directed at me. How can I understand you when I don't know what I'm dealing with?'

He grimaced as if stabbed by an unpleasant memory. 'I suppose I have to tell you if I want you to ever talk to me again.'

'I'm talking to you now.'

She remembered what she'd said about recalling unpleasant memories being like reliving them. But this had to come out—one way or another. Better it was with words than fists.

'Christmas Eve is the anniversary of my parents' deaths.'

She squeezed his hand. 'Dominic, I'm so sorry.' That explained a lot. 'Why didn't you say so before?'

'I…I didn't want people feeling sorry for me,' he said gruffly.

'People wouldn't have… Yes, they would have felt sorry for you. But in a good way.' Could all this Scrooge business have been solved by him simply explaining that? 'Can you tell me about it now?'

'There…there's more. It was cold and frosty. My parents went out to pick up the Christmas tree. A deer crossed the road and they braked to avoid it. The road was icy and the car swerved out of control and crashed into a barrier. That's how they died. Getting the damn Christmas tree.'

She couldn't find the words to say anything other than she was sorry again.

'It was…it was my fault they died.'

Andie frowned. 'How could it be your fault? You were eleven years old.'

'My aunt told me repeatedly for the next six years it was my fault.'

'I think you'd better tell me some more about this aunt.'

'The thing is, it really *was* my fault. I'd begged my parents for a real tree. We had a plastic one. My best friend had a real one; I wanted a real one. If they hadn't gone out to get the tree I wanted they wouldn't have died.'

'You've been blaming yourself all these years? It was an accident. How any competent adult could let you blame yourself, I can't imagine.'

'Competent adult and my aunt aren't compatible terms,' he said, the bitterness underlying his words shocking her.

'I keep asking you about her; it's time you gave me some answers.' Though she was beginning to dread what she might hear.

'She used alcohol and prescription meds to mask her serious psychological problems. I know that now as an adult. As a kid, I lived with a bitter woman who swung between abuse and smothering affection.'

'And, as a kid, you put up with a lot in the hope of love,' Andie said softly, not sure if Dominic actually heard her. She could see the vulnerability in that strong-jawed handsome face, wondered how many people he had ever let be aware of it. She thought again of that little boy with the dark hair. Her vision of Dominic's son merged with that of the young, grieving, abused Dominic. And her heart went out to him.

The words spilled out of him now, words that expressed emotions dammed for years. 'She was particularly bad at Christmas because that's when she'd lost her sister—which was, in her eyes, my fault. When she got fed up with me, she locked me in a cupboard. The physical abuse stopped when I got bigger than her. The mental abuse went on until the day I ran away. Yet all that time she held down a job and presented a reasonable face to the world. I talked to a teacher at school and he didn't believe me. Told me to man up.'

'I honestly don't know what to say…' But she hated his aunt, even though she was aware she'd been a deeply troubled person. No child should be treated like that.

'Say nothing. I don't want to talk about it any more. I'm thirty-two years old. That was all a long time ago.'

'But, deep down, you're still hurting,' she whispered. 'Dominic, I'm so sorry you had to go through all that. And I admire you so much for what you became after such a difficult start.'

Words could only communicate so much. Again, she felt that urge to comfort him. This time, she acted on it. She leaned over to him and kissed him, tasted bourbon on his lips, welcomed the scrape of his stubble on her skin. Immediately, he took the kiss deeper.

The kiss went on and on, passion building, thrilling her. But it was more than sensual pleasure; it was a new sense of connection, of shared emotion as well as sensation.

He broke the kiss to pull her shirt up and over her head. His shirt was already half unbuttoned. It didn't take much to have it completely undone and to slide it off his broad shoulders and muscular arms. She caught her breath in awe at the male perfection of his body.

She wanted him. Dominic had got what he wanted from Walter. Timothy was booked for the treatment he needed. She had promised herself to go after what she wanted— him—and now was her time. It might never be more than this. She knew it and was prepared to take that risk. But she hoped for so much more.

She hadn't known him for long but she had the same kind of certainty—that it could be for ever—as she'd felt for Anthony. A certainty she'd thought she'd never feel again. *For ever love.* Had she been given a chance for that special connection again? She thought *yes*, but could she convince Dominic she could bring him the kind of happiness that had seemed to evade him—that he deserved?

He threw his head back and moaned his pleasure as she planted urgent kisses down the firm column of his throat, then back up to claim his mouth again. He tasted so good, felt so good.

He caught her hands. 'Andie, is this what you want? Because we have to stop it now if you don't,' he said, his voice husky with need.

'Don't you dare stop,' she murmured.

He smiled a slow, seductive smile that sent her heart rate rocketing. 'In that case…' He unfastened the catch on her jeans. 'Let's see if we can get these jeans to misbehave…'

Satisfied, replete, her body aching in the most pleasurable of ways, Andie drowsed in his arms as Dominic slept. But she couldn't let herself sleep.

If she'd been a different kind of person she would have stayed there. Perhaps convinced Dominic to shower with her when they woke. She would enjoy soaping down that powerful body. Heaven knew what kind of fun they could have with the powerful jets of water in his spacious double shower. Then they could retire to spend the rest of the evening in that enormous bed of his.

But Andie was not that person. There was the Christmas Eve party she had committed to this evening. As the party planner, she was obliged to call in to see all was well. She also had to check the big tree had made its way there safely—though the eighteen-year-old daughter had texted Andie to thank her, thrilled with the 'real tree'.

There was nothing like the smell of pine resin and the beauty of a natural tree. As eleven-year-old Dominic had known. Her heart went out to that little boy who lived in the damaged soul of the big male, sleeping naked next to her, his arm thrown possessively over her. She was also naked, except for her engagement ring, shining with false promise under the lamplight.

She had agreed to see her family tonight. Tomorrow, Christmas Day, would be the first Christmas lunch she had not spent with them. She was surprised her father had taken it so lightly. 'You have to stand by Dominic, love. That party is not just a job for you now. You're his future wife.'

If only.

Reluctantly, she slid away from Dominic, then quietly got dressed. She would see him in the morning. Tomorrow was Christmas Day, a holiday she loved and he hated. Now she could see why. She ached to turn things around for him—if he would let her.

She looked at his face, more relaxed than she had seen it, and smiled a smile that was bittersweet. They had made love and it had been magnificent. But nothing had changed between them. Tomorrow she was facing the biggest party of her career so far. She would be by the side of the man she had fallen in love with, not knowing for how much longer he would be a part of her life.

When the truth was, she wanted Dominic for Christmas. Not just his body—his heart as well.

Somehow, tomorrow she would have to confess to Dominic the truth of how she felt about him. That she wanted to try a relationship for real. She hoped he felt the same. If so, this would be the best Christmas she had ever had. If not… Well, she couldn't bear to think about *if not*.

CHAPTER FIFTEEN

DOMINIC AWOKE ON Christmas morning as he was accustomed to waking on December the twenty-fifth—alone. It was very early, pale sunlight filtering through the blinds. He reached out his hand to the sofa beside him in the vain hope that Andie might still be there, only to find the leather on that side disappointingly cool to the touch. He closed his eyes again and breathed in the scent of her that lingered in the room, on his skin. Then was overtaken by an anguished rush of longing for her that made him double over with gut-wrenching pain.

He remembered her leaving his side, her quiet footsteps around the room, the rustling as she slid on her clothes. Then her leaning towards him, murmuring that she had to go. She had duties, obligations. He'd pulled her back close to him, tried to convince her with his hands, with his mouth why she should stay. But she'd murmured her regret, kissed him with a quick fierce passion, told him he had jet lag to get over. Then she'd gone.

All he'd wanted to say to her still remained unsaid.

Of course she'd gone to the other people in her life who needed her and loved her. The only commitment she'd made to him was based on the falsehoods he'd engendered and coerced her into. She'd played her role to perfection. So well he was uncertain what might be fact and what might be fiction. But surely making love to him with such passion and tenderness had not been play-acting?

He noticed the bourbon bottle on the desk, lid on, barely touched. This would be the first Christmas he could remember that he hadn't tried to obliterate. The first Christmas that he woke to the knowledge that while Andie might not be here now, she soon would be. And that his perfect, empty house would be filled with people. People who had known hardship like he had and whom he was in the position to help by making their Christmas Day memorable.

Not for the first time, he thought of the possibility of opening a branch of the Underground Help Centre here in Sydney, where it was so obviously needed. Profits from the joint venture with Walter could help fund it. He had much to learn from Walter—he could see it was going to end up a friendship as well as a business partnership.

For the first Christmas in a long time he had something to look forward to—and it was all thanks to Andie.

He hauled himself off the sofa and stretched out the cricks in his back. The sofa was not the best place to sleep—though it had proved perfectly fine for energetic lovemaking. He paused, overwhelmed by memories of the night before. *Andie.* Hunger for her threatened to overwhelm him again—and not just for her beautiful, generous body. He prayed to whatever power that had brought her to him to let him keep her in his life. He hoped she would forgive the way he'd behaved—understand why. And know that it would never happen again.

He headed down the stairs and stood in the entrance hall. Not a trace of the tree remained, thank heaven. He breathed in. And none of that awful smell. Andie had been well meaning but misguided about the tree—now she understood.

The ballroom was all set up, with tables and chairs adorned in various combinations of red and white. A large buffet table area stretched along the wall closest to the kitchen. He'd approved the menu with Gemma and knew within hours it would be groaning with a lavish festive feast. The dishes had been chosen with the diverse backgrounds of the guests in mind—some were refugees experiencing their first Christmas in Australia.

He still couldn't have tolerated a tree in the house but he had to admit to a stirring of interest in the celebrations— more interest than he'd had in Christmas since he'd been a child. Andie was clever—children would love all this and adults should also respond to the nostalgia and hope it evoked. Hadn't she said Christmas was about evoking emotion?

Thanks to the tragedy on Christmas Eve all those years ago, thanks to the way his aunt had treated him in the years that followed, the emotions the season had evoked for him had been unhappy in the extreme. Was there a chance now for him to forge new, happy memories with a kind, loving woman who seemed to understand his struggles?

Andie had said he could trust her, but after his display of anger over the Christmas tree last night would she let herself trust *him*?

There was a large Santa Claus figurine in the corner with rows of canvas, sunshine-themed goody bags stacked around it. Of course it should have been a tree—but the Santa worked okay too as a compromise. The sturdy bags could double as beach bags, the ever-practical Andie had pointed out to him. She had thought of everything. There were gifts there for the volunteers too.

The house seemed to hum with a quiet anticipation and he could feel his spirits rise. Christmas Day with Andie in his house must surely be a step up on the ones he'd been forced to endure up until now.

He swung open the doors and headed to his gym for a workout.

* * *

An hour later Andie arrived with the chef and his crew. Dominic had long given her a pass code to get in and out of fortress Vaucluse.

She was wearing working gear of shorts, T-shirt and sneakers. Later she would change into her beautiful new red lace dress and gorgeous shoes—strappy and red with tassels—in time to greet their guests. She took her dress on its hanger and her bag into the downstairs bathroom. As she did, she noticed the doors to the garden were open and someone was in the pool. She went out to investigate.

Of course it was Dominic, his powerful body spearing through the water. No wonder he had such well-developed muscles with vigorous swimming like this. She watched, mesmerised at his rhythmic strokes, the force of his arms and powerful kick propelling him with athletic grace.

She didn't say anything but maybe her shadow cast on the water alerted him to her presence. Maybe he caught sight of her when he turned his head to breathe. He swam to the edge of the pool and effortlessly pulled himself out of the water, muscles rippling. He wasn't even out of breath.

She almost swooned at the sight of him—could a man be more handsome? Memories of the ecstasy they had given each other the night before flashed through her, tightening her nipples and flooding her body with desire.

His wet hair was slick to his head, the morning sunlight refracted off droplets of water that clung to his powerfully developed shoulders and cut chest, his veins stood out on his biceps, pumped from exertion. And then there were the classic six-pack, the long, strong legs. He didn't have a lot of body hair for such a dark man, but what there was seemed to flag his outrageous masculinity.

She wanted him more than ever. Not just for a night. For many nights. Maybe every night for the rest of her life. There was so much she wanted to say to him but, for all the connection and closeness and *certainty* she had felt last night, she didn't know how to say it.

Her engagement ring glinted on her left hand. The deal with Walter was done. Dominic's Scrooge reputation was likely to be squashed after the party today. How much longer would this ring stay on her finger? What, if anything, would be her role in Dominic's life? She wanted to say something about last night, bring up the subject of the future, but she just couldn't. 'Happy Christmas,' she said instead, forcing every bit of enthusiasm she could muster into her voice.

He grabbed a towel from the back of the chair and slung it around his shoulders, towelling off the excess water. 'H… Happy Christmas to you too,' he said, his voice rusty in the way of someone unused to uttering those particular words. She wondered how long since he had actually wished anyone the Season's greetings.

He looked down into her face and she realised by the expression in his eyes that he might be as uncertain as she was.

Hope flared in her heart. 'Dominic, I—'

'Andie, I—'

They both spoke at the same time. They laughed. Tried again.

'About last night,' he said.

'Yes?' she said.

'I wanted to—'

But she didn't hear what he had to say, didn't get a chance to answer because at that moment the chef called from the doors that opened from the ballroom that Gemma and Eliza were there and needed to be buzzed in.

Dominic groaned his frustration at the terminated conversation. Andie echoed his groan.

'Later,' she said as she turned away, knowing that it

would be highly unlikely for them to get another private moment together for the next few hours.

Dominic found the amount of noise two hundred people could generate—especially when so many of them were children—quite astounding. He stood on the edge of the party, still at the meet-and-greet stage, with appetisers and drinks being passed around by waiters dressed as Christmas elves.

Santa Claus, otherwise known as Rob Cratchit, his Director of Marketing, sidled up next to him. 'It's going even better than I expected,' he said through his fake white beard. 'See that woman over there wiping tomato sauce off the little boy's shirt? She's a journalist, volunteering for the day, and one of your most strident Scrooge critics. She actually called you a multi-million-dollar miser. But I think she's already convinced that today is not some kind of cynical publicity stunt.'

'Good,' said Dominic. Strange that the original aim of this party—to curry favour with Walter Burton—seemed to have become lost. Now it was all about giving people who had it tough a heart-warming experience and a good meal. And enjoying it with Andie by his side.

'Good on you for dressing up as Santa Claus,' he said to Rob. Andie had been right—Rob made the perfect Santa and he had the outgoing personality to carry it off.

'Actually, *you're* the Santa Claus. I talked to one nice lady, a single mum, who said her kids would not have got Christmas lunch or a Christmas present this year, unless a charity had helped out. She said this was so much better than charity. You should mingle—a lot of people want to thank you.'

'I'm not the mingling type,' Dominic said. 'I don't need to be thanked. I just signed the cheques. It should be Andie they're thanking; this was all her idea.'

'She's brilliant,' said Rob. 'Smart of you to snap her up so quickly. You're a lucky man.'

'Yes,' said Dominic, not encouraging further conversation. He'd never been happy discussing his personal life with anyone. The thought that—unless he said something to her—this might be the last day he had with Andie in his life was enough to sink him into a decidedly unfestive gloom.

He hadn't been able to keep his eyes off Andie as she flitted around the room, looking her most beautiful in a very stylish dress of form-fitting lace in a dusky shade of Christmas red. It was modest but hugged every curve and showed off her long, gorgeous legs. He tried not to think of how it had felt to have those legs wrapped around him last night...

'Well, mustn't linger,' said Rob. 'I have to be off and do the *ho-ho-ho* thing.'

As Rob made his way back into the throng, Andie rang a bell for attention and asked everyone to move towards the entrance hall. 'Some of the children and their parents are singing carols for us today.' She'd told Dominic a few of the adults were involved in street choirs and had been happy to run through the carols with the kids.

There was a collective gasp from the 'audience' as they saw the children lined up on the stairs, starting from the tiniest to the teenagers with the adults behind. Again Andie had been right—the stairs made the most amazing showcase for a choir. Each of the choir members wore a plain red T-shirt with the word *'choir'* printed in white lowercase letters. It was perfect, gave them an identity without being ostentatious.

Andie met his gaze from across the room and she smiled. He gave her a discreet thumbs-up. Professional pride? Or something more personal?

The choir started off with the Australian Christmas

carol 'Six White Boomers' where Santa's reindeer were replaced by big white kangaroos for the Australian toy delivery. It was a good icebreaker, and had everyone laughing and clapping and singing along with the chorus.

As Dominic watched, he was surprised to see Andie playing guitar up on the balcony with two other guitarists. She was singing too, in a lovely warm soprano. He remembered that photo of her playing guitar in the hallway of her parents' home and realised how much there was he still didn't know about her—and how much he wanted to know.

When the choir switched to classics like 'Silent Night' and 'Away in a Manger', Dominic found himself transported back to the happy last Christmas when his parents were alive and they'd gone carol singing in their village. *How could he have forgotten?*

The music and the pure young voices resonated and seemed to unlock a well of feeling he'd suppressed—unable perhaps to deal with the pain of it during those years of abuse by his aunt. He'd thought himself incapable of love—because he had been without love. But he *had* been loved back then, by his parents and his grandparents—loved deeply and unconditionally.

He'd yearned for that love again but had never found it. His aunt had done her best to destroy him emotionally but the love that had nurtured him as a young child must have protected him. The realisation struck him—he had loved women incapable of loving him back, and all this time had thought the fault was his when those relationships had failed.

Andie's voice soared above the rest of the choir. Andie, who he sensed had a vast reserve of love locked away since she'd lost her boyfriend. He wanted that love for himself and he wanted to give her the love she needed. How could he tell her that?

He tried to join in with the words of the carol but his throat closed over. He pretended to cough. Before he made an idiot of himself by breaking down, he pushed his way politely through the crowd and made his way out to the cabana, the only place where he could be alone and gather his thoughts.

But he wasn't alone for long. Andie, her eyes warm with concern, was soon with him. 'Dominic, are you okay?' she said, her hand on his arm. 'I know how you feel about Christmas and I was worried—'

'I'm absolutely fine—better than I've been for a long time,' he said.

He picked up her left hand. 'Take off your ring and give it to me, please.'

Andie froze. She stared at him for a long moment, trying to conceal the pain from the shaft of hurt that had stabbed her heart. So it had come to this so soon. Her use was over. Fake fiancée no longer required. Party planner no longer required. Friend, lover, confidante and whatever else she'd been to him no longer required. *She was surplus to requirements.*

Dominic had proved himself to be generous and thoughtful way beyond her initial expectations of Scrooge. But she must not forget the cold, hard fact—people who got to be billionaires in their twenties must have a ruthless streak. And he'd reneged on his offer that she could keep the ring—not that she'd had any intention of doing so. To say she was disappointed would be the world's biggest understatement.

She felt as though all the energy and joy was flowing out of her to leave just a husk. The colour drained from her face—she must look like a ghost.

With trembling fingers, she slid off the magnificent ring and gave it back to him, pressing it firmly into the palm of his hand. Her finger felt immediately empty, her hand unbalanced.

'It's yours,' she said and turned on her heel, trying not to stagger. She would not cry. She would not say anything snarky to him. She would just walk out of here with dignity. *This was her worst Christmas Day ever.*

'Wait! Andie! Where are you going?'

She turned back to see Dominic with a look of bewilderment on his handsome, tough face. 'You're not going to leave me here with your ring?'

Now it was her turn to feel bewildered. '*My* ring? Then why—?' she managed to choke out.

He took her hand again and held it in a tight grip. 'I'm not doing a good job of this, am I?'

He drew her closer, cleared his throat. 'Andie, I… I love you, and I'm attempting to ask you to marry me. I'm hoping you'll say "yes", so I can put your ring back on your wedding finger where it belongs, as your *real* fiancé, as a *real* engagement ring. Just like you told me you wanted.'

She was stunned speechless. The colour rushed back into her face.

'Well?' he prompted. 'Andrea Jane Newman, will you do me the honour of becoming my wife?'

Finally she found her words. Although she only needed the one. 'Yes,' she said. 'I say "yes".'

With no further ado, he slid the beautiful ring back into its rightful place. To her happy eyes it seemed to flash even more brilliantly.

'Dominic, I love you too. I think maybe it *was* love at first sight the day I met you. I never really had to lie about that.'

She wound her arms around his neck and kissed him. They kissed for a long time. Until they were interrupted by a loud knock on the door of the pool house. Gemma.

'Hey, you two, I don't know what's going on in there

and I don't particularly want to know, but we're about to serve lunch and your presence is required.'

'Oh, yes, of course—we're coming straight away,' Andie called, flustered.

Dominic held her by the arm. 'Not so fast. There's something else I want to ask you. What would you like for Christmas?'

His question threw her. She had to think very hard. But then it came to her. 'All I want for Christmas is for us to get married as soon as possible. I… I don't want to wait. You…you know why.'

Anthony would have wanted this for her—to grab her second chance of happiness. She knew that as certainly as if he'd been there to give her his blessing.

'That suits me fine,' Dominic said. 'The sooner you're my wife the better.'

'Of course it takes a while to organise a wedding. Next month. The month after. I don't want anything too fussy anyway, just simple and private.'

'We'll have to talk to the Party Queens,' he said.

She laughed. 'Great idea. I have a feeling we'll be the best people for the job.'

She could hardly believe this was true, but the look in his eyes told her she could believe it. She wound her arms around his neck again. 'Dominic Hugo Hunt, you've just made this the very best Christmas of my life.'

He heaved a great sigh and she could see it was as if the weight of all those miserable Christmases he'd endured in the past had been thrown off. 'Me too,' he said. 'And all because of you, my wonderful wife-to-be.'

CHAPTER SIXTEEN

ANDIE FOUND HERSELF singing 'Rudolph the Red-Nosed Reindeer' as she drove to Dominic's house five days later. She couldn't remember when she'd last sung in the car—and certainly not such a cheesy carol as 'Rudolph'. No, wait. 'Six White Boomers' was even cheesier. But the choir had been so wonderful at Dominic's Christmas party she'd felt it had become the heart of the very successful party. The carols had stayed in her head.

It had only been significant to her, but it was the first time she'd played her guitar and sung in public since Anthony had died. She'd healed in every way from the trauma of his loss, although she would never forget him. Her future was with Dominic. How could she ever have thought he was not her type?

She didn't think Dominic would be burdened with the Scrooge label for too much longer. One of his most relentless critics had served as a volunteer at the party—and had completely changed her tune. Andie had committed to heart the journalist's article in one of the major newspapers.

Dominic Hunt appears more Santa Claus than Scrooge, having hosted a lavish Christmas party, not for celebrities and wealthy silvertails but for ordinary folk down on their luck. A publicity stunt? No way.

She suspected Dominic's other private philanthropic work would eventually be discovered—probably by the digging of this same journalist. But, with the support of her love and the encouragement of Walter Burton, she thought he was in a better place to handle the revelations of his past if and when they came to light.

Dominic had invited her for a special dinner at his house this evening, though they'd had dinner together every evening since Christmas—and breakfast. She hadn't been here for the last few days; rather, he'd stayed at her place. She didn't want to move in with him until they were married.

But he'd said they had to do something special this evening as they wouldn't be able to spend New Year's Eve together—December the thirty-first would be the Party Queens' busiest night yet.

She was looking forward to dinner together, just the two of them. It was a warm evening and she wore a simple aqua dress that was both cool and elegant. Even though they were now engaged for real, they were still getting to know each other—there was a new discovery each time they got the chance to truly talk.

As she climbed the stairs to his house, she heard the sounds of a classical string quartet playing through the sound system he had piped through the house. Dominic had good taste in music, thank heaven. But when she pushed open the door, she was astounded to see a live quartet playing in the same space where the ill-fated Christmas tree had stood. She smiled her delight. It took some getting used to the extravagant gestures of a billionaire.

Dominic was there to greet her, looking darkly handsome in a tuxedo. She looked down at her simple dress in dismay. 'I didn't realise it was such an occasion or I would have worn something dressier,' she said.

Dominic smiled. 'You look absolutely beautiful. Anyway, if all goes well, you'll be changing into something quite different.'

She tilted her head to the side. 'This is all very intriguing,' she said. 'I'm not quite sure where you're going with it.'

'First of all, I want to say that everything can be cancelled if you don't want to go ahead with it. No pressure.'

For the first time she saw Dominic look like he must have looked as a little boy. He seethed with suppressed excitement and the agony of holding on to a secret he was desperate to share.

'Do tell,' she said, tucking her arm through the crook of his elbow, loving him more in that moment than she had ever loved him.

A big grin split his face. 'I'm going to put my hands over your eyes and lead you into the ballroom.'

'Okay,' she said, bemused. Then she guessed it. The family had been determined to give her an engagement party. Now that she and Dominic actually were genuinely engaged she would happily go along with it. She would act suitably surprised. And be very happy. Getting engaged to this wonderful man was worth celebrating.

She could tell she was at the entrance to the ballroom. 'You can open your eyes now,' said Dominic, removing his hands.

There was a huge cry of 'Surprise!' Andie was astounded to see the happy, smiling faces of all her family and friends as well as a bunch of people she didn't recognise but who were also smiling.

What was more, the ballroom had been transformed. It was exquisitely decorated in shades of white with hints of pale blue. Round tables were set up, dressed with white ruffled cloths and the backs of the chairs looped with antique lace and white roses. It was as if she'd walked into a dream. She blinked. But it was all still there when she opened her eyes.

Dominic held her close. 'We—your family, your friends, me—have organised a surprise wedding for you.'

Andie had to put her hand to her heart to stop it from pounding out of her chest. 'A wedding!'

She looked further through the open glass doors to see a bridal arch draped with filmy white fabric and white flowers set up among the rows of blue agapanthus blooming in the garden. Again she blinked. Again it was still there when she opened her eyes.

'Your wedding,' said Dominic. '*Our* wedding. You asked to be married as soon as possible. I organised it. With some help from the Party Queens. Actually, a *lot* of help from the Party Queens. Jake Marlow and some other friends of mine are also here.'

'It…it's unbelievable.'

'Only if it's what you want, Andie,' Dominic said, turning to her so just she could hear. 'If it's too much, if you'd rather organise your own wedding in your own time, this can just turn into a celebration of our engagement.'

'No! I want it. It's perfect.' She turned to the expectant people who seemed to have all held their breath in anticipation of her response and gone silent. 'Thank you. I say I do—well, I'm *soon* going to say I do!'

There was an eruption of cheers and happy relieved laughter. 'Here comes the bride,' called out one of her brothers.

Andie felt a swell of joy and happy disbelief. It was usually her organising all the surprise parties. To have Dominic do this for her—well, she felt as if she was falling in love with him all over again.

But the party planner in her couldn't resist checking on the details. 'The rings?' she asked Dominic. He patted his breast pocket. 'Both ready-to-wear couture pieces,' he said.

'And this is all legal?'

'Strictly speaking, you need a month's notice of intent to be married—and we filled out our form less than a month ago. But I got a magistrate to approve a shorter notice period. It's legal all right.'

Her eyes smarted with tears of joy. This was really happening. She was getting married today to the man she adored and in front of the people she loved most in the world.

Her fashion editor friend, Karen, dashed out from the guests and took her by the arm. 'Hey! No tears. I've got my favourite hair and make-up artist on hand and we don't want red eyes and blotchy cheeks. Let's get your make-up done. She's already done your bridesmaids.'

'My bridesmaids?'

'Your sisters, Hannah and Bea, Gemma, Eliza and your little niece, Caitlin. The little nephews are ring-bearers.'

'You guys have thought of everything.'

Turning around to survey the room again, she noticed a fabulous four-tiered wedding cake, covered in creamy frosting and blue sugar forget-me-nots. It was exactly the cake she'd talked about with Gemma. She'd bet it was chocolate cake on the bottom layers and vanilla on the top—Gemma knew she disliked the heavy fruitcake of traditional wedding cakes.

'Wait until you see your wedding dresses,' said Karen.

'Dresses?'

'I've got you a choice of three. You'll love them all but there's one I think you'll choose. It's heavy ivory lace over silk, vintage inspired, covered at the front but swooping to the back.'

'And a veil? I always wanted to wear a veil on my wedding day.' This all felt surreal.

'I've got the most beautiful wisp of silk tulle edged with antique lace. You attach it at the back of a simple halo band twisted with lace and trimmed with pearls. A touch vintage, a touch boho—very Andie. Oh, and your mother's pearl necklace for your "something borrowed".'

'It sounds divine.' She hugged Karen and thanked her. 'I think you know my taste better than I do myself.'

It *was* divine. The dress, the veil, the silk-covered shoes that tied with ribbons around her ankles, the posy of white old-fashioned roses tied with mingled white and blue ribbon. The bridesmaids in their pale blue vintage style dresses with white rosebuds twisted through their hair. The little boys in adorable mini white tuxedos.

As she walked down the magnificent staircase on her father's arm, Andie didn't need the guests' *oohs* and *aahs* to know she looked her best and the bridal party was breath-taking. She felt surrounded by the people she cared for most—and who cared for her. She wouldn't wish anything to be different.

Dominic was waiting for her at the wedding arch, flanked by his best man, Jake Marlow—tall, broad-shoul-dered, blond and not at all the geek she'd imagined him to be—with her brothers and Rob Cratchit as groomsmen.

She knew she had to walk a stately, graceful bride's walk towards her husband-to-be. But she had to resist the temptation to pick up her skirts and run to him and the start of their new life as husband and wife.

Dominic knew the bridesmaids looked lovely and the lit-tle attendants adorable. But he only had eyes for Andie as she walked towards him, her love for him shining from her eyes.

As she neared where he waited for her with the cele-brant, a stray breeze picked up the fine layers of her gown's skirts and whirled them up and over her knees. She laughed and made no attempt to pin them down.

As her skirts settled back into place, their glances met

and her lips curved in an intimate exchange of a private joke that had meaning only for two. It was just one of many private connections he knew they would share, bonding and strengthening their life as partners in the years of happy marriage that stretched out ahead of them.

Finally she reached him and looked up to him with her dazzling smile. He enfolded her hand in his as he waited with her by his side to give his wholehearted assent to the celebrant's question. 'Do you, Dominic Hugo Hunt, take this woman, Andrea Jane Newman, to be your lawful wedded wife?'

CHAPTER SEVENTEEN

Christmas Day the following year.

ANDIE STOOD WITHIN the protective curve of her husband's arm as she admired the fabulous Christmas tree that stood in the entrance of their Vaucluse home. It soared almost to the ceiling and was covered in exquisite ornaments that were set to be the start of their family collection, to be brought out year after year. Brightly wrapped gifts were piled around its base.

Christmas lunch was again being held here today, but this time it was a party for just Andie's family and a few other waifs and strays who appreciated being invited to share their family's celebration.

The big Scrooge-busting party had been such a success that Dominic had committed to holding it every year. But not here this time. This year he'd hired a bigger house with a bigger pool and invited more people. He'd be calling in to greet his guests later in the day.

Andie hadn't had to do a thing for either party. She'd had her input—how could a Party Queen not? But for this private party the decorating, table settings and gift-wrapping had all been done by Dominic and her family.

After much cajoling, Andie had convinced her father to transfer his centre of cooking operations to Dominic's gourmet kitchen—just for this year. Although Dad had grumbled and complained about being away from familiar territory, Andie knew he was secretly delighted at the top-of-the-range equipment in the kitchen. The aromas that were wafting to her from the kitchen certainly smelled like the familiar traditional family favourites her father cooked each year. She couldn't imagine they would taste any less delicious than they would cooked in her parents' kitchen.

It was people who made the joy of Christmas and all the people she cherished the most were here to celebrate with her.

And one more.

The reason for all the disruption lay cradled in her arms. Hugo Andrew Hunt had been born in the early hours of Christmas Eve.

The birth had been straightforward and he was a healthy, strong baby. Andie had insisted on leaving the hospital today to be home for Christmas. Dominic had driven her and Hugo home so slowly and carefully they'd had a line of impatient cars honking their horns behind them by the time they'd got back to Vaucluse. He was over the moon about becoming a father. This was going to be one very loved little boy.

'Weren't you clever, to have our son born on Christmas Eve?' he said.

'I'm good at planning, but not *that* good,' she said. 'He came when he was ready. Maybe…maybe your parents sent him.' She turned her head so she could look up into Dominic's eyes. 'Now Christmas Eve will be a cause for celebration, not mourning, for you.'

'Yes,' he said. 'It will—because of you.'

Andie looked down at the perfect little face of her slumbering son and felt again the rush of fierce love for this precious being she'd felt when the midwife had first laid him on her tummy. He had his father's black hair but it was too soon to tell what colour his eyes would be.

Her husband, he-who-would-never-be-called-Scrooge-again, gently traced the line of little Hugo's cheek with his finger. 'Do you remember how I said last year was the very best Christmas of my life? Scratch that. This one is even better.'

'And they will get better and better,' she promised, turning her head for his kiss.

As they kissed, she heard footsteps on the marble floor and then an excited cry from her sister Bea. 'They're home! Andie, Dominic and baby Hugo are home!'

* * * * *

MILLS & BOON®

Christmas Collection!

Unwind with a festive romance this Christmas with our breathtakingly passionate heroes. Order all books today and receive a free gift!

FREE GIFT!

Order yours at
**www.millsandboon.co.uk
/christmas2015**

MILLS & BOON®

Buy A Regency Collection today and receive FOUR BOOKS FREE!

4 BOOKS FREE!

Transport yourself to the seductive world of Regency with this magnificent twelve-book collection.
Indulge in scandal and gossip with these 2-in-1 romances from top Historical authors

Order your complete collection today at
www.millsandboon.co.uk/regencycollection

915_ST19

MILLS & BOON®

The Italians Collection!

2 BOOKS FREE!

Irresistibly Hot Italians

You'll soon be dreaming of Italy with this scorching six-book collection. Each book is filled with three seductive stories full of sexy Italian men! Plus, if you order the collection today, you'll receive two books free!

This offer is just too good to miss!

Order your complete collection today at
www.millsandboon.co.uk/italians

0815_ST17

MILLS & BOON®

The Rising Stars Collection!

1 BOOK FREE!

This fabulous four-book collection features 3-in-1 stories from some of our talented writers who are the stars of the future! Feel the temperature rise this summer with our ultra-sexy and powerful heroes. Don't miss this great offer—buy the collection today to get one book free!

Order yours at www.millsandboon.co.uk/risingstars

0715_ST16

MILLS & BOON®

Cherish™

EXPERIENCE THE ULTIMATE RUSH OF FALLING IN LOVE

A sneak peek at next month's titles...

In stores from 20th November 2015:

- **Her Mistletoe Cowboy** – Marie Ferrarella *and*
  Proposal at the Winter Ball – Jessica Gilmore
- **The Best Man & The Wedding Planner**
  – Teresa Carpenter *and*
  Merry Christmas, Baby Maverick!
  – Brenda Harlen

In stores from 4th December 2015:

- **Carter Bravo's Christmas Bride** – Christine Rimmer
  and **Bodyguard...to Bridegroom?** – Nikki Logan
- **A Princess Under the Mistletoe** – Leanne Banks
  and **Christmas Kisses with Her Boss** – Nina Milne

Available at WHSmith, Tesco, Asda, Eason, Amazon and Apple

Just can't wait?
Buy our books online a month before they hit the shops!
visit www.millsandboon.co.uk

These books are also available in eBook format!